THE
WINTER
SISTER

THE WINTER SISTER

Megan Collins

ATRIA BOOKS

New York · London · Toronto · Sydney · New Delhi

ATRIA
BOOKS

An Imprint of Simon & Schuster, Inc.
1230 Avenue of the Americas
New York, NY 10020

First Atria Books hardcover edition February 2019

ATRIA BOOKS and colophon are registered trademarks of Simon & Schuster, Inc.

For information about special discounts for bulk purchases, please contact Simon & Schuster Special Sales at 1-866-506-1949 or business@simonandschuster.com.

The Simon & Schuster Speakers Bureau can bring authors to your live event. For more information or to book an event, contact the Simon & Schuster Speakers Bureau at 1-866-248-3049 or visit our website at www.simonspeakers.com.

Interior design by Alison Cnockaert

Manufactured in the United States of America

1   2   3   4   5   6   7   8   9   10

Library of Congress Cataloging-in-Publication Data

Names: Collins, Megan, 1984- author.
Title: The winter sister / Megan Collins.
Description: New York : Atria, 2019. |
Identifiers: LCCN 2018021281 (print) | LCCN 2018023654 (ebook) |
   ISBN 9781982100162 (eBook) | ISBN 9781982100148 (hardcover) | ISBN
   9781982100155 (pbk.)
Subjects: | GSAFD: Suspense fiction.
Classification: LCC PS3603.O454463 (ebook) | LCC PS3603.O454463 W56
   2019 (print) | DDC 813/.6—dc23
LC record available at https://lccn.loc.gov/2018023654

ISBN 978-1-9821-0014-8
ISBN 978-1-9821-0016-2 (ebook)

For Marc

Demeter had an only daughter, Persephone . . . the maiden of the spring. She lost her and in her terrible grief she withheld her gifts from the earth, which turned into a frozen desert. The green and flowering land was icebound and lifeless because Persephone had disappeared.

—Edith Hamilton, *Mythology*

1

When they found my sister's body, the flyers we'd hung around town were still crisp against the telephone poles. The search party still had land to scour; the batteries in their flashlights still held a charge. Persephone had been missing for less than seventy-two hours when a jogger caught a glimpse of her red coat through the snow, but by then, my mother had already become a stranger to me.

On the first morning of my sister's disappearance, Mom locked herself in her bedroom. I stayed in my room, too—my and Persephone's room—but I left the door ajar. For a long time, I watched the plows push through the foot of snow that had fallen overnight, and I kept imagining I saw Persephone out there, her fingers tapping on the window that fogged with my breath, and my hand opening it. Opening it every time.

The hours of that day were punctuated by my mother's sobs. In fourteen years of being her daughter, I'd never heard such a thing. Even on the fifteenth of every month—what Persephone, rolling her eyes, called "Mom's Dark Day"—there was only silence behind her bedroom door. Whenever she emerged the next morning, her eyelids were always swollen, but I had never actually heard her pain. But on this day, the first day, she cried so hard and so loud that I could swear I saw my paintbrushes quiver in their cup on my desk.

It wasn't until years later that I wondered why my mother didn't try to be strong for me, tell me that Persephone was just being Persephone and that she'd be home before we knew it. What did she know right then? What does a mother feel in her bones when her daughter stops breathing?

Aunt Jill came over with my cousin, Missy, at five o'clock that first day. The roads were clear enough by then, though the snow banks were as tall as our mailbox. Jill tried for fifteen minutes to reach her younger sister. She leaned her forehead against Mom's bedroom door and softly begged her to open up. When that didn't work, and the sobs continued, she plucked a bobby pin from Missy's bun and picked at the lock until the pin snapped between her fingers. "For Christ's sake, Annie," she said. Then she ushered my cousin and me to the kitchen where she splayed out Missy's issues of *Seventeen* and told us to sit tight while she called the police from my room.

Mom had already contacted the cops early that morning, her sentences sharp and shrill as she berated them for saying they'd "make a note of it" and that she should call back later if Persephone hadn't come home. Then she'd hung up with a long, tearful moan, and that's when she went to her room and shut the door. Even as the hours passed and daylight turned to dusk, she never did call them back. She stayed locked away, sobbing, the phone undisturbed on its hook.

Now, I could hear Jill spelling Persephone's name as she told the police that her niece had been missing for an entire day. But was she really missing? I'd seen her ride off with Ben the night before, just as the first flakes fell, and although I hated him more than I hated stiff paintbrushes or the loneliness of Mom's Dark Days, I hoped she was with him still—angry at me, maybe, but okay just the same.

"Tell them to check with her boyfriend," I told my aunt, stepping into the room. My voice startled her.

"Hold on a moment," Jill told the police. "What boyfriend, Sylvie?"

This was the second way in twenty-four hours that I betrayed my sister.

Ben was a secret—*our* secret, Persephone loved to remind me. The way he drove down our street and parked his car a couple houses down was a secret. The way Persephone opened the window in our room and straddled the sill until one foot touched the ground was a secret. And here were some more: how I'd keep the window open, just enough for her to slip her fingers under and pull it up when she returned; how, on many of those nights, I'd wake hours later to the cold shock of her snapping back my sheets. *Sylvie*, she'd whisper, her voice hoarse in the darkness. *I need you.* And then began the biggest secret of all.

"Ben Emory," I told my aunt. "The mayor's son. He graduated last year, and Persephone's been seeing him. But Mom doesn't know."

Jill frowned, the skin between her eyebrows wrinkling. "Why not?"

"We're not allowed to date. But Persephone sneaks out all the time to see him anyway. She left with him last night, about ten thirty."

Jill's eyes widened. "Sylvie," she said. "Why didn't you . . ." But then she shook her head, leaving the question unfinished, and put the phone back up to her ear. "She was last seen with Ben Emory," she said.

My pulse pounded as I walked back to the kitchen table, where Missy was braiding her hair to match a bright, glossy photo in one of the magazines. She was sixteen, the age smack-dab between Persephone and me, but she was carrying on as if this were a slumber party.

Why didn't you? Jill had asked, and it was a reasonable question. Why didn't I tell my mother about Ben the second I jolted awake that morning, the stillness of the house alerting me to Persephone's continued absence? I'd like to believe I was trying to protect Persephone's secret—*our* secret—but the truth, I know, is that I was trying to protect myself.

A little while later, Jill hurried into the kitchen to ask me for the names of Persephone's friends.

"Ben," I said.

"I called over there already. I had to leave a message because no one picked up. Who else?"

I shrugged, and then mentioned some girls I'd once seen Persephone with in the library as they worked on a project for school. Jill retreated back to my room, and I listened through the thin walls as, call after call, she reached a dead end: "Oh, they're not really friends? Okay, well thank you anyway. Let me give you my number just in case she . . ."

When she ran out of people to contact, Jill insisted we try to sleep—me in my bed, Missy in Persephone's, Jill on the lumpy couch in the living room. For a while that night, I kept myself awake, listening for the tap of Persephone's fingers on the window. All I ever heard, though, were Missy's kitten-like snores in my sister's bed, and the sound of Persephone's watch, ticking on somewhere in the room like a promise.

On the morning of the second day, I waited for Mom outside her door, sitting like a puppy that had been shut out. Normally, she was able to soothe me in ways that nothing else, not even painting, could. Her hand on my forehead was a cool washcloth, her voice a lullaby. We often played a game where she pretended to plant a garden on my face, using her fingers to show me where the roses would go (on my cheek) or where the lilies would be (on my forehead). "You're blooming," she'd say, and then she'd pretend to pick some of the flowers. "I've got three roses, two hydrangea bunches, and a stem of baby's breath. How much will that cost me?" She'd pinch her fingers together as if holding a tiny bouquet. "It'll cost you one hug," I'd say, and then we'd hold each other tightly, laughing at how ridiculous we were, how happy.

But when her door finally creaked open, her eyes were so swollen they looked as if they'd been punched. Her cheeks seemed to sag, and she was still wearing the bathrobe she'd had on the morning before when I told her that Persephone was gone.

She looked at me on the floor but didn't kneel down beside me or put her hand on my head. It was almost as if she knew what I had done, and hated me for it.

"Did she . . ." were the only words she uttered, and I felt how deeply I was failing her when I shook my head.

The doorbell rang just then, and Mom ran down the hall to the front door as Jill rounded the corner from the living room. They opened it together without a word, and I craned my neck to see between them. Missy was still asleep in my sister's bed, and I couldn't wait to tell Persephone that. "It was so weird," I would say. "She just kept *sleeping* as if it was a *vacation* or something. I mean, you're *missing*, right? But she's just snoring away in there." I could hear our laughter, even as I watched the police enter the house.

Two officers, a man and a woman, stood in the cramped entryway of our small two-bedroom ranch. They wiped their feet on the doormat, their hands on their belts like they were about to start line dancing.

"Are you Ms. O'Leary?" the male officer asked Mom.

"Yes," she said huskily. "Yes, that's me."

"And I'm Jill Foster." Jill stepped forward. "I'm the one who called last night."

"I'm Detective Falley," the female officer said, "and this is my partner, Detective Parker." She gestured to the man beside her, who was looking beyond us as if already trying to find clues within the walls of our house. "I wanted to let you know, first of all, that we followed up on what you reported to our desk sergeant, and we spoke to Ben Emory."

Mom stumbled backward a little. "What's he got to do with this?"

"We understand," Detective Falley said, "that he's the last person your daughter was seen with."

Mom spun around to look at me, and her eyes seemed grayer than usual, clouded by the horror gathering on her face. I looked at my feet, wiggling my big toe through the hole in my sock.

"Did you know about this?" she asked me.

I swallowed. "Yes," I said. "I saw her leave with him. She . . ." I paused, unsure of how far to go in my betrayal. Then I looked up, keeping my eyes on the detectives, neither of whom could have been more than thirty-five. Parker even had a small patch of zits around his nose.

"She sneaks out of the house a lot to see him," I said. "He's her boyfriend. They've been doing this for months."

Any color left on my mother's face disappeared. Her skin became as gray as her eyes, as gray as the cold light from the cloudy sky outside. "Boyfriend?" she asked, her voice quivering.

"This is Sylvie," Aunt Jill said to the detectives, gesturing toward me. "She's my niece. Persephone's sister."

Falley nodded. "Ben says he doesn't know where she is. Says they were driving around, got into a fight, and she demanded to be let out of the car so she could walk home. He says he let her off on Weston Road and then waited out the storm at his friend's house overnight. We checked with the friend's mother and she confirmed that Ben arrived around eleven p.m. and stayed until ten or so the next morning."

"Then where is she?" I asked. "And why would she want to walk home when it was snowing? Ben's lying! He has to know where she is."

The detectives looked at me. Aunt Jill looked at me. But Mom just stared into nothing.

"He says she was very adamant about leaving the car," Falley said. "Says she was opening the door and seemed ready to jump out if he didn't stop. According to him, he pulled over to try to calm her down, but then she got out and wouldn't get back inside. Says he got mad himself and finally drove off."

"What were they fighting about?" Jill asked.

"Sounds like typical relationship drama," Falley said. "He says she got angry when he snapped at her about something. It escalated from there."

I shook my head. The only part of Ben's story I believed was that he'd gotten mad at her. I had seen plenty of evidence of his anger; I knew he was dangerous, but I also knew that Persephone never shied away from danger.

"We're going to question him more about the fight," Parker finally chimed in. His voice was deeper than I expected, and this comforted me. I didn't know my father—my mother had always told me I'd been the product of a one-night stand, or a "one-night miracle," as she liked to say—but I always imagined that when he spoke, his voice was strong and unwavering, the way that Parker's was now.

"We drove around Weston Road, where Mr. Emory said he let her off, but we haven't found anything yet," he continued. "Please understand, though—we're doing everything we can to locate your daughter." He said this directly to Mom, who was leaning into the coatrack. She looked so fragile that the jackets and scarves tossed over the hooks seemed strong enough to bear her weight. "We're going to talk to the people who were operating the snowplows that night, see if they saw anyone walking around. In the meantime—can you think of anywhere she might have gone? Friends' houses? Places nearby that she frequents?" He pulled a small notepad out of his back pocket and clicked the top of a pen.

I looked at Mom, waiting to see if she'd answer, but her eyes were still locked on some distant air.

"I . . . there's . . ." I tried. Then I cleared my throat as Parker turned his attention to me. "Well, my aunt and cousin live just over in Hanover. But . . . they're here, so she's obviously not with them. Um, there's also . . ."

But there wasn't also.

"I don't know," I said. "The only person she really hangs out with anymore is Ben."

That's when the coatrack crashed to the floor. It landed across the entryway like a fallen tree, separating the detectives from my mother, Aunt Jill, and me. We all jumped backward. All except Mom, that is—because she'd pushed it over.

Next came the little yellow table where we dumped our mail and keys when we walked in the door. With one quick shove, it clattered to the floor, and Mom reached for one of the legs, snapping it off as if it were nothing more than a twig. We were all stunned, even the detectives, and it wasn't until Mom swung the table leg against the entryway mirror that Parker stepped over the coatrack and grabbed her arms. Mom struggled against him, her bathrobe opening, revealing the stained T-shirt she wore underneath, and when he tightened his grip, she screamed.

"Annie!" Aunt Jill cried. "What are you doing? Calm down!"

This only made her scream louder, her face reddening like a newborn's, and she kicked and twisted until Parker's hands loosened just long enough for her to escape. She jumped over the coatrack and ran down the hall. We turned the corner as her bedroom door slammed shut, Missy standing in the hall with wide sleep-filled eyes.

"Mom?" she said to my aunt. "What happened? Is Persephone back?"

Any answer Jill might have given was lost in the sounds coming from Mom's room. Furniture crashed. Throaty growls gave way to high-pitched screams. I recognized the squeak of her mattress as she—what? Pummeled her fists against it? Detective Parker marched forward and tried the knob. When the door wouldn't open, he looked back at us. "Falley," he said, and his partner nodded, steering me into the living room.

"Does your mother do this a lot?" she asked. She bent over slightly, staring into my eyes. "Has she thrown things and gotten angry like this before?"

I could hear Jill's voice pleading from down the hall—"Annie, please, open up. We'll find her, I know we will"—and I knew that Falley was waiting for me to say something, but I'd already forgotten what she'd asked. Who was that woman inside my mother's room? What rabid animal was making those noises?

"Sylvie," Falley said. "It's Sylvie, right?"

I nodded slowly.

"Have you ever known your mother to hurt your sister—physically?"

"Um," I said, "she . . . what did you say?"

"Annie, please. Open the door and let me be here for you."

"Ms. O'Leary, would you mind opening the door for a moment?"

"I said, have you ever known your mother to hurt your sister? Did she maybe hit her one time? Push her?"

I later learned that Falley was breaking protocol by asking me these questions—not because she felt that the situation was too urgent for all the red tape of recording devices and child psychologists, but because she was, in fact, a young detective. She'd only been promoted to that title six months before, and when she put her hands on my shoulders that day, they were shaking.

"Sylvie," she said, "do you understand what I'm asking you?"

Something about my mother. Something about somebody hurting my sister.

No one thought to look at my hands. But even if they'd noticed the splotches of blue and gray on my fingers, or the flashes of red near my nails, they wouldn't have connected it to Persephone walking toward Ben's car and not coming back. They wouldn't have seen it as evidence of a terrible crime. But *Sylvie*, she'd whispered the night before she disappeared, *I need you.*

As usual, I hadn't heard her return. I'd only woken to the feeling of my sheets and comforter being ripped off my body. "No," I groaned, trying to roll toward the wall.

"Yes," Persephone said, grabbing my arms and shaking me. "There's not much this time. Come on, you have to do this for me."

I opened my eyes to find my mother staring at me. That's what it seemed like, anyway, the two looked so similar—their large gray eyes, their blonde hair, their chins that came to a delicate point beneath their mouths. I knew that my sister and I had two different fathers, but with my brown hair and brown eyes and paler-than-pale complexion, it always surprised me how little I resembled the rest of my family.

Persephone leaned over and swung her head so that her hair tickled my face.

"I can do this all night," she said. She moved even closer to me, still swishing her hair around, but now the gold necklace she always wore fell forward, and the tip of the starfish pendant grazed my lips.

"Okay, fine," I conceded, pushing her hair, her necklace, away. "Show me."

Persephone turned on my bedside lamp and lifted the side of her shirt. "There's this one," she said, pointing to a fresh bruise the size of a quarter just beneath her rib cage. "But Mom won't see that one." She let her shirt fall back down and then showed me the inside of her right wrist. There were two more bruises rising toward the surface of her skin. "It's just these ones really."

I swore I knew the size of Ben's fingertips better than I knew my own. I sighed as I reached beneath my desk for the bucket of acrylic paints Mom had bought me for Christmas two months earlier. Grabbing some brushes and a Styrofoam palette, I sat back down beside my sister. Then I took her arm in my hand and turned it this way and that, assessing my canvas.

I worked in silence. I squirted Midnight Blue onto my palette and mixed it with Eggshell, not bothering to ask Persephone why she stayed with him. As I painted a moon over the first of the bruises, then crossed it with red-tinged waves that covered the other, I didn't remind her that I thought love should be painless, that it shouldn't be sneaking in and out of windows, or blood vessels bursting. We'd already had those conversations before, and they all ended the same way: "You don't understand. You don't know him. It's not what you think."

"Okay," I told Persephone, lifting my brush from her skin. "I'm done."

She smiled approvingly at the moonscape, and I rubbed at the colors that had bled onto my hands. There were always traces of my work on my own skin in the morning, and though my mother often commented on what I'd done to Persephone, praising me for the "beautiful little tattoos" I'd given her, she never seemed to notice the tattoos I'd given myself, the paint that screamed on my knuckles and fingers. When Persephone showered each day, she was careful to keep her concealed bruises away from the water. When I showered, I scrubbed and scrubbed.

"Sylvie." Detective Falley squeezed my shoulder gently. "Are you okay?"

The screaming had stopped. The hammering and crashing of furniture had stopped. Now, all I could hear from down the hall was the faint sound of paper being ripped, over and over, *ssshhhhk, ssshhhhk, ssshhhhk*. What could she be tearing in there? Photographs? Letters? Secrets? Later that day, when Mom finally left her room to use the bathroom, I crept across the hallway to find that it was a calendar she'd been destroying. Scraps of months lay scattered across the carpet like seeds in a garden, and among all those fragmented squares of dates, every fifteenth was circled in red.

"I'm really sorry about this, Detective," Aunt Jill was saying to Parker as they walked into the living room, where Falley still bent toward me with concerned eyes. "I don't know what to say."

Missy followed them. She was wearing one of Persephone's T-shirts, which snapped "I DON'T CARE." I hadn't seen her take it from our dresser the night before or I would have offered her some of my own clothes to wear. Missy shuffled in slippers—Persephone's slippers—toward the couch.

"Are you able to stay here for a while?" Detective Parker asked Jill. "With the family?" He shifted his eyes toward me.

"Of course," Jill said. "The girls have tomorrow off for Presidents' Day. I'm a teacher's aide—over at the middle school in Hanover?—so I'm off, too. We can be here, no problem."

"Good," Parker said. "Now, do you have a recent picture of Persephone we can take with us?"

"Yes!" Jill said. "I actually took out the photo albums first thing this morning. I was thinking of making some flyers to hang around town." She walked into the kitchen, which was open to the living room, and flipped through one of the faux-leather books on the table. "It would just feel better to actively *do* something, you know?"

She pulled my sister's senior portrait, taken earlier that school year, from its plastic sheath. In the photo, a painted bruise peeked out from Persephone's neckline, a shadow to anyone who didn't know, but to me, a focal point.

"So should I put the police station's number on the flyers," Jill asked, "or have people call us directly?"

Parker reached into his pocket and handed Jill a card in exchange for the picture. "Thank you," he said. "You can put that info on the signs. Though I should warn you that, with things like this, we get a lot of false information. Ninety-five percent of the calls that come in are useless."

"Well, that still leaves five percent," Jill replied.

Ssshhhhk, ssshhhhk, ssshhhhk. In my mother's room, paper kept ripping.

Clearing his throat, Parker rubbed his hand over the light brown stubble on his face. "Just a couple more things," he said, shifting his gaze toward me. "Is it okay if I ask you some questions, Sylvie, before we go?"

I looked to my aunt.

"Go ahead, Sylvie," she said. "It's okay."

I shrugged. "Yeah, that's fine."

Parker looked down at his notepad and clicked the top of his pen. "Your aunt reported that you saw your sister drive off with Ben Emory at about ten thirty the night before last. Is that correct?"

"Yes."

"And how did she seem just before she left? Was she angry, for example? Sad? Excited to see her boyfriend?"

I imagined what the expression on her face must have been as she looked at me through the window Friday night, her breath making ghosts on the glass as she called my name. She must have looked angry, annoyed. She must have looked ready to kill me.

"I don't know," I told Parker. "I guess she was . . . neutral."

He made a note on his pad. "Okay. Now, you also mentioned that she snuck out a lot to see him. Why is that?"

Everyone stared at me, the two detectives standing closest, my aunt and cousin on opposite ends of the room. So much seemed to hang on what I had to say, but how could a fourteen-year-old girl be expected to know what needed knowing?

"She's not allowed to date," I said. "Neither of us are. But I'm—I wouldn't date yet anyway."

"So your mother had no idea that your sister has been seeing Mr. Emory?"

"Well," I started, "she didn't know she was *still* seeing him."

"Go on," Parker prompted.

"My mom came home from the diner one night—she's a waitress; I don't know if that matters—and she found Persephone with Ben. They were just watching TV, I think, but it was the first time she'd ever brought a guy home, and my mom got upset. Persephone had broken the rule."

From there, after Ben had slinked out the front door, the two of them erupted at each other, Mom yelling at Persephone for her "blatant disrespect" and Persephone screaming right back about Mom "treating us like babies." At one point, Persephone knocked over a lamp with her wild gesticulations, and they both stared at it on the floor for a moment. Then Persephone tore off its flimsy shade and threw it across the room, where it whizzed by Mom's face and toppled some picture frames.

"Since then," I told Detective Parker, "Persephone's always just snuck out to see him."

"How well do you know him?" Falley jumped in.

"I barely know him at all. He graduated last year, so I've never even gone to the same school as him."

"And Persephone's a senior this year, correct?" Parker asked.

"Yes," Jill and I said in unison.

Falley took a step toward me. "The reason I asked, Sylvie," she said, "is because when we first got here, you seemed pretty sure that Ben had something to do with your sister being missing. Why is that?"

"I—what?"

"Has he ever hurt your sister before, or done anything that would put her at risk?"

"I . . ." I looked around the room. Four sets of eyes were latched onto me. "Like I said, I don't really know him."

"That wasn't the question," Parker said.

Why was I being interrogated? And where was the hot, bald light I'd seen on TV shows, the one that would shine on my face and sweat out all my secrets? At least then I wouldn't have a choice if I betrayed Persephone. As it was, though, the living room was cool and gray. The faces of the detectives remained serious, but kind enough.

Aunt Jill came to put her arm around my shoulder protectively. I leaned into her, grateful for the save, but then she whispered in my ear, "It's okay, Sylvie. Just tell the detectives whatever you know."

We're sisters, Sylvie, Persephone would always say. *And that's sacred.*

So I know your promise to keep this a secret isn't just words. It means something to you. Just like you mean something to me, and just like I hope—I really, really hope—I mean something to you.

Of course you do, I'd say.

Then prove it.

"I don't know if he ever hurt her." I looked at Falley and Parker, at Aunt Jill. I even looked at Missy, who sat with her chin resting on the palm of her hand. They were all listening to me, somehow sure that I had the right answers. "He just has to know where she is. She was with him that night."

Ssshhhhk, ssshhhhk, ssshhhhk.

Falley glanced back toward the hallway, listening to the muted sounds of my mother's rage. She looked at her partner before speaking.

"Sylvie," she began, "when your mother's acted like this in the past, did she—"

"My mother's never acted like this," I interrupted. "She's never had a daughter who's been missing before."

Silence spread through the room like a gas. Even the sound of paper paused, and I imagined it was because Mom had heard me defend her. I could almost feel the soft approval of her fingers stroking my cheek.

The detectives shared a glance, Falley tilting her head at Parker, her eyes asking a question I couldn't read. Then Parker nodded, closing his notebook and clicking his pen one more time.

"Thank you," Parker said. "You have our information. Please feel free to call us anytime."

He slipped his notepad into his pocket and headed toward the front door. Falley stayed behind a moment to put her hand on my shoulder. "You're being really brave," she said gently. "We'll find your sister. Don't worry."

Aunt Jill walked toward the entryway to see them out, and I sank into the couch cushions, which were still blanketed with Jill's makeshift bed.

"This is crazy," Missy said, the expression on her face one of slow understanding, as if she was just beginning to comprehend how serious the situation was.

Down the hall, behind my mother's door, the sound of shredding paper started up again.

2

That afternoon, we posted more than fifty flyers. Persephone's face smirked at us beneath a black, bulky "MISSING" as we worked our way through the center of town and neighboring streets. By the time we stapled the final sign to a telephone pole outside the post office, our fingers felt raw, even through our gloves.

When we got home, Jill pushed mugs of hot chocolate into our hands and encouraged us to "thaw out" in front of the TV. Missy put on a rerun of *The Real World*, which I watched without seeing, but at six o'clock on the dot, I changed it to the local news in case they mentioned Persephone.

As it turned out, my sister's disappearance was the lead story.

"The town of Spring Hill is in search of a missing high school student today," the anchor said. "Persephone O'Leary, eighteen, was last seen leaving her house on Friday night with her boyfriend, Ben Emory, the son of Spring Hill mayor and prominent land developer William Emory. Since then, police have been questioning neighbors and residents, including O'Leary's boyfriend, who, police say, dropped her off on Weston Road around eleven p.m. on Friday night."

"That's bad reporting," I said to Missy. "Saying 'police say' makes it sound like it's a fact that Ben dropped her off. But it's not a fact—it's Ben's story. And why didn't anyone talk to *us* about this?"

Missy shrugged. "Maybe they tried," she said, "while we were out. Maybe your mom didn't answer."

The thought of that chilled me, despite the steam rising from my mug. Could Mom have locked herself away so thoroughly that not even the ringing phone or doorbell could reach her? After we had gotten home, she finally let Aunt Jill into her bedroom, and although I couldn't hear what they were saying to each other, it made me feel better to remember that they were in that room together.

On the TV, the news anchor continued to speak over a video of people dressed in heavy coats and scarves, trudging in thick boots through the snowy woods by Emory Bridge.

"A modest search party is already underway for O'Leary, and people in town appear confident that they will locate the missing girl soon."

Missy and I looked at each other, the surprise in her eyes reflecting my own.

"Search party?" I said. "What search party?"

The footage switched to a close-up of a middle-aged woman in a knitted purple hat. Her nose was red and her breath danced in front of her lips as she spoke. I recognized her as Persephone's third-grade teacher, Mrs. McDonald.

"I organized all this myself," Mrs. McDonald said, almost proudly, to the microphone in her face. "I live near Weston Road, so of course I saw the police cars this afternoon, and as soon as I found out what was going on, I sprang into action. Called some friends together, alerted the press, and now here we are. We're a small group, and we've only just started, but we'll keep searching even after dark." She held up a flashlight and smiled to the camera. "We won't stop until we find her. She's one of Spring Hill's own, and that really means something."

Did it, though?

Spring Hill, Connecticut, was a town of about twenty-five thousand people, a good majority of whom lived in the big brick houses on the hilly northern side of Emory Bridge. People in neighboring towns came to Spring Hill for its frozen yogurt shops and its apple and berry orchards, and at Christmastime, they did their shopping at Spring Hill Commons. Then they drove around to look at the twinkling white lights on all the Ionic columns and wraparound porches, and when they returned home, they reevaluated their monthly budgets, trying to find some extra savings for a new swimming pool or a kitchen remodel, anything that would make them feel more like the residents of Spring Hill.

But we—Persephone, my mother, and I—had never been a part of that Spring Hill. We lived on the swampier southern side of Emory Bridge. We got our clothes at thrift stores in Hanover, wore out the edges of our library cards, and got free hot lunches at school. My mother had inherited our ranch from my grandparents, whom we had lived with, Persephone and I sleeping in the same bedroom as Mom, until they died in a car accident when I was three. From then on, I grew up with the narrowed eyes of the upper-crust Spring Hill residents on my back. "There goes Annie O'Leary's girl. Ugh, that woman. Always took handouts from her parents, still looking for handouts to this day. Our taxes even buy her kids' lunches at school. Meanwhile, Barry's working his fingers to the bone to make partner . . ."

So it surprised me that Mrs. McDonald was now claiming Persephone as "one of Spring Hill's own." I remembered her writing a letter home to Mom one time, urging her to "consider buying Persephone some new clothes that adhere to the current trends, so as not to alienate her from her peers and cause damaging social consequences." Mom had hung the letter on the refrigerator, right next to my splotchy kindergarten drawings, as a reminder, she said, of the people we never wanted to be. Now, I imagined her seeing Mrs. McDonald's face on the news and scoffing, "Attention-seeking snake."

"Do you know that lady?" Missy asked me.

"Not really," I said.

"She seems kind of excited."

"Yeah," I agreed. Then I added one of Mom's phrases: "This freaking town."

I clicked the power button on the remote, and for a few minutes, Missy and I sat in silence. In that time, the front door never opened. Persephone never walked inside, stamping the snow off her shoes, asking what had happened to the coatrack and table. Still, I listened for her grunt of annoyance as she noticed there was no longer a place to put her red winter jacket. I listened for it so hard that I didn't even register that Aunt Jill had walked into the room until she put her hand on my head and spoke.

"How are you doing?" she asked.

I looked up at her from my place on the floor, my fingers picking at the shaggy beige carpet. Her face was creased with an exhaustion I'd only ever seen on my mother the mornings after her Dark Days.

"I want to see Mom," I said. I started to push myself up off the floor, but Jill's fingertips on my shoulder stopped me.

"Not tonight," she said. "Your mother's finally sleeping. She wants to be alone."

But my sister was missing.

"She won't mind," I said. "It's just me."

I needed Mom's fingers on my forehead, planting and picking flowers as if my face were fertile, open land. I needed her to pull me into her, wrap her arms around me, and rock me like a child. I needed the lavender smell of her skin, the steady rhythm of her breathing. How would I fall asleep in a sisterless house for one more night without it?

"I'm sorry," Jill said, shaking her head. "Not tonight."

So Missy spent another night in Persephone's bed. So Jill spent another night on the couch. So I kept myself awake remembering Ben's face, how the danger lurked there in the scar that ran like a tendril of hair from the tip of his left eyebrow to the middle of his cheek. I'd only seen him a handful of times, his face pressed against our bedroom window on nights when Persephone was still applying her eyeliner in the bathroom, but I had him memorized. He had disheveled brown hair, which he sometimes pulled back into a short ponytail. Dark circles lingered under his eyes, as if he hadn't slept for days, and his mouth was always cocked at a half grin. When I finally fell asleep that night, it was to images of Ben, his fingernails—long and sharp in the dream—tapping on the windowpane until the glass shattered.

Somehow, I didn't wake up until the sun was high in the sky the next morning, and even then, I only opened my eyes because Missy was shaking me. "Sylvie," she said, "the police are here."

I threw off my blankets and jumped to my feet. Sure enough, from our bedroom window I could see a cop car in the driveway, the same two detectives fidgeting with their belts and stepping through snow to get to our front door. I had made it into the hallway before they even rang the bell.

Mom was in the entryway. Jill was in the entryway. Missy was dressed. It was as if they'd all been expecting this visit.

"Good morning," Jill said as Detective Falley and Detective Parker stepped into the house. She was trying to sound cheerful—or, at the very least, normal—but her voice trembled. "Can we get you anything? There's still some coffee in the pot."

"No," Parker said. "No, thank you. We, uh, we're here because—"

"Where is she?" I demanded. Mom glanced back at the sound of my voice, but her eyes were dim, as if she couldn't remember who I was.

Falley took a step forward, closer to the four of us. "I'm very sorry to have to tell you this, but we—we believe we've found Persephone's body."

Mom dropped to the floor, her knees folding beneath her. She put her hands flat against the dark gray tile and wailed. Aunt Jill put her hand on Mom's back, and when she looked up at the detectives, tears glossed her eyes.

"Her body?" Jill asked. "So she's . . ."

Parker and Falley nodded. Missy's hands gripped my shoulders and my throat went dry in an instant.

Jill stood up, leaving my mother sobbing in the fetal position on the floor. "What," she tried, "what happened?" I stared at Mom, but I couldn't bring myself to move.

Falley was also looking at Mom when she said, "We don't know for sure yet. She was covered with about a foot of snow, but it looks—it looks as if she was—gone, before that. She had . . . bruises on her neck. She appears to have been strangled."

No. No, no, no. No.

The word ran through my head, over and over, quiet at first, but then screaming. And in the years that followed, that was the moment when my memory of that day broke down. I could never remember when the detectives left, or at what point Mom stood up, walked to the barely stocked liquor cabinet in the kitchen, pulled down a bottle of something clear, and headed like a person on death row to her bedroom. I couldn't remember those last moments when Mom was Mom, before the years of empty vodka bottles, of a locked door and a dusty, stale smell throughout the house. Whenever I tried to piece together the minutes following Falley's words, all I could see was the night Persephone left.

She had gone out with Ben earlier than usual, about eight thirty. It was risky, because Mom had been awake, curled up on the couch watching TV, and she could have heard Persephone landing on the snow-covered mulch beneath our window. She could have seen a flash of headlights pass through our house. And on that night, despite all my promises to my sister, I was hoping she would. I was hoping that, finally, it could all be over—the bruises, the late-night painting, the cold air that slipped through the window I was expected to leave cracked open each night.

But Mom didn't notice. I could hear canned laughter floating down the hallway, could hear the squeaky old couch as she fluffed up pillows and repositioned herself. An hour later, I listened to popping sounds in the microwave, wondering if Mom would come to my room to offer me some of her snack. Then, just as my clock switched to ten twenty-five, as I saw Ben pull up to the curb two houses away, Mom turned off the TV, walked toward our room, and knocked lightly on the door.

"Good night, girls," she said.

I held my breath, waiting for her to open the door, to stick her head inside just in time to see Persephone, snowflakes in her hair, pull up the window. But my lungs began to burn, and I heard Mom's bedroom door close. Down the street, Persephone in her red coat was getting out of the car.

I acted without thinking. In a burst of motion that felt like one continuous movement, I closed the window that was supposed to be left open, turned the latch, shut off the light by my bed, and got under my blankets, facing the wall, my eyes wide open.

First, there was the crunch of shoes through snow, the sound muffled by walls and glass, but growing louder every second. Then, a fumbling of fingers against the window. Finally, a pause—was it one of anger or confusion or just mild annoyance? I'll never know—and then a tapping on the glass.

My heart pounded so hard in my chest that I thought I could see it disturb the blankets. Still, I waited it out, pretending to be fast asleep. Persephone would be mad, yes, and she'd likely pin me to the bed and squeeze my wrists until they bruised—but at least it would be *my* bruises, not hers. At least, after having to give up and ring the doorbell, after having to explain to Mom where she'd been, she would be exposed. Mom would take care of it. Mom would make sure that Persephone never snuck out again. And in that way, my sister would be safe, and I would never have had to utter a word.

What I didn't know, though, was that Persephone would not ring the doorbell. Once the tapping stopped, and she gave up hissing my name through the glass, I pulled my blankets back and crept toward the window to peer out. But I didn't see her trudging to the front door. Instead, I saw her running back toward Ben's car, fresh snow sparkling on her coat. She opened the passenger door and the two of them drove away, the car growing smaller and smaller until it turned the corner and disappeared.

And I didn't know it then, but if I'd just kept things the way they were supposed to be, if I'd kept the window open, the latch unlocked, if I'd kept on swallowing Persephone's secrets night after night, then I could have—I would have—kept my sister, too.

3

When Aunt Jill called to tell me about my mother's cancer, I was forcing down my second tequila shot in a bar on Thayer Street. It was my thirtieth birthday, and Lauren was buying. "All night," she said, "anything you want. None of this Sober Sylvie shit." I was wearing a black dress that dug into my thighs and black strappy shoes that dug into my ankles. When I stumbled outside to answer my phone, my jerky movements were less a product of the tequila than the four-inch heels that Lauren had forced me to wear ("Don't even *think* about putting on flats. That dress is a fuck-me dress, and a fuck-me dress needs fuck-me shoes."). I'd been working at Steve's Ink all day, so I hadn't had the energy to argue with her, or to explain that I didn't care that much about my birthday. With Lauren, it was easier to just wear whatever outfit she threw at me, drink whatever shots she bought me, and hope she found a guy she liked within the first thirty minutes. That way, I could feign queasiness and spend the last hours of my birthday alone in my bed.

I leaned against a telephone pole just outside the bar, watching a parade of young people—Brown students, most likely—marching inside.

Putting one finger into my ear, I tried my best to shut out the music that blasted through the door of the bar.

"Jill," I said. "Hi."

"Happy birthday!" she said. "I can't believe you're thirty years old. That must make me—what? Thirty-seven?"

I smiled, shifting my weight from foot to foot. "No way," I said. "Thirty-five. Tops."

"Great. I'll take it."

In the pause between us, I flicked through my brain for something to tell her, some recent activity or achievement that would prove to her that I wasn't "just floating," as she had said during our last conversation in September. But what was there?

"So," Jill said. "Anything new?"

I scanned the other side of the street, where a man sitting on the curb snuffed out a cigarette and then reached into his jacket pocket for another. Behind him was the Thai restaurant where Lauren and I often got takeout, and I looked at the flashing "OPEN" sign, my mouth watering. When I glanced back at the man a moment later, I was startled to find that his eyes were already locked onto mine. He cupped his hand over his lighter and lit a cigarette, his gaze lingering as he inhaled. I quickly looked away, busying my fingers by picking at an old staple on the telephone pole.

"Nothing much," I said to Jill. "I'm still at Steve's. Still living with Lauren. You know, same as last month."

"I don't know how you do it, working at that tattoo store."

"Tattoo *parlor*," I corrected her.

"Right. Parlor. It's just—all those needles, the blood. I wouldn't last a minute. Surely there must be something else you can do with your talents."

The man with the cigarettes stood up. He wiped his hands on his pants and walked down Thayer Street. A girl, coming from the opposite direction, sped up her pace to meet him. When they reached each other, they embraced, and the girl snagged his cigarette with a laugh. He put his arm around her and kissed her cheek as she took a drag.

I turned away, facing the bar again. He'd been harmless, of course—just someone waiting for his girlfriend to arrive. Lauren always told me I was paranoid, that the things that ran through my head on any given Tuesday could be lifted straight from the script of a Lifetime Original Movie. The ones where women are always at risk, and men, though beautiful and benign to the untrained eye, are always, inevitably, monsters.

"The needles and blood are no big deal," I said to Jill. "You get used to it."

"Okay," Jill said. "So are you just used to it, then, or do you actually like tattooing?"

"I like it," I lied, because it was easier than explaining the truth.

"Okay. Well, listen, Sylvie," Jill said, her tone suddenly shifting. "I know this isn't the best time for this. You're celebrating right now, I'm sure. But can we make some time to talk tomorrow? There's something I need to discuss with you."

There was an edge to her voice that I hadn't heard in years. For the first time since I'd walked outside, I registered the cool October air on my skin.

"What is it?" I asked. "Is it something about Persephone?"

"It's—what? No. Nothing like that." I could hear her, probably in her kitchen in Connecticut, sighing.

Sixteen years after my sister's murder, the case was as cold as her body must have been that night. But there were still days when I found myself hoping for some kind of news, some fresh lead that had come to light, some witness that hadn't found the courage to speak, until now. Never mind that it had happened on a street without many houses. Never mind that the snow had compromised the crime scene, made the chance of finding DNA evidence or fibers of clothing nearly nonexistent. After all those years, I'd never stopped waiting.

"Is it Missy, then? Something wrong with the baby?"

"No," Jill said. "No, no. She and Carl just went for an ultrasound last week actually. The baby's doing great. It's . . . about your mother actually."

A group of wobbly, laughing girls spilled out of the bar, and the sudden flare of music felt like a punch in the stomach.

"Listen," Jill said, "I can hear that you're busy. Let's just—"

"No," I interrupted, walking a few yards down the street. "It's okay. I can hear you. Just tell me."

I waited as Jill inhaled on the other end of the phone. Even with the muffled sounds of the bar surrounding me, I could still hear her slow, deliberate breath. I put my hand on the arm of a sidewalk bench.

"I've been taking your mother to a few doctor's appointments lately," Jill said. "She's been getting treated for what they thought was just acid reflux. But . . . well, new test results came back today, and it's . . . cancer. Esophageal cancer. I'm so sorry, Sylvie."

My fingers tightened on the bench's metal arm.

"Is that the one you get from drinking a lot?" I asked.

In the pause that followed, I could tell that Jill was surprised by my question. But what surprised me was that she hadn't been calling to tell me my mother was dead. In the months after Persephone was murdered, how many times had Jill and I pressed our ears against Mom's bedroom door, listening for some sound of life inside? How many times had I picked her lock, only to creak open the door and find her lying the way I imagined that people in coffins did? At a certain point— when our pleas did nothing, when the bottles continued to pile up in the sink, when the meals we made her never made it to her lips—I'd stopped seeing her as a withered plant that could be watered and sun- shined back to life. Instead, I'd started seeing the sagging stem of her spine for what it was: a sign that death was rooted within her.

"Uh, yes," Jill said. "Well, that's not the only cause of it, but . . . alcoholism can definitely be a factor."

My heart contracted. I tried to imagine my mother's face as the doctor told her the news, but whether her expression was one of fear or anxiety or relief, I couldn't tell; in my mind, she kept looking away.

"How long does she have?" I asked.

Again, there was a pause from Jill's end.

"She's starting chemo next week," she said. "Then, depending on how that goes, there might be another round before, hopefully, she can have surgery."

"Oh," I said. "Okay."

"It's not a death sentence just yet, Sylvie. But, I'll be honest—it doesn't look good."

I nodded, staring at the goose bumps that had risen to the surface of my skin. I wanted a sweater. I wanted my blankets and pillows. I wanted to crawl into bed.

"I'm going to be staying with her during the treatment," Jill continued, "in her house. But if you want to stop by sometime soon, that would be great. I'm sure she'd be happy to see you."

I heard, more than felt, myself chuckle. "No, she wouldn't," I said, and I loved Jill then for not trying to argue otherwise.

"Well," she said. "You should get back to your night. I'm sorry about the terrible timing, but I didn't want to wait too long to tell you."

"It's okay," I said. "I'm glad you told me."

"Let's talk more about this soon, okay? Will you call me if you have any questions?"

"Sure."

"Okay, Sylvie. Good night. Happy birthday."

In her last few words, there was a tinge of sadness that I knew was more than grief about my mother. I should have said more to her, asked her more questions—the whole conversation was over so quickly—and yet, it was exhausting trying to be what Aunt Jill expected of me. I couldn't pretend that, just by turning thirty, I was old enough now to have outgrown my feelings of motherlessness.

I knew that Jill understood, on some level, what those years had been like for me, but she hadn't lived them like I'd lived them. She couldn't know the ache of remembering how my mother didn't fight for me that first year, when Jill had declared that until Mom got her act together, I would stay with her and Missy. She never tried to get me back, never contacted Jill to see how I was doing. Every Sunday, when Jill and Missy and I went back to the house to check on her, stocking her cabinets with groceries and toiletries that Jill had bought with her own money, Mom cracked open her door, asked in a paper-thin voice if we'd brought any booze, and then shut us out again when we told her, our arms firmly crossed, no—no, we had not. "Well then what the hell did you come here for?" she yelled, a phrase that still jostled me out of sleep sometimes.

When I went back inside the bar, it took me only a few seconds to find Lauren. Her teal hair, which fell in loose curls around her shoulders, was like a spotlight in the dim room. She was talking to two guys in button-down shirts, each of them holding a beer, and when she saw me squeezing between the crowds of people, she began to laugh.

"Here she is!" she said, her voice straining to be heard over the music. "See, I told you the birthday girl exists!" She handed me a drink, something frothy and blue.

"Listen . . ." I started.

"Oh no you don't!" Lauren interrupted. She looked at the guys. "This is classic Sylvie. Watch. She's gonna try to go home early."

"I'm really tired," I said, moving so that I was standing between Lauren and the two guys. "Just—please. Don't make a big deal out of this. Looks like you've already made some new friends, and you said Jake and Jenna are showing up in a little while."

Something must have shown on my face. Lauren narrowed her eyes, and then pulled me away, using her elbows to create a space for us among the groups of people in the bar.

"What is it?" she asked, her forehead nearly touching mine. "Who was that call from?"

"My aunt. Nothing's wrong. I'm just tired, like I said."

She held my gaze before responding. "So you're not upset about something?" Her mouth fell open, as if she'd figured it out. "Is it about your cousin's baby? Is it okay?"

I forced myself to laugh. "No, no, the baby's great. I'm serious, Lauren. I'm fine. I just think those shots were a little much for me."

Lauren pursed her lips in thought, and then she nodded. "Well, that I believe. You're such a lightweight, it's embarrassing. Fine, okay, whatever. You go home and be eighty, and I'll stay here with Rob and—hey! Where'd they go?"

She looked back at the space we'd just left, the two guys lost behind a group of college students wearing purple fraternity shirts.

"You'd better go find them," I said. Reaching out to hug her, I added, "Be careful, okay?"

"Yeah, yeah. Okay, Mom," she said, and we went our separate ways—me back to our cramped but cozy apartment, and Lauren back to the nighttime buzz of Providence, Rhode Island.

It took me a long time to fall asleep that night. I was even still awake when, sometime after two o'clock, our apartment door opened. Lauren's heels clicked across the floor, followed by a thud as she tossed them off her feet. At the distinctive sound of chip bags opening, I considered getting up, putting my head in her lap on the couch, and telling her everything—or half of everything, anyway.

When we first met during orientation our freshman year at RISD, I was eager to detach myself from the person I'd been in high school. For those years at Spring Hill High after Persephone died, I stopped being Sylvie O'Leary. I was known instead, through whispers in the halls, as "Persephone's sister." Even as a senior, three years after everyone in my sister's grade had graduated, I still heard that phrase. It hissed from the crowd when I won Outstanding Achievement in Visual Arts at awards night, and it followed me, weeks later, as I crossed the stage to get my diploma. Some days, "Persephone's sister" was a comfort, a reminder that, no matter what had happened, I'd always be tethered to her. But most days, when I heard those words, it took everything I had not to buckle, not to see my fingers locking the bedroom window over and over, the click of the latch echoing in my head.

So in the early days of our friendship, when Lauren asked me about my family (first telling me all about her two "spoiled, obnoxious" brothers and her "embarrassingly boy-crazy" sister), I found myself giving her only the faintest sketch of my life: I had an alcoholic mother, I'd lived for several years with my aunt and cousin, and I had an older sister who'd died.

"Whoa," Lauren said back then, "I'm so sorry. How did she die?"

For a moment, my stomach tightened and my skin felt instantly cold. But then, as if my voice belonged to someone else, I heard myself reply.

"Car accident."

I thought of my grandparents' fatal crash—the crumpled Honda, the faulty airbags that hadn't deployed when they spun out on a patch of black ice and slammed into a tree. Persephone could have easily been in the car with them that night. They could have been taking her to get a hot chocolate at Spring Hill Commons. She'd have been seven at the time, and I, only three years old, might have stayed home with Mom, already blinking toward sleep at seven o'clock.

"But I was really young when it happened," I added. "I barely even remember her."

I held my breath for a moment, waiting to see if Lauren could sense the lies that hovered in the air, but she only frowned a little, said "I'm sorry" again, and that had been it. End of conversation. End of "Persephone's sister." As I exhaled, reveling in my revised history, my lungs felt lighter than they had in years.

After that, Lauren and I lived a thrifty but comfortable life together. We became roommates at RISD our sophomore year. "More like Rhode Island School of Detours," she quipped, but I, having scrambled for my scholarship, having painted some nights until the tips of my fingers bled, didn't view it the same way. She'd wanted to be a tattoo artist from the start (going to RISD was her parents' dream, paid for by their six-figure salaries), and when she got the job at Steve's she came alive in ways I'd never seen before. She designed new tattoos feverishly, leaving them on sticky notes around the apartment—on the toilet lid, an elephant with a trombone for a trunk; on the refrigerator, a light bulb with a ship inside; on the peephole of our door, a stained glass anatomical heart. Then she made me rate them, using a simple rubric of "Would you get this, yes or no?" It didn't matter that she knew I would never get *any* tattoo (a brief point of concern when she later convinced Steve to hire me, saving me from the monotony of art supply stores); she just wanted a chance to talk about what she was doing, because she loved it with a pure, uncomplicated passion—and I envied her that.

When I started my apprenticeship at Steve's, I came to understand what she liked about the job. It was creative, it required thought and skill, and it generated a considerable feeling of power; the tattoo artist, I soon learned, was not only the inflictor of pain, the drawer of blood, but also, on a good day, the fulfiller of dreams. None of that was why I kept up with the apprenticeship, though, or why I accepted the full-time job when I got my license.

After Persephone died, I kept on painting. At first, I wasn't sure why, given how the chemicals had begun to smell like bruises to me, but it became something I loved and loathed in equal measure. I loved it because of how easily you could hide your mistakes—one wrong shade of red, and you could just cover it with another; one leaf that didn't fall into place on a tree, and you could simply paint right over it, start all over. But still, there was always a catch. Even though no one would ever see your error, you never forgot it existed—a thing that haunted, a thing that whispered and gnawed at you beneath the paint. Tattooing was different, of course, but in the ways that mattered—bruise-scented chemicals, the masking of something old with something new—it was the same.

Now, outside my bedroom, the living room TV clicked on. I heard it surge to life and then quiet down as Lauren lowered the volume. But something stopped me from getting up and joining her, kept me staring instead at the moonlit cracks in my ceiling as my birthday slipped by. Somehow, it had happened again; another year had passed in which I'd grown older than my sister.

4

"Sylvie, I need you to come take care of your mother."

A few months after my thirtieth birthday, everything had taken a turn for the worse. I'd been laid off at work unexpectedly, winter had settled over Providence like an icy steel dome, and now, on a particularly brutal January night, Aunt Jill had no patience left for me. I hadn't been down to Spring Hill even once to visit my mother. In fact, I'd only been kept apprised of her treatments and condition because Jill had taken to calling me every Thursday night. Even for Thanksgiving and Christmas, which I usually spent in Hanover with Jill, Missy, and Missy's husband, Carl, I had made flimsy excuses. *Lauren's family invited me to Virginia* or *I can't get enough time off of work.* Swallowing down acidic guilt was safer, I felt, than seeing my mother. I imagined her attached to an IV bag, her eyes widening with an unspoken fear, and each time, the tenderness I felt for her scared me. It was risky— thinking of her in a way that made her easier to love.

Jill never called me out on my lies or excuses; she'd just sigh into the phone and say things like, "You can't stay away forever," or "She's your only parent, Sylvie."

I'm your only sister, Sylvie.

Back when I was living with Aunt Jill and Missy, I used to get jealous whenever Missy went to her dad's house for the weekend. I'd watch her pack a duffel bag with T-shirts and jeans and makeup, and I'd feel a tug at my heart that I didn't yet know was envy. It wasn't that I didn't love Aunt Jill, or didn't feel grateful that she'd swooped in to save me from my mother's darkness; it was just—having a father would have been nice, too. Useful, even.

All my life, it had been just Persephone, Mom, and me, and I had never felt the need for another parent. Still, when I watched Missy's dad pull up to the curb and honk his horn, when I saw Missy's ponytail bounce in the air behind her as she ran to the passenger side of his car, I wondered if things would have been different if one of our fathers—Persephone's or mine—had stayed in the picture. Maybe, I often thought, Mom had lost herself so easily because she had so few people who loved her; in that way, losing just one of us meant losing nearly everything.

Now, the phone pressed to my ear, and Aunt Jill waiting for my response on the other end, I had another, more selfish reason for wishing for a father. If there'd been someone else living in my mother's house, then the task of taking care of her wouldn't have fallen to me.

"I—can't," I said to Jill. "I meant to tell you, actually. I just got laid off at the tattoo parlor, so now isn't really the best time. I have to stay here to look for a new job, send out my résumé, hopefully go on inter—"

"No," Jill cut in, quick to refute the excuse I'd been crafting ever since Steve called me into his office the Friday before. "I'm sorry you were laid off—I really am, and I want to hear more about that later—but if you don't have a job, then this is actually the perfect time for you to come home."

"Yeah, but—"

"Sylvie, there's no 'but' about it. You know that Carl was deployed

last month, and that the baby is due next week. I have other responsi-
bilities, okay? Missy needs me, so I'm heading up to Boston to be with
her. If you hadn't been dodging my calls, then we would have had more
time to discuss this and it wouldn't have seemed so sudden. Now, I'll
drive down to your mother's whenever I can get away, but in the meantime, she needs someone to stay with her. Someone to drive her to her
appointments. Someone to help her when she feels sick."

Her voice wavered, and I closed my eyes as she cleared her throat.
"As you know, she finished up her first chemo cycle back in November,
but things haven't progressed the way the doctors were hoping. They're
starting her chemo again next week, and she can't drive herself to the
hospital. You have to do this, Sylvie. I know it's hard, but you have to
stop thinking only of yourself and just step up."

I'd never heard Aunt Jill speak to me that way before. I knew she
was exhausted and stressed and overwhelmed, but besides all that, I
could tell she was profoundly disappointed in me. In a way, the realization of that fact hit me even harder than hearing about my mother's
diagnosis had.

"You're right," I said. "I just—I don't know how to talk to her."

"So don't talk. Just drive. And cook. And clean. And help."

I hadn't been back to Spring Hill since I'd graduated high school.
On the few occasions I'd seen my mother since then, it was always at
Aunt Jill's, mere miles from the house I grew up in, but miles I was,
nevertheless, unwilling to travel. During those times, our tense barbe-
cues and forced family dinners, Mom pushed around the food on her
plate and said only the shortest sentences to me ("Fine." "That's interesting." "Huh."), and I was always uncomfortable, always aching, my mind
churning to conjure reasons for an early return to Providence.

"I just don't think Mom's gonna be happy to see me," I finally said.

"So what?" Jill shot back. "You think she's ever happy to see me?
Hell, the way she is—the way she's been to you and to all of us for all
these years—I'm never that happy to see her, either. But this is bigger

than that, Sylvie. You have to know that. And if you're not going to do it for your mother, then could you please—please—just do it for me?"

Can you please just do this for me? I'm your only sister, Sylvie.

I squeezed my eyes shut, willing Persephone's voice out of my head. Because it wasn't Persephone asking. It was, with a tone that was both defeated and desperate, Aunt Jill, who had signed my high school permission slips and gone to parent-teacher conferences, who had made my favorite meatballs when I got into RISD and sent me peanut butter cookies all through college. She was right, of course. Someone had to take care of my mother, and the only person left was me.

Lauren saw things differently, though.

"I don't get it," she said the next night as I packed. Her lips were set in a pout, and every time I folded another shirt and put it in the suitcase, she plucked it out and threw it on the floor. "Why can't your mom just hire one of those home-care nurses?"

I folded a pair of jeans, placed them on top of a stack of sweaters, and put my hand over the pile to keep Lauren's off of it. "My mom hasn't worked in years. I don't even know how she's managed to afford her vodka all this time—let alone her treatment."

Lauren groaned, throwing her body back on my bed and swinging her feet up onto the mound of shirts I had yet to fold. "Maybe your aunt can pay for home care, then."

"No," I said quickly. "I can't ask her to do that. She's been supporting my mother financially for years. She'd never admit it, but I know things are tight for her."

"Okay, fine," Lauren conceded, "but let's just think this through for a second. First of all, your mom randomly became a catatonic drunk when you were a teenager, and then she . . ." She stopped then, squinting at me. "What? What's that look about? Is it because I said your mom's an alcoholic? Because I'm sorry, but—"

"No," I cut her off. "It's not that."

It had been the word *randomly*. I'd winced when she said it. But, of course, that word was consistent with the story I'd told her of my life. In the version she knew, there was more than a decade between the time Persephone supposedly died in a car accident and the time Mom started drinking. How could I expect her to connect those dots and understand that, painful as it had always been, there was a reason my mother drank?

I thought about what it would be like to tell her the truth—that Mom was an alcoholic because the worst thing had happened to us, not a tragic but common death like a car accident, but the void of an unpunished murder. I pictured myself confessing that Mom was only half of what haunted me in Spring Hill, that I *did* remember my sister and it was the remembering that, all these years later, kept me awake some nights. But I knew how much it would hurt to speak the truth, to answer the questions that would definitely follow, to be pushed into explaining the whole story—the bruises, the paint, the window.

No one knew how I'd locked Persephone out that night—not Mom or Aunt Jill or the detectives. According to the official police report, Ben told them that he'd dropped her off around ten thirty, but then she'd quickly come back to his car and they'd driven off again. He never told them why she came back; the report had him stating that "she changed her mind."

Now, my throat ached at the thought of telling Lauren any of that. Still, she had seen me wince, and she stared at me now, waiting for me to explain.

"It just wasn't that random," I said, as casually as I could manage. "My mom's drinking, I mean. She was really messed up about what happened to Persephone, and she used alcohol to cope." Lauren's eyes widened and I quickly added, "Even though it had been years since her death."

"Wow," Lauren said, propping herself up on her elbow and looking at me with focused, earnest eyes. "You never bring up your sister." She paused for a few moments. "Do you want to talk about her?"

I forced a chuckle as I stared at the shirt I had folded. "No, I'm fine," I said.

I could feel Lauren's eyes lingering on my face, but I kept on placing clothes into my suitcase. Finally, she said, "Okay. But I'm just saying— reasons or no reasons, your mother has hardly been a mother at all to you for half your life. But now, when things get tough for her, you're expected to go play faithful daughter? How is that fair?"

I sighed, pushing the suitcase aside to lie down next to her. "You're right," I said. "It's not fair. But what choice do I have? Jill has to go be with Missy, and my mom's alone. I'm the only option she has left."

"Or . . ." Lauren said, "I could try to talk to Steve again. Maybe if you had your job back—"

"No. I don't want him to feel worse than he already does."

She rolled her eyes. "You're too nice for your own good, you know. You're giving up everything to go nurse your horrible mother, and you're worried about making the guy who fired you—after you gave *years* of your life to his business—feel just a little bit bad."

"You didn't see him when he was letting me go," I said. "He was close to tears. He kept saying that when business picks up again, he'd love to have me back, but he just couldn't afford it right now. He has a daughter going to college next year. How can you argue with that?"

I certainly hadn't been able to. I'd sat on the metal folding chair in Steve's office and nodded along to his reasons. I'd stared at the faded clock tattoo on his wrist and languidly wondered where I'd go from there. I knew of two other tattoo parlors in a four-block radius, but the idea of sending out résumés, of putting together a portfolio, exhausted me to the point where I'd gone home, crawled right back into bed, and didn't get up again until Lauren came home hours later demanding we talk about it.

"It's still bullshit," she said now. "You know the only reason he fired you instead of me is because I look the part, right?" She pushed up the sleeve of her sweatshirt, exposing her right arm, which was tattooed with a scene she'd designed based off *The Secret Garden*, her favorite book from when she was a kid. "I've got the tattoos, the dyed hair, the nose ring, and you're over here all 'My skin's never even seen the sun, let alone a needle and ink.' It's discrimination."

Lauren loved to claim discrimination. She did it at pizza restaurants when our order took a long time coming out, and she screamed it at female bartenders when they batted their lashes at men while pouring our drinks.

"It doesn't matter," I said. "What's done is done. Even if I still had a job, I don't know that it would change much. My mom's still dying."

The words came out louder than I'd anticipated. They bounced off the ceiling and walls. I hadn't said it like that before. I'd said, "My mom is sick," and "My mom has cancer," but I hadn't yet said what even the hopeful doctors probably knew: she was dying.

Lauren sat up, pulling her knees close to her chest. Then, after staring in silence at my suitcase, she grabbed a shirt from the pile on the bed and folded. "I'm sorry," she said, and then, quietly, "You're doing the right thing."

It was painful to remember, of course, but the truth was—I had once loved my mother so deeply that I couldn't imagine there being anything in the world that could complicate that feeling. Sometimes—it could be anytime, really; when I was just eating cereal, or loading ink into a tattoo gun—a memory of my mother, the way she'd been during the first half of my life, sharpened into focus. When that happened, I often had to brace myself, close my eyes until the familiar pangs in my chest subsided.

That night in particular, as I continued to pack after Lauren had gone to bed, one of my earliest memories suddenly swept through me, rushing into my mind like cold air through an open window.

I was four years old, and I was inventing constellations with Mom on our living room wall. Persephone watched us from the couch, her eyes peering over the third-grade science textbook propped against her knees. As I faced the wall, assessing my canvas, Mom passed me a thin paintbrush, then placed her palm on my shoulder. Even at such a young age, I handled that tool with reverence, with care; I understood that we were working together, the brush and I, to tell a story with stars.

"It's Persephone," I said, touching silver paint to our wall. Three slow, patient dots, then two more, then three again. I dipped the brush back onto the palette that Mom held out for me, then continued to constellate.

"This is your face," I explained, looking back at Persephone on the couch and pointing with the brush. "These are your legs, and this is your dust."

"What dust?" she asked.

"The disappearance dust."

My sister screwed up her nose the way she did whenever she heard an answer that didn't satisfy her. She chewed on the open tip of a Pixy Stix and waited for me to continue. The blue sugar on her lips made her mouth look cold.

"Go on, Sylvie," Mom coaxed. "What's disappearance dust?"

"It's magic," I said. "Now she's here, now she's not."

"What makes you think I have disappearance dust?" Persephone asked.

"You don't in real life," I said, "but in the stars, you're magic."

Mom knelt down so she could look into my eyes. "That's a beautiful idea, Sylvie," she said. She turned her head to look at my sister, who squinted at us, at Mom's hand on my arm in particular. "Don't you think so, Persephone?"

"No," my sister said, her tone sharp but still casual enough. "It doesn't make any sense. There's no such thing as disappearance dust."

Mom looked at the constellation on the wall, the scattered stars near the points that would be Persephone's hands, and smiled. "It's something your sister invented," she said, "and that makes it very special."

Persephone stood up off the couch, her textbook thumping to the floor. "It doesn't make any sense!" she insisted. "It's just stupid! Ooooh, look, I'm going to disappear." She spun around, shaking the remaining sugar from her Pixy Stix onto the carpet, and for a moment, it looked like it was snowing blue flurries in the living room.

As much as she tried to hide it, I could see the promise of a smile on my sister's lips. She meant to be biting, and sarcastic, and perhaps even hurtful, but she was only eight years old, and there is something about spinning freely in a room that just dissolves a child's anger. Persephone twirled and twirled until a single giggle escaped her lips, and then, just like that, she tripped. She fell to the floor, hands first, knees next, her science book caught between her feet.

I couldn't help it; I laughed. I laughed the way we did when we played in the snow together and made facedown angels, our cheeks stinging with the cold and the widths of our smiles.

"Shut up," Persephone snapped, her back arching like an animal as she struggled to get up.

"Hey—language," Mom warned. "Are you okay?" She reached for one of my sister's hands to try to help her up, but Persephone pulled away. Then, as if reconsidering, Persephone crawled back toward my mother and the two became mirror images of each other—the same blonde hair, same slender figure—kneeling together on the floor.

"Looks like a rug burn," Mom said, rubbing a finger against the textured red spot on Persephone's knee.

Persephone looked down and winced. "It hurts," she said. Then her icy eyes sparkled. "Can you kiss it and make it better, Mom?"

Mom sighed and stood up, brushing Pixy Stix sugar from her legs, still holding on to the paint palette. "You're too old for that," she said. "Come on, get up."

But Persephone made no effort to move.

"Please?" Persephone asked, and I was surprised to see that the sparkle in her eyes was just glittering tears. My sister was usually so much stronger than rug burns.

Mom turned away from the human Persephone on the floor to look at the one made of stars on the wall. "What do you think, Sylvie?" she asked. "Is it done, or does it need any finishing touches?"

"Maybe just . . ." I began, but I was cut off by what sounded like a growl coming from deep within my sister's body. I looked over at her just in time to see her spring from the floor and leap toward the wall, palm outstretched. She swiped her hand across the fresh paint, slashing silver through the constellation. For a moment, no one said anything. Then, Persephone made a sound—half sob, half grunt—and she stomped down the hallway. A moment later, I heard our bedroom door slam.

Mom's eyes were closed, the skin of her lids pinched together at the edges. "Why did she do that?" I asked, feeling hot tears gather in my lashes.

When she opened her eyes again, there was a smile in them. "Don't worry about it, okay?" she said. "It's just Persephone being Persephone. Now, look, come down here for a second."

She took the paintbrush from my hand and placed it on the end table. Then she swiped her finger across the tears that had spilled onto my cheek and she lay down on the beige carpet, waving at me to come join her. As I crawled beside her, I noticed that her hair mingled with the blue sugar on the floor, and that those specks looked like tiny jewels.

"Now, look up at the wall," she said, and pointed her finger toward the constellation we'd just made. There was something strangely beautiful about the way it had been ruined. Persephone's hand had made the disappearance dust streak across the stars meant to be her body, and it looked as if she was in motion, twirling in the sky like she'd done in the room minutes before.

"It's like we're looking up at the stars, and we're seeing Persephone," she said, "and just look at all the disappearance dust. I can still see it, can't you?"

I nodded my head but didn't respond, her words like a spell.

"My love for you, Sylvie," she continued, "is exactly like those stars. It's as eternal as each and every one of them. It goes on and on and on."

I smiled, growing drowsy on the floor as Mom spoke, and I nestled my head against her shoulder. We were safe right then, and happy, with blue sugar in our hair and a silver constellation on the wall. And because I wasn't Persephone's age yet, and I wasn't learning science in school, I didn't know that stars don't last forever. I had no idea that the light we see is just an echo of an old burn, or that, most of the time, it's the absence of a glow, instead of the glow itself, that goes on and on and on.

5

We lived on the side of Spring Hill without any highway access, so to get to the yellow ranch where Aunt Jill waited to "hand over the reins" (when she said those words on the phone, I couldn't help but imagine my mother as some leashed wild animal), I had to drive through the north side of town. Past Spring Hill Commons, where middle-aged women peered into shop windows, despite the flurries that dusted their heads. Past the churchlike Town Hall with its white columns and wide doors, its steeple that boasted stained glass windows and a large ticking clock. The benches on the town green were covered in snow so pristine it looked as if someone had laid thick white blankets over them. Even still, an older man had cleared a spot for himself to sit and, as if in prayer, he stared ahead at the gray life-size statue of George Emory, Spring Hill's Revolutionary War hero—and Ben Emory's great-great-great-etc.-grandfather.

Ben had been protected from the start—by his last name, his family's money, by the Emory estate that loomed on the highest hill in town. Spring Hill's own residents had even protected him. As soon as word got out that Ben was a "person of interest" in Persephone's murder, the news stories filled with people classifying the killer as an "out-of-towner."

Even the detectives, Falley and Parker, seemed to do little with the damning information I'd given them. A couple days after Persephone had been found, I worked up the courage to ask Aunt Jill for a ride to the police station, and she steered her car through a sprinkle of snow, swearing under her breath each time we slid on a patch of black ice. Then she sat with me inside the interview room, holding my hand as she, Falley, and Parker heard the secret I'd been hiding.

"I've been painting my sister's bruises," I started.

Parker and Falley exchanged a glance before Parker leaned forward. "Come again?" he asked.

I took a deep breath and looked at Aunt Jill, who, with wary eyes, nodded. "I lied to you guys the other day when you asked me if Ben ever hurt Persephone," I said. "After she comes—came—home from seeing him, she'd have bruises on her."

Parker wrote something on a yellow legal pad. "And you've been painting pictures of them?" he asked.

Falley put her hand on his, stopping him mid-scribble. When he looked at her, she shook her head, tucking loose strands of chin-length brown hair behind her ears. "I think she means she's been painting *over* them," she said.

They held each other's gaze until Parker cleared his throat and drew a line through something on the pad. "Right," he said.

"We saw the paint," Falley explained, folding her hands together over the table. "But just to clarify—do you remember what part of her body had bruises on it the night you last saw her?"

I swallowed—hard. It hadn't occurred to me that they'd already know about it, but of course her body would have been examined. She would have been naked on some long metallic table, her eyes closed, her blonde hair the only cushion for her head. Deft gloved fingers would have pressed against whatever was left of the paint, and the bruises beneath would have been exposed—ugly, menacing things.

"Sylvie?" Aunt Jill squeezed my hand. I looked at her, and she nodded toward the detectives, who waited for me to respond.

"Oh," I said. "Sorry. What was the question?"

"The bruises," Falley began again, her voice gentle and patient. "Do you remember what part of her body they were on?"

I tried to remember. All the daisies and seascapes and storm clouds and ladybugs were blending together. The bruises were usually on her arms, but sometimes it was her shoulder or hip bone or thigh. That final time, though—I closed my eyes, saw her leaning over me, her hair tickling my face, her starfish necklace nearly in my mouth—there'd been a bruise just beneath her rib cage, and two more on—

"Her wrist," I said.

Parker went back to making notes. "And why did you put paint on those bruises?" he asked.

I slipped my hand out of Aunt Jill's and scratched my wrist. "Because Persephone asked me to," I said. "She didn't want our mom to see."

"So this happened more than once?" Falley asked. "You painting over her bruises?"

Jill's eyes were on me, her gaze hot and unrelenting.

"That's what I'm trying to tell you," I said, keeping my eyes locked on Falley's youthful, encouraging face. "This happened all the time. Ben hurt her for months. He did this to her. I know he did. You have to arrest him."

My voice rose in pitch, but I didn't care. As much as my confession made me look bad, it made Ben look far worse—and that was all that mattered. He wouldn't get away with what he'd done to Persephone. He wouldn't be able to hurt some other girl and call it love.

"So I understand you're saying that your sister asked you to do this for her," Parker said. "But how come you never—"

"I don't know," I said, before he could finish what I'd already been asking myself for days. "I just—I don't even know anymore."

I turned to Aunt Jill, and the look in her eyes—not anger, not frustration; just bald, profound weariness—made something in me collapse. "I'm so sorry," I said to her. "I was so stupid. I should have told Mom about it the first time it happened. I can't believe I . . . I'm . . ."

She pulled me into a sideways hug between our chairs. My throat felt thick, my saliva viscous, but the warmth of her embrace was an immediate comfort, like burrowing under blankets on a cold night. As tears slipped from my eyes, the fabric of her sweater soaked them up.

"It's okay, Sylvie," she said. "You're doing the right thing now."

"That's true," Parker added. "We're glad you came to us with this information. We knew the bruises on her wrist and side had happened prior to the strangulation." I felt Jill's body tense up, in sync with my own. "But we didn't know if the two events were connected."

I narrowed my eyes at the sterile way he'd worded it—"the two events." Pulling away from Aunt Jill, I sat up straight in my chair. "They're connected," I said.

Parker nodded once. "We will follow up with this information, for sure."

It's not "information," I wanted to say. *It's the answer. The smoking gun.*

"Sylvie." Falley leaned forward. "Did Persephone ever give any explanation for what Ben did to her? Did she ever say how it happened, or why she stayed with him?"

I shrugged. "Just that they loved each other. And that it wasn't what I thought. She was always saying that—'It's not what you think.'" I shook my head as I realized for the millionth time how foolish I'd been. "But it *was* what I thought. Him killing her proves that."

I said these words into my lap, and when I looked up at the detectives, Parker was staring at me in a lingering, expectant way, as if he felt I was holding something back. But I wasn't—and that was the problem.

The truth was just that simple. My sister, according to her own twisted definition of the word, had allowed a man to love her to death.

The detectives launched into a list of questions then. When did she first come home with bruises? How many bruises did she usually have at a time? Where were these bruises? Here, look at this body I've drawn right here—please forgive me; I'm not an artist—and place an X anywhere you can remember her having been hurt. Did your sister ever say, or give any indication, that her boyfriend had been (a small pause here, a couple taps of a pen) sexually abusing her?

"Why do you ask?" Aunt Jill cut in sharply. "Was she sexually abused on the night she . . ." She glanced at me before adding the final word. "Died?"

Falley was quick to shake her head. "There's no evidence to suggest that," she said. "We just have to cover all our bases. It's standard procedure."

I had a hard time understanding how anything related to what had happened to Persephone could be considered "standard," but I answered the question anyway. "She never said anything like that."

"Okay," Parker said. "But their relationship *was* sexual in nature. Correct?"

"Detective," Jill said, her pronunciation reminding me of when lawyers yelled "Objection!" on TV. "Sylvie is fourteen years old."

Parker looked at Falley, who gave a quick, nearly imperceptible nod, and then turned back to Jill. "That's old enough, I think." He swung his eyes toward me. "But you don't have to answer the question, Sylvie, if it makes you uncomfortable."

It did make me uncomfortable—not because he was asking about sex, exactly, but because he was asking about *Persephone* and sex. It seemed like my sister's privacy had been violated so much already, and now, here was another layer being grabbed at and stripped away.

"I don't know," I said. But then I remembered the glow of her cheeks on nights when she'd stumble back through the window and, to my relief, wouldn't ask me to paint. She'd be smiling in a drowsy, contented way as she got ready for bed, and sometimes, I'd even hear her humming.

"I mean, she never talked about it," I continued, "but . . . yeah, probably."

Jill shifted in her seat as Parker nodded and scribbled onto his pad. "Okay," he said. "Thank you."

For a few moments, neither detective said anything. One of the light fixtures above us buzzed, sounding louder and louder to me until Falley finally spoke.

"Thank you, Sylvie," she said. "Unless there's anything else you think we should know, then that's all the information we need from you right now."

When I didn't say anything, still distracted by the sound of the light (it was kind of like the chorus of bugs Persephone and I always listened to through our open window on summer nights, laughing in our separate beds as we tried to harmonize with them), Aunt Jill slid back her chair. "Thank you for your time, Detectives," she said. The three of them stood, getting ready to shake hands.

"Wait." The word punched out of my mouth, reminding me that there *was* something else. "I—I just have a question."

Falley sat back down, folding her hands on the table. Then Parker and Jill sat, too. "Sure," Falley said. "Ask away."

"Well," I started, "I know you probably need all her clothes—you know, the clothes she was . . . found in—for evidence and stuff, but I—"

"Actually," Parker said, sharing a glance with Falley, "that's something we should talk to you about."

His tone made me feel uneasy, and I saw Jill's hands clasp tighter on her pocketbook. "What is it?" she asked.

"Well," he said, "it's just that, as you know, Persephone's body was covered in over a foot of snow. Because of all that moisture, much of the evidence that might have been on her clothes has been compromised. Hair follicles. Fibers. Things of that nature."

"Compromised," Aunt Jill repeated. "What does that mean exactly?"

"It means," Falley interjected, "destroyed. It's the same with the area surrounding the body. Tire tracks were covered up, and then plowed over. Any footsteps were buried. But—" She leaned forward, setting her earnest eyes on mine. "That doesn't mean it's hopeless. There are a lot of other angles we're investigating this from, and we'll still be keeping her clothes, just in case. Which means—to answer the question I think you were about to ask—we can't give any of that back to you. I'm sorry."

"Does that include her necklace?" I asked. "Or can we have that back?"

Falley tilted her head. "What necklace?"

"The starfish one," I said.

Our mother had given it to Persephone for her sixteenth birthday. When Persephone had opened it, she'd stared at it for a long time. "It reminded me of the Persephone constellation on our wall," my mother had told her. "All those stars Sylvie painted you as." Persephone had pulled the necklace from its box. She'd unclasped it and turned around, holding out each delicate gold end so Mom could put it on her. She'd then walked to the entryway mirror and we'd followed her, admiring how the starfish hung just below her collarbone.

She never took it off after that. She showered in it, went swimming in it during the summer, and often held the pendant absentmindedly between her fingers as we watched TV. Still, the night she had received it, she said to me in the dark as we were falling asleep, "Of course Mom got me a present that had more to do with you than me. She only thought to get me a star because *you* painted me that way."

She was always saying things like that, collecting evidence that our mother loved me more than her. I never really understood where she got this idea; sure, my quizzes hung on the refrigerator instead of Persephone's, but Persephone only got average grades. And yes, I always got to pick the movie we'd see when we'd splurge and go to the plush, air-conditioned theater at Spring Hill Commons, but Persephone always crossed her arms anyway, claiming not to care. Persephone's favorite theory to go on about, though, was that Mom had been madly in love with my father. Naturally, then, Mom favored me, because I reminded her of the man who got away. None of this was true, of course. Both of our fathers had been little more than flings, Mom had always said, even when we were too young to really know what a "fling" was. She was an independent woman, she'd told us, and she could love us more than a hundred fathers ever could. "Well," Persephone would whisper to me conspiratorially, "she can love *you* that much."

It comforted me, then, to see Persephone become so dedicated to the gift our mother gave her. This simple act of wearing the starfish necklace seemed to me an acceptance of the fact that Mom loved us equally. It didn't stop her from hypothesizing about my father, or suggesting that Mom's Dark Days were probably some anniversary related to their relationship, but then again, once Persephone had made up her mind about something, nothing could stop her. Not even her sister's pleas. Not even bruises.

"It's gold," I told Falley in the interview room. "And it has a starfish pendant."

Falley opened a folder on the table and flipped through some papers. She paused as she read, and then closed the folder back up.

"I'm sorry," she said. "Your sister wasn't wearing a necklace when we found her."

"Yes, she was," I insisted. "She never took it off. Ever."

Aunt Jill nodded. "That's true," she said. "I can't remember the last time I saw her without it. Could you check again please?"

Falley reopened the folder as Parker stood up. "I can call over to Evidence," he said. "Maybe it wasn't catalogued with the rest of her personal effects. I'll be right back."

I pressed my fingertips into my knees. Despite its name, the phrase "personal effects" sounded completely impersonal. What about her red coat with the third button missing? What about her black boots that she'd worn until they were gray?

Falley gave us a quick, sympathetic smile, tucking her hair behind her ears again. "This necklace," she said. "It was special to Persephone?"

"Yes," I answered. "My mom gave it to her."

"And she and your mom were close?"

"Um . . ."

I thought of the impatient tone that would creep into Mom's voice whenever Persephone used to ask for a ride somewhere. (*Seriously? I just got home from serving people all day long, and now you want me to serve you, too?*) I thought of the day Persephone got her license, how she bounced around the house, holding it up like a trophy she'd won. But Mom refused to let her use her car. (*If you think I'm letting a seventeen-year-old drive around wherever she pleases, you're crazy. I'll hide the keys if I have to.*) Persephone ran to our room then, slammed the door behind her, and even from the hallway, I could hear her screaming into her pillow. Letting myself in, I watched with wide eyes as she punched her fists against her bed, as she unclenched her fingers to claw at the quilt, her legs kicking, her face becoming bloodred.

Even when they weren't fighting, Persephone would talk about Mom like there was something wrong with her. "You know she drove your dad away, right?" she said to me one night just after we'd gone to bed. "I mean, that has to be it. I don't remember him or anything, but I bet you a million dollars she loved him so much that she suffocated him. Like how she's always doting over you. I don't know how you stand it." I shrugged in the dark but said nothing. I didn't really know what she meant.

"I don't know how to describe their relationship," I said to Falley. "I mean, they weren't, like, super close, but they also weren't, like . . . I don't know." I looked at my hands, knotted my fingers together. "Sorry."

"Oh, don't be," Falley said. "It's a complicated question. I don't know what I'd say, either, if someone asked me about me and my mother."

She laughed a little, and the sound was comforting. "But you're sure she was wearing this necklace the night she drove off with Ben? You saw it on her before she left?"

I remembered her coat, sprinkled with snow as she ran back to Ben's car. I remembered the jeans she'd put on earlier that night ("Ben likes these," she'd said), but I couldn't recall seeing the necklace. It was like asking me to remember if she'd been wearing socks, or if she'd brushed her teeth that morning. How do you remember a specific occurrence of something that happens every day?

"I guess, technically, I didn't see it on her," I said. "But she was wearing a coat. And anyway, I know she was wearing it. She was never not wearing it."

The door opened with a loud click as Parker returned. We all looked at him expectantly, but he just shook his head, keeping his eyes focused on Falley. "She wasn't wearing a necklace when her body was found," he said, "and there was nothing like that recovered at the scene."

"Then Ben must have it," I blurted. "Maybe it fell off her when he was strangling her. Or maybe he kept it as, like, a trophy or memento or something. Isn't that a thing murderers do?"

"Sylvie," Aunt Jill said, placing her hand on my leg.

"I'm serious," I said. "Don't murderers do that?"

Parker rubbed his chin, seeming to think carefully about how to answer my question. Finally, he said, "Sometimes. But that's more consistent with the behavior of a serial killer. And there's no evidence to suggest that this was the work of someone like that."

"Sylvie," Falley said, before I had a chance to respond. "If your sister was, in fact, wearing a necklace that night, and it's missing now, then we have to be open to the possibility that this was a robbery gone wrong."

"What?" I asked. "That's crazy. The necklace was gold, yeah, but it couldn't have been worth that much. You know my mom's a waitress, right?"

Falley shrugged. "Sometimes things look more expensive than they actually are," she said. She paused then, flipping open her folder and jotting something down on the inside cover. "Please be assured that we will look into this. It's a good lead. We can contact pawnshops, and—"

"Pawnshops? It won't be in a pawnshop. It'll be with Ben. I know it."

She paused—for only a moment, but I felt something cryptic in the lag time of her response. "We'll look into that, too," she said.

"In the meantime," Parker piped in, "it would be helpful to us if you could check Persephone's things when you get home. See if she took it off that day for some reason. See if it fell off and slipped under the bed or a pillow or something. Maybe it's in a drawer in the bathroom. You'd be surprised where missing things turn up."

I imagined Persephone then—how the sleeve of her red coat must have looked like a slash of blood in the snow, how the runner who first discovered her must have jogged in place, squinting at what he saw, unsure in the dull morning light if the sleeve belonged to a body, or if it was just some lost, discarded thing.

Even though I knew I wouldn't find it, I scoured our bedroom as soon as Jill brought me home. I banged drawers open and shut, I put my hands between Persephone's mattress and bed frame, I got onto the floor with a flashlight and searched between the clumps of dust under her bed, and I even picked through our trash can, wincing at the paint-smudged tissues. After searching, I felt a strange sense of satisfaction. The necklace wasn't there, so there was only one other place it could be—with Persephone's murderer. With Ben.

But the police never found it—not with Ben, or at a pawnshop, or on the ground that spring, when all the snow was melted and the detectives, in a last-ditch effort, returned to the place where my sister's body had been found. In fact, I had very little contact with Falley or Parker after that day in the interview room. They came over one morning, a week or so after Persephone's funeral, to ask for samples of Persephone's handwriting, but even as I handed them old birthday cards she'd written in for me, they wouldn't tell me why they needed them. After a while, I grew weary of calling them. I grew weary of Falley's voice on the phone, telling me kindly, but firmly, that although the investigation was ongoing, she had no new information she could share.

I was sure that Ben's father was protecting him. For as long as I could remember, Will Emory had been our mayor, and his pockets ran deep. He had inherited ownership of Emory Builders, which had been around since the turn of the century, and it was nearly impossible to throw a rock in Spring Hill without it flying over land that was either owned or developed by the Emorys. As mayor, he was able to use his wealth to an even greater advantage, keeping his hands in every aspect of town government, from planning and zoning to the police force. There were rumors that he would summon individual members of departments into his office, close the door, and use whatever tactics necessary to get what he wanted. No one in town ever seemed fazed by this, though; when it came to Will Emory, "any means necessary" was not a sign of corruption, but just another reason to revere him. *Look how resourceful he is*, residents said.

I'd only seen him on a handful of occasions. He was tall, with irises as dark as his pupils, giving him an unsettling shark-eyed gaze, and his sandy hair had streaks of gray in it. At Persephone's wake, which nearly every Spring Hill resident attended, regardless of how they may have treated us in the past, Will stood with his head bowed somberly, playing the part of the compassionate town leader. When he reached Mom in the receiving line, ready to offer his rehearsed condolences, her knees buckled suddenly, and Will caught her as she fell against him. He had a moment of uncertain stillness, and then he stroked her hair, looking around the room to be sure that everyone saw how comforting he was, how tender. Even then, cloaked in a practiced, artificial sadness, he came off as an intimidating man.

Over the years since then, election after election, town council members had come and gone, but Will Emory remained a constant as the mayor of Spring Hill. Even living in Providence, I'd kept up with him online. I wanted to read that he'd planned an early retirement, or that he'd finally lost the voting public's support—anything that would mean Ben no longer benefited from his father's immunity, his backdoor threats—but all I ever saw were stories about council meetings and ribbon cuttings.

It wasn't just Will Emory's position that gave Ben power; he had a long line of respected Spring Hill ancestors to stand behind him like an army of ghosts. The statue of George Emory on the town green was only part of his family's legacy. Emory Lane was named after Jackson Emory, one of the original colonists who settled Spring Hill in 1674, and Nathaniel Emory had built Emory Bridge back in the 1800s. Even Will's own father, Richard Emory, had been a popular congressman for several terms. Before that, he had expanded Emory Builders' niche from constructing modest houses in local towns to erecting million-dollar homes in vast subdivisions and leasing commercial spaces in strip malls throughout the state. The success of the company transformed the Emorys from a highly regarded, prominent family to town royalty presiding over a business empire. To convict Ben Emory of such a vicious crime would have been to cast a shadow on the entire town's history.

Now, sixteen years later, my sister's case was so cold that I imagined the folders and bags of evidence cracking like ice in the aisles of the police station basement. So much had changed since that day in the interview room, and yet, the details of my sister's death remained a mystery.

As I turned onto the street where Persephone and I had grown to be teenagers together, each making choices we couldn't unchoose, my heart thudded. My stomach felt weightless and heavy all at once. With only a few houses left before I reached our ranch near the end of the road, I caught sight of the cluster of hills where the Emory estate lurked. It was one of the many things that hadn't changed in the years

I'd been away—the Millers' blue house still had a broken shutter on the first floor; our street sign still sat crooked on its metal pole; and the place where Ben Emory had grown up still felt like a taunting, towering presence over the south side of town. I wasn't sure if it was the sight of that distant land, or the thickening flakes of snow against my windshield, but something in that moment made me shiver.

6

Before I could knock or ring the bell, the front door opened. I had been looking down, careful not to slip on the icy walkway, and it took much more energy than it should have to lift my head and meet Jill's eyes. She was smiling at me, dressed in a loose sweater that hid the weight she'd gained over the years, and I was so relieved that it was her instead of my mother that I rushed up the steps and threw my arms around her.

"Whoa," she said, squeezing me in that strong, enveloping way of hers. "Don't know what I did to deserve such a hello, but I'll take it."

Jill's face was a bright burst of joy in the snowy gloom of the afternoon. The consequence of avoiding my mother during her illness, I suddenly realized, was that I'd been keeping myself from Jill as well. Jill who made banana bread on rainy days. Jill who smiled.

"Well, come in," she said. "It's freezing out there."

I stepped inside and wiped my feet on the mat. Then I followed Jill to the living room, where it was so dark I could barely see. The curtains on the sliding glass door were closed, the lights were turned off, and when my eyes adjusted to the shadows, I didn't find Mom on the couch like I'd expected. She was probably squirreled away in her bedroom, and even though that meant I still had a few more minutes alone with Jill until I had to face her, some part of me felt stung by the fact that she hadn't even wanted to greet me.

Pulling off my scarf and shrugging out of my coat, I looked around for a place to put my things. Where had we hung our jackets? My memory offered up an image of Persephone bouncing through the doorway after school and flinging her red coat over the rack in the entryway—the same rack that Mom had knocked over when Persephone went missing. Her rage that day had momentarily paralyzed me, and even remembering it now, I could only stand in the middle of the room, my coat and scarf hanging limply over my arm as I stared at the carpet.

"So," Jill said, "here we are."

I nodded, knowing where this was going. The welcome was over, and now we had to get down to business.

"Is she in the bedroom?" I asked.

Aunt Jill cocked her head, her brow furrowing. "Who?"

Who? I actually laughed—the question was so strange. "Mom," I said.

Jill squinted and then her eyes slid past me, toward the corner of the room.

"I'm right here."

My lungs squeezed shut as I heard my mother's voice, huskier than I remembered, but undoubtedly hers. I saw then what I hadn't noticed when I'd entered the darkened room. Mom, or at least some version of her, was sitting in a recliner by the bookshelf. She was thinner than I'd ever seen her. When had been the last time? Two Junes ago when Jill dragged her to Hanover for another attempt at a family dinner? She'd been thin then as well, and had always been slender, but in the years since Persephone's death, the shape of her body had become less and less defined, more like a teenage boy's than a woman's. Now, though, all of her features seemed sunken. Her cheekbones protruded, and her neck looked like a thin stalk that could barely hold up her head. She'd lost her hair, too—her long, blonde Persephone hair—or at least that's what the scarf around her scalp suggested.

"I . . ." My throat felt dry all of a sudden; my vocal cords grated against each other. "I didn't see you there."

Aunt Jill laughed, the sound of it rich and rippling. "I guess not!" she said. "I was wondering why you hadn't said hello. Thought you were just being shy."

I looked at Mom, but her eyes were so masked by shadows that I couldn't see if they looked at me in return. "I didn't see you," I repeated.

Aunt Jill walked around the couch toward the sliding glass door. "It's because we've got these damn curtains closed," she said. "Is your headache any better, Annie?"

"No."

"Well." Aunt Jill ripped open the curtains, and for a moment, all I could see was crisp, blinding ivory. "We need some light in here."

Mom shielded her face with her hands and I saw how delicate her fingers looked, how easily it seemed they could break. When she lowered her hands, I noticed the brittleness of her skin, flakes gathering on the corners of her lips, the lobes of her ears. She had only wisps for eyebrows, making her forehead seem wide and vast as open land, and her cheeks looked sucked in. She was wearing a gray sweater, with large buttons down the front, and it was almost shocking how completely the shirt consumed her. She looked like a child playing dress-up in her mother's clothes.

I hadn't prepared myself for her deterioration. Every time I'd imagined seeing her again, I'd pictured her looking the same way she had when we were last at Jill's together—curveless as a cigarette, heavy bags beneath her eyes, but still, even through her bitterness, familiar. I never once considered that the bones of her wrists would stick so closely to her skin, or that the shape of her head would seem so alien. I hadn't thought to equate her illness with something that would vacuum her up inside.

"So." Mom's voice halted my thoughts, and I wasn't sure how long or how noticeably I'd been staring at her. "What do you think? Will I be gracing the cover of *Elle* magazine soon?"

My eyes widened. My mother had just made a joke. A dark, mirthless joke, its tone laced with acidity, but a joke nonetheless. What's more—she was speaking to me, and without Aunt Jill's prompting.

"Um . . ." I struggled for an appropriate response. "Not *Elle*, no. But maybe *Marie Claire*. And only if all the regular models are busy that month."

I winced, pulling the coat I was still holding even closer. Mom chuckled, though, and while it was a deeply cynical sound, it was the first time I'd heard any kind of laughter from her since before Persephone died. She rocked lightly in the recliner, her slippered feet pushing gently against the floor, and she was looking at me like she was performing an evaluation. I regretted then not having cut my hair like Lauren always urged me to do. It hung shapelessly down to my shoulders and, according to Lauren, gave me a look of "pathetic self-negligence—like a cat that's given up licking itself."

"Let me take your things," Jill said, reaching for my coat and scarf. As she padded out of the living room, I crossed my arms and looked around, pretending to be interested in whatever changes had been made to the house's decor over the years. But there were none. The couch was the same dusty brown it had always been, and the bookshelves of paperbacks and photo albums appeared unchanged. Even the TV had never been upgraded; it was small and boxy—nothing like the 48-inch flat screen that Lauren and I had in Providence—and on the wall beside that TV, Persephone's constellation. It was twenty-six years old, but somehow, the painted stars still held their shine; the slash of silver where Persephone's hand had angrily swiped was as vivid as the day it had happened. In smaller dots, like metallic snowflakes, the disappearance dust was scattered around the astral points of Persephone's body.

"You kept this," I said to Mom.

She'd been picking at the sleeve of her sweater. "Hmm?"

"Persephone's constellation."

Her lips tightened as she continued to look at her sleeve. She was plucking at something I couldn't see, and as the seconds passed by, heavy and slow, I realized she wasn't going to respond.

"So," Jill said, entering the room again, "should we go over everything? I need to get going in a little bit. I told Missy I'd be in Boston by dinnertime."

My heart quickened at the thought of Jill leaving, but I nodded and followed her into the kitchen. The small space, barely big enough for the table and chairs that were stuffed into it, was open to the living room, and I kept my eyes on Mom as Jill ticked off instructions.

"I've written everything down over here," Jill said. She spread out a few pieces of paper on the counter, and I watched as Mom continued her light rocking. "This is Missy's cell phone number, which I know you already have, but that's okay. This is the number for the cancer center at Brighton Memorial, just in case you have any questions. They're really great over there. During the first cycle of chemo, I was calling them up every other day, and they never got annoyed. This is the number for the pharmacy—try to talk to Fran if you can; she's the nicest of the three—and this is . . ."

The litany of numbers, the orderly way in which she'd prepared me for almost any kind of emergency—it felt like I was babysitting. Still, I was grateful. I didn't know the first thing about taking care of a sick person, and Mom was no child that I'd be watching for just a few hours.

". . . But they'll give it to you if you ask." Jill clicked the top of her pen. "Now, her appointments each week are on Monday and Wednesday. Her chemo always starts at ten a.m., but they draw blood first and take her vitals and everything, so you have to get there at nine on Monday, okay?"

But today was only Saturday, which meant I had nothing to do on Sunday but be alone in the house with my mother.

I looked at her, still rocking gently in the living room, her eyes focused on nothing. She seemed so fragile, as if by pushing her feet too forcefully against the floor, her bones would shatter. So why did I feel so afraid of her? What could she do to me now, in her weakened, skeletal form, that she hadn't ever done before?

"She should have a light meal before you leave on Monday morning," Jill said. "I usually make her scrambled eggs, but cereal would be fine, too. Whatever you want."

"And what about what I want?" We both looked over at Mom, who had turned her head toward us, the first indication she'd given that she'd even been listening.

"Well, okay," Jill said. "What do you want, Annie?"

Mom made a quick scoffing sound. "Not eggs," she said. "Not cereal."

Jill drummed her fingers on the counter, breathed in and out. "Well, what then? Just let us know what you want and Sylvie can go to the store tomorrow."

Mom cocked her head to the side, as if considering her options.

"Hmm," she said. "I'd like some orange juice . . ." Jill grabbed the sheet of paper with the hospital's information on it and started writing. "And some vodka . . ."

"Annie—come on."

"What?" Mom opened her eyes wide in a look of feigned innocence. "It'll be like a mimosa. That's breakfast, Jill."

Jill crossed out what she'd written, slicing her pen through the words "orange juice" as if she meant to obliterate the drink completely.

"I don't get it," Mom continued. "They pump me full of all this poison, but God forbid I enjoy a cocktail to make it all go down easier."

As Jill glanced at me, the annoyance in her eyes was clear as the crow's-feet that puckered her skin. "Your mother's quite the comedian when she's sober," she said.

And that was it, of course. She was sober. It hit me like the sudden twitch of a body nearly asleep. That was why she was speaking to us, why she seemed so different from the woman who could only mumble out half-responses at Jill's house two summers before. The vodka on her breath had been a constant for so many years that I hadn't considered how her cancer would change that. She was sober—she was finally, finally sober—but even so, she didn't feel like the mother I'd known before she started chasing her grief with alcohol. The mother from my childhood was peaceful, her voice as soothing to me as aloe on a burn, but this woman's words had edges; they were cold and comfortless, wrapped in barbed wire.

"I'm sure you already know this," Jill said to me, "but she can't have any alcohol. No matter what she says or does. Besides being absolutely horrible for her, it hurts her now, too." She turned her head back toward Mom. "Doesn't it, Annie?" She raised the volume of her voice, as if talking to someone elderly.

"If you say so, Jill," Mom said. "Thank goodness the chemo feels so good instead."

Jill ignored the comment, leaning her face close to mine, speaking just above a whisper. "Alcohol makes her feel like her esophagus is burning. Her words—believe it or not—not mine. That's how we first discovered something was wrong."

I nodded, trying to imagine my mother calling Aunt Jill one day, a tinge of anxiety in her voice as she confessed that the thing she'd relied on for so long felt like it was killing her now instead.

"Hey." Jill looked concerned. She circled her warm hand around my wrist, making me realize how cold I felt, even through my RISD sweatshirt. "Are you okay?"

"Yes," I said. "I just . . ." I lowered my voice, turning my back toward Mom. "I didn't expect it to be like this."

Jill tilted her head, rubbing her thumb into my palm. "Which part?"

"All of it, I think."

I knew I was being selfish. For the past several months, Jill had given up everything to take care of Mom—not to mention all the years she'd bought her groceries, paid her property taxes, handled general upkeep of the house, made sure Mom survived. Now, here I was, back home for only a few minutes, and already, I was buckling. How could Aunt Jill trust me with this? Even with her extensive notes and numbers, how could she expect me to know what my mother needed? I was in my thirties now—the deepening lines around my eyes reminded me of that every day—but suddenly, I felt more like a child than I had in years.

"It's gonna be fine," Jill said. And then, because she was always truthful, she added, "It's gonna have to be."

I squeezed Jill's hand and managed a smile. "I know," I said, though my nerves still felt taut as tightropes.

Her eyes lingered on my face before shifting over to the clock on the microwave. "I need to get going." She sounded apologetic—guilty, even.

"Okay," I said. "Are you sure you're gonna be all right to drive, though?" I looked toward the sliding glass door, and the sky still glittered with falling snow. "It seems to have picked up a little."

"Oh, she'll be fine," Mom said from the corner of the room. "Don't you know? Your Aunt Jill is a superhero, always swooping in to save people. Not even a blizzard could stop her." A wry smile crept into her lips.

"I've got four-wheel drive," Jill said to me, as if she hadn't even heard Mom speak. "It'll be a piece of cake."

"Yeah, of course," I agreed. "Tell Missy I'm thinking about her, okay? And let me know as soon as the baby's born."

A soft glow blossomed on Jill's cheeks at the mention of her soon-to-be grandchild. "You bet," she said. Then, with a slow intake of breath, she walked toward Mom. "Okay, Annie. Sylvie's gonna take it from here, all right?" I followed her into the living room, watching as she put her hand on Mom's shoulder. "Is there anything I can do for you before I leave?"

Mom shook her head, and as she did, I noticed a few strands of blonde hair still clinging to the nape of her neck. "I'm peachy," she said.

"Okay." Jill leaned down, kissing Mom's cheek, and I was surprised to see that Mom closed her eyes. She even lifted her hand to cup Jill's elbow, a gesture so tender that I felt as if I'd intruded on something by witnessing it.

"Love you," Jill said, and I saw when she straightened back up that her eyes were shiny with tears.

"Mmm," Mom replied.

Jill ran a finger beneath her eyelashes and then focused her attention on me. "Well," she said, "my stuff's already in the car." She stepped forward and wrapped me in a hug. "Oh, Sylvie. I wish I had more time to catch up with you. I'll be back to help out as soon as I can, though. I promise."

I nodded against her shoulder, and when we pulled away from each other, I whispered, "Okay." There was more I should have said, but in that moment, I knew I could only say so much before my voice gave away how urgently I wanted her to stay.

7

I'd been expecting our bedroom—Persephone's and mine—to look exactly the same. I'd imagined it like an exhibit in a museum, the artifacts of our childhood untouched—and for my side of the room, that was true. Besides the tightly made bed that I assumed Aunt Jill had been sleeping in, all of my things were precisely, eerily, the way I had left them. But Persephone's side looked plundered. Though her tag-sale dresser and her bed with its tattered quilt remained, everything else was missing—even the dream catcher that had hung above her bed, even the jewelry box full of chunky, colorful necklaces that she'd stopped wearing when Mom gave her the gold starfish.

The closet held only my things: school folders, forgotten stuffed animals, old dresses and coats. Persephone's clothes were gone, but the hangers that once held them were clinging to the wooden pole as if certain they still had a purpose. Where was her vial of dried lavender, which she'd smell sometimes after arguing with Mom? Where was her dark green afghan, which she'd draped around her body like a robe on winter mornings?

When I left home—first to go live with Aunt Jill, and then to Providence—Persephone's neat rows of lipsticks had still been on the bureau. I knew this because I used to open their caps, twist the sticks until their colors bloomed from their metal tubes, and mime the way my sister had put them on. It was always my own reflection that looked back at me, though, and never, as some childish part of me had hoped, Persephone's.

I couldn't imagine Mom getting rid of Persephone's things. That would have required her, in her glassy-eyed, boozed-up states, to gather boxes, sort through clothes, and face that her daughter was dead.

As soon as Jill had left that afternoon, Mom had turned on the TV and seemed absorbed in an infomercial on vacuum cleaners. For a few moments, I'd stood in the middle of the room, watching the flashes of "easy payments" and "limited time offer," but then I'd wondered if she'd turned the program on just so we wouldn't have to speak to each other.

"I'm gonna go get my suitcases from the car," I'd told her, and she'd only lifted her hand a little in response. Now, looking at Persephone's side of the room, scrubbed clean of her existence, I had the urge to march back into the living room, stand in front of the TV, and demand to know what had happened to all those scraps of my sister's life. The thing that stopped me, though, was the window.

After Persephone died, I'd kept the cheap venetian blinds drawn and closed, unable to look at the latch I'd locked that night. It didn't matter that the room was always dim as a result; I had to give myself a fighting chance in those months after it happened. Now, the blinds were wide open, and I could imagine Aunt Jill pulling the string to lift them up that morning, blinking at the cloudy light outside. I walked to the window and reached for the latch, switching it back and forth— locked, unlocked, locked again. It would have been so easy to let her back in that night. I could have played off the lock as a prank, and maybe we even would have laughed about it together. Instead, I now had to wonder if one of her last thoughts, with Ben's hands around her neck, with her breath trapped like a rock in her throat, was that I'd done this to her.

Turning away from the window, I hefted one of my suitcases onto my bed. As I unzipped it, my phone chimed with a text message. I pulled it out of my back pocket and was immediately comforted by the sight of Lauren's name on the screen.

"Okay, it's been a few hours," she wrote. "You coming back yet?" Then she sent a picture of a sticky note, on which she had drawn a little map of Connecticut and Rhode Island. Over Spring Hill, she'd placed a bold red X, the upper right point of which extended into an arrow that traveled all the way to Providence. There, she'd outlined a boxy little house with hearts for the door and windows.

"If you're home by Monday," Lauren added, "I'll give you a huge discount on this tat."

"And mess up my whole brand?" I joked. "I'm the tattooless tattoo artist!"

"Exactly! It's so unexpected. Steve would hire you back in a second. He'd be like 'OMG look at her commitment to the craft! And Lauren, YOU designed this stunner? I must give you a raise at once! An extra three thousand dollars a week, plus one puppy (pre-house-trained) every other month!'"

I laughed, and then covered my mouth to catch the sound. With the TV on, Mom probably wouldn't have even heard me, but it felt inappropriate, somehow, to be laughing in that house. I flicked my gaze toward the window latch again and I felt my smile go slack.

"That sounds just like Steve," I wrote after a few moments.

"Obviously," she replied. Then she added, "So how is it being back at your mom's house?"

I hesitated before responding. What could I say? That things were even stranger here than I'd imagined? That it wasn't just Mom that seemed skeletal, but my bedroom, too, Persephone's things having vanished right along with the muscle from Mom's bones? If I explained that to Lauren, I'd have to explain so much else. Instead, I wrote, "It's okay, I'm unpacking now, I'll update you later," and I let my phone slip onto the bed.

As I looked back toward my suitcase, my eyes swept across some of my old paintings that leaned against the wall in the corner of the room. I remembered bringing them over from Aunt Jill's just before I left for college. I'd planned to find a place to store them in the house, but in the rush of it all, my eagerness to leave, I never had. Now, unlike Persephone's things, they were still here, seemingly untouched. Kneeling in front of the stack, I blew a layer of dust off the top of the canvases and began to flip through them.

How easily it came back to me then, the single-mindedness with which I'd painted in the years after Persephone died. My grades had slipped, and the school psychologist said it was normal, that I was likely depressed. In those days, all I wanted was to move away from the black hole of my mother's grief, from the place where everything in my life had become unhitched.

The guidance counselor kept reminding me that college could be my fresh start, that even as an underclassman, it was never too early to start preparing for my future.

"Because you still have one," she said, "no matter what you've lost. You're still allowed to have dreams, you know. You're still allowed to chase them."

I winced when she said it—the cheesiness of it, the fact that my only dream was to go, get out, be gone—but I couldn't deny that college was the logical solution to my problem. I knew that I'd never be able to afford it—I didn't have enough money for a week's worth of groceries, let alone tuition—which meant I'd need to get a full scholarship somewhere. And with my missing homework assignments and late papers dragging down my once stellar GPA, the only chance I had left was art school.

Miss Keegan, the art teacher at Spring Hill High, had thought of me as her star student. "She's got it!" she said to my mother at the freshman art show, just one month before Persephone died. "I show her a new technique and she picks it up right away! I can't wait to see what she does in the next few years, once she really finds her voice." Mom had smiled at me, wrapping her arm around my shoulder, and Persephone had stood in the school gymnasium with her arms crossed, a freshly painted bruise hiding beneath the sleeve of her sweater. I'd believed, back then, that Miss Keegan was right; I would develop my own style, and someday I'd have gallery openings and pieces that sold for thousands of dollars. But when Persephone died, I couldn't bring myself to care about finding my voice as an artist any more than I could muster the motivation to study for tests and quizzes. All I knew was that if I did the work that Miss Keegan assigned, and made it seem as if it came from deep inside me (angry slashes of red on an otherwise soothing blue; a clay bust of my mother and sister, both heads supported by the same neck), then I could continue to fool her into thinking I "had it," that indefinable quality that makes someone an artist, instead of just good at art.

When I lived with Aunt Jill during high school, I spent my Friday and Saturday nights painting. While other girls my age went to the mall or had sleepovers, I was determined to create at least one new piece to show Miss Keegan the following week. Every Friday, she sent me home with a blank canvas (which I often suspected she paid for herself), and every Monday, I returned to school with a completed painting. "Motivated and highly skilled," I pictured Miss Keegan writing in a letter of recommendation, "Sylvie is the most prolific young artist I've ever known." On the nights I painted, Jill would often come into the guest room, watch me sweep my brush across the canvas, and she'd put her hand on my shoulder as if she was concerned about something she didn't know how to articulate. I continued painting even when she stood behind me like that. I couldn't rest until I knew the piece looked as if it meant something profound. Miss Keegan wasn't always convinced; sometimes, she would hold the canvas out in front of her, pushing her lips to one side. "Go deeper," she'd say. "What is this window supposed to show us exactly? What do you want us to feel?" Then, I'd take the painting back to Aunt Jill's, ignore my Algebra II homework, leave the assigned chapters of *The Things They Carried* unread, and paint Persephone into the picture, her body visible through the window, dressed in a red coat, walking away. When I did things like that, I had to ignore the pounding of my heart. I had to convince myself that it wasn't Persephone I was painting; it was my ticket away from home.

And in the end, it was worth it. I won the art awards, I won the RISD scholarship, I won a life without my mother. Only now, here I was again—a jobless tattoo artist, back at the very same place I'd made it my mission to leave.

"Looks like you haven't gotten too far."

The canvas I was holding slipped from my hand at the sound of Mom's voice.

"With what?" I asked, standing up and turning to face her in the doorway.

"Unpacking," she answered.

"I was just—looking at my stuff," I said. "Haven't seen any of this in a while."

"Hmm. Well."

She stared out the window as if something fascinating were happening out on our street. For a moment, I was jealous; when she looked through the glass, she saw the usual houses and snowy lawns dotting the road. She didn't spot Persephone lurking out there, unable to come inside, her icicle-thin fingers pressed against the panes.

"Mom, what did you do with Persephone's things?"

I held my breath as I waited for her to answer. Was she going to ignore me, pretend I hadn't spoken, the same way she had when I'd asked about Persephone's constellation in the living room?

"Oh," she finally said, her eyes still focused out the window. "I gave them to that boy."

Something heavy dropped into my stomach. That boy? The only boy with any connection to Persephone was Ben.

"What boy?" I asked, an edge to my voice I hadn't intended.

She waved her hand dismissively. "That neighbor boy," she said. "Her friend from down the street."

But the only friend Persephone had ever had on our street was Faith Dunhill, a girl who'd moved away at the end of eighth grade.

"Who are you talking about?" I tried again. "Ben Emory? He didn't live down the street."

Mom's head snapped toward me, and in a single second, the expression that passed over her face went from surprise to horror.

"Why—" she sputtered. "Why would you say that name?"

I studied the tears that had so suddenly sprung to her eyes.

"So, it wasn't him?" I asked.

"No!" She let out a quick sob of a sound, and she backed away from the door, her feet falling out of her slippers as she stumbled into the hallway.

Before I had the chance to stop her, she spun into her bedroom and slammed the door. I hesitated for a moment, then followed, twisting her doorknob several times, but each time, the brass handle clicked.

For some reason—despite what history should have told me, despite how desperately she'd run away—I was certain the door would open. And just like that, I was fourteen again. I slumped to the floor outside my mother's room, my skin prickling from a new charge in the air, as if, on the other side of that door, a dark and desperate storm cloud brewed.

"Mom," I called, my hand slipping from the doorknob and landing in my lap. "Mom, just let me in."

There was the creak of her mattress as she climbed into bed, then a rustle of blankets, and then nothing.

"Mom," I called again, even though I knew she wouldn't answer me.

For the next few minutes, I sat with my back against her door, my knees pulled up to my chest. My heart was a heavy, throbbing thing, and when I looked at my hands, I was surprised to find they were shaking.

8

The next morning, I woke to a call from Aunt Jill.

"Hey," I answered, my voice deeper than normal. I pulled the phone away from my ear to check the time. It was eleven thirty-two—the latest I'd managed to sleep since college—and I sat up sharply.

"Hey yourself," Jill said. "I'm just calling to see how things went yesterday and to make sure you're all set for tomorrow."

I grabbed a sweatshirt from the foot of my bed, struggling to respond as I pulled it on. "Things didn't go so well," I started to say, but the words stopped dead in my mouth as soon as I saw Persephone's bed. All through the night, I'd been careful to keep my body turned to the wall. I hadn't wanted to risk glimpsing what used to be the space where she slept. Stripped of all the belongings that once surrounded it, it looked so impersonal, so unhaunted, but I knew that if I squinted, I could still make out her ghost.

"Hello?" Jill prompted, but she sounded so far away.

I twisted to face the wall again, sinking down under my blankets as if going back to sleep. "Mom locked herself up," I said quietly.

"Oh Lord." I could almost hear Jill rolling her eyes. "What happened now?"

"I brought up Ben Emory."

There was a beat of silence as Jill hesitated. "Why?"

"Because when I asked her where all of Persephone's things were, she said she gave them to 'that boy.' I didn't know what other boy it could have been, so I asked if she meant Ben. Then she freaked out, and she's been in her room ever since. She didn't even come out for dinner."

The more I spoke, the wearier I felt. Instead of being refreshed from sleep, my body felt drained, weightless.

"It was crazy," I went on. "It was just like . . ."

Mom's Dark Days, I was going to say. But Jill didn't know about those. Persephone and I had never told her how on the fifteenth of each month, Mom would begin the day normally—sometimes even giddily—and then, just a little while later, the atmosphere in the house would change, and Mom would slink off to her bedroom, where she'd lock herself away for the rest of the day.

Persephone would tighten her lips then, watching Mom disappear down the hall. She'd help me pack my schoolbag and walk me to the bus stop. And we lived like that, month after month, until Persephone died and then all of Mom's days became dark.

"Just like what?" Jill asked.

"Just like after Persephone died," I said. "I told you I'd be terrible at this, Jill. It hasn't even been a full day yet, and I've already upset her so much that she's right back where she was. I'm sorry, I just don't—"

"All right, stop it." The firmness in Jill's voice made me flinch. "Do you think I expected you to walk right in, snap your fingers, and have everything be perfect?"

"No . . ."

"Do you think she never once locked herself away while I was taking care of her?"

"I don't know . . ."

"Sylvie, this is your mother we're talking about. She's not drinking anymore, so she's much more alert, yes, but she's still Annie. And I love my sister, I swear I do, but that woman has been a mystery to me for a very long time. So buck up. She's bound to backslide now and then. And just remember—when she gets like this: let the child pass out."

"Let the what?"

"It's something Grandma used to tell me, a million years ago, when I started babysitting. I was so nervous that they wouldn't listen to me and they'd threaten to hold their breath or something until I—I don't know—gave them cookies, or let them tie me to a chair and set the house on fire. So Grandma told me, 'Let the child pass out,' meaning— let them have their tantrum. Let them hold their breath all they want, because they'll only pass out and then wake up again a few seconds later."

I smiled a little. Jill always found a way to comfort me.

"Let the child pass out," I repeated. "Okay, I'll keep that in mind. But, Jill—do you know what boy she was talking about?"

Jill chuckled. "The boy she supposedly gave your sister's things to? No. In fact, you got a much more specific answer than I ever did. All she told me was that she'd gotten rid of it all. Like I said, she's a mystery to me."

"Okay, but—"

A creak from across the hall—the sound of Mom's door opening— forced me to stop. I jumped out of bed, like a soldier snapping to attention.

"She just came out," I whispered. "I should go."

With the phone still pressed to my ear, I cracked my door just wide enough to see Mom head into the living room, carrying a bowl with a spoon in it. She wore the same sweater and head wrap as the day before, but still, the smallness of her, the acuteness of her frame, was just as shocking as the first moment I'd seen her.

She'd had her tantrum, though—I'd let the child pass out—and now, at the sight of a cereal bowl in her hands, I felt a whisper of hope. She must have already come out that morning, or even late last night, and sick and skeletal as she looked, she had eaten something. This was a good sign.

"Okay," Jill said in my ear, and I realized with a jolt that she was still on the line. "Listen—just keep me in the loop about how things are going, all right?"

"I will," I said. "I'll talk to you soon. Love you."

Following Mom to the kitchen, I watched her place her bowl into the sink.

"Did you have some breakfast?" I asked.

Her only response was to turn the faucet on, watch the water as it collected in her bowl, and then turn it off. Walking closer to her, my bare feet winced against the cold kitchen tiles.

"Mom?"

The knuckles of her left hand were white from gripping the counter. As she stood there, staring into the sink, I thought I could smell something familiar rising off her skin—not a perfume, exactly, but a scent that was naturally, uniquely, hers. It reminded me of those nights she'd return home late from her shift at the restaurant and I'd already be in bed. She'd creep into our room so quietly I almost didn't hear her, and then she'd kiss my forehead, run her long, cool fingers down the side of my face. "Good night, my sweet girl," she'd say, and as I stood behind her now, my eyes closing as I breathed her in, I remembered how she would pull my blankets up toward my chin, tucking me in and making me safe.

"Mom," I said again. "Are you okay? Can I get you anything?"

She swayed a little, like a thin tree in a breeze, and just as I was about to put my hands out to steady her, she turned around. Her face was so close to me then, so significantly changed from those childhood nights I remembered, that I almost stopped breathing again. Her eyes were two moons, gray and opaque.

"I'm fine," she said abruptly, and then she moved to step around me.

As she walked back toward the cave of her bedroom, the ridge of her spine stabbed through her sweater. Soon she disappeared around the corner, and it was only a few moments before I heard her door close, heard the lock click from inside.

She didn't speak to me again until the next day, when the nurse at Brighton Memorial's cancer center hooked an IV into her arm. We hadn't spoken in the car, where the only sounds between us were that of a morning radio show, and we hadn't spoken when I checked her in at the hospital or when her blood was drawn and vitals were taken.

She'd replaced the head wrap she'd been wearing for the past two days with a shoulder-length blonde wig. She was wearing makeup, too—just some eyeliner and blush, maybe a hint of color on her lips, but it softened her features. She seemed less angular and washed out, and though the clothes she wore sagged against the edges of her body, she looked more like the woman I'd known before Persephone died. More like Mom.

Still, it was only when they led us into the chemotherapy room, sat Mom down in what looked like a dentist's chair with a small TV attached to it, and threaded the needle into her vein that she finally said a word to me.

"That person you were talking to on the phone yesterday," she said. "Was that your boyfriend?"

I snapped my eyes to the few other patients in the room, as if they would share my surprise at Mom's bizarre question. No one even glanced my way, though, and the nurse making adjustments to Mom's IV bag only smiled at me and offered a look that said, "Oh moms."

"No," I said. "It was Aunt Jill."

Mom nodded. "I see," she said, holding her arm out as the nurse strapped another piece of tape over the IV. "Have you spoken to your boyfriend yet?"

I opened my mouth to answer and then closed it again. Had Aunt Jill, for some inexplicable reason, told her I had a boyfriend? Or was she working off old information? Maybe she was thinking of Robbie Silano from a couple years back. Maybe Jill had mentioned that she met him one time when she came to visit me, and Mom just assumed we were still together.

"I don't have a boyfriend," I told her.

"Oh." Mom folded her hands together in her lap. "Well, you better hurry up, then," she said. "You're almost thirty."

The nurse—Kelly, she'd told me when she'd introduced herself— gave a quick, throaty chuckle, but I was too taken aback to respond myself. *Almost thirty*—even though I'd been thirty for four months. It shouldn't have bothered me—I hadn't received so much as a birthday card from her in years—but still, something heavy gathered in my chest.

"Oh, Annie, don't give her such a hard time," Kelly said, gently flicking Mom's shoulder with her hand. "She has plenty of time to find someone."

Kelly winked at me and I managed a smile.

"Easy for you to say," Mom replied. "Your wedding's in March, right?"

"March twentieth," Kelly said, nodding. "Good memory! I haven't even seen you since—when was it? November?"

"Good memory yourself."

Kelly smiled, leaning forward to press some buttons on Mom's TV screen. "Just don't be expecting an invitation to my wedding. I don't want Owen to take one look at your pretty face and then leave me at the altar."

"That's probably wise," Mom said. "I've been cultivating a new look lately that will be sure to drive men wild. I call it cancer chic."

I stared at the two of them in disbelief. As they joked together, Mom seemed so normal. With just a couple of sentences and a wave of authentic laughter, it was as if she hadn't spent most of the last sixteen years in self-imposed isolation, as if she hadn't just lost track of her daughter's age, and hadn't shut herself in her room at the mention of Ben Emory two days before.

"So I'm sure you remember the drill," Kelly said, "but since it's been a little while, I'll give you a quick refresher. This is your TV, and you can press these buttons on the side to change the channel. I'll be in and out to check on you, but you can press this other button over here if you need me at any time. We've got bottled waters in the little fridge over there—you're welcome to one as well, Sylvie—and there are some books and magazines on the bookshelves in the corner. Just have Sylvie get them for you if you want anything. Your job now is just to sit and relax."

Mom leaned her head against the back of the chair and closed her eyes as if she were going to sleep. "Ahhh," she said, "a regular day at the beach. Just bring me a piña colada and I'll be all set."

Kelly laughed, met my gaze, and pointed at Mom. "I love her," she mouthed, and then she turned around and left us there, Mom stretched out in her modified dentist's chair, hooked up to a bag and a machine, and me sitting down slowly, uncertainly, in the seat beside her.

As I glanced around the room, I realized that it looked nothing like I'd anticipated. I'd been picturing a small, dim space with a smell like a damp basement and a feeling of dread pushing down from the ceiling. This wasn't like that, though. It was bright and modern and clean, smelling faintly of citrus, and there were vases of fresh flowers throughout the room.

"Wow," I said, "this is a pretty nice place, huh? For—a treatment center, I mean."

Mom shifted her eyes toward me. "Oh yeah. It's a real five-star resort."

There was that acidic tone again.

"Well," I replied, "it just looks, and feels, a lot better here than I expected. It's—actually—how are you able to afford this, Mom?"

She shrugged. "I have health insurance. Jill nagged me to get it."

"So Jill's paying for it?" This made sense. Jill had paid for everything else that had kept Mom alive and comfortable over the years—food, carbon monoxide detectors, a new furnace when the one that was original to the house broke down and Mom barked, "Leave it, Jill. I don't mind the cold."

"No," she said now. "I'm not her child, you know. I pay for it myself."

"But how?" I pressed. "I mean, growing up, we lived paycheck to paycheck, and now you're just—"

"It's none of your goddamn business, okay?"

Her eyes were cool as metal as she snapped them toward me. A couple of other patients turned their heads my way before quickly returning to their screens and magazines.

"Okay," I said, "I'm sorry."

But I couldn't stop thinking about it. She'd done nothing in the last sixteen years but spend whatever money she'd had on alcohol. She shouldn't have been able to afford the type of health insurance that would cover her treatment. I decided to let it go for the moment, though; it was clear I wasn't going to get anywhere.

"You look nice, Mom," I said, changing tactics. "I like that wig on you."

She ran her hand over the unnaturally smooth hair on her head. "Jill picked it out," she said.

"It's nice. Do you always wear it when you leave the house?"

"Most of the time," she said. "No need to go around looking like a bald eagle." Her eyes were focused on her hands in her lap, her fingers rubbing at the knuckles that bulged beneath her skin. "I don't want anyone I know to see me the way I am now."

It was an unusually vulnerable thing for her to say, and I tried to appreciate that, but there was a nagging, bitter part of me that reacted differently. *You never cared how people saw you before*, it whispered. *You never cared that people at school always talked about how they'd seen "Annie O'Drunkie" walking to the liquor store in her nightgown, or how you showed up to my high school graduation with your hair a total mess and your stained clothes reeking.* But, I tried to remind myself, that was back then. She wasn't a drunk anymore; she was sober, and maybe sober, she'd regained her ability to feel exposed in the world.

"Can I get you anything?" I asked. "A bottle of water?"

Mom curled up her lip. "Ugh, no. Chemo makes water taste terrible. I could throw up just thinking about it."

"Okay," I said, scanning the room for other things to offer her. "How about a magazine, then?"

She shook her head. "I don't care about celebrities."

"Do you want to watch your TV?"

"I don't care about celebrities," she repeated. Then, cocking her head as if she'd just thought of something, she added, "But there was a book I was reading during my last chemo—whenever I could concentrate, anyway. Jill found it for me on the bookshelf over there."

She pointed to one of the pristine white shelves in the corner, and I stood up, eager to have a task to complete. "What book?" I asked.

"*Withering Heights*," she said.

"Oh—you mean *Wuthering Heights*?"

"That's what I just said."

"Right," I replied, smiling a little.

I walked to the bookshelf and ran a finger along the titles. There was no rhyme or reason to the way the books had been shelved; Michael Crichton was next to a Spider-Man comic, and a volume of Walt Whitman poems was stuck between *Dracula* and a book with a bright pink spine. Unable to find *Wuthering Heights*, I moved on to the other bookshelf, which mostly held old issues of *Time*, *National Geographic*, and *People*.

"I didn't see it over there," I said to Mom when I reached my seat again. "I'm sorry."

She looked at the other patients suspiciously, as if somebody were hiding the book from her. "But no one else in here is reading it," she whined.

"Do you want me to ask one of the nurses if they've seen it anywhere?" I asked, and I was surprised when she nodded her head vigorously.

"Okay," I said. "I'll be right back."

As I walked out of the treatment room and tried to orient myself in the bright, spacious lobby where the elevator had dropped us off that morning, I felt instantly more at ease. This was good, having a job to do. I could get books, I could get blankets, I could even try to find liquids that didn't taste as terrible as water. And, for all the stops and starts we'd been having, Mom and I had actually talked to each other for a few minutes. It hadn't been the warmest conversation in the world, but it was still something, and it was infinitely better than her being—

"Oof."

"Oh God, I'm so sorry."

I'd crashed right into a nurse, my forehead colliding with his chin.

"That was totally my fault," he said. "I wasn't watching where I was going. Are you okay?"

I kept my head down and my hand against my forehead, a wave of embarrassment flooding my cheeks.

"I'm fine," I said. "I wasn't watching where I was going, either. I'm sorry."

"Here, let me just . . ." He raised his hands as if to touch my face and then lowered them. "Can I?" he asked.

I nodded, then quickly winced as his cool fingers pressed against my forehead, targeting the exact point of pain.

"Yeah, that's gonna hurt for a bit," he said. "But I think you're gonna live."

"Oh, good."

I was about to apologize again, but suddenly, he jerked backward. That's when I got my first clear look at him—short brown hair, dark eyes, midthirties. I saw the scar along his cheek, the way it swept across the side of his face like a large comma, and I remembered that face—I remembered it in windows, in nightmares.

"Oh, shit," he said.

My skin went cold, my legs felt loose, and it was as if I were standing outside being blown about by the January wind. We stared at each other, and for the first time since it happened, we were face-to-face— the one who'd lost Persephone and the one who'd taken her away.

9

Persephone once told me that Ben's eyes were like black holes.

"In the most beautiful way possible," she'd clarified. "They're so dark and so deep, it's easy to get lost in them."

Her voice had been soft when she told me this, and all I could do was focus on the umbrella I was painting on her forearm, my grip tightening on the brush.

"And it's not only that," she continued. "His eyes are so dark they make everything else seem brighter. His skin. His hair. The air around you. And then, it's like, among all that light, there's just this pure, exquisite blackness. And it pulls you in."

She'd had her free hand latched onto her starfish pendant, sliding it back and forth across its chain as she waited for me to respond. But ever since she'd come home that night, climbing through the window and pushing up her sleeve, offering her bruised arm to me like a request, I'd been trying to tune her out. I'd had no desire to hear about Ben's eyes or his love for his grandfather or the way he laughed when she surprised him. I'd known that whatever Persephone said had no bearing on the person Ben really was; she'd only wanted me to believe there was something about him that warranted her return to him each night. She'd only wanted me to keep concealing the secrets that blushed blue and insistent on her skin.

As it turned out, though, she'd been right about Ben's eyes. The longer we stared at each other there in the hospital, the more weightless I felt, my body seeming to pitch forward, floating toward those two dark pools that kept pulling me in. Only it wasn't beautiful or alluring, as Persephone had tried to claim; it was dangerous, terrifying.

"You—you're Persephone's sister," he said, and I felt as if I were hearing his voice from underwater.

The walls were blotted out by darkness. The windows, too. I'd been wading into an ocean black as ink, and now I was drowning in it, unsure which way would lead me back to the surface.

"Are you a patient here?" he asked.

Here. Where was here? A woman named Kelly, a needle, *Wuthering Heights*. Then—Mom. Her wig and makeup. The bones of her fingers as easily broken as twigs.

"No," I said. "My mother."

The light was coming back into focus—slowly at first, and only around the edges. Then I heard voices, textures of conversation, people speaking to one another in some place other than darkness. There was a beeping sound, steady and measured, drifting toward me from one of the open rooms, and I forced myself to blink—once, twice, then again—my eyelids moving so rapidly they seemed to be forcing out tears.

The blackness split into two separate circles, each becoming smaller and smaller until they were back in Ben's eyes where they belonged. Finally, I could take in the rest of him again—the short hair, not long and ponytailed like it had been back then; the scar across his cheek; and the green scrubs with crisp sleeves.

"You're a—a *nurse?*" I asked, my voice rising. His fingers, which had touched my face just a minute before, were the same ones that had pushed into my sister's flesh, bursting her blood vessels, bringing up thumbprints of stormy blue. They were the same ones that circled her neck the night she died, pressing against her throat, crushing the air inside her. Now, I felt a hand squeezing my own neck, but when I reached up to tear it away, there was nothing there.

Ben nodded, but his eyes moved toward the windows to his right. He looked uncomfortable, guilty, as if he would claw through the glass just to have a way out. "Yeah," he said. "I'm sorry about your mom. I had no idea she was a patient here—I've only been here since December. What kind of cancer is it?"

"Esophageal," I said, the word shooting out of my mouth like a cannonball, an attempt to convey how my mother's sickness was entirely his fault. *If you hadn't taken Persephone from us*, I tried to say with my narrowed eyes, *then my mother would have never started to drink. If you hadn't strangled my sister, my mother's insides wouldn't have curdled and turned against her. If you hadn't given me something to keep secret, if I hadn't locked the window that night . . .*

"Ben." A voice cut through the monologue in my head, and I remembered that we weren't alone; we were in a hospital—a hospital where he worked, where people trusted him to draw their blood, to put his fingers against the tender flesh of their wrists and count their pulse. I could feel my own blood simmering at the thought of it.

A nurse stood with a manila folder tucked beneath her arm. She had an impatient expression on her face. "You've got Mr. Donaldson in Room 3," she said.

"Right," Ben replied, and he slid his dark eyes carefully back to me. "I'm sorry, I've got to . . ." His voice trailed off as he gestured to a corner room. "It was . . . nice seeing you, Sylvie."

Nice seeing you? I clenched my fists as he turned around and headed for Room 3—the room adjacent to the one where Mom sat, accepting her treatment, accepting, for the first time in years, an opportunity at life.

"Wait!" I called, nearly jogging to reach him in time. Ben turned around, his face almost pained, as if enduring a muscle spasm or migraine.

What would Mom do if she saw him? Just the sound of his name a couple days before had sent her reeling. I could easily imagine, then, how her eyes would widen at the sight of him, her fingers fumbling to rip the IV from her arm, her mouth releasing a sound more animal than human as she fell to the floor.

"Listen to me," I hissed. "You need to stay away from my mother. You've done enough to our family as it is, and if I ever find out that you so much as enter a room she's in, I will make it my mission to ruin your life as completely as you ruined ours. Do you understand me?"

I could feel the adrenaline rising like waves. I'd never spoken to anyone like that before, but as angry and desperate as I felt, I still savored the slight look of shock on Ben's face as he nodded.

"Now," I continued, "we're going to be back on Wednesday, so you need to stay away from us if you're here that day."

Ben cleared his throat, glancing over my shoulder. "I'm scheduled to work on Wednesday," he said, "but I . . . I'll make sure to stay out of your mom's way."

"You better," I said, and already I could feel the rock-solid strength in my voice crumbling. I had nothing else to say—no threats to make, no words that would come close to conveying what he'd done to us. All I had left was the ability to leave.

My feet unsteady, I walked back to Mom's treatment room and sat down in the chair beside her.

"Where's the book?" Mom asked.

We both looked at my lap, where my empty hands rested.

"They didn't have it," I said.

Mom sighed but didn't respond, and as the minutes went on, silence falling over us again like snow, I stayed rigid and alert, my eyes pointed toward the door.

They warned us about the anti-nausea medication. As we checked out, confirming Mom's appointment on Wednesday, the woman behind the desk passed us a prescription.

"Do you have any pills left over from your last cycle, Ms. O'Leary?" she asked.

"No."

"Okay, well this is the same medication you were prescribed before. If you did have any pills left over, the doctor said you could just use those and then move on to the fresh bottle. But since you don't, you're good to go with this."

Mom watched me tuck the piece of paper into my wallet, hopefully not noticing the tremble in my hands, and then looked back at the woman defiantly.

"I feel fine," she said.

"Oh, come on, Annie," Kelly piped in. She was filing a folder in a long metal cabinet behind the receptionist. Hitting the drawer closed with her hip, she crossed her arms over the front of her scrubs. "Don't be stubborn. You know how this works. There's a reason you don't have pills left over from last time."

Kelly turned her attention toward me and I tried my best to concentrate on what she was saying, even as my gaze kept bouncing around the room, searching every shadow and corner. "Your mom's probably right about feeling fine," she said. "A lot of patients actually feel great right after chemo because we've already administered an anti-nausea drug during the process. Don't let this fool you, though. She should still take the medication she was just prescribed, because once she starts to actually feel the symptoms, it's too late. She'd likely just throw up the pill if she took it, and then she'd be miserable."

She looked over at Mom, who was drumming her fingers in a slow, steady rhythm on the desk, staring off at a bland hospital-brand painting on the wall. "You remember all this from last time, right, Annie?" Kelly asked.

"Hmm," Mom said, her eyes still turned away from us. "Last time's kind of fuzzy."

Kelly leaned over the desk to speak to me in a soft conspiratorial voice. "She seems tired," she said, "which is also normal. Just let her rest while you go pick up the medication, and then give her a pill right when you get home. Sometimes it's best for the caregiver to be in charge of administering drugs. Some patients just try to grin and bear it, but if you ask me, there's no reason anyone should be in more discomfort than they have to be, right?"

I nodded, trying to smile, but my lips felt tight and heavy. The skin on the back of my neck bristled each time someone walked behind us or exited a room.

"If you have any questions," Kelly said, "you can call us at any time. I promise you there's no question too small. We've even had . . ."

I stopped hearing her. There he was, on the opposite end of the long reception area, walking beside a bald elderly man who was shuffling toward one of the treatment rooms. He had his hand on the man's back, as if to steady him, and the old man laughed up at Ben. Then the two of them disappeared together into a room, the door closing behind them.

My skin felt hot, as if the blood moving beneath it were made of lava. It was still impossible to comprehend—Ben Emory, the man who'd left a girl on the side of the road like a bag of trash, was a nurse now. He joked with patients, guiding them gently into rooms, and all the while, no one ever suspected what his hands could really do. Hadn't the hospital done a background check? Hadn't they seen that he was once a person of interest in a murder? The injustice of it made me shake, and I stared at the door he'd just closed, as if my gaze could burn a hole through it.

Maybe that was why, when I took Mom home, got her settled in her recliner with a glass of ginger ale and a blanket ("I'm not an invalid," she protested), I lied and said I'd be back in a few minutes. After picking up her prescription from the pharmacy, I drove past the turn that would have taken me home and headed instead for the Spring Hill police station, a place I hadn't been since I was fourteen years old. I pulled into the parking lot and got out of my car, stepping over patches of ice to make my way toward the entrance.

I'd believed, once, that justice was an infallible thing, that when I sat in an interview room and told the detectives about painting over Persephone's bruises, they would show up at Ben's door with an arrest warrant that very afternoon. But now, as I gripped the cold brass handles of the station's double doors, my heart hammered against my ribs at what I knew: justice was as flawed as any human; it was easily dodged and fooled. Ben had escaped it once. And I would make sure that he did not escape it again.

10

"I need to speak to a detective," I told the uniformed woman behind the glass window inside the station's lobby, my voice booming with urgency.

The woman looked at me, bored and unimpressed. "What is this regarding?" she asked.

"I have a . . ." I struggled to find the right word. "Complaint, I guess. Or a request."

She pulled a sheet of paper from a folder on her desk. "Do you wish to file a report?"

I shook my head. "No, it's not like that. I need to speak with Detective Parker and Detective Falley. Please—it's important."

It had been so long, but I still remembered their names. I remembered the stubble on Parker's chin and the way Falley tucked her hair behind her ears before she spoke. I remembered that they'd promised to find out what happened to Persephone, no matter how long it took.

The woman behind the glass raised one eyebrow, as if the detectives' names legitimized my presence. "What's your name?" she asked.

"Sylvie O'Leary."

She picked up a phone and punched a couple of numbers on the receiver. "Detective Falley doesn't work here anymore," she said to me. "She—yeah, hi. I've got a Sylvie O'Leary here. She says she needs to see you and that it's important." The woman listened, her eyes still focused on my face. "Okay." Hanging up, she gestured with a quick nod of her head toward a couple of chairs against a brick wall. "Detective Parker is on his way. You can have a seat over there."

"Thank you," I replied, but I didn't sit down. I only moved a few feet away from the woman's line of sight, pacing slowly in a small circle.

After a few minutes, a door opened and a man in a brown suit stepped into the lobby. He had gained a little weight over the years, and the stubble on his face was now gray, but other than those differences, he looked exactly as I remembered him. Even the way he held the door open seemed familiar, his arm stiff and outstretched as he looked at me with a solemn squint.

"Ms. O'Leary," he said.

When I was younger, he'd called me Sylvie, but the way he said my name now reminded me of how he'd stood outside Mom's locked door, trying to convince her to open up and answer his questions. Neither of us knew right then that she wouldn't be coming out, that she'd make a life inside those walls, shrinking into herself like a plant without light.

"Hi," I said, slipping past him through the doorway. "Thank you for seeing me."

He let the door close behind us and then led me down a long hallway with fluorescent lights that buzzed. Near the end of the hall, he held an ID card to a black keypad just outside a room. After a high-pitched beep and the sound of a bolt unlocking, he opened the door and gestured for me to head inside.

"We can talk in here," he said. "Please—have a seat."

As the lights switched on, illuminating the small, sparsely furnished space—just a metal table, two padded chairs, and a desk that held up a stack of boxes and folders—I had to swallow a lump that instantly swelled in my throat. The room looked exactly like the one I'd sat in with Aunt Jill, and it still gave me the prickly feeling of being a suspect, just as it had all those years ago.

The chair scraped against the floor as I pulled it away from the table. I sat down and waited for Detective Parker to do the same, but he remained standing, looking at his watch and passing his hands over his tie. "Can I get you anything?" he asked. "Coffee? Water? Stale doughnut, perhaps?"

I shook my head. "No, thank you."

"All right." He reached for the chair across from me and settled himself into it. "I'm afraid I have to preface this by saying that I don't have a lot of time. I have a meeting that I have to get to in a few minutes, but when I heard you were here . . . well, it's been a long time, hasn't it?" He folded his hands together. "So what can I do for you, Ms. O'Leary?"

"I—" Where was I supposed to begin? Looking at Parker's fingers, which he knotted and unknotted as he waited, I cleared my throat and took a breath. "I need you to reopen the investigation into my sister's death."

Parker nodded a little, as if expecting me to go on, but when I didn't, he sat back in his chair, his face gently sympathetic. "The investigation was never closed," he said. "The case is still open, but with no direct evidence or witnesses or new suspects, it's long been considered what we call a 'cold case.'" He used air quotes on the last two words, as if he assumed the phrase was foreign to me.

"I'm sorry," he added. "I know that's not what you want to hear, but I assure you we did everything we could to try to find out what happened."

"How is Ben Emory not still a suspect?" I asked, shooting forward in my seat. "Do you know he's a nurse now? A *nurse*. He's supposed to be helping people and making them better, and meanwhile, no one has any idea that he once killed somebody with his bare hands."

Parker's eyebrows lifted a little, but other than that, his face remained neutral. "I didn't know that," he said, "and I understand that that must be upsetting for you, given that you believed he was responsible for your sister's murder, but—"

"I didn't believe," I interrupted. "I knew. I still know."

"We were never able to find any evidence that connected Mr. Emory with the crime."

"What about his dad? The mayor. He's the owner of Emory Builders so you know he has tons of money. He could have easily paid someone to cover it up."

He paused for a second—just a tiny breath of hesitation, but one I noticed nonetheless. "That's a serious allegation, you know," he said, "but again, there was no evidence to suggest that."

"What about everything I told you sixteen years ago? Why—at the very least—wasn't Ben arrested for abusing Persephone? I told you and Detective Falley that the bruises on her body were from him. And what about the necklace that was missing when you found her—the one she never took off? Didn't you check to see if Ben had it? In his car? In his house?"

For a few seconds, Parker didn't speak, and I took the time to try to control my breathing. I needed to be calmer if I was going to get anywhere with this, but I kept seeing Ben in my mind, how deftly he'd placed his fingers on my face in the hospital, as if assessing injuries came naturally to him, as if he never could have dreamed of inflicting them himself.

"Ms. O'Leary," Parker said. "I promise you that we followed up on all the leads you gave us. We simply never found the necklace. Now, as for the bruises . . ." He paused again, as if carefully choosing his words. "We followed up with that as well, and Mr. Emory admitted responsibility. However, some information came to light that made us feel it was best not to press any charges."

I felt my lips open in surprise. "He actually admitted that he bruised her?"

"Yes."

"And you didn't charge him with *anything*—assault? Battery?"

"As I said, some information came to light, and—"

"What information? I thought you said there wasn't any evidence. I thought that's why this became a cold case in the first place."

As Parker looked at me, he took his time breathing in and then out. I clasped my hands together under the table, and for every moment he didn't respond, my fingers squeezed each other harder.

"It's true that there was no evidence directly associated with your sister's murder," he finally said. "But we became aware of some evidence, of a sort, regarding the bruises on your sister's side and wrist."

"What evidence?" I asked again.

Parker shook his head. "I'm sorry, but I can't really comment on that."

"But I'm her sister," I insisted, wincing at how effortlessly I still thought of Persephone in the present tense. "You're saying you can't even tell me why you eliminated Ben as a suspect?"

"No," Parker replied. "Let me be clear. Just because we didn't file any assault charges against Mr. Emory at the time does not mean that we'd eliminated him entirely. The fact of the bruises on your sister's wrist and the fact of your sister's strangulation were, we believed, two separate things—not necessarily connected, not necessarily unconnected. It was possible that the bruises on her neck and arm were inflicted by the same person, but then again, it was equally possible that they weren't. There were other people we were looking into at the time."

Other suspects? What would have been the point? Ben had a history of violent behavior against Persephone, and he'd been the last person to see her alive. It was so cut-and-dry that the thought of Parker and Falley investigating anyone else seemed almost laughable. And maybe that was the problem—they'd never found anything conclusive against Ben because they'd been too busy inventing additional suspects, searching for evidence in places it would never be found. My breath quivered with a slowly budding rage.

"Who else were you looking at?" I demanded.

Again, Parker shook his head. "I'm sorry," he said, "but we can't release details like that in an open investigation, not even to the victim's family."

"Why not? Don't we have rights in this?"

"You do," he said. "And if we were to make an arrest, you'd be the first to know. But think of it this way. If I gave you a name, what's to stop you from trying to track that person down? Or going to the media? Either of those actions could interfere with the investigation."

"But there isn't an investigation anymore."

"I understand why you would feel that way, but as I said, the case is still open."

I dug my fingers into my leg. We were going around in circles.

"Then can you at least tell me about my sister's bruises?" I asked. "Don't I have a right to know why you didn't charge Ben with anything, especially since he admitted to hurting her?"

Parker opened his mouth, uttered the beginning of a word, and then closed it. Looking at his watch, he tapped its face with his fingers in a pensive, rhythmless way. "Ms. O'Leary," he said, "as you just noted, Mr. Emory was never charged with a crime, which means that, just like you or me or anyone else, he is entitled to his privacy. It would not be appropriate to divulge the details of his personal life. I can understand that may be frustrating, but I'm sure you'd expect the same treatment if you were in his shoes."

"You're worried about his privacy?" I blurted. "My sister is dead."

"As I—"

"You can't just bring him in for questioning again? Just to see if maybe there's something you guys missed? I just—I don't think he should be able to work with sick people. It's not safe."

"I'm sorry," Parker said. "We can't bring someone in for questioning without a reason. Now, please be assured, Ms. O'Leary, that if something were to happen that seemed to link Mr. Emory to this case, then, yes, of course we would question him again. But as it stands . . ." He shrugged.

I could feel him building a wall between us—one that, clearly, I wouldn't be able to penetrate. But why would Parker need to hide the truth from me? Why was he more concerned with protecting my sister's abuser than arresting her killer?

Despite the room's comfortable temperature, I braced for a shiver. As it shook through me, I felt the determination and anger that had been spurring me on just moments before melt into hopelessness.

I picked up my purse. "Okay," I said, standing up.

"Listen," Parker said, rising from his chair. "I know this isn't what you wanted to hear. I'm sorry I couldn't . . ." He trailed off, his eyes lingering on me, and then he patted the pockets of his pants. "Here." He took out his cell phone and reached into his suit jacket for a small notepad and pen.

"You mentioned my former partner—Detective Falley," he said, tapping at his phone, then writing something down. "She left the department a few years ago, but—" He ripped out the sheet of paper from his notepad and handed it to me; he'd written "Hannah Falley" at the top, along with a phone number. "You might want to talk to her if you've been left feeling unsatisfied here. I'm not saying she'll be able to tell you much more than I already have, but I will say that she's no longer bound to certain . . . rules. Just tell her that you got her number from me."

I stared at the paper. Falley wasn't a detective anymore; she couldn't arrest Ben or even interrogate him, so what could she possibly do for me? But as Parker stood in the doorway, waiting for me to follow him out, I folded the paper anyway and stuck it in my purse. "Thanks," I mumbled, and he nodded in response.

When I got back to my car, I sat there for a while, the cold air hardening around me like a cube of ice. I watched people pull into the parking lot, walk toward the doors of the station, and disappear inside. I watched officers exit through the same doors, head toward squad cars, and take a left onto the main road, some with their lights flashing, some not. At a certain point, a text came in from Lauren, and my phone startled me with its chime.

"Best news ever," she'd written. "Tankard now does half-off apps and drinks on Mondays! Come home for the night and we'll app it up!"

Home. I read the word over and over. Where was that exactly? In Providence? There, Lauren and I split orders of mozzarella sticks at bars with scratched and sticky tables. We swapped stories of our day's clients as we picked at cheese stuck on our plates. We laughed about the guy who wanted a tiny squirrel on one earlobe and an acorn on the other. We cringed about the girl who wanted "is terrible in bed" under the tattoo of her ex-boyfriend's name.

But here, living in Spring Hill, my sister had once shattered all Mom's perfume bottles, once ripped pages from the book Mom was reading, once threw forkfuls of spaghetti on the floor—all in retaliation for things I couldn't even remember. Here, she'd been wild-eyed and passionate and alive, right up until the last time I saw her—red-coated and running from our house, right back to Ben.

"Wish I could be there," I responded to Lauren, and I turned the sound off on my phone so I wouldn't hear the alerts for any other texts.

Another twenty minutes passed before I drove back to the house, minutes in which I shivered and pulled my coat tighter but refused to turn on the heat. What had Persephone's skin felt like when they found her? She'd been dead for days, buried beneath layers of snow, so when someone first touched her—the police, or an EMT, or the jogger who discovered her, maybe—did it feel smooth but glacial, like touching a window in winter?

The moment I opened the front door, I could see that Mom wasn't in her recliner anymore. I headed down the hallway, the bottle of her pills rattling inside the pharmacy bag, and when I reached her bedroom door, I was surprised to find it ajar. "Mom?" I asked, slipping my head inside.

I hadn't seen her room in a very long time. With the door so often locked after Persephone died, it had become forbidden territory. Now, as I looked around, I was struck by how dark it was, the shades pulled down and the curtains drawn. Still, there was just enough light from the hallway to see that things hadn't changed much since I was a teenager. There was the same bed with the same floral comforter. The same dresser with a top drawer that never fully closed. Even the smell was as I remembered it—musty and stale, but sweet, too, like roses that had been left to rot.

I heard a noise like an animal retching. "Mom?" I called again, following the sound to the bathroom, where she kneeled on the tile in front of the toilet. Her back was to me, her wig off, and her head was a globe of thin veins that pulsed when her body heaved.

I was too late. I hadn't listened to the nurse; I hadn't returned right away with the pills. Now Mom would be miserable; she'd just throw the medication right up—and I hadn't even considered that as I sat in the police station parking lot, letting my skin grow colder and colder like some useless punishment.

"Mom, I'm sorry," I said. "I—"

But then she snapped her head toward me, and the sight of her cheeks, smudged with eyeliner, slick with sweat, made the words evaporate like snow on my tongue.

"Where the hell were you?" she spat, and as she stared at me, squinting through a dry heave, I saw that her eyes were the darkest gray they'd ever been. They looked shadowed and leaden, the color of clouds about to rain.

11

On Wednesday, I visited Persephone. I hadn't been planning to do it until I jolted awake from a dream in which she crawled into my bed, her body so cold that, even through layers of sleep, I felt myself shiver. "You never talk to me anymore," she said, her breath as solid as icy fingers on the back of my neck. "I've been here all along, but you keep ignoring me." In the dream, she was crying, her tears the color of bruises, watercolor streaks of blue and gray. Then, with only the slightest waver in her voice, she said, "You did this to me, Sylvie," and my body jerked in response, sending me shooting up in bed.

I hadn't actually been to her grave since the day we buried her, so when I got to the cemetery, I had to weave through rows of headstones, my boots leaving tracks in the snow as I searched for her name. My memories of her burial were foggy. Mostly, I remembered Mom, who cried so loudly that the priest had to pause his prayers. She was wild that day—sobs as jarring as a car crash, debris of tears all over her face—and though I preferred any show of emotion to the silence she'd been keeping behind her locked door, I was hurt, too, that she never once composed herself enough to come to me, never once untangled herself from Jill's arms to gather me in her own.

When I found Persephone's grave, I was surprised to see a bouquet of white roses lying on the snow in front of the stone. The flowers looked fresh, the petals still clean and crisp, as if they'd only been there for a day or two. Bending down to pick them up, I turned them over to check for a note, struggling to imagine who might have left them. But then, like a surge of electricity passing through me, I remembered a night when Persephone came through our window, a single white rose clutched in her hand.

"Look what Ben gave me," she said.

I closed the window behind her, shutting the cold air out of our room, and watched as she brought the flower to her nose and breathed in its scent. Shrugging out of her coat, she touched the petals to her face and dragged the rose from her temple to her chin. Then she placed her finger against a thorn, as if its sharp point were incapable of piercing her skin.

"It's just one," she continued, "so Mom won't get suspicious, and he said he got it in white because—okay, this is a little corny, but I swear he was so sincere—because the color is as pure as the way we love each other." She laughed quietly, careful even in her giddiness not to wake Mom. "I don't know, he said it a lot better than that. I wish sometimes we could just stop and record moments, you know? I mean, he always says we—ouch!"

She sucked in her breath as she stared at her finger. A bright bead of blood blossomed on her skin. We stood together in the space between our beds, neither of us moving to grab a napkin or tissue, and I was stunned by how beautiful it looked, how the tiny wound reminded me of the first drop of paint on a canvas.

"Wow," she said, and then she lifted her finger and swept it across the petals.

"What are you doing?" I asked, watching as she twirled the rose in her hand, leaving smudges of red among the luminous white.

"I don't know," she said, and she dropped her finger, smiling faintly at the flower. "It just makes sense like this, I think." Then, pulling down the collar of her shirt, she revealed a dime-sized bruise just below her clavicle. "Take care of this for me?"

Still holding the bouquet at Persephone's grave, I realized that my grip had crinkled the plastic wrapping. I dropped the roses into the snow and took a few steps backward, any peace I might have found now lost. My eyes darted around the cemetery, my body tense as the strings of a tightly tuned guitar. Was everything Ben did now—becoming a nurse, leaving flowers—just a calculated effort to try to soothe his guilt? Or, I wondered, the thought sliding through me like a stiff, paralyzing drug, was he sending me a message, telling me that he wasn't just going to disappear, that even though Persephone was dead, he wouldn't leave her or my family alone?

"Why are you driving so fast?" Mom asked an hour later as I barely braked at stop signs on our way to the hospital.

"I'm not," I said, pressing my foot more firmly on the gas. "I'm just trying to get you there on time."

"On time?" Mom smoothed down the hair of her wig before leaning back against the headrest. "At this rate, we'll be twenty minutes early."

"That's fine. Maybe they'll take us early."

"They won't," she insisted. "Everything's on a schedule there. And I hate waiting. It's bad enough having to sit in that chair for a couple hours—just waiting, waiting, waiting while I get the damn treatment. Now we're going to be waiting beforehand, too." Crossing her arms, she turned her head to stare out the passenger window like a sulky teenager.

"Well, listen," I said. "About that." I reached into the back seat and felt around until my fingers closed around the handle of a plastic bag. Pulling it forward, I plopped it gently into her lap. "I got you something."

"What is it?" she asked, staring down at it apprehensively, like it was a dog that might bite her.

"It's something I picked up yesterday," I said. "Just open it."

Up the road, a green light switched to yellow and then red. As I slowed to a stop behind a line of cars, Mom reached into the bag and pulled out a copy of *Wuthering Heights*, which I'd bought while running errands the day before. It had a dark blue hardcover and its pages looked as if they'd been dipped in gold.

"Is this because you feel bad about the other day?" she asked.

"What do you mean?"

The light switched back to green, and I eased my foot back onto the accelerator.

"Being late with the pills," Mom said. "Making me throw up."

"No, Mom, I told you—there was a line at the pharmacy and I saw someone I knew from high school. I've already apologized a hundred times about that."

I'd had to lie to her, of course—just another item on the growing list of ways I'd failed her since I'd been home. But I couldn't tell her where I'd been without explaining why, and I wasn't about to let her know how dangerously close she was to Ben each time she got her treatment. That was my problem and mine alone—even more so now that I'd seen the roses—and I was going to handle it.

"I know that," Mom said. "Which is why you don't have to be giving me books. You've been attentive enough as it is the last two days. Annoyingly attentive, I'd say. If you're not careful, you're going to end up as bad as Jill."

I wasn't sure how heating up soup, getting her crackers, and periodically asking her if she needed anything qualified as "annoyingly attentive," but I brushed past the comment anyway. Turning a corner, the hospital came into view ahead of us, and I accelerated toward the entrance to the parking garage.

"Well, I didn't get you the book because of that," I said. "I got it because you wanted to read it on Monday and they didn't have it. I just thought you might like to have your own copy."

Mom turned the book over in her hands, as if looking for the latch to a secret compartment along its edges. "I don't really like hardcovers," she said, putting it back into the bag.

I took a left turn, driving faster than I should have down a ramp into the garage. As I pulled sharply into a space, the book slid off Mom's lap and onto the floor. She glared at it, its pages thrust open against the dusty mat, but she made no movement to pick it up. When we got out of the car, I watched as she closed the door behind her, leaving the book locked inside.

It didn't take me long to find Ben. Once Mom was settled into her chair in the treatment room, her IV taped to her arm, I told her I had some questions for the woman at the front desk. She stared out the window and lifted her hand in a slight, listless wave as if to dismiss me.

I walked around the cancer center, glancing into every open door for a glimpse of Ben. I wanted to seem strong when I saw him, fierce and invulnerable, but my pulse was already betraying me. When I finally found him, coming out of a closed room, a pen clamped between his teeth as he stuffed a paper into a folder, my knees buckled a little, and I forced myself to remember the roses in the snow, how intrusive they were, how thorned and threatening.

"Ben." I called his name before my throat had the chance to tighten up like a fist.

Ben's eyes latched onto mine and his mouth opened just enough for his pen to clatter to the floor.

"Hi," he said. "I thought you didn't—"

"I don't." We were standing only a few feet apart. "Did you put roses on Persephone's grave?"

Ben tilted his head, his brows furrowing. "Yeah," he said. "I always do."

Stiffening my jaw, I was afraid that if I didn't keep speaking, it would set like concrete. "What do you mean you always do?"

He shifted his weight, looking around the large space, its couches and windows, its doors to rooms where people suffered and survived. "I've been leaving her roses for years," he said. "Ever since . . ." He cleared his throat as I narrowed my eyes. "But when I saw you on Monday, I realized that I hadn't done it in a couple months, so I brought some over yesterday."

A nurse squeezed between us then, glancing up at Ben as she passed, and a wave of nausea rose within me. "And it's always white roses," I said.

Ben nodded. "Yeah, because—"

"Because they're as pure as your love for each other?"

Again, his brows furrowed, a crafted look of confusion distorting his features. "What?"

"That's what you told her the first time you gave her a white rose. Persephone said you chose that color because it was as pure as the way you loved each other. I know this, because she told me things."

I wanted that last sentence to make him nervous, make him wonder how much else I knew about their relationship, but he surprised me by chuckling, lifting a hand to cover his face. "Oh God," he said. "Did I really say that? Okay, that's embarrassing, but, uh, no. That's not why I keep getting white roses. I just remember she liked them."

"Well, you need to stop," I snapped. "Don't you think you've done enough? Do you think that when we visit her grave, we want to see any evidence that you've been there? You got what you wanted—you're free, the police have nothing against you—so just leave us alone, okay? And for God's sake—leave Persephone alone, too."

I started to spin around, but Ben's fingers latched onto my wrist, tugging me back toward him. "You think I killed her?" he whispered. His dark eyes were shining like the ocean at night.

I looked down at my wrist, how his fingers dug into my skin, and as I did, he looked, too, then immediately let go. "Sorry," he said. "Sorry. But, seriously, you think I'm the one who killed her?"

I couldn't read his expression. It seemed to flicker between bewilderment and anger, caution and aggression. His nostrils flared as he breathed, but whether it was out of nervousness or fury, I couldn't tell.

"Of course I know you killed her," I whispered back, rubbing at my wrist. It was red where he'd grabbed it, but it didn't look like it would bruise. "Do you think I'm stupid?"

For some reason, I wasn't afraid of him right then. Even though he'd grabbed my arm, I felt something like empowerment. For the first time, I was able to speak the truth to his face, to tell him how disgusting and cowardly I knew him to be, and it felt good—exhilarating, even. It felt like I was finally protecting Persephone the way I should have done all along.

"It wasn't me," he said, shaking his head vigorously. "In fact . . ." He tucked his folder under his chin and patted at the pockets of his scrubs. "Shit, I think I left it in my locker. Um, do you think we could go somewhere for a few minutes?"

He looked toward the reception desk, where a couple nurses stood together, one staring at us with interest, the other stern, resting her fist on her cocked hip.

"I'm not going anywhere with you," I said.

"No, it's just—that's my supervisor over there." He gestured toward the women. "I can take my break a little early, and we could go down to the cafeteria—it's public, so we wouldn't be alone or anything, if that's what you're worried about. I have something I want to show you. I found it a few weeks ago, and I brought it today, on the off chance I got to talk to you again. I was wondering if you could help me understand it."

"Ben," I said sharply. "I don't want to help you do anything."

"No, I know, I get it," he said. "But what I'm trying to say is that I realized something—or, at least, I think I did—and I think it will help you understand what happened that night." His eyes flicked toward the nurses again. "Please?"

I didn't want to admit it, but part of me was curious to know what he was talking about. He had a fumbling desperation that made me think it might be useful to let him keep rambling. He wanted to show me something—after my meeting with Parker, the word *evidence* flashed in large letters in my mind—and maybe, while trying to convince me of his innocence, he would slip up, mention a detail that only Persephone's killer would know.

"Fine," I said after a moment.

"Really?" His face instantly relaxed. "Oh man, thank you. I'll meet you in the cafeteria in a few minutes. It's on the third floor."

He was walking backward as he said this, his eyes fixed on mine, but just before he turned around, I could have sworn I saw him smile.

12

I chose a table by the window. The cafeteria wasn't very full—only a few families and a couple doctors—but I still felt more comfortable knowing that, if anything happened, there would be witnesses.

Ben waved as he walked in and slid into the seat across from me.

"Thanks for coming," he said.

I stared at him, suddenly unwilling to speak unless I absolutely had to.

"Well, okay, so . . ." He pulled a photograph out of his pocket and pushed it toward me across the table. "Do you know anything about this?"

I recognized Will Emory right away, even though he couldn't have been more than twenty-five years old in the picture. He was tall like Ben, with the same dark eyes, and he was standing in front of a red sports car. Clinging to his arm, staring up at him with a smiling, lovestruck expression on her face was—I shot forward, bending over the picture.

"What the hell is this?" I asked.

"I was hoping you could tell me."

"That's my mother," I said, pointing to the woman. I was almost breathless looking at her—the long blonde hair she used to braid into place, the smile that used to greet me when I came home from school.

"I know," Ben said. "I didn't really recognize her at first—it's not that great of a picture—but then I noticed how much she looks like Persephone here."

It was true—not just because of the length of her hair or the color of her eyes; it was her posture, too, her height, her frame—and as I stared at the picture, I ached for them both.

Ben flipped over the photo, pressing Mom's beautiful beaming face against the table. "Look," he said, pointing to the bottom corner, where someone had written a date inside of a heart.

Those bulky loops, the way the ink curved up at the end of each word—I recognized the handwriting from notes she used to leave on my pillow or in my lunchbox. "My mother wrote that," I said. "But—what is this? She didn't even know your dad."

"Apparently she did."

"Where did you find this?"

Ben nodded, as if he'd been expecting me to ask that question. "In my grandfather's house. Well—no, I guess it's mine now. Do you know where my dad lives? The big house on the hill?"

"Yes."

"Well, there's this guesthouse in the back that my grandfather lived in while I was growing up. He died when I was nineteen, and the house just sat empty for years after that. I moved in a while ago, and I've only recently had time to start going through some of the things that are stored there. I was actually looking for my grandfather's stuff, but I found this box that had my dad's name on it, and the picture was just loose in there with all these high school track and field trophies, yearbooks, graduation tassels, things like that. I don't know if it was something my grandfather was storing for my dad, or if it was things my dad boxed up and kept there after the house became empty. Either way—there it was."

"There it was," I repeated, careful to keep my voice dry and even.

"And look," Ben pressed on, pointing at the date on the bottom corner again. "This date—it's about a year and a half before my parents got married."

"So?"

"So . . . I don't know. Do you think they dated—your mom and my dad? Before my parents were together? I mean, look at how she's looking at him."

He flipped the picture over again, and the warmth in my mom's eyes brought a stinging feeling to my own. She had been like that once—open, loving, her laughter like a song. She would hum while doing the laundry. She would tend to her rhododendrons in the front yard, talking to the bees that buzzed around her as she worked.

"And this heart she drew around the date," Ben said, turning the photo once more. "It just—it seems pretty obvious they were together once, right? And, if that's true, well—my dad has a way of making women hate him."

"What are you talking about?" I asked.

Ben looked toward the window. "My parents have been divorced since I was eighteen," he said. "And it happened pretty suddenly." He paused, squinting at the trees in the distance outside. "I mean, I knew they fought—a lot—but one day I came home and my mom had all these suitcases packed. I asked her what was going on and she told me she was moving to Portugal."

"Portugal?"

Ben nodded. "She has a cousin there that she was close with when they were kids. I'd never even met her at the time, but . . . anyway. She said I was eighteen now, and she'd stayed longer than she should have, but she'd wanted to make sure I wasn't negatively influenced, or something like that. And so she just left. And anytime I've talked to her or visited her, if I so much as mention my dad, she goes crazy. She yells about how she doesn't want to hear a word about him, how he's a terrible human being, on and on and on like that, and I mean, she just hates him."

He looked at the back of the photo again, tracing the heart with his fingertip. "And it's not just her," he continued. "Since they got divorced, my dad has dated all kinds of women, and they all end up hating him, too. Just last month, I was in the guesthouse and I heard one of them screaming at him at the top of her lungs. Then I heard a car screeching away. So I don't know what he does to them exactly, but like I said, he has a way of driving women crazy."

He rubbed at the ink where the date had been written on the photo, as if it hadn't been dried and set for decades, as if his fingers were strong enough to erase any record of the past.

"Maybe he was abusive," I said. "Left marks on them."

Ben snapped his head up to look at me, and my heart clenched. His features hardened and his jaw tightened, the movement of the bone seeming to ripple through his scar.

"No," he said, his voice resolute. "No, it wasn't like that. He didn't hurt them. Not physically, anyway."

"How can you be so sure?" I asked. Then, drawing in my breath, imagining each molecule of air as a tiny source of strength collecting inside me, I added, "Like father, like s—"

"Look," Ben interrupted, his eyes like two dark marbles staring out at me. "I was just telling you that to try to explain how—well, I think it could be the same thing with your mom. If she dated my dad and ended up hating him, then it would make sense that she wouldn't want Persephone to date me. Right?"

"That had nothing to do with *you*," I said. "Persephone wasn't allowed to date *anyone*."

He cocked his head to the side. "Are you sure about that?"

"Yes," I said, but even as I sat there, my arms crossed, there was a part of me that wondered. All those years ago, when Mom came home to find Ben with Persephone, she kicked him out and began yelling. I'd always attributed that to Mom's anger that her dating rule had been broken, but thinking of it now, it was as if she'd known for a fact that Ben would only hurt Persephone, as if she could see right through to the very core of him—and maybe what she saw was Will. A man who—what? Had driven her crazy? Had left her beaten and bruised as her daughter would be?

It was so difficult to fathom, even with the evidence gaping up at me. The only time I'd ever seen them interact was at Persephone's wake. Beyond that, she'd never mentioned him. Then again, she'd never talked about any of the men she'd been with, not even the ones she went out with sporadically when Persephone and I were kids. On those occasions, she'd have Aunt Jill come over to watch us, be gone for several hours, and then return to tuck us in, the smell of garlic overpowering her flowery perfume. If I asked her anything about how the date had gone, she'd just smile, skim her fingers over my face, and kiss me on the forehead. She had a history of silence, I realized, even before Persephone had died. She'd had so many secrets stored inside her, it was a wonder I'd ever felt close to her at all.

"And the other thing," Ben said, "is that . . ." He was speaking more slowly, and he was shifting around, the plastic chair creaking each time he moved. "Well, it has to do with the night Persephone died."

My eyes widened before I had a chance to stop them. "Yeah?" I prompted.

"Well, we had this fight. It—she'd—okay. Let me start over." He took a deep breath, rolling his shoulders back and forth as if preparing for a workout. "I dropped her off like I always did, but something was wrong. She couldn't get back into her room."

He paused to look at me, his black-hole eyes lingering on my face just long enough to suggest he knew what I'd done. I stared back at him, biting down on the inside of my cheek.

"So she came back to the car," he said. "And she got in, explained what had happened, and told me to drive. So I did, and . . . I told her that I thought we should try to talk to her mom. I said if we were just upfront with her about our relationship and told her how much we meant to each other, then everything would be out in the open, and she wouldn't have to keep sneaking in and out."

He shook his head, closing his eyes for a second. "But she didn't want to do that. She was like, 'It's a waste of time, my mom's horrible, she'll never listen.' So I asked her why she wasn't willing to fight for us, and things—escalated from there. I should have known they would. She was already pissed when she got in the car." He slid the photograph in circles on the table, his eyes avoiding mine. "Eventually, she demanded I let her out. It was snowing, though, and she was a mile from her house. I told her no, and I was going to start heading back to her street, but then she just—went wild. She was kicking the dashboard, unbuckling her seat belt, yelling at me to stop the car. I'd—I'd never seen her like that, so I did what she said. I let her out."

His Adam's apple bobbed up and down inside his neck as he swallowed. He scratched his shoulder, looked out the window, squinting at the sun as it emerged from behind a cloud, and then, for the briefest of moments, his eyes flicked back toward me. "And then I was pissed off, I guess," he said. "So I drove away." He stared at the table, his voice worn down to a whisper. "I fucking drove away."

I didn't know how long the tears had been in my eyes, but when he finished speaking, I felt them spill over my lashes and onto my cheeks. The girl he was describing was, without a doubt, Persephone—my Persephone—who could swoon over a white rose, but could just as easily scream at our mother and pummel pillows in our room. I could picture her raging against the inside of Ben's car, slamming her fists against the window until he did what she demanded. She was like that, always needing to get her way. But where was that rage, that fight, whenever he hurt her? Why had she returned to him at all?

I swiped a hand across my cheek, wiping the tears onto my jeans. "Why are you telling me this?" I asked.

He flipped the photo back over so that the side with Mom and Will was facing up. He tapped her face three times. "Ever since I found this picture," he said, "I just keep thinking how—if your mom had just come out with it, if she'd just been honest with Persephone about why she didn't want her to see me, then maybe we could have talked through it. I could have told her that I wasn't like my dad, and then—we wouldn't have been fighting that night, and then—"

"So you're saying this is all my mom's fault?"

Just like that, my eyes were dry and my chest flared hot with anger. I dug my fingernails into my palms.

"No," Ben said, shaking his head. "I'm just looking for some way to feel—less guilty, I guess. I think of Persephone every single day, you know."

"Good! You should! You should never stop thinking about how you hurt her. You should be so filled with guilt that it's impossible to get out of bed every day."

I thought of Saturday mornings when I lived at Aunt Jill's house, where I burrowed beneath the blankets, curled like a baby in a womb. I thought of mornings at RISD, where I'd make last-minute decisions to skip class, choosing instead to sleep until dinner. Even living with Lauren, there were days when she had to bang on my bedroom door to get me up for work. On those days, I wouldn't even be asleep; I'd just be staring at the ceiling, holding the sheets to my chin, my heart beating so fast I thought she'd be able to hear it from the hallway.

Ben narrowed his eyes. "You still think I did it?" he asked. "Even after I just explained what happened?"

It was true I'd been drawn in by his story, seduced by the ways I recognized my sister in it, by the way his voice chipped like old paint as he told it. But this was Ben—the same guy who somehow convinced the police not to press any charges. It was strange how surprised he seemed that I didn't believe him, but then again, he was used to getting away with what he'd done.

"I believe you about the fight," I said. "But I know you didn't just drop her off on the side of the street. Come on. It escalated, just like you said, and then . . ."

Even now, I couldn't just say, *You strangled her.* I still had such a hard time grappling with that image—Persephone's eyes going frantic, her hands clawing at the fingers on her neck. I couldn't see the moment when she went limp as a rag doll in the car; I could only see her body thrown onto the snow, her throat already purpling.

"I have to go," I told him, pushing back my chair. "I need to get back to my mom."

As I stood up, Ben shook his head. "And so, what?" he said. "The fact that she was being stalked means nothing to you? You blame me, her boyfriend, over—fucking Tommy Dent?"

My hand froze over the strap of my purse. "What?"

I hadn't heard the name Tommy Dent in a long time. He was a boy who'd lived a few houses down from us, and I knew very little about him, just that he was two years ahead of me in school and he was always getting into trouble for something—shoplifting, smoking weed in the woods, lighting rats on fire. Mom always told us to keep away from him, but she'd done so in a dismissive way—"Tommy Dent is a bad seed; steer clear of him"—which was nothing at all like the intense, fiery way she'd yelled at Persephone when she saw her with Ben.

"Sorry," Ben said, "I didn't mean to sound so—aggressive or whatever. I just don't understand it. I mean, they questioned Tommy, too, you know. And he's the one who was always stalking Persephone, so I just, I don't understand why you're so convinced it was me. I *loved* her, Sylvie."

His eyes were wide as he stared up at me. I blinked, my lips parting, but for some reason, I couldn't form the words I needed to say. Picking up my purse, I backed away, bumping into the chair as I did. "I have to go," I reminded him.

"But—" He stood up, too, and I hated how I had to look up to meet his gaze. "You knew he was stalking her, right? That he was always watching her, always leaving her all these crazy little notes?"

"I have to go," I repeated.

As I walked toward the exit, my legs felt weak and wobbly. Because I hadn't known; she'd never told me. Persephone, who'd pointed out her bruises, who'd shown off the rose that had to be kept a secret from Mom, who'd made me agree to a pact as her one and only sister—*Just keep the window open. Just a crack, okay?*—had never told me that someone else was a threat to her, that someone else meant to do her harm.

13

That afternoon, I tried to remember everything I could about Tommy Dent.

I pictured his messy blonde hair, and I remembered how he'd sometimes toss rocks at cars as they drove down our street. There'd been a rumor that his mother chased him around their house with a baseball bat whenever he got in trouble, and his father had supposedly overdosed on heroin when Tommy was a baby. But beyond that, I didn't know much, and the only clear memory I had of Tommy wasn't even really about him.

"I just saw Tommy Dent hacking at the Townsends' flowers with an axe," Mom had said to us, unloading groceries in the kitchen. "He's a bad kid. I better never see you girls hanging out with him."

I was twelve years old at the time, still in middle school. Tommy went to Spring Hill High, and we'd never really interacted with each other, not even to wait at the bus stop, since the high school started thirty minutes before the middle school did. Everything I'd ever heard about him seemed to corroborate Mom's statement, though, so I just nodded in agreement, certain that she knew what was best for us. But Persephone, who rode the bus with Tommy every day, rolled her eyes and stomped off to our room.

"What's the matter?" I asked, following her in before she had a chance to slam the door, as she so often did in those days.

"Mom, obviously," she said. "Mom's the matter." She pulled a scrunchie out of her hair, her eyes set fiercely on the mirror above her dresser, and reset her ponytail, smoothing back each blonde strand until they were all firmly pushed into place.

"What do you mean?" I asked. "Are you friends with Tommy Dent or something?"

"What?" Persephone looked at me in the mirror, her eyes sharp and narrowed. "Of course not. Tommy Dent is weird."

"Then I don't get it."

Spinning around to face me, she sighed. "No, I don't think you would," she said. Then she sat down on her bed, leaning her back against the headboard and crossing her arms over her knees. "It's just how Mom is, and I'm sick of it. She's always making these proclamations, like 'Oh, Tommy Dent is a bad person,' or 'Your teenage years are for friendship, not love,' or, today at the store, when I picked up a box of hair dye, just because I've been *considering* adding some highlights, she was like 'Hair dye is for people with low self-esteem, Persephone.' She acts like she knows everything about everything, and that what she says is the ultimate truth. And if you even try to convince her that something might not be exactly the way she thinks it is, then watch out. Because then you're just being disrespectful and hurtful and the worst daughter on earth."

I sat down at the foot of her bed and picked at some lint on my T-shirt. Without looking at her, I said, "I don't really think she's like that."

"Of course you don't," Persephone scoffed. "Because you're her perfect child who gets perfect grades and still snuggles in bed with her like a five-year-old."

I could feel myself blushing. I knew I was too old to be climbing into my mother's bed, pressing my back against her body so she'd wrap her arm around me, but it was a childhood comfort I hadn't been willing to let go of yet. I loved the faint floral scent of her sheets, the way she hummed sometimes instead of snored, and I loved how her thick curtains kept out the moonlight, making the darkness rich and enveloping. Still, I hated when Persephone thought of me as a child. At sixteen, she was wearing makeup and buying her own bras and taking driver's ed, and I sometimes felt as if the older she got, the more the years between us widened.

"Sorry," Persephone said, stretching her leg out to nudge me with her foot. "I didn't mean that. It's just—I swear, Sylvie. Sometimes it's like you and I have two different mothers."

I never knew what she meant by that. I knew that Persephone fought with Mom in ways that I never did; I knew that Persephone believed that Mom loved me more—but that was just misplaced jealousy, remnants of whatever she'd felt when Mom first told her that she was going to have a sister.

"But anyway," Persephone said, "it's not fair for Mom to go around saying who we can and can't hang out with. I'm not running down the street to be Tommy's friend or anything, but if I *were* friends with him, she'd just have to deal with it. I mean, she doesn't even know him. Like, yeah, he does stupid things, but one, he doesn't have a dad, and two, everyone's heard the stories about Mrs. Dent chasing him with a bat. But Mom doesn't care. To her, he's just a bad kid, and that's it. End of story."

End of the memory, too. That day in our bedroom was the only time I could recall Persephone even mentioning Tommy. Detective Parker had said there'd been other suspects, but could our neighbor, who'd barely factored into our lives, really have been one of them? If he'd been sending her threatening notes or following her around at school, wouldn't I have known about it? If she could talk to me about Ben, the guy who was abusing her, why would she never once tell me about a boy who was supposedly stalking her? It was highly possible that Ben had lied about Tommy, that he'd just been trying to shift the focus away from himself. But there was an itch—a pulsing, persistent itch right beneath my skin—that made me keep trying to remember.

"That neighbor boy." Mom's phrase snapped into my brain like a puzzle piece clicking into place. She'd said it so casually, as if I wouldn't question why she'd given Persephone's things to "that neighbor boy, her friend from down the street." My stomach soured at the thought that she might have been talking about Tommy. But Tommy and Persephone weren't friends and Mom had never liked him. Sure, she'd done a lot of out-of-character things since Persephone died, but I couldn't imagine that giving away her daughter's possessions to a virtual stranger could be one of them.

Then, of course, there was the other thing gnawing at me—Mom and Will Emory. I hadn't asked about the photograph on the way home from the hospital. I couldn't figure out how to bring it up without revealing that I'd been talking to Ben—and anyway, Mom had seemed reluctant to speak to me in the first place. She'd had her arms crossed over her seat belt and her chin kept drooping toward her collarbone. When I asked her if she was feeling okay, she only nodded softly before mumbling, "I'm just tired, all right? Keep driving." Her voice sounded muted and far away, and her words seemed brittle as dried leaves. Watching out of the corner of my eye as she leaned her head against the window, I decided that I would just ask Aunt Jill about Will. After all, she was Mom's sister, and sisters were supposed to know everything.

Now, with Mom in the living room napping in her recliner, I sat down on my bed and picked up my phone, where there was a new text from Lauren on the screen.

"Work is stupid without you," she'd written. "Someone asked for the Chinese symbol for clarity and I had no one to roll my eyes with.

Home is stupid too. Watching Friends dubbed in German isn't as funny when you're not there."

My eyes lingered on her message. On a normal Wednesday, Lauren and I would be leaving work in a few hours and then we'd park ourselves on the couch for some TV and takeout. I ached a little, remembering it—the comfort of it all, the simplicity of that routine.

"I miss you too," I wrote. Then I pulled up Jill's number and pressed the button to connect the call.

After the fourth ring, I heard the click of her voicemail. I waited for the familiar and clipped "Hi, it's Jill, leave me a message," but her outgoing message was one I'd never heard before.

"Hi there—Jill here! Sorry I can't answer the phone right now, but I'm busy *waiting to become a grandmother*! That's right—it could be any day now, so I'm either out shopping for the baby or helping Missy prep for the baby or—God, if I'm lucky—holding the baby! You can leave me a message, but I don't know how good the reception is on cloud nine!"

There was a quick girlish laugh just before the beep, and I immediately hung up. The energy in her voice was dizzying. It felt like, wherever she was, folding tiny clothes into drawers in a nursery or driving Missy to a doctor in Boston, the sky was a soothing unbroken blue, completely empty of the plump gray clouds that hovered over the houses on our street. I hadn't heard her voice sound that way—so chipper and buoyant—in a long time, and hearing it bounce so easily against my ear, I knew that my questions about Will and Mom would have to wait. She was only one state away, but even still, she was in a whole different world, one of cheerful excitement and trips to the doctor that ended in smiles instead of dread. After taking care of Mom for months—for years, really—Aunt Jill deserved that joy. She deserved to remain in her blissful, hopeful present—not to be dragged back into her exhausting sister's past.

I reached for my purse and dug around for the piece of paper that

Detective Parker had given me on Monday. He'd told me that I should contact Detective Falley if I was unsatisfied by his answers to my questions, and now, with Aunt Jill a temporary dead end, I realized that *unsatisfied* was the perfect word to describe how I'd been feeling—not just that afternoon, but for days. Ever since I'd come back to Spring Hill, it seemed that our past—Persephone's, Mom's, and mine—had been circling around me while remaining tauntingly out of reach, and after my conversation with Ben in the hospital, I could feel it slipping even further away. I got up and paced around the room, the slip of paper with Falley's number gripped between my fingers, and decided that if I wasn't going to find out about Will that afternoon, then I at least needed to know about Tommy.

14

I didn't recognize her when I first walked into Spoons, the diner on the southern edge of Spring Hill. I'd looked for the same Detective Falley I'd met sixteen years ago—chin-length brown hair; a gentle, almost timid demeanor; a soft, uncertain smile—but the woman who stood up from a table to greet me had dark-framed glasses, a stylish pixie cut, and she grinned at me so widely it was as if I were some long-lost relative. I almost walked right by her, thinking she must be smiling at someone just behind me, but then she put her hand on my arm as tenderly as a mother would.

"Sylvie," she said, and when my eyes met hers, I recognized them as the ones that had once looked at me with such kindness, the two of us standing in my living room as Mom raged behind the closed door down the hall, as Jill and Detective Parker tried to coax her out.

"It's good to see you," Falley continued, gesturing for me to have a seat at the booth where she'd been waiting. "Thanks for accommodating my crazy schedule." She said this with a quick, almost nervous laugh as we each sat down, as if *she'd* been the one to request a meeting with *me*, as if it had been *her* voice that nearly shook on the phone that afternoon. "I just dropped my daughter off at ballet, so we have some time to chat."

I nodded. I'd been able to hear her daughter laughing in the background when I called her. "It's crazy over here right now," Falley had said over the sound of a faucet turning on. "But I'm happy to meet you in a little while—say, six thirty? Do you know Spoons?"

Spoons was where Mom had waitressed for most of my childhood, the green and yellow of her uniform as familiar to me as the colors of a beloved sports team. She'd always come home smelling like french fries and gravy, and sometimes, on the best nights, she'd walk through the door holding a stack of take-out containers. We'd open them up, inhale the aroma of cheese and salt and meat, and we'd eat our burgers on the living room couch, some made-for-TV movie making me and Persephone laugh with our mouths still full.

But I hadn't told Falley this. I'd been too relieved that she was willing to speak to me so soon, and I'd just told her that, yes, I knew where Spoons was, and I'd be happy to meet her there. Now, though, taking in the forest-green walls and metal napkin holders, the framed photographs of utensils, and the plastic menus that looked as if they hadn't changed since I was a girl, I regretted that I hadn't just suggested the Dunkin' Donuts across the street. Mom was whole here, able to smile at customers and take their orders, to attend to people's needs. How easily I'd once taken such miracles for granted.

Clearing my throat, I tried to smile at Falley. "Thanks again for meeting with me, Detective," I said. "I wanted—"

"Uh, uh, uh," she interrupted, wagging her finger from side to side. "Call me Hannah, okay? Just like I told you on the phone. I'm not a detective anymore. We can dispense with formalities."

She smiled again, her face so open and encouraging that I felt myself relax, even if only slightly.

"Sorry," I said, and she shook her head, dismissing my apology. I put my hands on the table and tore tiny pieces off my paper place mat. It was a habit I'd had for a long time, with napkins or straw wrappers or place mats like this, and one I usually didn't even notice until Lauren would lose her patience, clamp her hand over mine, and demand I stop making a mess "like some OCD rodent."

Dropping the edge of the place mat and brushing the shreds I'd already made to the side, I put my hands in my lap. "I'm sure you were surprised to hear from me," I said, and my eyes latched onto a waitress a few tables away, the green of her uniform much brighter than Mom's had been by the time she worked her last shift.

"Actually," Falley said, "Ryan Parker called me the other day and told me he'd given you my number. He said you'd probably try to get in touch with me, and to be honest, I was happy you did. I've kind of always hoped our paths would cross again."

"You did?" I asked, leaning forward. Falley nodded, opening her mouth to say more, but the waitress slapped two plastic cups of water onto the table and pulled out a pad of paper.

"What can I get you ladies?" she asked.

"Just a coffee for me, please," Falley said.

"Coffee," I echoed.

"Easy enough," the waitress said, and walked away, her eyes never having once met ours.

Mom used to say that true customer service was all about eye contact. *You have to look at the person,* she'd tell me. *It's important to foster that human connection, because that's what keeps people coming back. If they'd wanted someone to not even look at them, they'd have gone to the drivethrough across the street. So you have to actually care—and that starts with getting to know the color of their eyes.*

Falley's eyes met mine so intensely that I had to look away, focusing instead on my fingers as they found the place mat and tore.

"Yeah, so, as I was saying," she said, "I've thought about you a lot over the years. Your sister's case was . . . brutal. I was still kind of a rookie. I don't know if you knew that, or could tell, but I was. Ryan and I were only sent out that day because a couple of the more senior detectives were on vacation. That, and . . ." She paused, as if she wasn't sure she should continue.

"And what?" I asked.

"They just didn't think her disappearance would amount to much. She was eighteen—a legal adult. Old enough to leave and be on her own. Not to mention that it was Spring Hill, and there hadn't been a murder there since the seventies." She shook her head and took a sip of her water. "But obviously—what happened to your sister—it was all much more than that." She folded her hands together over the table and leaned forward. "And I promise you, Sylvie, I wasn't the most experienced detective, but I worked my fingers and toes to the bone on that case. I did everything I could—we both did—but it just wasn't enough. I'm still so sorry about that."

She wasn't smiling anymore. I could see that behind her tightly closed lips, she was biting the inside of her cheek, and now I wondered if her expansive grin when I first arrived had been to overcompensate for how nervous she was to see me.

"I still dream about the case," she continued. "I think about you. Your family. How badly we failed you. How badly we failed your sister. I'm not going to pretend it's the sole reason I left the force—the case had been cold for ten years already once I did—but it stayed with me. Made me wonder, if we can't catch the bad guy in a situation like that, if we can't give the victim some justice and the family a little peace, then what's the point of being a cop in the first place? What's a badge and a pair of handcuffs if you can't use them to make things right, you know? I mean, I—"

We each moved back as our waitress returned with two coffees and a bowl of creamers. She set them down between us without a word, and the smell that rose from the mugs was instantly familiar to me. When we were really young, Persephone and I would sit at the counter for hours after school, our legs dangling from the stools, waiting for Mom's shift to be over. "That coffee smells gross," Persephone would say as we watched a waitress reach for the pot. "Like cinnamon skunk." She'd hold her nose and we'd laugh while the waitress rolled her eyes, and I wouldn't tell her that, secretly, I liked it, that there was something to its pungent, nearly sweet scent that comforted me because it meant that Mom was nearby.

"Anyway," Falley said. "I know you said on the phone that you wanted to ask me some specifics about the case, but I just wanted to get that out of the way first. I wanted to finally be able to tell you that I'm sorry—and not as a cop, but as a human, I guess."

She reached for a packet of sugar from the dish at the end of the booth. When she stirred it into her coffee, the movements of her fingers were stiff and jerky, as if she was gripping the spoon too hard. Part of me wanted to tell her I didn't blame her for what happened, to watch the relief slip over her face like a veil, to see her smile come shining back, but another part wanted to stay in that moment, where someone was taking responsibility for the ragged, loose ends of my life.

"Thanks," I finally said, and I saw the corner of her lips lift just a little before she took a sip from her mug. "But, uh—" I cleared my throat, then drank from my water, leaving my own coffee untouched. "The reason I wanted to meet with you is to ask if you remember a Tommy Dent?"

Falley hesitated for only a moment before she nodded.

"Yes," she said. "He was a suspect."

I felt my stomach contract, and I had to lean back against the booth.

"Why?" I managed.

Falley ran her finger over a dark stain like a burn mark on the table. "For lots of reasons," she said. "But we started to look into him because of Ben Emory. When we first questioned him, he told us that Tommy had been stalking Persephone."

"And you believed him?" I asked. "Just like that?"

She shook her head, scratching at the stain with her thumbnail. "No," she said. "But it's the kind of thing you can't just ignore. We had to look into it."

"What else did Ben say?" I asked. I could feel the sandwich I'd eaten an hour earlier rocking in my stomach.

"As I recall," she began, putting her elbow on the table and rubbing at the back of her neck, "he said that Tommy used to leave notes in Persephone's locker, saying—weird things. I don't remember exactly, it's been so long, but stuff like . . . what she'd been wearing that day, or what she'd eaten for lunch. 'Good choice going with the egg salad today.' Things like that. Nothing overtly threatening."

She paused, her eyes sweeping over my face as if trying to gauge my reaction. But I couldn't react. Couldn't even move.

"Go on," I urged after a moment.

Falley reached for her coffee and took another sip.

"Ben said that, some nights, when he dropped Persephone off, he'd see Tommy out on his front steps, just watching Ben's car go by. Almost as if he'd seen Persephone go out and had been waiting for her to return. Because of that, Ben always waited until he saw Persephone get safely back inside the house, and then he'd stop in front of Tommy's house and glare at him until he went back inside, too."

"How chivalrous of him," I said, but even as the words came out, I was remembering how, on that very last night, with snow just beginning to frost the streets, Persephone hadn't given up on our locked bedroom window and rung the doorbell instead, as I'd planned. She'd returned to Ben's car—which hadn't left, which still had its brake lights on.

"He said," Falley continued, "that he thought maybe Tommy saw Persephone leave with him on the night she went missing, and that maybe he decided to follow them. He said it was possible that Tommy saw Persephone get out of his car on Weston Street after their argument, and maybe he . . ."

She trailed off, the end of her sentence as clear as the water I reached for and drank, its iciness spreading along the walls of my stomach.

"That's a lot of maybes," I said when I set down the glass, and Falley nodded.

"We thought so, too. But after her body was discovered and we went to question Tommy, we saw that he was—" She shook her head slightly as if unsure of what words to use. "He was just very strange. We went to his house and the first thing he did was take us to his bedroom, as if he wanted to give us a tour. And his room was kind of creepy. There were all these posters of guns and samurai swords and other weapons. And it was dark in there. The windows were covered with, like, cardboard or something, except for a few holes that had been made to let some light in. And then—" She shuddered a little. "There was this doll."

"A doll?" I asked.

She nodded. "It was creepy. Not really the doll itself so much as the fact that it was so 'one of these things is not like the other,' you know? It was a porcelain doll, in perfect condition, and it was lying on his bed against the pillow. I remember it had this shiny golden hair, and it was wearing a pink satin dress with little lace frills at the collar and wrists. And then he—he introduced us to it."

"To the doll?"

"To the doll. He said her name was Molly—God, I've never forgotten that—and then he just . . . stood there, waiting for us to say something, like 'Nice to meet you' or something. It gave me the willies, if I'm being honest."

I shrugged one shoulder. "So he was weird," I said. "That doesn't mean he had anything to do with what happened to my sister." Still, my heart thudded.

"It was more than that," Falley said. "When we actually got down to questioning him, he was so . . . interested. He was just really, really interested in what had happened. And not in a devastated way, or in a 'Wow, this happened so close to where I live' kind of way, but as if he was really fascinated by it. He kept asking us questions—what did her body look like? How was she positioned? Was her lipstick smeared? Had she been wearing lipstick at all? It definitely raised a red flag."

I'd been tearing my napkin to shreds. There was a pile at my fingertips I hadn't noticed I'd been making.

"Well," I said, "wouldn't those questions suggest he didn't know how she looked that night, which would suggest he didn't do it?"

Falley shrugged. "Not necessarily. Sometimes people want recognition for what they've done. It was almost as if he was toying with us, baiting us toward seeing some piece of evidence."

She leaned forward then, pressing her hands flat against the table and lowering her voice. "In fact," she continued, "when we were questioning him, I noticed that he was playing with this hair tie. A scrunchie, actually. Remember those? He had this black scrunchie in his hands, and he kept stretching it out, tying it around one wrist and then the other, and I could see that there were these long blonde hairs tangled up in it."

The skin on my arms prickled. "Oh my God," I said. "Did you test the hairs to see if they were a match?"

Falley straightened up and shook her head. "Didn't have to. When we asked him where he got it, he said it was Persephone's. Said he found it in front of her locker when he was slipping in a note one day."

"So the notes were real?"

"Yep. He said . . . oh, how did he put it?" She put her elbows back on the table and rubbed her temples. "He said he wrote her notes all the time. Said he knew what it was like to feel lonely and he wanted her to know that he noticed her."

"But Persephone wasn't lonely," I objected—a little too quickly, maybe. "She was noticed all the time."

Hadn't I known by heart the map of veins in her wrists, even when they were shadowed by bruises? If I had the chance, couldn't I still recognize the catch of breath in her throat as she woke up in the morning? Hadn't I known exactly who she was, even if I never knew about these notes?

"Oh, I'm sure it was all a load of crap," Falley said. "Everything that kid said. I don't think he was totally there, you know?" She tapped the side of her head with her finger.

"So then . . . what happened?" I asked. "If he all but admitted to stalking her, and he said the scrunchie was hers, which—by the way, I highly doubt he just found it in front of her locker—then why wasn't he arrested? Did he have an alibi or something?"

Falley chewed on her bottom lip, held my gaze, and then shook her head. "I really shouldn't be telling you all this, especially since it's still an open case. But—God, I feel like I owe you something. And what are they going to do? Fire me?" She chuckled dryly before continuing. "He had no alibi. He wouldn't tell us where he was that night. When we asked, he said 'Out.' That's all he said, every time. Just 'Out.'"

I felt the ghost of an old rage lift its head inside me. It scratched at the inside of my stomach with long, uncut claws. "Then why wasn't he arrested?" I asked. "What more did you need?"

"Evidence," Falley said. "We needed evidence." She took a deep breath and clamped her lips together, a look of discomfort or disgust gathering on her face. "We only had a few of the notes. Ben gave us some he'd managed to hold on to, but he told us that Persephone usually just threw them away. Tommy admitted that the notes we showed him were his, but the ones we had couldn't prove malicious intent. The scrunchie didn't do anything for us because we couldn't prove where he got it. And his lack of an alibi—well, it could have meant he did it, or it could have meant he was just a petulant teenager bucking against the system by refusing to answer our question. Believe me, Sylvie, any case we tried to build against him would have been thrown out the second it reached the prosecutor's desk. That's just how things work, and it's a big reason why I left. There's too much red tape and not enough stock put into hunches and gut feelings. And I get it. We can't put people away on intuition. But it's still just frustrating and demoralizing, to say the least. I mean—God, sorry—" She waved her hands in the air, as if trying to erase what she'd just said. "This isn't about me and my crap. I'm sorry."

"So it was your gut feeling," I said slowly, "that Tommy Dent killed Persephone."

Falley opened her mouth, her response practically visible between her lips, but then she closed it again and looked down at her coffee.

"I don't know who killed her," she said. "But it was my gut feeling that Tommy knew more about what happened to her than he let on."

I nodded, as if I understood that kind of feeling, as if I was finally able to comprehend that someone other than Ben might have been the one to kill her.

"And what made you think that?" I asked.

Falley's eyes flicked toward the ceiling, and I couldn't tell if she was avoiding looking at me or just pausing to consider the question.

"A lot of it was just his demeanor," she said. "Something was off. It was as if he didn't really get that we were questioning him because he was a person of interest in the case. It was like he thought our questions were meant to get his opinion, like he was some sort of police consultant. Like he—like he could lead us to a detail that would blow the whole thing open. He kept asking questions that didn't make any sense to us, like 'Did you take any blood from the body?' or 'Did you check her pockets for house keys?' And he was *particularly* insistent about—"

She stopped, her eyes widening and her mouth drooping open, suddenly aware, it seemed, of what she'd been about to say.

"Insistent about what?" I asked. "Come on, what was it?"

Falley reached for her coffee and took a long, slow sip. My heart measured out the seconds as I waited. Then she cradled the mug with both hands, holding it close to her chest, and shook her head. "It's nothing, really. More nonsense, I guess. It's just—he kept saying, 'Talk to the mother.' Over and over throughout our interview. 'Talk to the mother. Talk to the mother.'"

"Whose mother?" I asked.

She set the mug back on the table but kept her hands circled around it. "Yours," she said.

15

I felt something push me backward, something with strong, insistent arms. I closed my eyes at the impact, but when I opened them, there was nothing in front of me but air. Falley was looking toward the door at the front of the diner, as if she were regretting ever agreeing to meet with me in the first place, and my fingers trembled under the table.

"Talk to my mother?" I asked. "Why? About what? Talk to her, like—question her? Talk to her, like—a suspect?"

Falley nodded slowly. "Yes," she said. "And we did question her. She never told you that?"

I was beginning to think I could fill a hundred pages with all the things my mother never told me.

I ignored Falley's question, let it evaporate in the air like the steam from our coffees. "What would you have had to question her about?" I asked.

As she hesitated, her eyes bounced across my face.

"It's actually pretty standard procedure," she said. "You always have to question the parents. And with your mom, we were concerned about the way she acted when we first came to your house."

"She was devastated," I reminded her.

"I know," Falley said, "but at that point your sister was still only missing. And of course she should have been upset—any mother would be—but the way she acted, it was like she was positive that Persephone was never coming back."

"She was out of her mind with worry," I said. "Doesn't it make sense that she'd jump to the worst-case scenario?"

Falley nodded. "Sure. And she was never really a serious suspect, not once we questioned her."

I couldn't picture it. Questioning Mom meant she would have had to emerge from her darkened bedroom, taking in the light from the sliding door in the living room, squinting as it fell across her face. Questioning her meant she would have had to speak, string words together, one after the other, like the popcorn and cranberries she used to make garlands with every year for our Christmas tree. But Mom didn't speak in words, not in the days immediately following the news of Persephone's murder. Hers was a language of sobs and silence that I couldn't understand.

"What happened," I asked, "when you questioned her?"

Falley shrugged. "Not a lot. It was . . . the saddest day of my career, I think. I couldn't sleep for days afterward because I kept picturing her face. During our interview, I kept looking at her and thinking, 'This woman is beyond shattered.'"

I nodded. That was the right word—*shattered*. I thought of Mom in her recliner that night as I put on my coat to go meet Falley. She'd been watching TV and hadn't even asked where I was going. I'd looked at the bones that protruded from her hand as it held the remote, and it hadn't been hard to imagine that even beneath the gentlest grasp, those bones would easily break.

"So you saw that she was perfectly normal, then," I said. "For someone who had just lost their daughter, I mean."

Falley put her spoon in her coffee and stirred. She raised one shoulder in a noncommittal shrug. "Well," she said, and didn't continue.

"What?"

She let go of the spoon and shook the hand that had been holding it, as if she'd been writing for hours and suddenly had a cramp. "I don't know, Sylvie," she said. "I feel terrible talking about your mom this way. What she went through—what you both went through—is unspeakably horrific, and who knows how I'd react if the same thing happened to me. It's just, there was something about her behavior that day that didn't seem right."

"Not right how?"

"Just—" Falley tilted her head in thought. "I don't know. She was obviously devastated, but she didn't necessarily seem surprised. I remember that she was acting almost as if she'd expected this to happen."

"Expected what? For her daughter to be killed?"

Falley shook her head. "No," she said. "To lose her."

I dipped my fingers into my glass of water and placed them, dripping and cold, against my wrist. There was something about icy water above a place of pulse, Mom had taught me once, that always made her feel calm.

"So what happened with Tommy Dent?" I asked, steering the conversation away from Mom. "He just went on to live his life like normal? Have a family? A job? Not a care in the world?"

Falley winced, briefly and only faintly, but I noticed it just the same. "Not exactly," she said. "Up until about a year ago, Tommy was in prison. He got out last March and he's been living in a trailer park in Hanover ever since. I only know this because, uh—" She chuckled, but the sound was filled with disappointment. "I've learned you can't ever really leave the job behind. I've kept tabs on him. Even though I probably shouldn't anymore."

"What was he in prison for?" I asked.

"Sexual assault."

I admired how quickly she said it.

Reaching for my water again, I finally started to see it. Tommy might have followed Persephone that night, just like Ben said. He might have driven far enough behind them that, with the snow coming down, his headlights would have been difficult to see in the rearview mirror. Maybe when Persephone stormed out of Ben's car, Tommy saw his opportunity. Maybe he drove up beside her and offered her a ride. She wouldn't have taken one, though. She would have rather walked all the way home just to be able to hold it over Ben's head later. *You were being so stupid,* I could imagine her saying, *that I chose trudging home in a fucking blizzard over being in that car with you for one more second.* Maybe Tommy grew angry when she declined the ride. He seemed to think they had some sort of connection—two lonely souls in a town too self-absorbed to care for them—so maybe he saw her refusal as a betrayal. Maybe he got out of the car, reached for her, but slipped on the slickening road. Still fuming from her fight with Ben, Persephone might have laughed at him then, and the next time he reached for her, his hands might have been stretching toward her neck.

"So you never really thought it was Ben who did it?" I asked.

Falley shrugged. "With boyfriends, there's always that suspicion. Call it sexist, call it history, but it's there. I don't know, though. My instinct was always that he didn't do it."

Still, he wasn't innocent, and night after night, I had agreed to be his accomplice.

"But what about the bruises?" I asked. "When I talked to Detective Parker the other day, he said you guys decided not to file any assault charges against Ben, even though he admitted that he'd been the one to hurt her. Why would you do that?"

I saw the exact moment she closed up. It was like watching a flower unbloom, tucking in its petals until it was nothing more than a tight, protected bud.

"I can't speak to that," she said. "I'm sorry."

I lunged closer to the table. "What do you mean you can't speak to that? You just told me everything about Tommy. Come on, Fal—Hannah. Please. Just tell me why you didn't arrest him for hurting her."

She shook her head, and I could tell by the way she folded in her lips that she wasn't going to answer me. "I told you about Tommy," she said, "because I think you have a right to know. If he did kill Persephone, or even just knows who did, then he's a danger to you. Now that he's out of jail, I don't want you running into him somewhere, completely in the dark."

"But Ben could be a danger to me," I insisted. "He—listen. The only reason I'm even back in Spring Hill is because my mother is sick. She has cancer, and I'm here to take care of her. And I—"

"Oh, that's awful," Falley said, the taut lines around her eyes instantly softening. "I'm really sorry to hear that."

"Thanks. But—the point is, Ben's a nurse now. A *nurse*. And he works on the same floor where my mom is getting her treatment twice a week." Falley's eyebrows shot up. "I know, right? So you see why this is important. I'm going to be around him a lot. And I know you don't think he killed Persephone, but you do know that he abused her, he told you he did. So what's to stop him from hurting me, too?"

Falley looked down at her mug, and when she met my gaze again, her eyes seemed cautious but resolute.

"I don't believe Ben abused your sister," she said quietly. "At least not in the way you think."

I jerked backward. *It's not what you think.* That's what Persephone had always said.

"What other way could there be?" I asked. "She had bruises. Ben said he gave them to her. That's clearly abuse."

She shook her head. "I'm sorry. I shouldn't have said that."

"But what did you mean?"

"I'm sorry," she repeated. "I can't tell you about that. It's just, you have to understand, I worked your sister's case for a long time. In some ways, it feels like I'm still working it. And I didn't know her, but I feel like I did. All the interviews and searches, all the dead-end leads we followed. You start to get an idea of a person. And that idea of her, it's real to me, Sylvie. *She's* real to me."

She picked up her mug and took a slow, measured sip. "I think there are things she didn't tell you," she said, setting her coffee back on the table. "Things we learned over the course of the investigation. And I know it probably doesn't make sense to you, and it probably doesn't seem fair, but I'd feel like I was betraying her if I told you what you want to know. And I already betrayed her once by not solving her case. I can't do it again."

I opened my mouth to push back, to insist that I had a right to know whatever it was she thought Persephone had kept from me, but in that moment, the guilt on Falley's face was palpable. And I knew, better than anyone, how guilt kept you in debt to the dead.

"I'm sorry, Sylvie," she said. "The last thing I wanted to do tonight was upset you, but clearly I have." Her fingers fidgeted with the handle of her mug, and then she lifted her wrist, making a show of checking the time. "Maybe I should just get going. I'm, uh, I'm sorry to make this so short, it's just—Alyssa likes it when I'm there to watch her dance. I told her I couldn't make any promises tonight but I'd try." She dug into the purse beside her on the booth and pulled out her wallet. "Of course, to a six-year-old, 'I'll try' means 'Yes, honey, I'll definitely be there.'"

She took out some money and looked around the room. "Where is that waitress with the bill?" she asked. "Terrible service here, huh?"

Mom used to draw flowers on people's checks before dropping them at their tables. No matter the season or weather, she'd sketch a rose or a daisy right beside the amount they owed. Persephone said she was manipulating the customers, buttering them up so they'd give her a larger tip.

"You can go, I'll wait for the check," I told Falley. "Just one more thing, though. I'm not trying to make you feel worse about this than you already do, but I have to ask: That's it, then? No one will ever pay for what they did to my sister? Ben will go on being a nurse? Tommy will go on living in his trailer, unless he hurts someone else? I just—" I shook my head and bit my lip. "I mean, what about Persephone's necklace? The gold starfish. The one I told you guys about after she died. Did you ever even check to see if Tommy or anyone else had it?"

Falley flattened her money out on the table, placed the saltshaker over it, and then put her wallet back in her purse. When she looked at me again, I could have sworn her eyes were glistening.

"When we were trying to build a case against Tommy," she said, "we got a warrant to search his house. He seemed fine with it, not nervous or anything like people usually are. But he watched us the entire time, following us from room to room, and he had this smile on his face that I'll never forget." She blinked and the sheen on her eyes went dry. "We never found anything."

I nodded, my fingers reaching for the place mat. I was tearing at one of the clean, untouched corners when Falley placed her hand gently over mine. The warmth was like a soothing balm to my chapped knuckles; it made my throat tighten, my eyes sting. Then she leaned forward, her body arching halfway across the table.

"Doesn't mean it wasn't there, though," she said.

16

Even though I hadn't left her a message, Aunt Jill called me back. I woke up on Thursday morning to the phone shouting in my ear, and when I rolled over to silence it, it took me several shrill seconds to find it under my pillow. I'd been up late doing research in bed—scrolling through web results of "Thomas Dent, Spring Hill, Connecticut," or "Thomas Dent, Connecticut, sexual assault"—and I must have passed out in the middle of it all. Now, I fumbled to get ahold of the phone, my fingers stiff and clumsy.

"Hi, Jill."

It was the second time in a week that I'd been sleeping when she called. I tried to sound steady and focused when I answered, as if I'd been up for hours and had even made Mom breakfast, but my throat betrayed me, filtering out my voice in thick, scratchy waves.

"Hi yourself," Jill said. "What do you think you're doing, calling me and not leaving a message? I was going to call you back last night, but I didn't notice the little notification thingy until after ten o'clock, and Missy told me you would have left a message if it were important. But you can't do that to me, okay? Not with your mom the way she is. If you call, you leave a message, got it?"

"Okay," I said. "I'm sorry. How's Missy doing?"

"Good, good, her due date is today, you know."

"Oh, wow," I said. "So it could be any minute, then, huh?"

Jill chuckled. "Only if you listen to Missy. She's sure it's going to be today, but I keep telling her that first babies always come late. I wouldn't be surprised if, a week from now, we're still waiting for the little lady to arrive."

I heard Missy groan from somewhere behind Aunt Jill. "Oh my God, don't say that." Then, louder, as if leaning closer to the phone, she added, "I'm the hugest woman who's ever lived, Sylvie!"

"Don't listen to her," Jill said. "Surely the circus has huger women."

When Missy responded with a squeaky, indignant "Mo-om!" I tried to laugh, but the sound came out of me in a whisper. I wanted so badly to be with them, helping to prepare the nursery, listening to Aunt Jill and Missy go back and forth.

"Anyway," Jill said. "What did you call about yesterday? Did everything go okay with Annie's session?"

Still lying in bed, I fidgeted with my blankets, picking at lint that wasn't there. If I closed my eyes, I could see the picture of Mom and Will that Ben had showed me in the hospital the day before. She'd tilted her face toward his like a flower toward the sun, and she'd clung to his body like ivy on a brick wall. Once again, questions bubbled up inside me, ready to come frothing out.

"Um," I started. "No, yeah, everything went fine yesterday."

"Okay. Good," Jill said. "And that's why you called? To tell me things went well?"

"Well . . . not exactly. No." I set my eyes on the thin space between my closed door and the floor. "It's just . . . I have a question."

"Uh-huh," Jill prompted. "Go on."

I listened for the TV, or a faucet turning on, or a creak in the floor, anything that would tell me where Mom was at that moment.

"Well, it's about"—I lowered my voice—"Mom. And Will Emory. I don't know if you remember who that is, but he's the mayor. And Ben Emory's father."

She paused. "I remember."

"Okay, well . . ." The house was unnervingly quiet, like a street after snow has stopped falling. "I was just wondering if you knew anything about Mom and Will. Like, did they go out or anything?"

Jill sighed against the phone, and her breath sounded like the air outside on nights when I left the window cracked for Persephone. "Yeah, they dated," she said.

"Oh," I replied, trying to sound casual. "Why'd you sigh about it? Was it a bad relationship? Did he hurt her or something?"

"Yeah, he hurt her quite a bit, actually."

I swallowed, imagining blue fingerprints like smudges of paint on Mom's skin. "Bruises?"

"No," Jill said after a moment's hesitation. "No, not that kind of hurt. I was away at college when she was with him. I never even saw them together—not until he came to Persephone's wake. And by then, it had already been over between them for—what? Twenty years?"

I pulled back my blankets and got out of bed, the floorboards cold against my feet. Pacing around the space between Persephone's bed and mine, careful to keep to the large oval rag rug that had been there for as long as I could remember, I posed my next question.

"Was it serious?"

"Eh," Jill said, her voice like a shrug. "It was to your mother, but I don't know about him. They started dating in high school—senior year, I think? Then he went off to some fancy university and your mom stayed in Spring Hill so she could go to community college. She'd only applied to one school—one that was close to where Will wanted to go—and she hadn't gotten in. So he broke up with her soon afterward. The distance was too hard, I guess."

She coughed for a second, and I stopped pacing, watching my toes dig into the rug. When she continued, my feet resumed their steady march between the beds.

"Anyway," she said, "maybe a year or so later, he ended up getting married to some girl he'd met at school. Your mom was devastated. I think she thought they'd eventually get back together, once he graduated and came back to Spring Hill. Instead, he came home with a wife. She used to call me up back then and just cry into the phone about it."

I tried to picture it—Mom crying over a boy. All my life, she'd been the one to leave men feeling jilted and disappointed. There was one who'd shown up at our door once, a couple days after they'd been on a date, and he'd had a look on his face like he wasn't sure how he'd ended up there. "Send him away," Mom had told us from the couch with a dismissive wave of her hand, and Persephone and I had had to stand in the doorway and explain that it was nothing personal—our mom just didn't do second dates.

"Did she . . . lock herself up in her room?" I asked. Her closed door was the only way I knew how to measure my mother's grief.

"I don't know," Jill said. "As I said, I wasn't really around. But you know, to me, it was a good thing—Will getting married—because she finally stopped waiting around for him. She sent out some more applications, transferred to a four-year college, finally started—"

"Mom went to college?"

As far as I knew, she'd always been a waitress, drawing flowers on people's checks, maintaining eye contact even with those who looked down on her for her faded green uniform, her sauce-splattered shoes.

"Well," Jill said, "briefly. You know what I mean. Just that one semester before she got pregnant."

I froze midstep, my legs locking into place. "Wait, what?" I asked. "Mom went to college . . . and met Persephone's dad there?"

Jill was silent for a moment. "Well—yeah," she said. "Annie never told you any of this?"

"She always said he was a one-night stand. She said both of our fathers were one-night stands."

"She actually used those words?" Jill asked. "When you were a *kid?*"

"Yeah."

"Oh, Annie," Jill said, as if Mom were on the line with us and could hear the disappointment in her sister's voice.

I remembered knowing that phrase—one-night stand—before I was even old enough to fully grasp its meaning. I remembered how literally I took it, imagining my parents in an open field beneath a sky dusted with stars, standing together until morning came and they went their separate ways. I couldn't expect Aunt Jill to understand how, as a child, that phrase had been a comfort to me. How could she know that, for me, being with Mom had been like sitting in the sun on a cloudless spring morning? Never mind the Dark Days. Never mind the shifts she had at the diner, the dates she had with men whose names we never knew. When she was with me, she was all that I needed. I was warm and safe and loved, and a father—someone more than a one-night stand—would only distract her from me, only pull the sun from my sky.

"Well, sure, she had some of *those* over the years," Jill said, as if unwilling to use the phrase that Mom had taught me without a second thought. "*Your* dad, for example. Definitely a quick fling. He wasn't from town. He was in and out, and Annie didn't seem to mind. But Persephone's father—I don't really know how long that lasted. Less than a semester, I guess. They met in her classical mythology course, which I only remember because that's why she named Persephone the way she did."

"*That's* why she named her Persephone?"

I'd grown up knowing the myth, of course. Mom had told it to us one day when Persephone marched into the house, complaining how the kids at school were teasing her about her "stupid, weirdo" name.

"It's not weird," Mom had said. "It's ancient. Here, I'll tell you the story." But I didn't know that she'd chosen the name as some kind of homage to Persephone's father.

"Well, yeah," Jill said. "Why? What did you think was the reason?"

"I never really thought about it."

I'd always just accepted that the name was like Persephone herself—beautiful and uncommon.

"So wait—what happened with Persephone's father, then?" I asked. "If Mom actually had a relationship with him, then why wasn't he a part of Persephone's life?"

How strange that, before now, I'd never even considered him—the man whose blood had been in Persephone's veins. When I covered her bruises at night, I never once thought of him, never wondered if his skin, when wounded, blushed the same shade of blue.

"He didn't know about her," Jill said. "Annie never even told him she was pregnant. She just moved her stuff back into the house and went back to waitressing. Our parents begged her to tell him, but she was adamant. Actually, that's why she decided on the name Persephone in particular. She said he wasn't good enough to be her child's father, so she was rescuing Persephone from a life in the Underworld." She paused, as if hearing the words for the first time. "Gosh, she could be so dramatic."

"So she never even gave him a chance?" I asked. "Why would she do that? Why wasn't he 'good enough' in her eyes?"

Jill sighed, and I stepped outside of the rug's perimeter, my feet more prepared for the coolness of the floor. "It's simple," she said. "He wasn't good enough because he wasn't Will."

"But that's stupid," I protested. "You said yourself that, after Will got married, she got over him." I walked by the closet, the dresser, the light switch, my hand skimming along the surface of things as I went.

"No," Jill said. "I said she stopped waiting around for him. Stopped loving him, though? I don't know. I'm pretty sure she only, uh . . . got with . . . Persephone's father to try to get over Will."

So was that it, then? Was that why Mom had only allowed herself those brief flings? Because her heart had long ago been given to Will Emory? Because all she could do after that was lend it out like a library book, something to be borrowed for a short period of time and then safely returned? That would mean, then, that she'd loved him so much longer than she should have. I hated to think of her like that, pining away for Ben's father—of all people—wasting any chance she'd had on finding someone else to love. Now, it was too late. She was a different person—no longer the sun, as she'd once seemed, but a cloud, one that always held the threat of a storm, and I knew very well how much it hurt to love somebody like that.

"Sylvie?" Jill said.

"Yeah?"

"Where is this coming from? Why are you asking about all this ancient history?"

"Oh, um, I don't know, I guess I just—ow."

My hip bumped against the post of Persephone's footboard. I hadn't been paying attention to where I was going—I'd been speaking slowly, stalling as I scurried around my brain, wondering if I should tell Aunt Jill about running into Ben—and I'd jostled the bed out of place.

"Ow?" Jill said. "What happened?"

"Nothing," I said. "I was . . ."

The end of the bed had only moved about an inch, but it was enough to reveal the edge of something—a box, it looked like, peeking out from underneath Persephone's long blue quilt. I knelt to the ground and slid the rest of it out, pulling it onto the rug. As soon as it was free of the low frame of the bed, the two sides of the box's unsealed top popped open.

"You were what?" Jill asked.

I saw Persephone's green afghan before I registered anything else in the box. It was the one that had always been draped along the foot of her bed, the one she reached for in the middle of the night whenever she got too cold. I pulled it out and brought it to my nose, inhaling its scent, feeling its threads tickle my face in a way that felt profoundly familiar. It didn't smell like her, but it made me feel closer to her, just the same.

"Uh, Jill?" I said. "Can I call you back later?"

"What? What's going on?"

"Everything's fine," I said quickly. "Love you."

I set the afghan aside and dropped the phone on top of it. When I reached into the shallow box again, I pulled out a necklace—some old chunky thing—and a bottle of lotion that looked thinned and yellowed with age.

"What the hell?" I whispered to the room, as if Persephone herself were watching and would answer me.

I closed the box's flaps, looking for a sticker or label, something to explain why these three very disparate items had been packed away to-gether and shoved under Persephone's bed. Besides her blue quilt, these were the only things I'd seen of hers since I'd been home.

In the upper left-hand corner of the box's top, Mom had written our address. I noticed that first because of how thick the letters looked, as if she'd traced over them with her pen several times, wanting to make sure that, if the package didn't make it to its intended recipient, it would at least make it back to her. Then, in the middle of the right flap, there was another address, and when I read it, my breath caught in the back of my throat.

"Tom Dent," it said, followed by a house number and street in Hanover.

17

Grabbing the empty box, I marched across the room and pulled the door open with so much force that it banged against my dresser.

"Jesus," Mom barked at the noise, her voice guiding me to the living room.

Her chair was in a reclining position, and she held the copy of *Wuthering Heights* I'd given her the day before.

"Well," Mom said, not bothering to lift her eyes from the page, "it's about time you got up. Or is taking care of me in my time of need a vacation for you?"

"What the hell have you been doing?"

She actually jumped at the question.

"Jesus," she said again, covering her ears. "I was only kidding, Sylvie. Sleep as late as you want."

"I'm talking about this," I said, and I held up the box, facing the side with Tommy's name on it toward her. She squinted as she read it, then returned her eyes to the book.

"Oh," she said. "I told you I gave him your sister's things."

"No." I shook my head so hard that a bone in my neck cracked.

"You said you gave them to 'that neighbor boy.' You were talking about *him*? Tommy Dent?"

"He goes by Tom now, Sylvie."

I laughed, a quick indignant sputter, and I paced around the living room.

"Okay," I said, "we'll get to how you know *that* in a second. But first—why would you give him Persephone's stuff? He didn't even—he was—I don't understand what would possess you to do that."

"Would you calm down for half a second?" She pulled the lever on the recliner and the back of her chair shot forward. "It's not the end of the world, all right? It was just part of a deal we had."

I stopped moving, glanced down at Tommy's name on the box, and then set my eyes on Mom. "A *deal*? What kind of deal?"

Straightening the scarf she wore around her head, Mom sighed. "He started coming over a couple years after your sister . . ." She let the sentence hang in the air, heavy as wet clothes drying on a line. I glared at her until she continued.

"He used to mow the lawn for me. Clean the house. And in exchange, I'd—"

"You'd give him her stuff?" My voice was so shrill I could imagine the neighbors' dogs howling in response.

"Yes, well, they were friends. And I hadn't known that. I'd always thought he was a bad seed, but it turns out he really cared for her. So he'd come over and we'd talk."

"You'd *talk*?" As far as I knew, she'd always been too drunk to carry a conversation. Couldn't even handle the words *happy birthday* each October. "Talk about *what*?"

Talk to the mother, Tommy had told the detectives. Now, the sentence drummed in my head as I waited for her answer.

"About her," she said, as if it should have been obvious. "He wanted to know every memory I could think of. Didn't matter how small. It was very sweet, actually."

"Oh, I'm sure!" I scoffed. "But that doesn't explain why you'd give him Persephone's stuff."

"I just told you," she said. "I gave it to him in exchange for his time."

"Why wouldn't you just pay him?"

"He didn't want money. He just wanted to be able to choose a few of your sister's things each time. So I let him." She shrugged. "Two birds, one stone. It—her stuff—I needed it gone."

The hair on my arms rose. He had been in our house, our bedroom. He had fondled Persephone's things. I could picture him pressing the nozzle of her cheap drugstore perfume, spraying it into the air as he closed his eyes, inhaling. And Mom had let him do this—over and over. But even as that realization gathered in my mind, there was something else Mom had been saying that made my chest feel tight.

"Say her name, Mom."

I took a step closer to her, and she blinked up at me.

"What?" she asked.

"You keep saying 'your sister' or just referring to her as *her*, but she had a name and I need you to say it. I don't think I've heard you say it once since she died."

"That's not—" She tried an unconvincing, paper-thin chuckle. "You're being ridiculous."

"I'm not," I said. "Say her name."

The name she'd chosen, just a young woman inspired by her classics course in college. The name she'd picked because she, like the goddess Demeter, had wanted to rescue her daughter from a life in the Underworld—which, apparently for Mom, was any life with a man who wasn't Will.

She stared at me for what felt like minutes.

"Persephone," she finally said, and it was barely more than a whisper.

I set the box on the coffee table and crossed my arms. "Good," I said coolly. "Now—back to Tommy. I know you're lying."

"What? No, I'm not. I gave it all to him."

I shook my head. "Not about that. About him mowing the lawn and cleaning the house. I know for a fact that Jill paid a landscaping service and cleaned the house herself. So what was the real deal? What did you get in exchange for your dead daughter's possessions?"

She shrank into her chair, pulling her book toward her chest as if to defend herself.

"If you must know," she said, her voice creaky and low, "he gave me pills."

I hesitated. "Pills? What kind of pills?"

"Oh, I don't know the fancy names," she said, sounding annoyed. "They were painkillers mostly. The good stuff."

Even though it probably shouldn't have, this actually surprised me.

"You used pills?" I asked. "Did—did Jill know?"

Mom lowered her book onto her lap, her finger still pressed like a dried flower between its pages. "Not at first," she said. "But later, after Tom stopped coming around, she . . . found me. Withdrawals were a bitch."

The living room clock counted the seconds of my silence. "I can't believe she never told me," I said, more to myself than to Mom.

"I asked her not to."

And we O'Leary women—we keep our promises to our sisters.

Something hot flickered in my chest. "This is so . . ." I started—but then I stopped. I didn't know what this was. I could barely keep up with all the things I'd learned so far that day, let alone find the words to define them.

Talk to the mother. I heard it again, that absurd suggestion that Mom knew something about Persephone's murder. Was this why he'd urged the detectives to talk to her? Because he'd been talking to her himself, dropping pills like coins into her palm each week? Did she say something to him once, the drugs just beginning to blunt her edges, that made him think she was worth investigating?

No. I shook the thought from my head. Mom said Tommy didn't start coming around until a couple years after Persephone died. There was no reason, then, for him to have thought of her when talking to the police.

"You know it was all bullshit, right?" I said. "Everything Tommy said? For one thing, he and Persephone weren't friends. He barely even knew her. He just left all these creepy notes in her locker. He—"

"That's not true," Mom said. "They were good friends. He told me they used to hang out all the time after school. I just never knew about it because I was always working."

"They *never* hung out," I insisted. "That last year? When we were all in the same school? She came home with me on the bus and then she'd do her homework or watch TV until—"

Until Ben came to pick her up, I was going to say, but Mom, as if sensing the dark, choppy waves I was wading into, quickly cut me off.

"And why would Tom lie?" she asked. "Why would he want mementos of her if he hardly knew her?" Mom reached for a bookmark on the end table, slid it between the pages she'd been marking with her finger, and snapped the book shut. "That doesn't make any sense. You're just mad I gave those things to him and not you."

"Damn right I'm mad," I agreed. "I'm mad you gave him her stuff, and I'm mad you gave him her stuff for *pills*. God, did you really have no—" I stopped, another thought overlapping the others. "Also, even if they *were* friends, why would you give her stuff to *him*, and not to *me*?"

Mom shrugged and rested her head against the back of the chair. Closing her eyes, she said, "I didn't think you wanted it. You were out of here the first chance you got, weren't you? You never asked for any of it."

"I didn't think you'd just give it away!"

Her arms hung limply at her sides, her palms turned toward the ceiling. She was clearly exhausted. Still, I couldn't stop myself from charging forward.

"He was a suspect, Mom. In Persephone's murder."

She opened one eye and looked at me before closing it again.

"That's insane," she said. "I would have heard about that if it were true."

"When?" I demanded. "When you were locked in your bedroom? When you were passed out drunk? When you were on *drugs*?"

"Sylvie," Mom said, touching her forehead, "you're being very loud. And I wasn't *on drugs*. I was just taking painkillers."

"He raped a girl," I told her, remembering the details I'd collected during my research the night before. "Twelve years ago. He was at a party and he found some girl passed out in one of the bedrooms, and he raped her."

Mom shook her head, her eyes still closed.

"That doesn't sound like Tom," she said.

"No? That doesn't sound like your drug-dealing friend, Tom?" I couldn't keep the condescension out of my voice. It dripped over every word, thick and sticky. "He spent the next eleven years in prison, so clearly he did it. He—"

My pulse seemed to pause. Turning back to look at the box on the coffee table, I read the address again.

"Wait," I said. "This is a Hanover address. He's only lived there since he got out of prison last year. But you said—you said you had your little deal with him a couple years after Persephone died, when he would have still lived down the street, right? So how did you know where to send this?"

Mom opened her eyes, looked at her fingernails, and slid one beneath the other as if cleaning it of dirt. "He called me, all right?" she said. "He told me his new address. Not a big deal."

"When?" I asked. "When did he call you?"

"I don't know, sometime early last fall. I hadn't heard from him in years."

"Eleven years, to be exact?" I pressed. "Because he was in prison?"

She took a deep breath, rubbed the arms of the chair with her hands, and then gripped the edges. "I don't know how long it had been," she said, her voice pinched. "I wasn't keeping track. All I know is he called me up and said he wanted to resume our deal. He told me it was going to be harder this time around to get my pills, so he wanted a gesture of good faith that I was ready to start things up again."

She put a finger in the air as if to stop me from speaking. "And before you get all high and mighty," she said, "I wasn't even sure that I wanted those pills again, but I figured it would be good to have some options. So . . ." She exhaled loudly. "I told him I'd send him a package. But as I'm sure you saw, there wasn't much left. I'd already given him most of it."

I pushed my toes into the carpet, my fingers into my arms. "That didn't strike you as strange?" I asked. "He's supposedly this great, honest guy in your book, but he demands this—'gesture of good faith,' as you called it?"

Mom waved away my question. "Oh, he was always a little strange," she said. "Sweet. But strange."

"So why didn't you send it to him?" I asked. "Why was the package just sitting under Persephone's bed, with his address already on it?"

"I was going to send it," she said. "I had it ready to go, obviously. But then the doctor called and told me I had to come in, and then I got my CV, and—"

"CV?"

"Cancer verdict. Anyway, you know your aunt—she steamrolled over the whole situation. Moved right in, whether I wanted her to or not. Started watching my every move. So I hid it—I didn't want her asking all her damn questions—" She flashed her eyes toward me and narrowed them. "And then I just forgot about it. Tom never called me again. So there—are you happy? I've told you everything. Now leave me alone so I can take a nap."

As I dug my fingernails deeper into my arms, my throat burned with betrayal. She had let Tommy into our house, ushered him into our living room, but me—me she'd closed her door on. No matter how long I'd waited in the hallway, begging her to open up, she'd kept herself locked away from me. Now, she settled farther into her chair and closed her eyes, sealing me from her sight the same way she'd always sealed me from her room, and I took a step forward, unwilling to be shut out anymore.

"Why didn't you ever tell me you dated Will Emory?"

The change in her body was instantaneous. Her limbs stiffened for a moment, her eyes shooting open like a person shaken from a dream. Then her fingers dug into the arms of her chair, and her face became gnarled with agony.

"What are you—" She looked at me as though I had punched her, as though my fist were still raised in the air, ready to strike again. "Why would you say that name?"

I went rigid then. "What do you mean?"

"That name! Why would you say it?"

It was the same thing she'd cried on my first day back, when I'd asked if Ben Emory was the "neighbor boy" she'd given Persephone's things to. The look she'd given me then had been similar, too—the same cornered-animal eyes, same quiver in her chin—and it occurred to me, only now, that the name she'd been objecting to that day hadn't been Ben at all—but Emory.

"I just want to know why you never mentioned that you dated him."

She stood up from her chair, her arms shaking with the effort of pushing herself up, and before I could leap forward to stop her or help her, she stumbled toward the hallway, reaching for the walls like someone without sight.

"Mom," I called after her, but she disappeared around the corner. "Mom, we're not doing this again."

With a few quick steps, I caught up to her, just as her hand stretched toward her doorknob. Grabbing her arm gently, I had to swallow my surprise at how little there was to grasp; her arms felt thin as broom handles.

"Come on," I said, but she pulled and pulled and pulled, and I loosened my grip for fear that she'd hurt herself.

"I don't want to talk about it!" she cried, and she pushed her door open, threw herself into her dark, shrouded room, and shoved her body back against the door to close it again.

"Mom—no."

I twisted the knob just in time, heard her groan as she held her place, and then felt the pressure lessen as she backed away. The door swung open easily, and as the light from the hallway gushed into her room, she crawled onto her bed, then clutched her legs to her chest like a child.

"Mom," I said. "What's going on?"

She rocked back and forth, her cheek pressed against her knee. "I don't want to talk about him," she said. "How do you—how did you even know?"

I took a couple steps toward the bed. Reaching out slowly, I put my hand on her back, trying to be as tender as I could manage, but her spine arched away from my touch.

"I asked you a question," she snapped. "How the hell did you know?"

For a few seconds, I watched the tears gather in her eyes. I was struck by how fragile and beautiful they looked, their delicate sheen seeming to turn her eyes to glass.

"I ran into Ben," I started. "Will's son. Persephone's . . . yeah. And he showed me an old picture of you and his dad. It was clear something went on between you guys, so I asked Jill about it and she confirmed that you used to date him."

Mom blinked up at me, tears spilling onto her cheeks. "You ran into Will's—you ran into his son?"

I nodded and then swallowed, hoping she wouldn't ask me where I'd seen him, hoping that, if she did, I'd be able to offer a convincing lie. She didn't need to know, I reminded myself. It would only make her chemo even more difficult each week. I didn't know if she'd react the same to Ben being at the hospital as she had just now to the mere mention of Will's name, but looking at the hollow of her collarbones, how scooped-out they seemed, I knew it was a risk I wasn't willing to take.

"Why didn't you ever mention him?" I asked her softly.

She leaned her forehead toward her knees, and when she spoke, her words fell into the space between them. "I don't like to talk about it," she said. "It hurts just to . . . just to hear his name."

With slow, careful movements, I sat down in front of her on the bed. "What happened between you guys?" I asked.

She shrugged, shaking her head. "We were in love," she said. "We were in love, and . . ." She sniffled, wiping her nose. "He broke my heart. What more do you need to know?"

Everything, I wanted to say—*Tell me everything about loving a man so hard that, even decades later, it brings you to tears*—but instead, I moved a little closer and kept my voice gentle.

"How did he break your heart?" I asked. "What did he do?"

She lifted her head and met my eyes, her gaze so intense that I felt it on my skin. From all the way down the hall, I could hear the clock ticking, counting time as if it were endless.

"Stop sniffing into my life," she finally hissed. "There's nothing there. Nothing."

Pushing back with her hands and feet, she moved toward the headboard. She crossed her arms over her chest and turned her head to look at the windows. I looked, too, for just a second, as if there was anything to see there but curtained darkness.

"I'm not sniffing," I objected. "I just want to—God, Mom, I just want to feel like I actually know you. I don't think that's too much to ask. So, come on, what happened? Jill said he married another woman."

The air blew out of Mom's lips in a quick scoff. "He only married her because he got her pregnant," she said. "It should have been me. He loved *me*."

"Okay," I said, "but you guys were broken up. Right? I mean, he was at college, and he met someone else, and—"

"We weren't together," she spit out. "But we still belonged to each other."

I paused. My mother—the woman who left men with their mouths watering at our front door, who said second dates were for people who lacked independence—was talking about Will as if they had a lifelong commitment.

"I'm sure that was . . . hard for you, then," I said, my words like feet tiptoeing across a cold floor. "You thought you'd be together forever, but he chose someone else."

"Oh, please," she said. "He didn't choose her. That was all Richard, I'm sure of it."

"Richard?"

"His father," she reminded me, and I remembered his name on lawn signs, back when I was a kid and he was running for reelection to Congress.

"He chose *her* for his son," she continued, "because she was of perfect breeding with perfect hair and perfect behavior. Just like a show dog."

She gave a quick, bitter chuckle before continuing. "It wouldn't do," she went on, "for him to be with me. Diner waitress. Student at the *community* college. How embarrassing for the *family*. How embarrassing to the legacy of Emory Builders, if the boy being groomed to take over ended up with someone like *me*. No, no. Richard wouldn't have that. So he found Susie Perfect, planted her at his son's school—probably paid her damn tuition—and welcomed her into the clan with open arms. A baby? Oh, how wonderful! A daughter-in-law who irons her underwear? What man would settle for anything less!"

Something thick and constricting coiled around my stomach. The more she finally spoke about it all, the more she sounded—paranoid. Delusional, even.

"But, Mom," I said. "That doesn't really make sense, right? I mean, it couldn't have all been his dad, because, well, he still got her pregnant, didn't he? He still chose to marry her after that. Don't you think that if he *really* wanted to be with you, he could have figured something out? He could have been a father to Ben *and* . . . I don't know—eventually married you, I guess?"

Her eyes widened, and in the span of a few seconds, moved through a spectrum of emotions—first disbelief, then surprise, then anger—before finally brimming with a simple, broken sadness.

"Like I said," she whispered, "he broke my heart."

She stared past me, her eyes landing somewhere on the wall, and I wondered what scenes from her life with Will were playing out in front of her there. Inching closer to her again and taking a deep breath, I prepared myself for my final question—the sole reason her past with Will Emory mattered to me at all.

"So is this why you didn't want Persephone to be with Ben? Not because of your dating rule, but because—because of who Ben's father was? And how he'd hurt you?"

Her eyes flicked away from the wall, and when they found mine, the ache inside them was as visible as the leaden gray of her irises.

"Yes," she said.

Yes. The air became heavy, making it difficult to reel in my breath. Yes, Ben had been right—again. Yes, Mom could have just told us about Will from the start. *Yes*—what I said to Persephone when she asked me to paint her bruises. Yes when it was her wrist, yes when it was her arm, yes when it was her rib.

"Do you realize," I said shakily, "what you did by not telling us? You turned them into fucking Romeo and Juliet, Mom, when maybe, if you'd just told her that you'd dated Ben's father and he'd hurt you and you didn't want the same thing to happen to her, then maybe—"

"Stop."

"—things would have been different. Maybe she would have told Ben that things were—I don't know—too complicated for them to be together. Or maybe you guys would have talked about it like normal human beings and you'd realize that she was allowed to learn her own lessons, make her own—"

"I told you to stop it!" she cried, and the look in her eyes was no longer one of remembered misery. Instead, there was a knifelike sharpness to her stare that made me swallow the rest of my words.

"You have no idea," she said, "what it would have taken for me to talk about it. What it still takes, now. So don't tell me what I should have done, or how things would have been different if I'd just been honest, because . . . well . . . you should know, huh?"

She glared at me but didn't continue.

"What are you talking about?" I asked, and seeing the piercing accusation in her eyes, I felt my throat tighten.

"You weren't so honest, either."

Come on, Sylvie, it's just one tonight. Yes when it was her hip. Yes when it was her shoulder. Yes when I was tired and cold and wanted nothing more than to stay wrapped in the cocoon of my bed. *Don't ever tell Mom, okay? You have to promise me, Sylvie*—and I kept my promises to my sister, every one until that final night. Now, my breath started coming in shallow little gasps.

"Isn't that right, Sylvie?" Mom pressed.

You have to leave the window cracked, just a little. You'll be the best sister ever if you do it. But Mom didn't know how I'd broken that particular promise—she couldn't. She must have only meant how Persephone snuck out to see Ben, how I kept that from her until it was too late. Because nobody knew how I held the latch in my fingers on that final night, then clicked it into place. No one had seen me jump into bed when I saw Persephone coming; no one knew how long she tapped at the glass, certain, at first, that I'd just made a mistake. Now, my eyes were so blurred that I could barely see Mom in front of me anymore.

I'm your only sister, Sylvie. I could still hear her say it. *You have to do this for me, and you can't ever tell.* The tears fell hot and fast down my cheeks as Mom watched me, knowing how I'd betrayed her. Yes when it was her arm. Yes when it was her leg. Yes when I still thought we had a thousand more nights, and in one of them, I'd finally say no.

As the first sob wrenched its way out of my body, I pitched forward, dropping my head into my hands.

"You're right," I said, gulping for air between words. "I'm sorry. I'm so sorry. I don't know why I—I didn't know she'd . . ."

My chest heaved and sank as I collapsed under the weight of such old, lingering grief. I fell against Mom, my head landing in her lap, but I couldn't move, couldn't adjust my position; I could only curl into myself like I'd once curled up in her womb.

"I'm sorry," I whispered, tasting the tears on my lips. "I'm sorry. I'm sorry."

"Shhh," Mom said, and I felt her hand, light as a petal, on the top of my head. She ran her fingers through my hair, slowly and gently, and then placed them on my forehead and started all over, stroke after stroke after stroke.

"It's okay," she said as I cried against her stomach. "We all played our part, Sylvie. We all played our part."

18

Somehow, living in Providence, I'd found myself in a place of ease. Strange, now, to think of it, now that I was so far from that world, sucked instead back into the one I'd thought I'd peeled off of me like a sunburn. It had only been a few weeks since my last shift at Steve's, but already, I could barely remember how to load the ink into the gun. I could remember wiping beads of blood from flesh, but when I pictured those moments, wearing those blue latex gloves, it was someone else's hand I saw.

I texted with Lauren on Sunday, trying to get back to that place. Mom and I were barely speaking. After spitting and sobbing more words to each other on Thursday than we had in sixteen years, we'd spent most of the next few days in the living room—together, watching TV, but silent. Now, while Mom flipped through channels, I huddled up with my phone on the couch, texting Lauren about Wolf Bro, the nickname we'd given to one of her clients. He was a guy in his midthirties who always boasted about the women he'd "beasted" over the weekend, and he'd been scheduled to come back that week for session three of his wolf tattoo.

"Ugh," Lauren wrote. "Wolf Bro now wants a full moon done over his entire right pec, because—exact quote—'a true wolf needs something to howl at.'"

"Genius," I replied.

"I know, right? Because how else will the chicks at the gym know what an animal he is in the sheets?"

"Haha."

"I swear, it took everything I had not to scream at him that no self-respecting woman would ever fuck a guy with a wolf tattoo."

"Haha," I typed again, but I didn't even smile.

I tried to be engaged in the conversation. I tried to picture us in our apartment, handing a bag of Doritos back and forth as we laughed about Wolf Bro. I even saw us swiping orange crumbs onto the floor and joking that Claude, our fictional French housekeeper, would vacuum them up later. But every time I went to type a response to Lauren, to embed myself deeper into the comfort of that fantasy, I found myself nearly writing what was really on my mind instead, all the unanswered questions I'd collected over the last week: What had Tommy Dent wanted with Persephone's things, and what had happened to them after all this time?

And why had he told the police to *talk to the mo—*

"So how's it going with your mom?" Lauren texted, and I was grateful to be yanked away from the skipping record of those questions. "Is it weird between you guys?"

"Yeah," I responded quickly. "It's really weird."

"Is she acting like you're her personal bartender instead of her nurse?"

"No, she's actually sober. Apparently it hurts when she drinks now, because . . . cancer."

"Oh, that makes sense," Lauren replied. "So then have you guys talked about it? How she drank herself into oblivion for half your life?"

"There's nothing to talk about really," I said. "I already know why she did it."

"So?? That doesn't make it right! Yes, she lost a daughter, and that's really tragic, but so many parents have lost children, and they don't just shut down forever. They mourn, of course, but they eventually move on. It was so selfish that she didn't find a way to do that—for YOUR sake at least!"

Even through text, Lauren's tone was sharp and unforgiving, same as it always was when she talked about Mom. I knew she spoke that way out of fierce loyalty to me, but as I read her message again, I couldn't help but feel that it was a little unfair. And that wasn't Lauren's fault. It was mine.

"It was hard for her to move on," I wrote. "She never got any closure."

"Don't make excuses for her," Lauren replied. "No one ever gets closure when they lose someone they love."

"Yeah . . . but it was the way she lost her . . ."

I felt my heart thumping then. It was picking up speed as I snuck closer to the truth—truth I'd hidden since the beginning of our friendship, truth I'd painted over as if it were a bruise.

"I'm not saying it wasn't awful," Lauren said. "A car accident is so unexpected. But it doesn't give her a free pass out of living."

"It wasn't a car accident."

I'd typed it so quickly that I barely realized what I was doing. But now I had said it. I'd scratched off the paint of that lie. I could almost see it under my fingernails as I gripped the phone in my hand.

Taking a deep breath, I typed out the rest. "She was murdered. And they never solved the case."

The second I pressed Send, I felt dizzy, and I leaned my head against the back of the couch to steady myself. When I looked at my phone a few moments later, the space where Lauren's response would be was empty. There wasn't even a typing icon, and I stared at the screen until one finally appeared.

"What??" she wrote after a minute.

"I'm so sorry I lied to you," I rushed forward. "I just couldn't bring myself to talk about it before. The lie was so much easier. I know that sounds stupid, but . . . ugh. I'm so sorry."

"Murdered how?" she replied, much faster this time.

"Strangled."

The temperature in the room seemed to drop by twenty degrees. I imagined I could look up at the ceiling and see snow beginning to fall.

"Holy shit," Lauren said.

"Yeah . . ."

"And they don't know who did it?"

I brought my fingers to my lips and breathed against them, trying to warm myself. But soon, I shivered anyway, and my hands began to shake.

"Nope," I responded.

"Wow," Lauren said. "This is . . . I don't even know. That's a really huge thing to never tell me."

I didn't respond. Instead, I kept my eyes on the phone, where the typing icon flashed and disappeared, flashed and disappeared, over and over again. I slouched down on the couch, huddling deeper into myself as I waited for her to hit Send, and I tucked my icy hands into the sleeves of my sweatshirt.

"But I GUESS I can understand why you never talked about it," Lauren finally wrote, and I released a breath I hadn't realized I'd been holding. "That's some heavy shit for a toddler to go through."

For a moment, I blinked at her text in confusion. Then I recalled the rest of the lie I'd told her, the paint that still remained. And right away, I knew I could fix that. I could tell her I'd been fourteen years old when I lost Persephone—old enough to know and love her, old enough to be baffled by her, too.

"Do you want me to call you right now?" Lauren asked. "I have so many questions but it seems weird to talk about it over text. I don't want to overwhelm you or anything, but I'm just over here like OMG where did it happen, where were YOU when it happened, etc. etc."

I remembered Persephone hissing at me through the window that night. I remembered holding the blanket tighter over my head, ignoring her so hard that she walked away. And then I remembered what I'd always known; paint is stubborn. It clings instead of chips, and even after more than a decade, it has to be scraped and scraped and scraped. But right then, my hands were stiff with cold, and my entire body was trembling.

"I'm so sorry," I managed to type, "but I have to help my mom with something. Can we talk about this later? Tomorrow maybe?"

"Uhhh sure . . ." she replied after a moment, and I looked over at Mom, asleep in her chair.

The next morning, Mom brought *Wuthering Heights* to chemo. I watched her as she read, trying to distract myself from my conversations with Lauren—both the one I'd stumbled through the night before, and the one I still needed to have. Each of them filled me with a light-headed anxiety that made the words in Mom's book seem to blur.

Clearing my throat, I forced my eyes to focus, and I saw that the corners of several pages were folded down. It seemed so unlike her—flagging a passage with the intention of returning to it later—and for a moment, I had to resist the urge to rip the book from her hands, comb through those pages, and see what had moved her so much that she felt the need to mark them.

"You know," I said, "I had to do a paper on that book in high school, but I barely remember it. Is it good?"

She didn't look at me when she responded.

"It's not that it's good," she said distractedly. "It's just true." The page she'd been reading made a whispery sound as she turned it. "Be quiet, though, okay? I can't concentrate if you're talking to me."

"Sorry," I said, and I turned my attention toward the entrance of the room. I jolted then, seeing Ben walk by. He glanced in casually, but as soon as he noticed me, he hurried away down the hall.

I looked at Mom, who held the book so close that it blocked her face entirely, and then I stood up and followed him into the reception area.

"Ben," I whispered, and when he turned around, there was a twinge of pain—or guilt—in his eyes, as if it hurt him just to look at me.

"Hey," he said, coming to an abrupt stop. "I wasn't trying to get in your way or anything. I forgot this was your mom's chemo time."

"That's not—"

"But while you're here, can we talk for a second? I want to apologize."

I paused. "About what?"

Cupping my elbow gently with his palm, he led me toward a window in front of some chairs. "I'm sorry about what I said to you last week," he said.

"Um," I started, "you're going to have to be more specific."

"About Tommy Dent," he said, shaking his head, as if disappointed with himself. "I was a jerk about it. It's obviously a sensitive subject, and I sort of threw him in your face."

I rubbed the toe of my shoe into the carpet, keeping my eyes on my feet as I responded.

"Actually," I said, "you might be right about Tommy."

When I looked back up at him, his brow was furrowed, his dark eyes slightly squinted. "You're going to have to be more specific," he echoed.

"I think he—" I stopped, knowing that once I said it, I wouldn't be able to take it back. "I think he might have killed my sister."

The words thudded against the air, louder than I'd intended, as I finally said the thing I'd only been able to imagine in sporadic flashes so far. My breath became sharp yet shallow, my skin suddenly hot. I lifted my hand to my forehead, and then my body loosened, my arms flopping to my sides.

"Here. Come with me," Ben insisted. He put his hand on my back and I allowed myself to be led away from the windows and down a hall. We walked until we reached a door marked "Staff Only," and then Ben nudged me inside.

At first, it was dark, but I could sense that the room was small, and when Ben flicked on a light switch and my eyes recovered from the shock of brightness, I saw that we were standing in a tiny bathroom. Ben slid the silver lock into place, and I had to blink away the image of my bedroom window, the old white latch so easy to turn that it made betraying my sister seem almost natural.

Ben pumped some brown paper from the towel dispenser and held it under the running faucet. "Here," he said. "This will help." Pushing my hair to one side, he held the cool, wet paper to the back of my neck.

For a moment, the dampness soothed me; it eased the prickling darkness that was swarming my vision. But then, registering the slight pressure of Ben's palm as he cupped the base of my skull, I saw Persephone in my mind, pulling back her shirt to expose a fresh purple bruise just beginning to burn beneath her skin.

I jerked away from him, and the wet paper towel slapped onto the tile. I took in the door with its silver lock, and I reached forward to snap the lever backward. "What are you doing?" I demanded.

Ben bent over to pick up the towel and tossed it into the trash can. "Nothing," he said. "You just got so pale all of a sudden, I thought you were going to faint." He gestured toward the door. "Sorry—I locked that out of habit, I guess."

When I didn't respond, he put his hand on the door handle and opened it a little. "Do you want to go back out there?" he asked. "It's just—you got kind of loud, and . . . the cancer center isn't really the place for phrases like 'killed my sister.'"

He laughed then, quickly and uncomfortably, but it was still a kick to my stomach.

"So which is it?" I shot at him. "I looked like I was going to faint, or I was too loud?"

He blinked at me—once, twice—and then he returned his hand to his side, letting the bathroom door fall closed. "Both," he said. His eyes roved over my face. "How are you feeling now? Do you want to sit down for a second?"

He reached behind me and closed the lid on the toilet seat. Feeling ridiculous and stupid, but also a little unsteady, I sat down on top of it and put my elbows on my knees, my head in my hands.

"Did you have breakfast this morning?" he asked.

I pictured Mom's plate, the food only pushed around instead of eaten, and how my stomach had growled as I scraped the cold, dry leftovers into the trash just before we left for the hospital.

"We only had two eggs left," I muttered. "I need to go shopping."

"Oh man," Ben said, "I hate grocery shopping. Such a pain in the ass."

I lifted my head just long enough to give him a look, and he took a small step back in response, leaning against the counter. "Sorry," he said. "Not important. But, look, now that we're on the same page about Tommy, I'm just curious—what made you come around? It was just last week that you were accusing *me* of killing her."

I stared at the floor and mumbled toward the tiles, "A lot has changed since last week."

"Okay," Ben said, his feet shifting. "Like what?"

I hesitated, unsure of how much to tell him, how much to admit. He was Ben Emory—all I had to do was think his name and my pulse would quicken—but there was so much swimming in my head right then, so much lapping at my brain and ready to overflow.

"Well," I said, "that picture you showed me. You were right about it. You were right about my mom and your dad."

"About how they dated?"

"Yes, that. But also how he hurt her. How they were together and it ended badly and that's why my mom never wanted Persephone to be with you."

I heard Ben take a breath. "Shit." My gaze was still focused on the grout between the tiles—it wasn't safe, in such a small space, to look him in the eye—but I knew that his body had stiffened.

"Sorry," he said after a moment. "That's not a very articulate response. It's just—" He ran his hand over his face, his features sagging as he dragged his fingers against them. "I wish she'd told us that back then. I'm *not* my father."

There was a sudden edge, cool but sharp, that slid into his voice, and it was enough to remind me of where I was, who I was with. In that tiny space stood a man who, murderer or not, had once hurt my sister. I picked my head up to glance at the door. It was only a few feet away from me. I could reach it in less than a second if I had to.

"Why didn't she just explain that to Persephone?" he asked, his tone softening. "I don't—I don't understand."

My eyes coasted back toward the floor, though my body remained alert. "She said it hurt too much to talk about it."

Ben didn't say anything to that, and even I couldn't blame him.

"I don't know," I continued, more to myself than to him. "Maybe I should have done more—back then. Maybe I should have questioned things. I mean, Persephone was almost eighteen when my mom saw you guys together—how much longer could the dating rule really apply to her? I should have found that odd, but instead I just accepted it. I just trusted that my mom knew what was best."

"You were a kid," Ben said. "That's what you were supposed to do."

I shrugged. "I guess," I said. Then I straightened a little. "I'm just surprised I never figured this out. I mean, even after she died, there were signs."

"Signs? What kind of signs?"

I flicked my eyes toward his face, then quickly looked at the trash can. "You weren't at Persephone's wake, were you?" I asked, though I already knew the answer. I'd spent those brutal hours with my fists clenched, my eyes narrowed, scanning the crowd to see if he dared to show up.

Ben shifted his feet. "No," he said. "I didn't want to upset anyone. I figured you guys would have heard that I left Persephone on the road that night, and . . ." He cleared his throat. "No, I didn't go."

"Well your dad did," I said. "And I hated that, because he was *your* dad. But it made sense, I guess, because the other council members were there, too—except my mom only shook hands with them. But when she saw your dad, she just . . . collapsed against him, and he sort of . . ." I gestured with my hand to demonstrate. "Gently patted her hair. I didn't think about it back then, but now, it's like—it was the kind of thing you'd see between people who have history."

I paused, remembering the way she'd gripped his arms, how her tears had seemed swift and endless. "I don't know," I added. "I just think that if I'd actually thought about it, then maybe I would have put things together. It would have been too late, obviously—but still."

Ben was silent for a moment. "Well, if we're going by that logic," he said, "then I should have figured it out a long time ago, too—even before Persephone died."

I tilted my head to look up at him, but he was staring at the wall. "Why?" I asked.

He crossed his arms, squinting a little. "Your mom came to my grandfather's funeral," he said. "My dad's dad."

Richard Emory? But Mom had just spoken about him with such venom in her voice.

"It was soon after Persephone and I started dating," Ben continued. "Soon after your mom said that we couldn't. And when I saw her there, I thought maybe things had changed. Maybe she was coming around to the idea of the two of us. Maybe Persephone had mentioned that my grandfather had died and how—how close he and I were, and maybe your mom was trying to, I don't know, offer her support to our family? I mean, she didn't actually speak to me that day, but still. I asked Persephone about it, but she said nope, nothing had changed, your mom still didn't know we were together. She couldn't even believe your mom had been at the funeral in the first place, so it was just this weird, inexplicable thing. But now . . ."

I watched his face, saw the realization of something gather in his features, and I waited for him to continue. When seconds passed and he still hadn't spoken, I rolled my eyes.

"But now *what?*" I prompted.

He shook his head slightly. "My mom had just left my dad, not that long before my grandfather died. So maybe . . . maybe your mom came to the funeral to see my dad, and to see if—now that he wasn't married—if there was . . ." He trailed off.

"There was what?"

"Space for her again?"

He framed the words as a question, but when I snapped my head up to look at him, I could tell that, already, he believed them as fact.

"Are you serious?" I asked. "You think your father's so great that my mom came crawling right back to him the second he became available again? Do you really think that anyone could be that pathetic?"

Ben scratched at his cheek, the one with the scar that cut across his skin. "I don't think my father is so great," he said.

"But you think my mother is pathetic?"

"What? No, I—"

"Then what are we talking about here?"

I stood up, latching my eyes onto his, and I waited to see who would last the longest, who would be the one to see the other look away. Even though the darkness of his irises, so close in color to his pupils, made my neck prickle, I knew that it had to be me. I crossed my arms and shifted my weight, and in a few more seconds, his gaze dropped to the floor.

"I just think," he said, "that it's possible to love someone for a really long time, even if you can't be with them. I mean, I still love—"

He stopped himself before he said her name. I narrowed my eyes to slits.

"Let me start again," he said. "I don't think your mom would be pathetic if she still loved him. Love is love. You can't just kick it to the curb, even if sometimes you wished like hell you could."

But it had been nearly two decades from the time Mom and Will had been together to the time Mom went to his father's funeral. I couldn't imagine loving someone that long—not when they were just a memory, a wound, a thing that was already gone. How could a love like that remain so constant, dependable as the change of seasons or the months in a year? I pictured the pages of a calendar turning, the squares of days that my mother might have wasted holding out for a ghost. I envisioned her marking each date with a small, carefully drawn heart—the third, the twelfth, the twenty-first, all days she might have loved him—and then I felt my breath catch in my throat.

"Did your dad ever have Dark Days?" I asked.

Ben tilted his head. "Dark what?"

"The fifteenth of every month—does it mean anything to you? Did you ever notice your dad acting strange on those days?"

He bit his lip, seeming to consider it, and then slowly shook his head. "No," he said. "I don't think so. Not that I can remember anyway. Why? What's the significance of the fifteenth?"

I sighed. "I have no idea. Just this weird thing with my mom. Guess I'll add it to the list of all the other mysteries about her, right after why the hell she loved your dad and why she trusted Tommy Dent."

I felt him watching me through the beat of silence that followed. "What do you mean she trusted Tommy?" he asked. "Trusted him about what?"

I rolled my eyes. "It's so stupid," I scoffed, "but apparently he told her that he and Persephone—"

My shoulder bumped against the paper towel dispenser, and I stumbled a little, startled at how close I'd been to it.

Ben's nearness in that small room made the space even tighter. Still, I couldn't risk taking the conversation into the hallway where Mom might hear us. Her chair was close to the door; she might recognize my voice down the hall—or worse, recognize one that reminded her of a man she once knew.

"Apparently," I tried again, "he told her that he and Persephone had been really good friends."

Ben looked at me as if I'd just insulted him. "That's insane," he said. "I told you the other day—he was stalking her. He'd, like, wait outside his house for me to drop her off at night. He left her all these notes that were just—" He shook his head, as if trying to shake away the memory. "They were *not* friends."

"I know that," I said. "But my mom believed him for some reason."

"That's insane," Ben repeated, rubbing the back of his neck. "But I don't get it, why would he tell her that—besides the fact that he's crazy."

I shrugged wearily. "He wanted Persephone's things."

Ben stared at me blankly. "I'm sorry, I'm not following."

"Me either," I said. "All I know is that after Persephone died, Tommy visited my mom a bunch and fed her a story about how the two of them had been such good friends. He said he wanted to have some mementos of her—and somehow that worked, because my mom ended up giving him basically all of Persephone's stuff."

Ben paused. "She what?"

"Well," I said, "technically she traded it."

His eyes clouded, as if a fog had rolled in front of them. "Traded it for what?"

I tried to picture Mom's body succumbing to the pills. Was it different from how she'd slump against the headboard after too many drinks? Did her nerve endings start to feel like beginnings, like she could float

away from her skin and hover near the ceiling, watching, with only mild curiosity, the sad hollow woman below?

"She—had him do stuff around the house," I said. "Cleaning, mowing, et cetera."

Ben took his time absorbing my answer. "Tommy did chores for your mother. And in return, she gave him her daughter's things? That can't be it. There's got to be more to it than that. Did you try asking her—"

"Look," I interrupted. "My mom hasn't been well for a really long time. After Persephone died, she fell apart. She wasn't thinking clearly. But yeah, she gave him all of Persephone's stuff. And I don't know why he wanted it or what he planned to do with it, or if he even still has it, but that's what happened."

Ben was quiet for a while, staring at something just to the right of my head. When he finally spoke again, his voice sounded deeper than before. "Well," he said, "we should find out."

I waited for him to clarify, but he just kept staring into space.

"Find out what?" I asked.

He looked at me, briefly, as if he'd almost forgotten I was there, and then he returned his gaze to the wall. "Find out why he wanted her stuff," he said. "Find out what he planned to do."

"Oh yeah? And how do you expect to do that? You can't exactly go back in time and spy on him."

His brows knitted together. "No, not spy. Talk. I think we need to talk to Tommy Dent."

A sound—not quite laughter, not quite breath—squeezed through my lips. "You mean, like, visit him? Go to his house?"

Ben nodded in a slow, unhurried way. "Yes."

"No way," I said. "I'm not going anywhere near Tommy Dent. Do you have any idea what kind of—how he—he raped a girl! He was in jail for eleven years."

"I know," Ben said coolly.

"He doesn't even live on my street anymore."

"I know. He lives in Hanover."

I narrowed my eyes again. "How do you know that?"

He looked right at me, and beneath the fluorescent bathroom lighting, his irises seemed as dark and solid as coal. "It may be news to you, Sylvie—that he killed Persephone. But I've believed it was him from day one."

The light above us flickered. I glanced at the sink, the door, the toilet, anywhere but his face. "Okay," I said, "but—"

"And it's weird, right? That he wanted Persephone's things? I mean, it's suspicious as hell. I could maybe see him wanting some kind of keepsake, given how obsessed he was with her, but all of it? No. I don't think so. There's something not right there."

"There's something not right with *Tommy*," I said, and Ben nodded.

"I know. Which is why we should go see him. Maybe after all these years he's got his guard down. He thinks he got away with it, that he's untouchable. We can ask him about it and see if he slips up. Maybe he'll tell us something we can take to the police."

I allowed myself to imagine it—sneaking off down a hallway while Ben distracted Tommy, finding his bedroom, rummaging through drawers until my fingers latched onto a box. It would be small, no bigger than a cell phone, no thicker than a couple of inches. I saw myself open it, saw the lid lift away, and inside, coiled on a piece of cloth, I saw a gold chain, a pendant shaped like a star.

"I don't know," I said quietly. "I don't—"

"I have the day off tomorrow," Ben cut in. "We could go then. Early afternoon, maybe? I could pick you up and we could drive there together."

"Pick me up?" I heard myself ask, my voice distant and soft.

His car on the street, still running. A plume of exhaust in the air. My sister going back to him, and back to him, opening the door and slinking inside.

"No," I said, snapping to attention.

"But we could—"

"There's no we! I'm not going with you to Tommy's!"

He'd been using that word—we—as if we were teammates or partners or even on the same side. I glared at him, trying to make my eyes as sharp as possible, and the flicker of determination on his face slowly dimmed to embers.

"Okay," he said after a moment, and he put up his hands in a gesture of surrender. "Sorry."

"I need to go."

I stepped forward and yanked open the door, Ben dodging to the side so it didn't hit his feet. I blinked as I entered the hallway, trying to orient myself.

"Sylvie, wait," Ben said.

When I turned around, he was stepping into the hall and pulling a pen from his pocket. "Here, let me just . . ." He looked around and tore off a strip of paper from a nearby bulletin board. Using his palm as a writing surface, he scribbled something down.

"Here. Take this."

He held the paper out to me, and I could see, as it dangled from his fingers, that he'd written a series of numbers on it.

"You're giving me your phone number?" I asked. "Seriously?"

"In case you change your mind," he said.

I thought about refusing to take it, just walking away and letting him stand there, stupidly watching me go, but something about that felt childish. It was just a piece of paper; I could put it in my pocket and throw it away when I got home.

"I'm not going to change my mind," I promised, and when I reached out to take it, my fingers grazed against his. I pulled back quickly, as if recoiling from an electric shock, and he smiled at me—kindly, one might think, a little sheepishly even. If he had been anyone else, I might have smiled back as a measure of habit.

As he headed off down the hall, I watched him get farther away.

Then I saw him round the corner and finally disappear. I had to get back to Mom—I knew that I did—but my feet wouldn't move. The feeling of his skin was still singeing mine. Ben's fingers—I knew what they could do, the colors they coaxed from blood. Stuffing his number into my pocket, I made myself remember. I made myself think of what they'd done.

19

Missy went into labor that afternoon, though I didn't hear about it until well after dinner when Jill sent me an alarming text. "Baby's coming. Complications. Prepping for emergency C." I imagined the panic in Missy's eyes, her hand reaching for Jill's as the nurses wheeled her toward an operating room.

"Oh my god," I wrote back. "I hope everything's okay. Let me know when you can."

Mom and I were in the living room again, me scrolling through my phone, her gently rocking in her chair. I didn't want to tell her about Missy. I didn't know what the word *complications* might trigger in her— if she'd think of the baby being motionless and blue as it was lifted from Missy's body, then think of Persephone's lips, motionless and blue under layers of snow. Still, she needed to know. Her sister and niece were enduring something terrifying together, and if there was anyone who knew about the ways a person's body could betray them, it was Mom.

"The baby's coming," I told her. "There were complications, though, so they have to do a C-section."

Her eyes didn't move from the TV; the rhythm of her rocking didn't stutter.

"Mom? Did you hear me?"

"Hmm?"

"The baby. Something's wrong. They have to do a C-section."

She still didn't look at me, but after a moment, she said, "What baby," her inflection as flat and nonchalant as if she were asking me to clarify a detail in the show we were watching.

I paused, studying her face. "Missy's baby," I said.

"Oh," Mom said. "Her."

She put her heels on the floor and the chair stopped moving.

"Yeah . . ." I said. "Do you want me to send Jill a message for you? You can just tell me what to say and I'll text it to her."

"No, that's okay," Mom said, and the rocking resumed.

"I don't mind," I insisted. "It doesn't have to be long. Just something to let her know that you're thinking about her and hoping everything goes well."

"No," Mom said again. "I don't think so."

I leaned forward, trying to get her to turn her head and look at me. "Why not?" I asked.

She shrugged. "I have nothing to say."

"What do you mean you—" I stopped, my chest tightening. "You can literally just say 'Hey—I'm thinking of you guys. Hope Missy and the baby are okay.'"

"Why don't you say that, then?" she asked. "From you."

"I already did say that from me."

"Then why do I need to say it, too?"

The question shoved me backward. I hadn't known my mother could still surprise me. I hadn't thought that, after all the ways that Jill had been there for her, Mom could deny her sister the smallest of gestures in return. Her apathy was a door slammed shut, her refusal a lock she clicked into place. My skin felt warm, flushing with familiar bitterness, and I swung my eyes toward the wall. I didn't want to look at her, didn't want to see the show that interested her more than the anxiety her family was experiencing.

That wall, though—it, too, made something churn inside me, the Persephone constellation still studding it like silver thumbtacks. That constellation had been my own creation, but when I looked at it now, all I could see was Persephone, how her hand reached out in a spurt of anger, how she growled when she wrecked it, more animal than sister. I'd painted the constellation myself, but after that moment, it had never been mine again. Whenever I saw it, it only reminded me of the darkness that swirled inside Persephone, how something as harmless as painted stars, and Mom's appreciation of them, could turn her smile into a snarl. For decades now, that constellation had belonged to my sister, and as I stared at it, imagining I could still see her fingerprints in the paint, it almost surprised me that Mom hadn't carved it right out of the wall, hadn't given it to Tommy Dent in exchange for a few hours of fog.

All at once, the TV seemed to blare from the speakers. I fumbled for the remote and then shoved my finger onto the mute button.

"Hey!" Mom protested. "I'm watching that!"

"Mom," I said sharply.

She looked at me, her eyes wide with the injustice of her show being silenced, and my nerves sizzled, ready to ignite.

"Do you have any idea how selfish it is," I started, "that you can't even offer your sister a single encouraging word right now?"

She sighed, reaching down to scratch her ankle. I looked away when it seemed that all she scratched was bone. "Come on," she said. "It's not as serious as you're making it out to be. Millions of women have had C-sections, Sylvie."

"Well, this is Missy's first. And Jill's probably out of her mind. You know how she worries. You know that she—"

"Oh, I know how she worries, all right."

My fingers curled into fists.

"Exactly," I said. "You know better than anyone, don't you? Because for half of her life, she's been worrying about *you*—an alcoholic who goes catatonic at the slightest mention of anything hard."

It felt good to finally say it—and terrible, too. Terrible that it was true, terrible that we'd once been so gentle with each other, curling up in bed together, singing and giggling as if both of us were children, and now—we were here, a place where all the edges were sharp.

"I don't want to fight with you, Sylvie," Mom said, but there was something about her voice—too even, too contained—that made me think she did.

"Jill has done everything for you," I pressed on. "She did your grocery shopping, your laundry, she made sure your house was taken care of, she took you to your doctor's appointments, your chemo. And that's only in the past few months. She also took care of me when you were too drunk to be my mother, helped me get into RISD, helped me—"

"Oh, right," Mom interrupted. "RISD. Are you sure it was art you studied and not theater? You're being incredibly dramatic."

"She stepped in the second you fell apart."

"I lost my daughter, Sylvie."

"And I lost my sister. You don't think that was hard? I needed you, and you weren't even there. You were ten feet away but there might as well have been an ocean between us."

The corners of my eyes burned, but I blinked the sensation away. "Jill took care of everything. She dealt with the police and the reporters and the TV stations. She cooked me dinner, talked to my school, planned the entire funeral. And oh! Speaking of funerals, what the hell were you doing at Richard Emory's?"

It caught us both off guard—how quickly my track had changed. Mom jumped a little in her chair, and even I felt a jolt as my muscles tensed. I hadn't meant to bring it up—not right then, at least—but now that it was out, the question remained, humming with expectation.

"How do you even know about that?" Mom asked, her eyes so narrowed it was as if she'd caught me in her bedroom snooping through her things.

"I ran into Ben again," I said. "He was at . . ."

But I didn't have to finish, didn't have to decide between the truth and the same old lie; Mom's eyes flashed with fury, and she plowed through my hesitation.

"Seriously, Sylvie? You haven't been able to find a man on your own, so you move onto your sister's boyfriend?"

The words stung like a slap across the face, the kind that keeps vibrating on the skin. My mouth dropped open, but there was nothing to pass through the space where my breath had tumbled out.

"You don't know what men like that can do to you," Mom continued. "They suck the blood right out of your heart until all you're left with is a heap of raw meat. No—not even meat. More like a raisin. A twitching, shriveled raisin where your heart's supposed to be."

I struggled for a response. "Ben and me—we're—it's not like that."

"Oh, of course it's like that," she stormed ahead. "Listen to you— 'Ben and me.' Well, let me tell you, little girl. The apple doesn't fall far from the Emory tree. It never does. Don't be such a fool as to think he might be different."

Our eyes locked like the antlers of two panting animals, and I felt like the weaker one. Mom was all bone and tendon and spine, but in that moment, I believed she could snap me in half if she wanted to. She was fueled by something—anger or resentment or pain—and it was so potent I could feel it radiating from her body. My only weapon, I was sure, was to keep on digging at the thing that had set her off.

"Then why did you go to Will's father's funeral?" I asked. "If the Emorys are so horrible, why would you ever step foot in a service for one of them? Why bother paying your respects to Will at all?"

I saw the second that she loosened, her hands unclenching from the armrests as she sagged back into her chair. Just like that, I noticed, I was the stronger one again.

"Because I love him, obviously," she said. "He'd had a loss, and I love him."

"Still?" The word shot out of my mouth. "You love him *now*, present tense? Even after he hurt you so badly? Even after what you just said about your—your twitching raisin?"

"Yes," she said quietly, dropping her gaze into her hands. "Even after that."

"Why?" I demanded. I heard the clock on the wall ticking, the refrigerator's buzz and hum. I saw her right hand squeeze her left, her knuckles going white.

Finally, she shrugged. "I don't know," she said. "It just won't stop."

Her voice was a leaf letting go of its branch, gentle as an exhalation, but I shook my head, unsatisfied. "I don't understand," I said. "It's been—how many years?"

I thought of the date scrawled on the back of the picture of Mom and Will.

"Like, thirty-seven?" I asked. "It's been thirty-seven years since you dated him?"

Mom shrugged again. "That sounds right," she said, turning her head away from me to stare at the muted TV. "But it doesn't matter how long it's been."

"How could it not matter? How could you not have moved on in all that time? Mom, this—this isn't good for you."

She watched the screen awhile before she spoke. "Haven't you ever been in love?"

I straightened my spine, glanced at the TV as if it were another person in the room that she might have been speaking to.

"I mean—I guess," I said. "I've had relationships. And they've ended. And I've always moved on."

"No," she said, her eyes still focused on the screen in front of her. "Not that kind of love. I'm talking about love that feels like—like your bones are filled with light."

I flicked my eyes toward the Persephone constellation, where all the edges of her body were formed by stars. After so many years, she still remained there, a painted skeleton simulating brightness.

"Um," I said, "I can't say that I have. But still—"

"Well, what about me, then?"

When I looked back at Mom, her eyes were already clamped onto mine. Lit by the lamp beside her, they seemed almost metallic—more silver than gray.

"What do you mean?" I asked.

"You still love me, right?"

The question made my heartbeat stutter. It was a moment before I could answer. "Why would you ask that?"

"Well," she began, "here you were just now, cataloguing all my faults. I'm an alcoholic. I shut down. I shut you out. Jill had to step in because I was 'too drunk to be your mother.'" She air-quoted the phrase, her tone slightly mocking.

"But," she added, "you still love me, don't you?"

I hesitated. My mind flashed between memories of her fingers on my face—her scent a floral, lingering thing I could still smell while I was at school—and memories of her fingers choking the neck of a bottle as she dragged herself into her room.

"That's not the same," I finally said.

"Of course it is," she insisted. "I hurt you, Sylvie. I know that I did."

I felt my throat hollow out. What Mom had just said—it wasn't an apology exactly, but it was the closest thing I'd ever gotten to one.

"It's the same with"—Mom paused and then swallowed—"me and Will. I can't stop loving him just because he hurt me, not when I loved him so deeply to begin with. And it's not only that, it's . . ."

Her eyes became distant, as if she could see right through me to the kitchen, to the houses down the street, to the gray and shimmering past.

"I still dream about him," she said, and even her voice was in another place. "Ever since it ended, I have these dreams. They're so real, I can—I can hear his voice. And not in a vague, dreamlike way. I can actually hear the . . . grit of him. I can remember his voice in my dreams better than I can when I'm awake. I can feel his fingertips on my skin. I can smell him, even. Like leather and mown grass. And every time, every dream, no matter what he's done—I always take him back."

Her eyelids fluttered, and her head shook back and forth so slightly I wasn't even sure she was controlling the movement.

"Then I wake up," she said. "And I lose him all over again. He's gone and I'm—still alone, but with a fresh new ache. The wound, it's—never fully closed, you know. Not with those dreams. Not with—"

She pressed her lips together, cutting off the sentence as cleanly as scissors cutting through thread. Then, as slowly as I'd ever seen, she stood up from her chair and wavered a little where she stood.

"I'm going to bed," she said. "You've made me so tired."

I watched her turn around, her feet soundless on the carpet.

"Mom, wait."

It reminded me of something—the way she'd described her dreams, the effect they had on her in the morning. I could easily imagine her waking to a world without Will, remembering what she'd lost, and then curling into herself under the sheets. She'd be unable to face the day after that, unable to open the shades or even leave her bed.

She looked back at me, but her gaze was limp, falling more against my collarbone than my face. "What?" she asked.

"What was the fifteenth?"

The clock continued ticking as she paused. "Huh?"

"The fifteenth of every month. What happened then?"

In an instant, her eyes sharpened; a tendon in her neck went tight. "How do you know about that?" she asked, and it was the second time in one conversation that she'd uttered that question, the same accusatory tone lacing her words.

"Persephone used to call it your Dark Day. Every fifteenth—or

nearly, anyway—it was like you were a different person. You'd just . . .
disappear."

She turned away from me again, and I watched the stiff, unyielding
board of her back.

"What was it, Mom? Tell me."

The silence became so dense for a minute that it swallowed all
other sounds—the clock, the refrigerator, the blood drumming against
my temples. I felt like I was impossibly close to something, and that if
she'd just answer me, she'd become less like the question mark that had
too frequently punctuated my past. She could tell me what it was—the
fifteenth, the Dark Day—and I could finally know her. We could know
each other, maybe, again.

"You really want to know what it is?" she asked quietly.

"Yes," I breathed.

"It's . . ."

I stopped my lungs, listening.

". . . none of your fucking business."

She left me then, moving away down the hall, and my shoulders
sunk so low they seemed to become edgeless. In a moment, I heard her
bedroom door close and then lock, a sound I knew as well as my own
voice.

"Idiot," I muttered to myself.

After a few minutes, I turned off the TV and the lights, checked
the dead bolts, and headed into my own room—that somber, sisterless
place. Glancing at Persephone's bed, I felt something in me throb. The
box for Tommy Dent was still there, right where I'd tossed it on Thursday. I averted my gaze and crossed the room to crawl into my bed. My
eyes traced the cracks in the ceiling, and at some point—maybe an
hour later, maybe just fifteen minutes—I heard my phone vibrate with
a text.

"Everything went great," Jill wrote. "Missy and Baby are just fine.
She doesn't have a name yet, but she's gorgeous."

Then a picture came in—a little blurry and off-center, but it showed a tiny pink body in a tiny white blanket tucked up against Missy's neck. I smiled at the image, putting my finger on the baby's cheek.

"She's perfect," I wrote back to Jill. "I can't wait to meet her."

"We'll come visit you and Annie as soon as we can," Jill replied—and I picked my head up, staring at the wall as the edges of an idea came together in my mind.

"Or I could come to Boston," I wrote. "It's probably easier that way. I could stay for a weekend, days when Mom doesn't have treatment."

I was instantly comforted by the possibility of it. I would cradle this new little human, and Jill would hum in the kitchen, stirring pots of food that, even three rooms away, smelled delicious. I'd help with the laundry and the cooking, I'd watch the baby so Missy could nap, and Mom would be fine back at home. She'd probably revel in my absence, breathe it in like a scent she wanted to savor. For days, there'd be no one to pester her with questions, no one who cared enough to try to understand who she was, and I'd be in Boston, a city even farther from home than Providence, and whenever a bedroom door was closed, the person behind it would never turn the lock.

"No," Jill wrote, and the fantasy crumbled as quickly as I'd built it. "I need you to be there with your mother."

The walls in my room crept closer. The house itself was shrinking, shriveling up like the raisin Mom believed was her heart.

"I'll call you soon," Jill wrote. "We're going to Skype with Carl and show him his beautiful daughter!"

I let my phone slip from my grasp. Then I lay with my arms at my sides as if strapped to my bed with restraints. A few moments later, another text came in, and instead of Jill again, it was Lauren.

"Hey," she'd written, "I looked up your sister's murder and I think we should talk."

I sucked in my breath, held it for a moment, and then slowly let it out. So now she knew—when Persephone died, how old I'd been, how much I'd kept from her about who I really was. I should have figured she'd do some research; Lauren wasn't the type to wait for information.

Nausea roiled in my stomach, my hands suddenly clammy. I knew what she'd ask me now: *Why didn't you tell me?* But the only way to defend my decision was with the indefensible, the details that all the articles hadn't reported. And how could I explain the window, the lock, the taps on the glass that I'd heard that night but hadn't answered? How could I expect her to know the truth and love me anyway?

I turned off my phone without responding. Rolling onto my side, I blinked a few times at Persephone's bed, and studied the flaps of Tommy's box, splayed open like begging hands. His name stared out at me in bold black letters, reminding me that I was not the only one who'd done my sister wrong. At the very least, he had watched her, left her notes, and then after she had died, he'd conned his way into taking her things. But what exactly had he wanted from her? And what had he done with her scarves, or the jeans she'd once drawn on, or her starfish necklace? My fingers twitched with the need to touch them all.

I stared at the space beneath Tommy's name, where the address of his house was neatly written. Each word was clear and unmistakable, as if I'd always been intended to see it and know exactly where he lived.

Sitting up in bed, I swung my feet over the side and felt my pulse begin to pound. My heart was not a raisin—it was furiously pumping inside me—and I knew now it wasn't Boston I needed to drive to; it was Tommy's.

20

The sign announcing my arrival to Pewter Hinge, the trailer park where Tommy lived, called the place "a luxurious mobile home community," and I wondered if I'd been wrong to picture Tommy's trailer as little more than a dirty boxcar. I'd imagined dishes competing for space in the sink, a sheetless mattress kicked into the corner of the room. I'd imagined all of his spaces, even the road itself, to be dark and neglected, but the piles of shoveled snow beneath the sign were reflecting the afternoon sunlight, and I had to pull down my visor to keep from being blinded.

Just before I'd left the house that afternoon, I'd received another text from Lauren. "Come on, Sylvie," she'd said. "Don't ignore me. Let's talk." But I didn't want to talk, I wanted to do, and now my phone sat in my cup holder with the ringer turned off as I navigated the rows of trailers, all with the same awning-covered doors and muted siding. As soon as I found Tommy's, confirming the address with the piece of paper I'd gripped to a moist crinkle, I squeezed the steering wheel with both hands.

A navy BMW sat in front of his house. It was a scratched older model, but it looked wildly out of place. Parking behind it, I grabbed the package that Mom had made for Tommy and got out of the car. As I walked toward the front door, I measured my breaths, and when I climbed up the steps, I kept my teeth clenched together, my toes curled tight in my boots. An icy wind swirled around me as I knocked.

For a few moments after Tommy opened the door, I could only blink at him—the bulk of his body, broader than I remembered; the sandy hair that was already thinning; the goatee that seemed coarse as a broom. He looked nothing like the scrawny boy who once lived on my street. He blinked at me, too, taking in my face, the box in my arms, the entire length of my body, and then he laughed, loud and explosive as a car with a broken muffler.

"Jesus," he said. "Special delivery?" He nodded toward the package.

"Um . . ." I looked at his eyes, a deep but murky brown. "You probably don't remember me, but I used to—"

"I know who you are," he said. "And I didn't kill your sister."

My mouth fell open, cold air rushing along my teeth. He was grinning at me, seeming to find pleasure in my surprise, the smile slinking farther up his cheeks as he continued to look me over.

"What?" I said. "I didn't even . . ."

He took a step back and opened the door as wide as it would go, allowing me a glimpse into his living room. I squinted into the shadows, and when I saw what Tommy was gesturing toward, I stiffened.

There, standing in front of a chair, as if it were the most natural place in the world for him to be, was Ben.

"What are you doing here?" I hissed at him.

He looked a little embarrassed, rubbing the back of his neck and staring at the floor, but there was something else in his expression, too—annoyance, maybe? Frustration? I didn't have time to untangle what I was seeing. He started toward me, and when he reached the door, he turned to Tommy.

"Mind if I step outside with her for a second?" he asked.

"Oh sure," Tommy replied. "But hurry back, okay? I can tell this is gonna be fun."

He was still grinning, and as Ben came out onto the steps and grabbed the knob to close the door behind us, Tommy moved to keep us in his view, craning his neck until the door was fully shut.

I marched down the steps, gripping the box to my chest, and Ben followed, the two of us stopping on the stretch of curb in front of the BMW—which, I realized now, belonged to him.

"What are you doing here?" I asked him again.

He crossed his arms over his sweater—his coat must have been inside; he must have made himself right at home in Tommy's trailer—and his breath resembled smoke as it slipped through his lips.

"What are *you* doing here?" he fired back. "You said you didn't want to go anywhere near him."

"I don't," I said. "But I realized that I have to, okay? I need some answers."

"Well so do I," he replied. "But if you changed your mind, then why didn't you call me?"

"Because we're not a team, Ben."

He shook his head, then glanced at my car, tucked into the space behind his. "I can't believe you came here alone. That's so dangerous."

"*You* came alone."

"Yeah, but—"

"But what?" I pressed. "I can take care of myself, you know."

"That's not the point," he said. "We have no idea what this guy is capable of. And you—you're Persephone's sister. Who knows what that might trigger in him. You could've gone in there and . . . and he might have . . ."

"He might have what?"

"I don't know. That's the problem. I just . . . I want you to be careful."

He let out his breath in a rush, as if it had been spooled up tight inside him. As the muscles in his face relaxed, the expression he'd had drained away. His eyes became softer around the edges, and I wondered, for only a moment, if his frustration just now had been out of a feeling of protectiveness for me, the little sister of the girl he claimed to love.

His brows knitted together. "What?" he said. "Why are you looking at me like that?"

"Huh?" I blinked and glanced over his shoulder at Tommy's door. It was still shut, but I could imagine Tommy with his ear pressed against it on the other side. "Nothing. I'm not—looking at you like anything. How long have you been here anyway?"

He shook his head. "Not long. You showed up maybe ten minutes after I did."

"Oh." I shifted my weight, repositioned my hands under the box. "Well, what have you guys talked about so far?"

Ben looked at his shoe while he flattened a clump of snow. "A whole lot of nothing. He's very amused by it all. My questions. My showing up in the first place. It's one big joke to him." His foot shot out and kicked at the hardened snow along the curb. Then he looked at what I was carrying. "What is that? You brought him something?"

I glanced at the box. "No," I said. "Well—kind of. It's leverage."

He nodded, as if that were all the explanation he required. "We're gonna need it," he said. "That guy's a piece of work. But, who knows, maybe you'll have better luck with him. You're her sister—that might . . ." He put his finger near his temple and swirled it in the air. "Scramble him all up."

"You just told me five seconds ago that that would be a bad thing," I reminded him. "You said I might trigger him."

"Right," Ben said, "but I'm going to be in there with you, so it's okay. I'm not going to let him hurt you."

I rolled my eyes. "Would you please spare me the chivalrous bullshit? I'm pretty sure I can handle Tommy Dent. You can just go home, all right? I came here to speak to him by myself, and that's what I'm going to do."

I said it with all the confidence I could muster, but the truth was—I didn't actually want to be alone with Tommy; he was so much bigger and gruffer than I remembered. When I started walking toward the front steps, as if to carry on by myself and leave Ben behind, there was a tiny part of me, somewhere so deep I wouldn't have even known where to find it, that was relieved when Ben wrapped his hand around my arm and steered me back toward the curb.

"Listen," he said. "This isn't about me trying to be some sort of gentleman. I know you're strong. Just look at what you've been through." He gestured to the space around us, as if all my life experiences had happened in that cold and biting air. "But Persephone was tough, too. And . . ."

His face tightened, as if he'd tasted something he wanted to spit out. "Let's just agree to work together," he said. "We can have each other's backs, okay?" He stuck out his hand. "Deal?"

His fingers—they were long and thin, twitching slightly in the air as he waited for me to place my palm against his. I remembered the print of them on Persephone's skin, the purple ovals he left on her each night. But I remembered them on my own skin, too, the way he'd held the paper towel to my neck in the hospital the day before—firm but gentle. He could have hurt me right then, could have pressed down harder until my skin ached with the promise of bruises, but he stopped when I'd protested. He'd watched the towel fall to the floor and then, instead of grabbing me the way I'd always imagined he'd grabbed Persephone, he just calmly bent over and picked the towel off the ground.

"Okay," I said, and I slid my hand into his.

We shook on it then, our eyes locked together, and in that moment, I couldn't tell what was more powerful—the reassurance that, no matter what Tommy did, I'd be safe, or the feeling that, with Ben's hand in mine, I was betraying Persephone all over again.

21

Tommy's trailer was tidier than I'd expected. It was almost disarming how neatly everything was displayed. He didn't appear to have much, but everything he did have—magazines, a few movies, a small bowl that cupped some change—seemed so meticulously placed that I feared what would happen if I accidentally disturbed something. Even the patch of laminate floorboards beneath his TV stand looked recently dusted, as if he'd known we were coming and had left no space untouched.

"Why do you think I killed Persephone?" Tommy asked.

He was rocking in a recliner that looked eerily similar to my mother's, while Ben and I sat in the two remaining chairs in the room. I stared at him, my eyes growing wide. Her name in his mouth sounded wrong, misshapen. He lingered too long on the s, like his tongue was savoring the taste of each syllable. The sound paralyzed my vocal cords.

"You used to stalk her," Ben jumped in, "and you just served a prison sentence for assault against a woman. It's two plus two, Dent."

Tommy crossed his arms and leaned back in his chair. "That girl was nothing," he said.

A muscle in my eyelid spasmed. His flippancy jostled loose the words that had been crouching inside me.

"What did you do with my sister's stuff?" I asked.

Tommy cocked his head. "What stuff?"

"Don't play dumb," I snapped. "My mother told me she gave you Persephone's things. I want to know what you did with them." Then, my voice wavering slightly, I added, "Do you still have them?"

He sucked in one of his cheeks and his eyes crept over my face.

"How *is* Annie?" he asked, practically purring my mother's name, and as I flinched, another grin spread onto his face as greasily as butter in a hot pan.

"Answer the question, Dent," Ben said.

Tommy looked at Ben, then back at me, and for a couple seconds, his head pivoted between the two of us. Then, with a sound that gurgled up from his stomach, he laughed.

"What's so funny?" Ben asked.

Tommy's body pitched forward, his arm clutching his stomach, and he wiped his hands over his eyes in a theatrical display of amusement. "Oh, nothing," he said. "It's just—" He paused to allow for an aftershock of chuckles. "You're fucking the little O'Leary now, too?"

Something flashed in Ben's eyes, as clearly as a blade glinting in the light. His hands balled into fists.

"Hey, man, I get it," Tommy continued. "She's a good stand-in for Persephone, isn't she? I mean, they don't look anything alike, but there's still something kind of similar there, don't you think? There's definitely an essence."

Even though he was speaking to Ben, Tommy's eyes latched onto my skin like a pair of leeches. I could feel him trying to drag the blood from my veins, keep me troubled and tense.

Ben was sitting at least four feet away from me, but I sensed how tightly he was wound. It was calming, somehow, to see his jaw clench. It reminded me that we needed to keep our cool.

"Look," I said, cutting Ben off just as he opened his mouth to speak. "Our . . ." I searched for the right word, but after several seconds, I was still unable to find one that fit. "It's none of your business. I came here today because I'm willing to make a trade. I hear you like those."

I picked up the package from my lap and shook it, the necklace and lotion bottle rattling around inside. "I have some of Persephone's things right here. If you just let me look through the stuff you have of hers, maybe we could make an exchange. You could have these new things, and I could have back some of the things that mean something to me."

Tommy's eyes swelled with interest.

"It's just . . ." I softened my voice. "My sister and I were really close, and I never got to keep anything of hers. There are certain things that would be nice to have. Things I really loved."

I could see him getting reeled in, his lips parting, just like a fish on a line. "Like what?" he asked.

"Like this necklace she had. It was gold and had a starfish pendant. It meant so much to her, and I'd do anything to have it as a way to remember my sister. Please. If you have it, just—at least let me see it."

I looked away from him as desperation crept into my voice. When I glanced at Ben, I saw that he was already looking at me, nodding his head a little, a wince of pain in his eyes. He seemed to be trying to tell me something—that he knew that necklace, too, maybe, and that the thought of it was comforting and annihilating all at once, just as it was for me.

Tommy shrugged. "Sorry," he said. "I never got a fish necklace."

"Not a fish," I corrected. "A starfish."

"Never got one of them either."

Disappointment sank into my bones, but I wasn't really surprised by his denial. He was playing with me, and I had to keep at it.

"Well," I said, "can I just look through the stuff you do have?"

Half a smile wormed up his face. "Sorry," he said again. "I don't have it anymore."

"Any of it?" The question barged out before I could balance my tone, and his eyes flickered with recognition of his power.

"Any of it," he confirmed.

"Well, where did it go?" Ben asked.

Tommy glanced at Ben, but then snapped his eyes back to me. My skin grew cold beneath his stare.

"I gave it all away," Tommy said.

"Where?" I asked, and I was surprised to hear Ben's voice overlap my own with the same question.

Tommy's smile grew wider, filling out both his cheeks. "I'm not at liberty to say," he taunted.

"That's bullshit," Ben said.

"Is it?"

Tommy reached toward the coffee table. He placed his fingers on a shiny issue of *Gun World* and moved it a fraction of an inch. Apparently satisfied, he leaned back in his chair and resumed his amused watch of my face.

"Well, did you pawn it or something?" I prompted. "None of it was valuable."

He chuckled. "Value's in the eye of the buyer," he said. "Don't you think so, Ben?"

Tommy turned his head sharply to look at Ben, whose eyes widened like a kid called on in class. "Uh," he said, stretching out the syllable as he returned Tommy's gaze, "I wouldn't know."

Tommy nodded. "Sure you wouldn't," he said.

I looked between the two of them, watched them glare at each other like ancient rivals, and my stomach churned. There was a glimmer of history in that stare, as if this wasn't the first time they'd shared it, and Ben's nostrils flared as he breathed.

"What is he talking about?" I asked him. "Do you know something about this?"

Ben didn't answer. He kept his eyes bolted to Tommy's.

"Ben," I tried again, a note of panic rising in my voice. "Do you know where Persephone's things are?"

He broke the stare, the spell, whatever was passing unsaid between them, and he met my eyes with a squint in his own. "No," he said, sounding offended by the question. "Of course not. He's crazy."

"Crazy man with all the answers," Tommy said, and we turned to look at him. "According to you two, at least. Why else would you both come banging on my door today?"

His eyes flicked toward the box. "What's in there anyway?"

"Don't worry about it," I said, drawing the package closer. "What did you want with her stuff in the first place? Or was it always your plan to sell it?"

Tommy rolled his eyes—bored, it seemed, to be back on that topic. "Your sister and me were the same." He leaned forward, raked his eyes across my face. "I deserved to have some reminders of her. And your mother agreed."

My pulse thrummed against my wrist, but I focused on keeping my muscles as stiff and unyielding as possible. I was unwilling to give him the reaction he wanted—not even a twitch, not even a shaky inhalation.

Finally, he added, "I didn't sell it until the money ran out."

"What money?" Ben asked. "Your family didn't have any money."

"No, you're right," Tommy said. "My family wasn't rich. Not like yours, Benji. Not like Daddy Emory in the big fancy house on the hill. Must be nice, huh?" He slid his hands over the armrests of his chair, petting them as if they were animals. "But I had ways of getting what I needed."

I thought of the drugs he'd given to Mom, how her cupped hands were probably not the only ones he'd dropped some pills into. What other exchanges had he made? How much had he profited off of other people's suffering?

"Okay," I said, letting him hear my impatience as I tapped the box with my finger. "So your money ran out, and then what happened?"

He continued stroking the chair, tilting his head while he looked at me. "Like I said, I sold it all. To someone who needed it more than I did."

Ben and I glanced at each other.

"To *someone*?" I asked. "Who? Who else could have possibly wanted her stuff?"

"Not wanted," Tommy said. "Needed." Then he slammed his eyes toward Ben. "You wouldn't know about need—would you, Emory? Sylvie, though." His gaze slinked back to my face. "She knows. She and Persephone both knew. Persephone needed more than you could ever give her, Benji. She didn't need a joyride every other night behind her mother's back. She needed companionship."

"And that was you, huh?" Ben said. "A real companion?"

Tommy shrugged. "I let her know what she needed to know. I let her know that somebody saw her."

"You let her know you stalked her," Ben said. "She showed me all those notes, you know. She thought you were pathetic."

Tommy continued, unfazed by Ben's words. "I see you, too, Sylvie," he said. "And—I have to tell you—you're not going to make it."

My lips parted, the breath between them unraveling. "What?"

Tommy nodded. "If you keep going like this," he said, "you're not going to make it. There's so much pain inside you, I can see it clear as day. Your inner feng shui—it's all fucked up."

He chuckled then. "I mean, Jesus," he went on. "Just look at your eyes. It's like you're already half dead."

Ben moved forward in his chair. "Are you threatening her, Dent?"

"Hey, man," Tommy said, holding up his hands. "It's not me she has to worry about. I'm not the one whose girlfriend ended up dead."

Ben stood up, the movement so sudden that it made me jump, distracting me from the chill threading through my veins.

"I think we should go, Sylvie," he said.

"Go?" My voice sounded hollow as I looked up at him. "But we haven't even . . . he hasn't even told us anything yet."

"Yeah, Ben," Tommy chimed in, "I haven't even told you anything yet."

Ben's fingers contracted into a fist, but he kept his eyes on me. "Come on," he urged. "I was wrong, okay? We're not going to get any answers from him. He's spewing nonsense. He just wants to mess with us."

He tried to pull me up, but when his hand circled my arm, I jerked away from him. "No," I said. "I'm not—I can't go yet. He has to tell—" I leaned forward, searching Tommy's face for some weakness, some fragility, something that would let me speak to him on a level we could both understand. "You have to tell me what you know."

The corners of Tommy's lips curled up. "What about your mother?" he asked. "Did she tell you what *she* knows?"

I straightened up, my spine like an elastic snapping into place. "What are you talking about?"

Talk to the mother—that's what Tommy had told the detectives— and now, here he was, making the same ridiculous insinuation that Mom knew something about what happened to Persephone.

"It's really not my place to say," Tommy answered, his grin nothing but teeth, a film of saliva glazing his lower lip.

"Then why bring it up at all?" Ben challenged. "See, Sylvie? It's nonsense."

Tommy looked up at Ben, who towered above him. "Let's just say," he started, "that Annie lied to the police. I was the one who told them to talk to her. I was the one who knew they should. But she didn't exactly tell them the truth."

"How would you even know that?" I asked. "How would you know what she did or did not tell them, and how would you know if what she told them was the truth?"

Tommy shrugged. "I have my ways," he said. "A person on the inside."

"*You* have a person on the inside," I scoffed. "On the inside of what—the police?"

He didn't answer, but a low, reverberating chuckle emanated from his throat.

"You're lying," I said. "You don't know a thing about my mother."

"Oh, I don't? I guess I just imagined it, then—all those long, intimate chats we had."

He chewed on the word *intimate* as if it were a delicious bite of food.

"I guess I don't know anything about what kind of pills she prefers, huh?" he continued. "Or how long it takes for her to just—"

"Stop!" Anger ballooned inside me, squeezing out the fear and hesitation. I leaned forward as far as I could, the package on my lap thudding to the floor as I stared him in the eyes.

"Don't say another word about my mother," I said. "I know what you're doing. I know you're just trying to distract me from figuring out what *you* did and what *you* know."

"Is that so?" Tommy said.

"Yep."

"Well—please, Sylvie—tell me what else I'm doing. This is so informative."

He leaned forward, too, his face coming so close to mine that I could see the web of veins pulsing through his eyelids.

"Dent . . ." Ben warned, taking a step closer to Tommy.

"For one thing," I said, "you're lying about Persephone's stuff. You didn't sell it to anyone, that's ridiculous—no one in their right mind would want it. So it's here, isn't it? I know it is. And I'm going to give you one more chance to come clean about everything."

Tommy smiled as he inched even closer to me, the excitement on his face dripping with vulgarity. "Or what?" he asked.

I saw pockmarks on his cheeks—ghosts of old acne and the scrawny teenage boy he'd once been. I saw strands of gray in the wiry hair of his goatee.

"Or this."

I stood up, marched through the kitchen, and entered the hallway beyond it. It was dim back there, and it took a second for my eyes to adjust enough to make out the bathroom to my left, the shaded bedroom to my right.

"Sylvie," Ben said, and I could feel him following just behind me.

"Not now," I snapped. I walked into Tommy's room, flicking on the light switch by the door, which illuminated a space as tidy and spare as his living room had been. There was a twin bed, its comforter pulled taut toward the headboard, a dresser with a watch and a comb on it, and a couple of plastic bins stacked in the corner.

"What is she doing?" Tommy asked as I rushed toward the bins. His laughter bubbled up in pitch.

"Sylvie, come on." I felt Ben's hand on my arm, but I pulled away and tore off the lid on the highest bin in the stack.

"It's in here," I mumbled, rifling through shirts and blankets, tossing each item on the floor as soon as I confirmed that it hadn't belonged to Persephone. When I reached the bottom of the bin, I picked it up and threw it over Tommy's bed.

"She's insane!" he said, his voice dancing with delight as I looked inside the bottom bin. A stack of blank paper, a couple magazines, journals packed with indecipherable handwriting—but nothing I recognized. I held up the bin and shook out the rest of its contents, Tommy's laughter in the background only spurring me on.

"Sylvie," Ben said again, his voice a little firmer this time.

"No," I said. "Not until . . ."

There was a closet door on the opposite side of the room. I waded through bins and papers to rip it open. The shallow space was barely big enough for a person to stand in comfortably, and lined up inside was a vacuum cleaner, a broom, and a mop. The only thing hanging from the pole at the top was a gray button-down. As I slammed the door, I grunted.

Ben was making his way around the bed, Tommy covering his cackling mouth as he watched me, and I dropped to the floor, lying with my stomach flat against the carpet. Reaching underneath the bed, my hand flailed around in empty space until it bumped against something hard and rigid, wrapped in cloth.

Ben knelt down beside me, rested his hand on my back. "Come on," he said. "Let's go."

"No!" I said. "There's something . . ."

My fingers hooked around it and yanked it out from under the bed. I used my other hand to push myself up off the floor and didn't look at what I was holding until I was kneeling in front of Ben. We stared at it, Tommy's laughter cutting off like a needle jerked from a record, and after taking in the shiny pink satin, the waves of blonde hair, the unblinking gray eyes framed by lifelike lashes, Ben and I looked at each other.

"Is that hers?" he asked.

"No," I breathed, remembering what Falley told me she once saw in Tommy's bedroom. "It's his."

"Don't you fucking touch her," Tommy shouted, lunging forward and pouncing on the bed to snatch the doll from my hand. The mattress groaned as he landed on it, and after pulling the doll away from me, he clutched it to his chest. He stroked its hair, smoothed a wrinkle from its dress, and when he spoke again, his voice was strained.

"Get out," he said.

"Sylvie, let's go." Ben took my hand and pulled me up as he stood. He started leading me toward the bedroom door, but I resisted, watching what looked like tears gather in Tommy's eyes.

"No, wait," I said, and I took a step back toward the bed. "Tommy, I'm sorry I upset you. I'm sorry I . . . touched your doll. Please, just—tell me what you did with Persephone's things. Tell me what you know, and then we'll leave, I swear."

Tommy narrowed his eyes, squeezing out a single tear that slithered down his skin. "My doll?" he said, his voice pinched. "Are you fucking serious right now? You think she's just a doll? Just a fucking *doll?*"

He jumped off the bed, the doll slipping from his grasp and landing facedown on the comforter. When he started to charge at me, I drew in a quick gulp of air, but then he fell, tripping over one of the many things I'd thrown around the room.

Ben grabbed me by the arm—much more tightly now—and pulled me out into the hallway, back through the kitchen, and toward the living room.

"No," I protested. "No, stop, Ben. I didn't even get to check the dresser, I have to—stop!"

He dragged me toward the trailer door, and when he opened it and pulled me through it, the cold air lashed my face, his fingers digging so deep into my arm I could already picture the bruises they'd leave. Then he slammed the door behind us, finally letting go of me at the top of the stairs, but the momentum sent me sputtering down the steps, and my feet landed hard on the slush that coated the sidewalk.

"What the hell?" I demanded. "Why did you do that?"

He walked down the steps, shaking his head. "He's insane, Sylvie," he said. "He was coming after you."

"That?" I asked, gesturing toward the trailer. "He tripped! He's a clumsy idiot. He couldn't have hurt me. And I still had the dresser drawers to check. I could have found something!"

My chest heaved through my words; my throat tightened with missed opportunity. I felt tears burrowing in the corners of my eyes.

"You weren't going to find anything," Ben yelled. "There's nothing to find in there."

I opened my mouth to respond, then quickly closed it. There was so much certainty in the way he spoke, as if it wasn't even possible that a single item of Persephone's could still be with Tommy. But

I hadn't even checked the dresser or kitchen cabinets before Ben had hauled me from the trailer, his hands and arms constricting as a straightjacket.

"How do you know there's nothing?" My heart was beating hot and wild. "What was going on between you two in there? He seemed to think you knew a lot more than you've said."

"What? I have no idea what he meant by any of that. He's just crazy. He's completely unhinged. Didn't you hear what he said about that doll? It's like he thinks it's a person or something. And did you get a good look at the thing? It looked like . . ."

He trailed off, but it didn't matter. I knew what he was going to say. It looked like Persephone.

"He seemed to know something about you," I persisted, pushing the doll out of my mind. It didn't matter right then; Ben was only deflecting. "And what was with the way you two were glaring at each other? Have you spoken to him before—before today, I mean?"

Ben shivered against the cold.

"Damn it," he said, ignoring me as he looked back toward the door. "I left my coat in there. Oh, whatever, it doesn't matter. We have to get out of here, Sylvie."

"I'm not going anywhere until you answer me!" I didn't care how loudly I yelled it. *Let there be witnesses*, I thought. *Let there finally be people who see and know the truth.* "Are you in cahoots with Tommy?"

"Cahoots?" Ben repeated. "No! Before today, I hadn't even seen the guy since I was, like, nineteen."

"But you've spoken with him," I said. "Haven't you?"

The tears welling in my eyes were hot as my heart. I wiped them away as soon as they spilled onto my cheeks. I couldn't let Ben think I was breaking, or that these were tears of fragility. They were angry tears, furious tears; they were how-could-I-be-so-stupid tears.

"No," Ben said, looking at me now with a careful blend of curiosity and concern. "I haven't spoken to him, either."

"Then what was he talking about?" I spit out the question, my voice thick and warped.

"I honestly don't know," Ben said. "He was messing with me. He was messing with both of us. He's just crazy, Sylvie. That's all."

"Maybe," I said, brushing my cheek with the back of my hand. "Or maybe I'm the crazy one for thinking for one second that anyone but you killed my sister."

"What?" Ben fired. "Sylvie—"

Something inside me spurred me forward, and I pushed him, watching with satisfaction as he stumbled backward.

"Hey," he protested, but I pushed him again—only, this time, I slipped on the slushy ground, and I nearly fell. He grabbed me by the elbows then, as if trying to stabilize me, and I punched at him instead, my fists landing on his chest with feeble, impotent thumps.

"You did it!" I cried. "Just admit it! Just tell me the truth!"

I could hear myself sobbing, could feel my arms growing weaker and weaker the harder I swung them.

"You know I didn't kill her, Sylvie," Ben said, his voice quiet and gentle, like someone trying to lure an animal into a trap. "I loved her. God, I—I loved her so much."

"If that's true, then why did you hurt her?" My fists bumped against his chest while he held me. "Why did you abuse her all the time?"

Ben let go of my arms and took a step back. I wobbled, trying to regain my balance, and when I looked at him, my breath coming out in uneven gasps, I saw that he seemed stunned.

"Abuse her?" he asked.

"The bruises!" I pointed to my wrist, my neck, my ribs. "She had them everywhere. All the time."

"No," Ben said, slowly shaking his head.

"Yes! She showed me every single one. She made me—she asked me to paint over them, so nobody would know. You must have seen that. You must have known that I knew."

"No," Ben said again. "You don't understand. She . . ."

"She what? Deserved it? Provoked you? Don't even think of saying that."

"No. No, of course not. She . . ."

"She *what*, Ben? *What?*"

"She asked me to bruise her!"

I took a step back, the tears on my face seeming to freeze.

"What?" I said. "No—no, she didn't. That's insane. Stop lying to me!"

Ben's head drooped, his eyes staring at the ground. "It's true," he said, and he sounded so defeated, like he'd lost something just now and knew that he'd never get it back. "It—the bruises—the whole thing— it's not what you've been thinking."

My eyes widened. The familiarity of that phrase, the gnawing ache of those words—night after night, *It's not what you're thinking, Sylvie*— made my throat sting and swell.

"She asked me to bruise her," he said again. Then, his eyes lifting tentatively toward my face, he straightened his posture, shuffled his feet.

"I have proof," he added. He took a step toward me, his black-hole eyes, with all their gravitational pull and imprisoned light, looking deeply, imploringly, into mine.

"Proof?" I heard myself ask.

"Yes," he said, inching toward me again. "But you're going to have to trust me, okay? It's at my house. Will you come with me please, so I can show you?"

22

The thought of being alone with Ben in his house on the hill—where he knew all escape routes, where there'd be no one around to hear me if I screamed—made the hair on my arms stand on end. Even through my coat, I could feel the goose bumps swelling on my skin.

"No," I told him. "How could you ever even prove that?"

I shivered, the cold air wrapping around me as I stood on the curb, and I shifted my eyes toward Tommy's trailer. I had a feeling he was watching us, his gaze like an icy hand against my cheek, but when I glanced over Ben's shoulder at the windows, the curtains remained undisturbed.

"It's in a letter," Ben said. "But you'll have to read it yourself, or you won't believe me."

"A letter from who?"

He paused. "From Persephone."

My breath snagged on the back of my throat. A letter from Persephone?

After she died, I tried so hard to resurrect her voice, scouring my room for notes she'd once written me. All I managed to find, though, were my two most recent birthday cards from her—one still on my desk, where it had been propped since October, and one I'd tossed into a drawer. The font of the words inside each card was so distinctly hers, and I stared at the series of too-short paragraphs, memorizing the curves of each letter. A couple days later, when the detectives returned and asked for samples of Persephone's handwriting, I was reluctant to hand the cards over, even though Falley and Parker had assured me they'd return them.

As Ben and I stood in front of Tommy's trailer, I remembered that moment—"We just need our guy to examine them," they told me, the only explanation they offered—and I found myself staring at Ben's face, my lips slightly parted. When I'd spoken to Falley and Parker over the last week, they'd both said that evidence had emerged that led them to not press assault charges against Ben. Was it possible that this "proof" Ben wanted to show me was the evidence that neither of them had been willing to discuss with me? And if that evidence was a letter from Persephone, wouldn't they have needed something, all those years ago, to verify its authenticity?

"Did they—" I tried. "Did the police ever do, like, a handwriting analysis of this letter you're talking about?"

Ben cocked his head to the side. "You knew about that?"

"No, I . . ." Despite the cold, my palms felt sweaty. "The detectives—they asked me for samples of Persephone's handwriting once. But they never said why."

"Oh," Ben said. "Yeah, this was why. I showed them the letter—to explain about the bruises—and they had to make sure I didn't forge it."

My eyes widened, my breath shaky between my lips. "Okay," I said. "I'll do it. I'll go back to your house and read Persephone's letter."

The Emorys' driveway was steep, flanked on either side by evergreens that stood in lines like soldiers on guard. It could have been the shade those trees provided, or the fact that the afternoon was quickly slipping toward evening, but I could have sworn that everything grew darker the higher I drove up the hill.

I followed Ben's car past the main house, that brick monstrosity I'd never seen up close before, and I tasted something bitter on the back of my tongue. Will Emory, the man who had so thoroughly unraveled my mother, could have easily been inside there somewhere, drinking a cup of coffee or scrolling through his tablet, completely indifferent to the pain he'd caused—not only to Mom, but to all the other women whose hearts he'd unstitched throughout the years.

A couple hundred feet past the mansion, Ben veered off into a circular driveway and pulled up in front of a small cottage that looked remarkably different from the main house. The guesthouse, as he'd called it, had immaculate white siding and pale blue shutters. For a moment, the setting sun winked through the trees and glazed the house with a glow resembling candlelight.

I parked behind Ben, leaving a few feet of space between our cars in case I needed to leave quickly. When I stepped outside, my muscles stiffened against the cold. My breath flared out before me, frosting the air, and I saw that Ben was already at the front door of the cottage.

"Thank you for coming," he said, as if I were a guest at a party he was throwing. He opened the door and crossed the threshold. "I know this was a lot to ask."

He gestured for me to come inside, and if it weren't for the heat I could feel from within the house, I might have paused a bit longer before following him in. As he closed the door behind me, my eyes swept across the house. There was a bedroom to our left through a set of French doors, a dining room to our right, and in front of us a hallway that led to a shiny white kitchen. Off of the kitchen there were two closed doors—a bathroom, I supposed, and maybe a closet as well—but from where I stood, I couldn't see an exit other than the door I'd just come through.

"It's not much," Ben said, seeming to notice that I was studying the layout. "And actually, most of it's a dumping ground for stuff my dad doesn't want in the main house anymore. But I don't know." He shrugged. "I like it."

I turned to him, my gaze as sharp as I could manage. "So where's the letter?"

"Right," he said. "In here."

He opened one of the paneled glass doors to our left and stepped into his bedroom, flicking on the light switch as he moved toward a dresser in the corner. I followed him in but stayed near the doorway, my eyes creeping over his navy comforter, the silver laptop on his nightstand, the retainer box propped against an alarm clock. In front of the window overlooking the driveway, there was a cluttered desk holding up stacks of textbooks, and the back of its chair was draped with clothes.

"Sorry about the mess," Ben said as he bent down to open the bottom dresser drawer. "This is actually supposed to be the living room, you know. But I like the French doors." He chuckled. "My dad says I'm compromising the integrity of the guesthouse—his exact words, by the way—because I don't have a real living room and I'm just using the back bedroom for storage."

He pulled a shoebox out of the drawer, and as he straightened back up, he held it as if its contents were fragile. "I don't know why I felt the need to tell you that," he said, looking at me. "I think I'm just nervous."

"Why?" I asked, crossing my arms as I watched him sit down on the edge of the bed. He removed the lid from the box, and I could see that there were folded pieces of paper inside.

"Because . . ." he started, his voice sounding farther away than just the few feet of space between us. "It's been a long time since I've looked at any of her letters. We, um, we couldn't call each other back then, because your mom didn't—well, you know."

He dug through the contents of the box until he found what he was looking for, a crisply folded sheet of paper that seemed a brighter white than the rest.

"We wrote each other these letters so we could have them when we were apart," he continued. "And this one in particular . . ." He held it up to show me, waving it in the air before unfolding it. "This is the one I gave to the police. It's not even the original—they still have that, I think—but they let me keep a copy after they confirmed it was real."

The paper was splayed open in his hands now. I could see Persephone's handwriting, and it took everything I had to blink away the sudden stinging in my eyes. Ben stared at the letter, his eyes flicking back and forth across the page.

"What are you doing?" I asked.

"Sorry, I'm just reading it." He turned the paper over, and after a few more seconds, he straightened his back and looked at me. "Maybe this was a bad idea."

"Why?" I snapped, taking a step forward. "Doesn't paint you as innocently as you remembered?" I reached for the letter, but he leaned back and held it flat against his chest.

"No," he said. "That's not it."

Again, I tried to grab it, but he stopped me, curling his fingers around my wrist—not tightly, not aggressively, but the insistence in his touch froze me just the same.

"Sylvie, stop. Just wait."

I jerked my hand out of his grasp and crossed my arms again. He turned the paper over. I waited for what felt like a minute, but just as I leaned forward, ready to try once more to pluck it from his hands, Ben straightened his arm and held out the letter.

"Here," he said. "Just—remember how young she was when she wrote this, okay? She was only a teenager, and I'm sure you remember how teenagers can be."

"What are you talking about?" I asked, snatching the letter.

The second I saw her words and her writing up close, I was transfixed, a white noise humming in my ears.

Ben, Persephone wrote, and I could hear his name almost as clearly as nights when she whispered it into the darkness of our room.

Ben,

I'm writing this in fifth period because Mrs. Keller is clueless and I'm never gonna get stoichiometry. I wish I were with you right now. I know I'm seeing you tonight, but that feels like years away.

I've been thinking about what you said the other night, and I want you to know that I love you for worrying about me, but you don't have to. I love our routine. I wouldn't ask you to keep going or to hold me harder if I didn't. I love that I can still see your fingers on my skin when I get home, and I love how much it helps me. Because it does. It really does. Sometimes I feel like I'm going to explode with all the anger and pain that's thrashing around inside me, but then I have your hands.

Some girls cut, you know. I've seen the scars on their thighs when we change for gym, and I've been to enough health classes to get the reasons why they do it. I know it's kind of the same as what we do, but at least the bruises are temporary. Those ugly scars will be on those girls for life.

Anyway, it's like this: in the moment, I can concentrate on the physical pain of you holding me, and somehow, that allows me to forget the real pain, the deeper one. Then, later, I have your fingerprints on my skin. Even after I cover them up, I know that they're there as a reminder of your love. They let me know that I'm actually not unloved, even though I am unloved by the person who's supposed to love me most.

She was at it again this morning. We were eating breakfast and I tried to tell her about the B+ on my English paper (thanks again for helping!), but she just ran her hands through my sister's hair and said,

"That's nothing. Sylvie got a perfect score on her science test." She was looking at my sister like she couldn't believe her luck that she was the mother of the most perfect human being on earth and I swear I had to stop eating, it was that disgusting.

I know I should just accept that this is how she is, but it really hurt me that she said that. You saw how much work I put into that paper. I actually read the book this time! But she told me "that's nothing." I mean, who says that to their daughter?? And my stupid sister just sat there smiling at my mom like that's a totally normal thing to say. I get that she's just a kid, but it makes me so mad how she just goes along with every cruel thing my mother says to me and she always defends her. It's such a betrayal. I bet if I brought it up to her tonight, Sylvie would say, "She didn't mean it like that." But how else could she have meant it??

Anyway, I'm rambling. My point is this: all that stuff with my shitty mother and my little sister, it all just . . . dissipates (damn straight that's an SAT word!) whenever your arms are around me and you're pressing my skin to the bone. Plus, it helps you too with everything you're going through, that's what you've said. And I want to help you. I want to be there for you the same way you're there for me.

I have to go now. The bell's gonna ring soon. I can't wait to see you tonight. (But I guess by the time you read this, I'll have already seen you! Lucky me!)

Loving you endlessly,
Persephone

I stared at the curves of her name, the way the end of the *e* looped back up and around to cross over the *h*. It was my sister's signature, distinct as a fingerprint, and it was scrawled on a letter that had called me her betrayer.

But what, exactly, was the betrayal? My love for my mother? My determination, as a young girl, to see only the best in her? If that was it, then what had she thought of the locked window? What was the word for something stronger than betrayal?

And had she been that bad, our mother? I didn't remember the moment she mentioned in the letter, but I trusted it was true. The flippancy in saying "That's nothing" to a daughter offering her something—a chance to connect over an accomplishment that should be celebrated together—felt like the mother I knew now. Was it possible, then, that she'd always been so harsh and dismissive, and I simply hadn't seen it?

Sometimes, Persephone would say to me, *it's like you and I have two different mothers.* But we didn't. We had one mother, one woman who had birthed us both. Maybe it was just the two of us who'd been different— one who saw her clearly, and one who saw her impossibly, as a garden constantly in bloom.

She didn't mean it like that. Those were the words that Persephone had imagined I'd say, and they rang true to me, too. I was always thinking of Persephone as having a darkness inside her that kept her from absorbing Mom's light. How ferociously she'd swiped her hand across the constellation I'd made of her, how thunderously her words could roar across our house as she and Mom shouted at each other. But what if it had always been Mom's darkness, to begin with, that had slid like a cloud over Persephone, denying her a view of the sun and other stars, blacking out what she should have always been surest of—that she was worthy, that she was loved?

And when I said those things—*She didn't mean it like that* and a thousand other excuses—did she see that as me taking sides? When she tried to open the window that final night and found it wouldn't budge, did it confirm for her a suspicion that I, too, didn't love her? When she marched back to Ben's car, was she not just furious with me, as I'd always thought, but also deeply wounded?

It all just dissipated, she'd written—all that pain and rejection, from Mom, from me—when Ben's arms were around her, when he pressed her skin to bone. I shook my head, standing in the room of the man who'd held her and hurt her, and I tried to will away the dizziness that was whirling right through me.

"Are you okay?" I heard Ben ask.

When I blinked my eyes away from the letter, I saw that he was still sitting on the edge of his bed, his face as blank as a clean sheet of paper.

"I don't understand," I said.

Ben closed his eyes and nodded. "I know," he said. "That's why I was having second thoughts about showing it to you. It wasn't your fault, though. You know that, right?"

I had a breath of hesitation, and then I squinted until my eyes were slits that I could barely see him through. "What wasn't my fault?"

"The whole situation," he said. "The bruises and all that."

"Obviously it wasn't my fault," I snapped. "It was *your* fault."

Ben cocked his head to the side, his brow furrowing. "I know, but I just mean—did you read the whole thing?" he asked. "The part where she—"

"Are you being serious?" I cut him off. "Let me get this straight. She had the impulse to self-harm, but instead of actually doing it herself, she wanted *you* to do it—and you *did*—and that's supposed to prove that you're innocent? That's supposed to make it all okay? What happened exactly? Did she say, 'I'm thinking of cutting,' and then you said, 'Wait, let me just give you all these bruises instead'?"

"No," Ben protested. "No, it wasn't like that. It was an accident, at first."

"An accident," I repeated. "You just accidentally held on to her so hard that she bruised?"

"Well . . ." He flipped over his palms so they faced the ceiling and he stared into them. "Kind of," he said. Then, rushing into the next sentence, he looked at me and added, "But it was complicated."

"I'm sure," I said, crossing my arms.

"No, really, it was. I don't know where to start to try to explain it."

"The beginning usually works."

"Yeah, but the beginning," he said. "I don't even know where that is." He shook his head. "Listen. Long story short, I was really messed up at the time. I was—"

"Drunk?" I demanded. "On drugs?"

"No," he said. "Not that kind of messed up. I was emotionally messed up, I guess. Things had been happening, and I was crying one night. And not just crying, but, like, all-out uncontrollably sobbing. And Persephone was trying to comfort me. She pulled me into her arms and I held on to her, and I was gripping her so hard, just bawling into her neck, and . . . I didn't even know about the bruises until I saw them on her the next day. I apologized a million times, I felt so terrible, but she said no, she liked it. She said she wanted to do it again. She said we could help each other."

He looked at me, his eyes locking me into their magnetic darkness. "I was in so much pain," he said, "that I actually agreed to it. And then it just became this ritual. Every time we saw each other, we'd—I don't know—share our pain, I guess."

My throat contracted, my breath quickening. The shame in his eyes was so palpable I had to turn my gaze away. I even wondered how my own eyes looked, the word *betrayal* staring unblinkingly up at me from the letter still clutched in my hand.

"I just," he continued. "I loved the way it felt, you know? Holding on to something so tightly that you know it can't leave you. I don't know if you've ever felt that kind of desperation to keep something you love before, to make sure it will always stay with you, but it's a powerful feeling, and it made it easier for me to convince myself that we really *were* just helping each other."

He cleared his throat, and when I glanced back at him, he was look-ing just past me, his eyes focused on the gathering darkness outside the window.

"I know now," he said, "that it was fucked up. I've known that for a long time. What we did back then, it was unhealthy. It was wrong. Even if we both thought we wanted it, thought it was healing us, it was actually damaging. But I didn't get that then. I couldn't see beyond my grief. I was just so grateful."

His fingers trembled, the tips of them flickering like flames.

"I mean, here was a girl I loved," he continued, "who was willing to bear my pain." He scratched his cheek with his shaking fingers. "She shouldn't have had to, though, no matter what she said. I know that. I know that."

Then he met my eyes again with a look so pained and penetrating it felt like a hand reaching between my ribs and grabbing onto my heart. "I know that, Sylvie. I know it now and I've known it for a while, but by the time I did it was too late. I—God, I fucking . . ."

He stood up and walked toward the French doors, placing his hand on one of them before glancing back at me. "I'm sorry," he said. "I need to—" His gaze darted around the room. "I'll be right back."

He disappeared down the hallway, and in a few moments, I heard a door open and close. Then there was only silence.

I looked at the letter, the words blurred together, and I let the con-fusion wash over me, disorienting as waves that crash and pull against a body at sea. Listening to Ben, watching the weight of memory drag him down, my anger toward him had quickly melted into—something else, though I had no idea what to call it. Pity? That didn't seem right. Understanding? No, that wasn't it either; there was still so much I didn't understand. But that look in his eyes when he'd spoken of his pain, his regret—I knew it, I recognized it, I'd seen it countless times in mirrors, in pictures, in self-portraits I was assigned in college.

"Your eyes seem so sad here," my professor once said, evaluating my work. Then I'd looked at the painting and found what I'd just seen in Ben—the ache in him throbbing, as if the air he was breathing was something he didn't believe he deserved.

And then, standing alone in his bedroom, not even sure if he was coming back, I knew what I was feeling, what had swooped in so suddenly to replace my anger.

It was belief. Simple, unguarded, lightweight belief.

He had loved her *and* he had bruised her. He had stained her skin with his pain, and she had let him—encouraged him, even. He had believed her when she said he was helping her, that Persephone could exchange her own pain for another, and when he finally stopped believing it, it was too late. There was nobody to hear his apologies, nobody to forgive him, nobody to bear his grief or love.

So strange to even think it, but I believed him. I did. I did. I believed that you could love someone so much, and still, you could hurt them. I believed that a heart could pound with pain and love at exactly the same time.

23

When Ben returned, he was holding a glass of whiskey.

"Sorry," he said once he swallowed. He nodded at the drink. "I just needed this. Memory Lane is a difficult road to walk." He chuckled briefly, then shook his head, sobering. "Do you want some? I could go make another."

I thought of Mom—how quickly she'd turned to alcohol to dilute her difficult emotions, how cowardly I'd always felt that was—but then I imagined how the whiskey would feel on my tongue, warm and velvety.

"Sure."

"Cool," Ben said. "I hate drinking alone. Be right back."

I unbuttoned my coat and sloughed it off like a snake unpeeling from its skin. Then I placed it on the bed and sat down beside it, crossing my legs and uncrossing them, crossing and uncrossing again. I didn't have the energy to keep standing, but my nerves felt too frayed to let me sit still.

Ben held a glass out toward me as he walked back into the room. He took another sip from his own. As I accepted the whiskey from him, our fingers brushed together, and reflexively, I jerked away, the liquor sloshing against the sides of the glass. He looked at me, his eyebrows raised, but he didn't say anything, just sipped and then sipped again.

"Thanks," I muttered.

He nodded, and I drank, feeling the satisfying burn of the whiskey at the back of my throat as I swallowed. Silence settled like dust over the room, and I kept my eyes pointed down toward the whiskey, cupping the glass as if it contained tea leaves I knew how to read.

"There's something I don't understand," I finally said.

As I glanced over at Persephone's letter beside me on the bed, I kept my eyes unfocused just enough so that the edges of each word became imprecise, one after another blurring together.

"You told me," I started, "that you were messed up when it happened. Right? That's how you put it? Messed up?"

Ben nodded, the movement as slow and full of effort as if there were an anchor hanging from his neck.

"And my sister wrote that she wanted to help you with what you were going through, so what was it, exactly? What made you hold on to her so hard in the first place?"

He brought his glass to his lips, took a gulp that nearly emptied it, and then slid to the floor, his back against the dresser, his legs straightening out in front of him. Releasing a long, heavy breath, he set his whiskey down beside him on the carpet.

"It was a lot of things," he said. "But, for starters—I told you how my mom moved to Portugal, right?"

I nodded.

"Well, when she left," he continued, "I had just graduated high school. And I had no plans. I wasn't going to college or anything—because, you know . . ." His voice deepened, as if imitating someone else. "It was clearly my goal in life to be an utter disappointment to my father and bring shame to the family name."

He cleared his throat. "Anyway, my mom gave me the option to come with her. But Portugal? Europe? I didn't know anyone there. And besides, my grandfather was here—right here, actually, living in this guesthouse—and he and I were really close. I didn't want to leave him."

He paused, glancing down at the remains of his drink. "And thank God I didn't." His shoulders lifted and sagged with a barely audible sigh. "He died a little while later. He had a stroke, and—things deteriorated very quickly. It happened in October of that same year, a few months after I started dating Persephone."

Again, I nodded, the pieces of Ben's past falling together for me like snow into piles—Richard Emory had died and Mom had gone to his funeral. *He'd had a loss*, Mom had said of Will. *He'd had a loss, and I love him.*

"So, with my grandfather dying," Ben said, "so soon after my mom left, it just—it felt like everyone I loved was leaving me." He rubbed at the back of his neck. "And it really messed me up for a while. Like, it hurt some days just to get out of bed."

I remembered mornings like that—how the sun could feel like a wound bleeding into my bedroom, how my mother's bed was no longer a cocoon I could join her in, and how that made it even easier to stay buried for hours in my own.

"So, that first time it happened," Ben went on, "with Persephone and the bruises—I was holding on to her not just as a shoulder to cry on, but because I couldn't bear the thought of *not* having her to hold on to."

He shook his head, swept his hand over his face as if trying to wipe the memories off. "I was floundering," he said. "Lost. I wasn't seeing things as clearly as I should have. I mean, all I had at home was my dad, and that was . . . not the best thing to have."

I tightened my fingers around my drink. "What do you mean?"

Ben shrugged, his gaze falling onto the carpet. "We've never had a great relationship," he said. Then he lifted his hand to his cheek and ran a finger along the curve of his scar. "He gave me this, you know."

My eyes widened. I realized that I'd never even wondered about the scar's origin or tried to imagine his face without it. How blank it would seem. How normal and benign.

"What happened?" I asked.

Ben looked up at the ceiling. "It was stupid," he said. "I was twelve and acting out. My mom had asked me to do the dishes but I wanted to play video games. We argued for a while until my dad just—snapped. I remember him yelling, 'You'll do as you're fucking told,' and then he threw a knife at me."

My mouth dropped open. "What?"

"I was actually pretty lucky," Ben said. "It could have been a lot worse."

"But—" I paused, fumbling for words. "But that's insane!"

Ben nodded, slowly and rhythmically, his gaze lingering in the air above us. "Yep."

I inched forward on the bed. "So what happened?" I asked. "Did your dad get arrested or anything?"

Ben laughed, the sound startling me as it erupted from his mouth. "No," he said. "My parents took me to the hospital and they told the nurses I'd had an accident while playing with a knife."

"And your mom just went along with that?" My chest was heating up.

"She didn't want to, of course," he said, "but my dad convinced her that the scandal would be damaging for all of us." He chuckled. "I still remember him using that exact word—*damaging*. He was in the front seat on the way to the hospital, and he was yammering on and on to my mom about what would happen if she were to say anything—the damage to Emory Builders, the damage to our reputation, the damage to *my* legacy and inheritance that he'd supposedly spent his whole life building. Meanwhile, I was just sitting there in the back seat with a bloody rag to my face. Talk about damage."

"Well, why didn't *you* say anything?" I asked. "To a doctor, or a nurse."

Ben shook his head. "You don't know my father. He can be incredibly manipulative. And he can turn on the charm like that." He snapped his fingers. "By the time we got to the hospital, he'd twisted things around so much that I started apologizing profusely. He made me believe it was all my fault, for refusing to do what I was told."

I stared at Ben's scar. If Will had done that to his own son, how easily might he have done something like that to Mom, someone who had no ties to him but the tenuous ones of the heart? I felt grateful in that moment that he'd chosen Ben's mother over mine, that he'd committed to his family in the house on the hill and laid his destruction on them instead. Mom was lucky, I thought now, to have escaped Will Emory with only an aching void inside her.

But then I looked at Ben's eyes, how they winced with remembered pain, and I felt guilt as sharp as a blade across my face. It wasn't my mother that the worst of Will had happened to—but it was still Ben's mother, a woman who had known enough to flee him when she could, and it was Ben himself, the person sitting in front of me, the person who, I was beginning to concede, was maybe as human as anyone else.

"Anyway," Ben said, "it was years later and everything, but when my mom left and my grandfather passed, it was hard for me to be alone with him." He touched the scar again. "Since this happened, he's never been violent with me like that—not physically anyway—but I've seen bursts of that same rage, usually when he's not getting what he wants, with business, with the town, with me. He's like a child in that way."

"Then why do you still live with him?" I asked. "Or on his property at least."

Ben picked up his drink, swirled it around, and then sucked the rest of it down. He set the glass heavily onto the carpet.

"After Persephone died," he said, "my life kind of went off the rails. Or, I don't know, maybe it was already off the rails. Like I said, I wasn't going to college or anything. I hadn't taken high school very seriously, and there wasn't a single university that would take me—not the ones deemed *fit for an Emory* anyway. So my father wanted pretty much nothing to do with me, and for years, I lived in this dingy little apartment I could barely afford—working at a gas station during the day, delivering pizzas at night. At some point, I finally realized I was in a really dark place. I got promoted to assistant manager at the gas station, and it was like a wake-up call. I knew I didn't want that life. Nothing against people who work at gas stations—retail, customer service, that's hard, honest work—I just knew I wanted something different."

His eyes latched onto Persephone's letter beside me on the bed. "But the good thing about the promotion," he continued, "was that it came with health insurance. So I started seeing a therapist—which was probably long overdue—and he actually helped me out a lot. I told him about Persephone and everything that happened. Loving her, bruising her, letting her out of the car that night instead of just insisting I drive her back home."

His voice became sharp, edged with a regret I could almost taste on the tip of my tongue.

"Anyway," he went on, "I finally realized I wanted to do something with my life that would—in some way, at least—make up for the horrible mistakes I'd made. I knew I'd been trying to help her, to heal her in the way she said she needed, but I'd been hurting her, too. So I wanted to help people for real this time, and eventually that led to me wanting to become a nurse. The only problem was—I couldn't afford to pay for school. My father had cut me off the second I moved out of the house, and all the money I earned went into my living expenses. I couldn't get any loans, either, because I didn't have the best credit. So, when I finally admitted to myself that I had no other option, I returned to my dad—tail between my legs, the whole thing—and I asked him for a loan. And he surprised me by saying that a loan would not be necessary; he'd pay for my education himself."

He smiled a little before continuing, but it was a wry and wavering smile. "Only, there was a catch, because with my dad, there's always a catch. He said he would pay for my education *if* I moved back to the house."

Ben paused, his shoulders sinking so noticeably it was as if his father's hands, heavy with ultimatum, were pushing them down.

"Why?" I jumped in. "Why would it matter to him where you lived?"

"Well," Ben said slowly, seeming to take his time choosing his words, "an Emory male is not a true Emory unless he's under the thumb of his father. It's like my family is one big revolving door of power. And at a certain point, it becomes the elder Emory's job to ensure that the younger Emory—the Emory heir—will continue on in a manner befitting the family name. Take my dad and my grandfather. I've never seen a tenser relationship in my life. My grandfather was great with me—kind and funny and we always got along—but with my dad, he was different. He was critical, demanding. He was disappointed in him because, in terms of his political aspirations, my dad only ever wanted to be mayor. Unlike my grandfather, who was a congressman for years, my dad just wasn't interested in anything that took him away from this town."

Ben sighed, as if talking about his family history were the most tedious thing he could imagine. "It turned out okay, though, because my dad did what he always does. He manipulated the right people, pulled the right strings, made some significant changes to the town. Profits soared at Emory Builders, too. It was brilliant, actually. As mayor, he could bully his way into getting whatever the business needed—permits, land, et cetera. So, in the end, he accomplished what my grandfather wanted the most—his name being stamped into the Spring Hill history books just like all the other Emorys before him. But still, like I said, there was always this tension between them."

He traced his scar with his finger again—only, this time, it seemed more like a force of habit. "Runs in the family, I guess. I'm an extension of my father, see, and he's not a successful Emory male if he doesn't have an heir to mold into someone just like him—a political figure, or the next great leader of Emory Builders, or both. And right now, he's playing the long game. He knows I have no interest in any of that, but this way, he's letting me indulge in my 'childish whim,' as he says, while still keeping me under his thumb. I'm sure he thinks that, living in the guesthouse, getting all the perks of our family lifestyle day after day, eventually I'll come around and decide to do something more honorable."

I cocked my head to the side. "More honorable than working with cancer patients?"

"Something more public," Ben clarified. "Something with a better salary. Something at the family company. It's my destiny, don't you know?"

Despite the space between us—me on the bed, him on the floor, separated by at least a few feet—I saw his eyelids twitch, the skin there, thin as a moth's wing, kicking with spasms. As his words lingered in the air, his gaze drilled deeper and deeper into the carpet.

"But, actually," he said, "it hasn't been all that bad living here. I thought I'd hate it. My father was manipulating me, and I knew it. But school was expensive, and I didn't really have another option. I still plan to pay him back—I don't want to owe my father a thing—but it's been okay. Plus, I don't see him too much. Every now and then, we pass each other in the driveway, and we wave, and we roll our windows down, and he guilts me into having dinner with him, where he'll talk about how I'm not living up to my potential—but mostly, I just work a lot."

I nodded in acknowledgment and took a sip of my drink. I felt its warmth course through me, lighting me up from inside.

"So anyway," Ben said, letting out a long, abundant breath, "that's my life story."

He laughed then, briefly but heartily, the sound welling from somewhere deep in his body. I looked at him, surprised—the bellow of his laughter seemed disproportionate to the comment he'd made—but then I heard myself laugh a little, too, cracking a tension I hadn't realized was still hovering over the room.

When our laughter subsided, there were a few beats of silence, during which I wondered where to look, what to say. Then my stomach let out a low, rumbling grunt that swiftly crescendoed into a growl. The flush in my face was immediate, and I raised my glass to my lips again, trying to cover the pink I felt burning in my cheeks.

"Oh thank God," Ben said. "I'm so hungry, too." He put a hand against the dresser to steady himself as he stood. "I think I have a frozen pizza in the kitchen. You interested?"

I looked back at the clock on Ben's nightstand. It had been hours since I'd wolfed down half a sandwich before heading off to Tommy's. And it might have been the alcohol radiating through my veins, or even just the hunger I was suddenly aware of like a gaping hole in my gut, but as I stood up from the bed, I didn't think of Persephone or bruises. I thought only of dough and sauce and cheese—how that seemed like all I needed in that moment—and I found myself nodding, my mouth actually watering in response.

"Sure," I said. "Pizza sounds good."

24

We didn't speak much as we ate. Sitting at the white marble counter of Ben's breakfast bar, we inhaled slice after slice of mediocre—yet wholly delicious—pizza, taking breaks only to drink long, thirsty gulps of the beers we'd opened while waiting for the oven to preheat.

"Okay," Ben said after a while, a single slice remaining on the pan between us. "I think I'm ready to come up for air."

He wiped his hands on a napkin and tossed it onto the counter. Shifting his weight on the tall, low-backed chair, he looked at me and crossed his arms. "So," he said, "your turn. I want to know about you."

I swallowed the bite I'd been chewing and set my crust on my plate. "What about me?" I asked, reaching for my beer.

"Well," he said, "I feel like I told you everything there is to know about me, but I don't know much about you. I don't even know what you do for a living."

"Oh," I said. "Well, I'm sort of between jobs right now—that's the fancy way of saying 'unemployed,' right? I was a tattoo artist until I got laid off."

"Oh, that's awesome!" Ben said. Then he shook his head. "Not the getting laid off part. I mean being a tattoo artist. That must be so cool. Do you like it?"

I thought about it, and then I answered him honestly. "No. I mean, I don't hate it. But I don't enjoy it, either. My roommate, Lauren—we worked at the same place, and she's in love with it."

I pictured the sticky notes she'd place around the apartment—a phoenix in transition from ash to bird, a woman's eye with thin, barren trees for lashes. I pictured her face as she worked on someone's arm or calf or shoulder blade, the way her eyes would smile even as her lips pursed in concentration.

"She would marry tattooing if she could," I added, and then I cleared my throat, my voice too loud as it bounced off all the gleaming white surfaces in the kitchen. "I think that maybe I've always been a little jealous of that. I just can't imagine being that passionate about a job."

I slid my finger up and down my beer bottle, watching clear, glistening tracks of condensation emerge. "It's only been a few weeks since I was laid off," I said, "but it feels like a lifetime ago that I ever did that. It seems like it was someone else entirely."

Ben tilted his head and knitted his brows together. "So how'd you get into tattooing in the first place, then? Is it something you have to go to school for?"

"You have to do an apprenticeship, get certified," I said, shrugging. "But I originally went to art school. And then after that, I basically hopped on board my best friend's plans because I didn't have any of my own."

"Art school," Ben said. "That's cool. What kind of art do you do?"

"I don't do any art," I said quickly.

"Oh. Sorry, I just thought—"

"Yeah, it would make sense," I cut in, "for someone with a degree in fine arts to actually *make* art, but I don't know." I continued to trace the condensation on my beer, my fingertip wet and cold. "The truth is, I have no idea what I want to do with my life."

I was buzzed by now, clearly—I was making admissions to Ben that I'd barely even articulated to myself. As I pushed my half-empty bottle a couple inches away, the beer and lingering whiskey kept unthreading thoughts that, up until now, had been knotted up inside me.

"My life is totally directionless," I said. "In high school, I painted every day so I could get into RISD. At RISD, I painted every day so I could get a degree. And for years now since then, I've just been . . ." I searched for the correct word, thumbing through my brain until I landed on the one that Aunt Jill had often ascribed to me. "Floating."

Ben shrugged. "That's okay," he said. "You're—what? Thirty? That's about the age I was when I figured things out. Before that, I never cared about a job, but now that I'm a nurse, I love going to work. It's hard, but I love it."

Looking at him then, I saw that, even with all their darkness, his eyes seemed earnest and encouraging, as if he truly believed that I, too, had a calling, and that mine was a path that would reveal itself in time. After a couple seconds, I had to look away from him.

"Yeah," I said, "well, what you said before—about becoming a nurse to make up for your mistakes with Persephone? I think that, for me, doing tattoos is similar—only, in the opposite way."

His eyes squinted in confusion. "What do you mean?"

I took a deep breath. "I think I only stuck with tattooing to *remember* my mistakes. Because if I remembered them, then I could keep punishing myself. Because I should be. I should be punished."

Ben shook his head. "I don't under—"

"You know I painted over Persephone's bruises, right?"

He hesitated, looking away from me to stare at his drink, but then he nodded.

"I shouldn't have done that," I rushed on. "I shouldn't have kept it a secret. But she asked me to, and so I did. And I always thought that covering her bruises, keeping her secret—I thought it led to what happened that night, because, as you know, I believed it was you who killed her. So tattooing—inking pictures onto people's skin—it reminds me of what I did. Which is good. I don't want to be able to forget. I don't deserve to."

A crease of concern spread across Ben's forehead. "You were a kid," he said. "You can't carry that. You didn't do anything wrong, Sylvie."

I shook my head so hard that my hair flew across my face. "You don't understand," I said, brushing it back behind my ear. "You don't know what I did."

Standing up, I pushed my chair away from the counter and took a step back. My heart was a clenched fist knocking against my ribs; the air felt too thick, my throat too small. I could feel a film of sweat, sudden and slick, on my forehead, and I could see her in her red coat, the snow just beginning to dust her shoulders as she trudged back toward Ben, as she got in his car and never looked back. *It's such a betrayal,* she'd written.

"Sylvie," I heard Ben say, but my eyes were blurring and I was already walking away from him, stumbling down the hallway and toward the front door. I could see the handle, could almost reach out and grasp it. I could see the dead bolt, the latch that wasn't locked.

"I have to go," I mumbled, vaguely looking around for my coat but then deciding, somewhere in the fog beginning to envelop me, that I didn't need it. It wasn't as cold outside as it had been that night. My body wouldn't freeze; my body would not be buried in snow.

"Sylvie," Ben said again, and I felt his hands on my shoulders. When he turned me around to face him, his eyes looked into mine so deeply I wondered if he could see her, too—her blonde hair tinted almost pink by his taillights, her boots leaving ghosts of herself on the ground.

"Talk to me," Ben said. "It's okay. It's okay."

He guided me into his bedroom and flicked on the light switch, a yellow glow flooding the carpet, the walls, the air. Sitting me down on the bed and taking the space beside me, he kept his hand on my back, rubbing it up and down. "Shh," he soothed. "It's okay. It's okay."

It wasn't until a tear, fat yet weightless, splashed onto my hand that I realized why he kept saying that. My cheeks were wet, I registered now; my shoulders were shaking and my lungs kept sucking in air.

"Whatever it is," he said, "it can't be that bad. You were a kid, Sylvie. Just a kid."

"It doesn't matter how old I was," I spat. "She's dead because of me. Because I—" A burning sob raged through me. "I locked her out!"

Ben was silent, watching me.

"I was—I was always supposed to keep the window open. Just a crack. That's all she needed to get back in, but I—I was sick of it. I didn't want to cover for her anymore. I wanted our mom to know what was happening to her. Only I didn't—I didn't think that—I only locked it because I thought she'd come to the front door. I thought she'd have to ring the doorbell and wake up my mom and they'd have a fight but then everything would be out in the open. I didn't know she'd—I had no idea . . . oh God."

I slumped forward, my face falling into my hands. Tears slipped between my fingers, and as I endured the sobs that spasmed through my stomach, my throat, my lungs, I felt Ben's body tense up beside me. Even his hand on my back went stiff.

I straightened up, wiping at each of my cheeks, and I looked him in the eyes. "I locked her out," I confessed again. "She couldn't come back that night because I locked her out."

Ben pulled his hand away from me and placed it on his lap. For a while, he just sucked on the inside of his cheek, the one that was scarless and smooth, and I watched his pulse as it throbbed against his neck.

"I locked her out," I repeated.

Now that I'd finally come clean, now that—for the first time in my life—I'd spoken the words out loud, I couldn't stop saying them. It was as if my tongue were a diving board, and they kept lining up, one after another, to jump right off.

"I locked Perseph—"

"So what?" Ben snapped his head to look at me.

I blinked, tears catching in my eyelashes. "So *what?*" I said back. "So *everything.*"

Ben shook his head. "No. It doesn't matter. You locked her out, okay, but what about Persephone?"

I stared at him, watching how the light in the room pooled and swirled in his eyes. "What about her?"

"It was *her* decision to come back to my car. She could have rung the bell, like you said, gotten in trouble and that would've been it. But she didn't. She got in my car instead. And we fought. She said she hadn't been able to get back in, and I told her we should just tell her mom so this wasn't such an issue in the future, but she said no. She got angry. She demanded I let her out."

I narrowed my eyes, my tears stalling on my cheeks. "Are you saying this was *her* fault?"

"No. Not at all. Because the next thing that happened was that I *did* let her out. And if I could redo anything in my life, that's the one thing I'd take back. But even if I did take it back—even if I'd found a way to calm her down and then drove her home again and she'd figured out how to sneak inside—would it matter? Would she still be alive today?"

"Yes," I said, and Ben tilted his head to the side.

"I'm not so sure about that. Because, just like she made the decision to get out of my car, and I made the decision to let her, someone else made the decision to kill her. And if it was Tommy, then he could have done it another time, too. He was stalking her, Sylvie. He was biding his time. He—"

He stopped himself, taking a deep breath before continuing.

"What I'm saying is—Persephone made a decision to sneak out, to come back to my car, to demand to be let out, and I made a decision to let her go, and you made a decision to lock the window because you were tired of covering up a dangerous situation. But only one person made a decision that night to hurt her. To kill her. You were—God, Sylvie—you were only trying to *help* her. You were trying to *keep* her from getting hurt. Why the hell would you blame yourself—let alone punish yourself—for that?"

My lips parted to say something, and then closed, parted and closed, parted and closed. I was stunned into stillness, my hands half open, half fisted in my lap. I was stunned by the reflections of light I could see in those obsidian eyes, the ones my sister had called black holes, the ones that seemed to make their own gravity as they pulled me toward their gaze.

He was right.

I actually laughed when I realized it, my breath gushing out of me as if it were water that had filled my lungs to bursting. In an instant, I felt lighter, pounds and years lighter, and I was about to press my hand to my mouth, dam up the laughter that was coming and coming in an otherwise somber room, but then I changed my mind, let the sound spill from my body until nearly all of it had been drained.

"Uh . . ." I heard Ben say. "What's so funny?"

All this time, I'd remembered locking the window as something I'd done *to* Persephone. But Ben was right—God, he was so right, it felt wonderful and terrible at once—I'd locked the window *for* her. I'd locked it because I'd loved her, deeply, and I'd wanted to save her from herself, wanted to protect her from boyfriends and bruises and misinterpretations of love.

But still—and here, the laughter dried up, quick as the stopping of a faucet—I had lost her.

The tears flowed again as I collapsed against Ben, boneless as a pile of laundry. For whole moments, whole minutes maybe, I continued to cry, crumpled up in his arms.

That loss—the absence of Persephone—had always been an ache so fierce that, at times, it was difficult to breathe. I felt it now, again, my lungs gasping to keep up with the pace of my tears, and I missed her. I missed how she scrunched up her nose when looking in the mirror, how she hummed whenever she brushed her hair. I missed the pinches and Indian burns we'd given each other, just kids with no understanding yet of bruises, of what it would take to want them, of what it would take to cover them up. I missed movie nights and buttered popcorn, missed rewinding again and again to rehear the lines we loved. I missed kicking each other under the table at breakfast, both of us stifling smiles that threatened to give us away. There were so many things—millions of tiny, essential things—that I'd been too busy living my life to appreciate and cherish. How many times had I crawled into bed with my mother, when my sister, alive and just as warm, had a bed to crawl into, too? She might have pushed me away, grumbled her annoyance into her pillow, but when she placed her hands on my arms or my shoulders or my back, they would have had blood coursing through them, round and round again.

I straightened up, and Ben's arms loosened as I wiped a hand across my nose. When I met his eyes—eyes that Persephone had gazed into each night, eyes that she'd said she could get lost in—I saw that our faces were very close. I could feel his breath on my lips.

"I know," he whispered, and his voice was so fragile it sounded like my own. "I miss her, too. I miss her all the time."

I kissed him then. Without thinking, without understanding, I pressed my mouth against his. I cupped his face and felt the ridge of his scar beneath my fingers. He'd been wounded there, hurt by a parent who was supposed to only love him, and I kissed him harder for that. I could feel his surprise in the shape of his mouth, the initial stiffness of his lips, but then he kissed me back, lifting his hand to cradle my neck, and my nerves became electrified. Something in my body roared back to life.

I gripped him closer, pulling him down with me to the bed. I felt the weight of him, his chest rising and falling in tempo with my own, and I wrapped my legs around him, fastening his body to mine.

His lips were softer than I would have expected, and as our mouths moved together, breathy and slick, I slipped my hands under the back of his sweater, felt the heat of his skin against my palms as I pulled him even closer.

His thumb stroked my cheek as he kissed me and kissed me again, and I struggled with his belt, trying to unbuckle it without unthreading my lips from his. He leaned back then, his breathing heavy and rhythmic, and he peeled off his sweater, undid his belt, and slid out of his pants. I tugged my shirt over my head and pulled my jeans and underwear down together. When he came back to me, his skin already beading with sweat, he wrapped his fingers around the straps of my bra and slipped them down over my shoulders, kissing each inch of my body he revealed.

I didn't want his mouth that far from mine. I put my hands on the sides of his face and guided him back to my lips. We kissed each other again—and again and again and again—until he finally entered me, and I gasped, his mouth trailing down to my neck, where he breathed hot and hard against my skin.

As I pressed my fingers into his shoulder blades, as I turned my head to run my lips along his scar, I didn't stop to wonder why tears still dampened my cheeks. I only thought of all the parts of my sister that Ben alone had known—parts secret and mysterious, parts I'd never been able to reach. Then I felt the rhythm of him inside me for the miracle that it was; with every gentle but insistent thrust, he was pushing Persephone back, back, back into me.

25

The lights were still on when I got home. I wiped my feet on the mat and paused at the front door, pressing my back against the wood as the imprint of Ben's body continued to hum inside me. The air felt taut, as if stretched over too small a space, and I closed my eyes to the accusations I could imagine Mom hurling at me: *Where the hell were you? I've been here alone for hours, wasting away. I guess it means nothing to you that I'm sick.*

But when I walked through the entryway into the living room, wincing in anticipation, I was surprised to find that she wasn't in her chair. All the lamps were on, casting a buttery glow on the furniture and walls. Even the Persephone constellation, usually shadowed by the nearby TV, was perfectly spotlighted. I stared at it—that angry, silver swipe of my sister's hand—and quickly looked away.

When I saw the time on the microwave in the kitchen, I knew why Mom wasn't there. It was eleven thirty-two. I'd stayed with Ben even longer than I'd thought, and Mom was asleep. Of course she was—she had chemo in the morning—and if I had even a chance of enduring her eye rolls and complaints, her acidic comments bookended by silence, then I needed to get some sleep myself.

I switched off the lamps, each of the bulbs lingering a dull orange before snuffing out completely, but the darkness didn't take. There was still another light, coming from somewhere down the hall. As I got closer, I saw that Mom's door was open, the light spilling out. Tiptoeing into the doorway and resting my shoulder against its frame, I found her asleep on top of the bed, bald as a baby and curled up like one, too.

I watched the flicker of a vein on her head, how it forked across her skull like pale blue roots. Then, her arm twitched, responding to something from deep within the folds of sleep, and I noticed her fist, tightly balled and clutching something. Taking a couple steps into the room, I saw that it was a tissue—that, in fact, the bed was littered with tissues crumpled up around her, fist-like themselves.

At the foot of the bed was a lidless shoebox stuffed with what appeared to be small white envelopes. I glanced back at Mom's face, noted her pink, swollen eyelids, the hints of dried tears on her cheeks, and I looked at the box again. My heart sputtered, seeming to understand something before my mind could catch up, and I reached for the box, my movements as slow and soundless as dust floating through air. Palms flat against the cardboard, I lifted it up and snuck back into my room, where I switched on the light and carried the box to my bed. For a few moments, I could only stare at all those envelopes lined up like entries in a card catalogue.

I picked out one at random. "Annie – January 15," it said, and then a year. I did the math quickly—I would have been four years old when Mom received this; Persephone would have been eight. I plucked out another envelope ("Annie – October 15," it said, with the same year as the first) and then another ("Annie – May 15," dated two years later). Flipping through more and more, I saw that there were ones with years that predated the first one I'd picked up, and ones with years when I hadn't even been alive yet. But every single one arrived on the fifteenth of the month—Mom's Dark Day.

Envelopes scattered around me, I pulled out another from the box (I'd been seven for this one, Persephone eleven), and I looked inside. A strip of paper no bigger than a credit card said, "I can't stop thinking about you." For a second, I let my eyes trace the bulky handwriting, and then I reached for another (I'd been two, Persephone six) and read the note inside: "I took my son blueberry picking yesterday and remembered that stain on your lips." I fingered the top edges of the envelopes until I stopped on one that was closer to the end of the box (I'd been thirteen, Persephone seventeen), and when I opened it, I read his words: "In my dream last night I was kissing you."

Will's words, of course. So now I knew. On the fifteenth of each month, he'd sent my mother a letter—no stamp, no address, hand-delivered apparently. "I miss your face," one said. Then Mom would glide through the hallway like a ghost, turn into her room, shut the door. "The other day, a song came on the radio that reminded me of you and I had to pull over on the side of the road for ten minutes." We'd press our ears to her door, pancake batter dripping from the wooden spoon that Persephone held up in the air, and we'd hear nothing but the sound of our own breathing. "I love you. I'll always love you. Only you." Darkness would swallow the house as we'd wait in the living room, still in our pajamas, the rumble of our stomachs reminding us to turn on the light, heat up the leftover pancakes, have breakfast for dinner. "It's not enough to just remember you." The next morning, she'd emerge from her room, the creak of her door a sound that pulled us from dreams, and her eyes would be puffy. Then she'd kiss us on the tops of our heads—Persephone just a peck, me a kiss of hard I've-come-back-to-you lips, her palm lingering under my chin, Persephone's eyes lingering on Mom's hand.

"Those are mine."

Her voice made me jump—not because Mom was there, in my doorway, and who knew for how long, but because of the anger trembling in each word. I looked at her, her arms crossed, a gnarled twig of a woman.

"These notes," I said. "They're why you had your Dark Days."

"My *what*?"

"Every fifteenth, you'd slink off to your room and not come out until the next day."

She was silent then, her lips pinched so tightly together they almost disappeared.

"So this was why," I continued. "Because Will would write you these notes. And then you'd miss him, I guess. You'd miss him so much you'd abandon us."

She unsealed her mouth to scoff. "Abandon you? Please. You girls could take care of yourselves."

"Because we had to," I said. "You can do nearly anything when you *have* to."

Mom rolled her eyes.

"He was toying with you," I said. "You know that, right?"

"What are you talking about?"

"Sending you these notes—with no intention of actually seeing you. He just wanted to know you were still under his thumb. He was manipulating you."

"And what makes you think he had no intention of actually seeing me?"

I hesitated, the answer so obvious. "Because you never saw him."

"Like hell I didn't."

Her eyes blazed, practically scorching my skin with the heat of their conviction, even from across the room.

"What?" I asked.

"You think you have it all figured out, but you don't know anything."

"When would you have seen him? The only time I ever saw the two of you together was at Persephone's wake."

She shrugged. "I saw him now and then."

"When?" I asked. "Where?"

"We made arrangements."

"You made arrangements. How? Through these?" I picked up a couple of envelopes, then loosened my grip, letting them slip back onto the bed like leaves floating to the ground.

She shrugged again. "Guess you didn't pay close enough attention when invading my privacy."

I stared at her—her nearly translucent skin thin as an onion's, her eyebrows all bone, her gray eyes like clouds holding in their rain—and I saw her look at the notes that were scattered all around me. Her lips twitched, as if she wanted to say more.

Running my fingers over the letters still in the box, I grabbed a few at a time. "My new secretary is named Annie," one said. "I find all sorts of reasons to say her name." Without bothering to return it to its envelope, I dropped that note and went on to the next: "I saw you with your kids last week. You were checking out at the grocery store when I walked in. I had to stop myself from whisking you away." I dropped that note and went on to the next: "I'm aching to see you." I dropped that note, and as it fluttered on to the bed, it turned itself upside down, revealing another message, the handwriting cramped and small in the corner. "This Thursday," it said. "2 p.m., usual place."

I glanced up at Mom. Even as her mouth held on to a tiny, satisfied smile, her eyes brimmed with anxiety. I dug back into the notes I'd already read, flipping them over to see the words on the opposite side of each one. "Saturday night, 9:30 p.m., usual place." "Next Wednesday, 3:30 p.m., usual place." "Tomorrow, 8 a.m., usual place."

"You were having an affair with him?" I blurted. "All that time?"

"Oh, don't look so scandalized," Mom said, but she wasn't even looking at me; her eyes were stapled to the wall behind my head. "It was just a few times a year."

"Just a few times a year? He was *married*."

"And that was his business, not mine. If his wife couldn't make him happy, then that was her problem."

My mouth fell open. "*Her* problem? Oh my God, Mom—who *are* you?"

"I'm the woman who loves him."

She tightened her crossed arms, her body rigid, as if she were solid as a deeply rooted tree—not the hollow stalk, easily snapped by the wind, that we both knew she really was. I held myself back from responding right away. I wanted the words she'd just said to reverberate in the air, mock her with their absurdity.

I looked down at the notes again. "What's the usual place?" I asked.

"Does it matter?"

I pictured them in the back seat of a car, like two teenagers with no better options. I pictured them in Will's office, his wife unknowingly on her way with the bagged lunch he'd forgotten at home that morning.

"No," I said. "But—when were you even meeting up with him? I feel like I'd remember that."

And then, all at once, I did. I remembered those nights she'd come into my bedroom after one of her dates, tucking me deeper into sleep, her skin bringing the scent of peonies into the air. I remembered mumbling questions about the men she'd had dinner with, and I remembered her shushing me as if I were a baby beginning to fuss.

All those nights, she'd been going out with Will? I shook my head at the thought. She couldn't have been. I'd seen some of the men she dated. There was that one who pulled into our driveway in a red Ferrari and Mom rolled her eyes as the three of us peeked at him through the curtains. We watched him check his reflection in the side-view mirror and nod his approval before heading toward the door.

"The men I went out with were just distractions," Mom said now, as if reading my mind. "They were few and far between—fewer and farther than I let you think. I hardly dated anyone but Will. Sometimes I did—here and there, just to make him jealous, or just to feel like I was calling the shots—but mostly, it was him." Her eyes glazed over and her voice became brittle. "All him."

She slouched a little, her arms dropping to her sides, the knot of her body beginning to loosen. I watched her waver slightly, like a branch swaying with a breeze, before she placed her hand on the dresser to steady herself.

"So you understand what he was doing to you, then," I said.

Mom squinted. "Doing to me?"

"You just said you went out with other men to feel like you were calling the shots. Because you were completely powerless, right? Completely under Will's control, at the whim of *his* desires. If he wanted to see you, he didn't ask when you were available. He told you when and where, and you just—you just showed up!" I laughed—a dry, abbreviated chuckle. "I mean, didn't you have any respect for yourself?"

The silence she offered was enough of an answer, and as another thought pushed its way to the surface of my mind, gasping for attention, my stomach clenched.

"Oh my God," I said. "Is this still going on?"

Mom shook her head so slightly it was as if she didn't move it at all. "No," she said, but her voice was distant.

"You're lying!" I screeched. "You're still seeing him, aren't you?"

I thought of Ben's scar, how Will had thrown a blade at his son and sliced the boy he was into two—one who had trusted his father and one who never would again. I raked my eyes over Mom's body, searching for signs of Will's damage on her skin. She was pale as milk and there were bruises on her arms—but that was because of her sickness, that was because of the chemo. Right?

"No, I'm not still seeing him," she hissed, and when her eyes connected with mine, there were tears in them. "The last time we met up, your sister was still alive, okay? The last time I even saw him was at her wake. Do you think I don't wish I'd seen him since then? That we were together right now? But look at me. I've hardly left the house in the last sixteen years, and he's never asked me to."

Her eyes fell to the floor again, a tear sliding down the sharp curve of her cheek. "He doesn't love me anymore. He's forgotten I even exist."

I was struck by how young she sounded—like a lovelorn teenager, or like Lauren when she got attached to someone who then began ignoring her texts. "He's over me," she'd always say, her tone nearly theatrical.

I shook my head, glancing at Will's letters on the bed. "I don't get it," I said. "These notes are clearly connected to your Dark Days—the dates prove that. But shouldn't they have made you happy? I mean, he was sending you a letter once a month telling you how much he wanted to see you. Isn't that what you wanted?"

"Do you see two hundred and sixteen notes in there?" Mom snapped.

I paused. "What?"

"It wasn't once a month. The notes weren't, anyway. And *that's* what broke me, if you really have to know. Eight, nine, ten times a year—I'd go to the mailbox, take out the envelope, and there'd be no note inside it at all. It was . . . Jesus, it was brutal. I'd wait for weeks for the fifteenth, for his middle-of-the-night courier or whoever the hell he sent, and then, most of the time—nothing. He'd completely shut me out." She turned her head to look at the wall, crossing her arms once again. "You can't possibly know how that feels."

Laughter burst through my lips. "I can't possibly know how it feels to be shut out? Are you ser—" But then I stopped. "Wait."

I rewound the words she'd just said, playing them back in my mind.

"Why would there be an envelope in the mailbox if there wasn't a letter?" I asked.

Mom stared at the wall, her mouth firmly closed.

"What else was in the envelopes?" I tried.

When she still didn't answer, I riffled through the notes again, picking out envelopes in the box I hadn't yet touched. I opened them up and shook them out, as if whatever else had been in them were still inside. But all that slipped out were the same strips of paper with the same handwriting I was already beginning to hate.

"I still have dreams about us at the lake."

"I ate our favorite pizza last week. It wasn't the same without you."

"I saw you outside the movie theater with another guy. I wanted to kiss you right in front of him."

"Couldn't get to the bank in time to make the withdrawal. I'll—"

My pulse sped up. I tightened my grip on the note, crinkling it a little. Then I started over.

"Couldn't get to the bank in time to make the withdrawal. I'll get it to you tonight. Wear the green dress."

I flipped the paper over. "Usual place. 8:30."

"He was giving you money?" I asked. "Why?"

Mom drummed her fingers on her arm as if she were bored, but her eyes flicked nervously across the wall.

"Was he buying your silence?" I pressed. "You got to have your affair with him but you couldn't let anyone know?"

She opened her mouth a little, but she didn't respond.

"It couldn't have been very much," I said. "We lived paycheck to paycheck."

Finally, she shrugged. "I saved it."

"For what?"

She pinched her lips together, resuming her silence.

"Is that how you've been paying for your treatment?" I asked.

"My insurance pays for my treatment."

"Right," I said. "But you told me you pay for your own insurance— and since you don't have an income, that's never made any sense to me. Is this how you've been able to afford it?"

Her eyes crept toward me. "I'm tired of this conversation. Give me back my box."

"No." I picked up the box and held it to my chest, protecting it as Mom took a few steps and reached out her hands. I was close to something—I could feel it. There were tremors of it in the air, beckoning me closer, or warning me to turn back.

"Does he still send you money?" I asked.

She dropped her arms. "What?" There was genuine surprise in her voice. "No."

"Yes, he does. He has to be. That's how you keep affording everything."

"No, he doesn't! I told you already, I saved everything he ever gave me. And anyway, why would he send me money now, huh? He's had no reason to for a very long time."

"Why not? Because the affair's been over since Persephone died?"

There was a beat of silence before she responded. "Yes."

She was lying—or, at the very least, withholding. There was something I was still missing. I could almost make it out; it pulsed beneath her skin like a vein.

"So he really hasn't given you a single dime since . . ."

The rest of the sentence crumbled in my mouth. I clamped my lips shut, holding the words tightly between my teeth. Then I swallowed them, sharp as a jagged crust of bread. I was struggling to put it all together, but every part of it was blurred. Will had sent my mother money for years, and had only stopped when Persephone died.

"Oh my God."

I was forgetting how to breathe. I couldn't get my chest to expand or contract.

"Oh my *God*."

"Sylvie, please . . ."

"He's her father, isn't he? Will Emory is Persephone's father."

As I looked her in the eyes, I drank the air in shaky, uneven gulps. Silence spread through the space between us, and I watched as she walked toward Persephone's bed, her steps like an old woman's. Easing herself onto the blue quilt, she sat down without a squeak or groan from the decades-old mattress.

Then, finally, in a voice as creaky as a coffin being pried open, she answered, "Yes."

26

"Oh my God."

"Please stop saying that."

"You never told us!" I cried, shooting up from my bed. "How could you—why wouldn't you—"

"I promised Will I'd keep it a secret," Mom cut in. "He was married when I got pregnant. Do you have any idea what a scandal like that would have done to him? It would have rocked his whole family, his whole career! He was already campaigning at that point. He was going to be the youngest mayor this town ever had. So he asked me to keep it quiet."

"And you agreed to that?" My voice was so shrill I barely recognized it. "You agreed to keep your daughter in the dark and accept his hush money?"

"It wasn't hush money! It was money for Persephone—child support, if you want to call it that. I was saving it up for her in a college fund, letting it accumulate interest. Really, Sylvie. Do you think so little of me that you honestly believe I'd blackmail him into giving me money to keep our secret? I loved him, and he needed this from me. I would have done it for free!"

"Persephone wasn't a *secret*, Mom. She was a human being. She was your fucking daughter."

"And she was *his*, too. He had a right to be part of that decision."

"No, he didn't," I spit out, shaking my head. "No, he did not have even an ounce of—"

I stopped, my mind pummeling off the track it was on and hitching onto another. *She was his, too*, she'd just said. But Ben was also his. And Ben and Persephone had been each other's. Ben had probably put his hand on her cheek when he kissed her, like he'd just done to me. He had probably run his fingers through her hair, grazed his teeth against the skin of her shoulder. And just as his tension and desire began to brim over, he must have pressed his hipbones against Persephone's, then drained himself into her, gasping and grunting for breath.

"Do you, do you have any idea what this means?" I sputtered. "Persephone—she—she *dated* Ben. She dated her—oh God, I can't even say it—her *brother*."

"Half brother," Mom corrected.

"Oh, well never mind, then, I guess that—"

I sucked in a breath. It hadn't even been an hour since I'd left Ben's house, since he'd brushed his lips against my cheek at the door, a gentle acknowledgment of what had passed between us—our bodies cresting and falling together on the bed, my legs clinging to his waist as I pulled him deeper and deeper inside me.

My heart was pounding when I asked my next question. "Mom," I started. "Is Will my father, too?"

"No," she said quickly.

"*Is* he?"

"No! Your father is a man named Eddie. I don't even know his last name. I have no idea where he lives or who he is really."

I watched her for a while, looking for the slightest tremor in her expression. Nothing happened, though, not even when I focused on the pulse that ticked in her temple, the dry skin at the corners of her mouth. She was telling the truth, I conceded—the bland, unpretty truth—and relief flooded my veins like a drug. But then, in just a few seconds, my anger snapped back into place, boiling me up inside.

"But Persephone *is* Will's," I said. "And so is Ben. And they were *together*. How could you let that happen?"

"Obviously I didn't know it was happening. I told her she wasn't allowed to see him."

"But you never told her why!" I fired back. "So she had no idea when she saw him . . . when she went out with him . . . that she—she—"

"I didn't know she was still seeing him! That's not my fault!"

"Yes, it is. It absolutely is."

She shook her head, her eyes darting back and forth across the rug between the two beds. Her forehead wrinkled; her mouth sagged at the edges.

"And you know it is," I added. "I can see it all over your face. You're not stupid, Mom. If she'd known he was her brother, then she never would have been sneaking out to see him. Which means she never would have been out the night that somebody killed her. You know that! You know it!"

Mom covered her face with her hands, shielding herself from my words. "Stop it!" she cried. "I know! I know! Jesus, just—stop, okay? I know."

Then, for almost a minute, she wore her palms like a mask, her breath muffled and raspy. I watched her, noticed the knobs of her knuckles—even larger now, it seemed, than just a few days ago—and I waited for her to speak again, my throat and wrists quivering with pulse. Finally, Mom dropped her hands into her lap, and I saw there were tears in her eyes, tears on her cheeks and chin.

"I never claimed to be perfect," she said, her voice all gravel. "I know I've made mistakes. Why the hell do you think I drink?"

I'd never heard her speak like this—acknowledging her faults, her addictions—and I grasped at the chance to flash a light down the endless cave of that subject. I wanted us to enter it together, even if it meant we'd never find our way out. I knew her question had been rhetorical, but I answered it anyway.

"Because you couldn't deal with losing Persephone," I said.

"Oh, I always knew I'd lose her," she scoffed. "I just didn't know how or when. But I couldn't—I *can't*—deal with the part I played in it."

She looked down into her hands, her fingers curling toward her palms like shriveling petals.

"What do you mean you always knew you'd lose her?"

She shrugged. "I lost her father. And even on nights when I had him, he was never really mine. It made sense that I'd lose her, too."

I narrowed my eyes. "How does that make sense?"

Mom clenched her jaw so tightly I could almost hear her teeth grinding together. Then, wiping at the tears that lingered on her cheeks, she said, "You don't know anything about the Emorys. About Will's father. He was ruthless. He did everything he could to make sure that Will stayed away from me and married someone else. If he'd ever found out Persephone was an Emory, who knows what he would have done to get her in his grasp."

I shook my head. "That doesn't make any sense. You said Will wanted Persephone to be kept a secret because she'd be a scandal to his family. And now you're suggesting they would try to take her from you?"

She let out a breath. "Both things were possible," she said. "It was possible that if the town knew about Will having a daughter with me, they would turn on him in a second. You know how Spring Hill is—all holier-than-thou types. I'm sure they'd be able to overlook it if the affair were with one of their own—but *me*? South Side Annie O'Leary? No way. They'd eviscerate him. They'd send a strict message that those from the north side of town do not sully their reputations by fraternizing with diner waitresses."

She paused to breathe again, taking the air in sharply, as if stringing together so many words had exhausted her.

"But it was also possible," she continued, "that, regardless of the scandal, Richard Emory would want his granddaughter. That he wouldn't be able to stand the idea of an *Emory*—someone from such a *godly* bloodline—slumming it with the likes of me. That he'd find some way to portray me as an unfit mother, bribe or blackmail the right people, and take her away from me. And obviously I couldn't let that happen. I couldn't let Persephone live with *Richard*. It would have been like sending her to the Underworld!"

My mouth was open, ready to respond, but at the mention of the Underworld, I froze. *She said he wasn't good enough to be her child's father,* Jill had remembered Mom explaining about the man she'd met in her classics class. *So she was rescuing Persephone from a life in the Underworld.*

"Did Jill know about this?" I demanded. "About Will being Persephone's dad?"

I braced myself for the possibility that Jill might have lied to me. It seemed so unfathomable; she'd always been honest with me about everything. Still, Jill was an O'Leary woman. She would know how to keep her sister's secrets.

"No," Mom said. "Jill thought it was someone from college. I told you, I couldn't tell anyone."

"Not even your sister?"

"Especially not my sister! You know Jill. If I'd told her, she'd have barged right into the situation and tried to fix everything. But she'd only have done more harm than good. Just imagine if she told Richard to stay away from the baby! He'd have snatched Persephone up in an instant."

I crossed my arms over my chest. "Come on," I said. "He wouldn't have taken her."

"Yes, he would have!" she cried. "Will told me so himself!"

I paused. "What?"

"He told me that if his father ever found out, Richard would do anything he could to make sure I never saw Persephone again."

I felt my skin flush, my pulse quickening again. "He was lying to you," I said. "Manipulating you. He would have told you just about anything to make sure you didn't screw up his career. I mean—just—think about this, Mom!"

"I *have* thought about it! I spent every day of Persephone's childhood thinking about it. You have no idea what it was like—especially those first few years. Every time the doorbell rang, I was terrified it was Richard—that he'd found out somehow, and he'd be there on the front steps with some fancy court order in his hands. Every time a car slowed down in front of our house, I was sure it was one of Richard's people spying on me. When Persephone was a baby, I couldn't—I wouldn't even take two steps from her in the grocery store for fear that Richard would pop up out of nowhere and snatch her from the cart!"

"That's ridiculous," I said. "You were her mother. You had rights. This was just Will messing with your mind. You have to see that!"

She whipped her head from side to side. "My rights meant nothing. You don't know what Richard did—what he must have done—to get Will away from me. Will would never have picked that—that *woman* over me, not if he'd had a choice. Richard did something—blackmailed him in some way. He—"

"You think he blackmailed his own son into marrying someone else and having a child with her? Mom, I'm sorry, but you're just being paranoid."

"No, I'm not. It's what happened, Sylvie. It's how he was. Richard took Will away from me, and if he found out the truth, he would have taken Persephone, too. Will would *never* lie to me about something like that."

She took a deep, ragged breath, the air hissing in her throat. "So that's why we kept it a secret. We weren't just protecting Will. We were protecting Persephone."

"Maybe *you* were. Because Will had you all twisted up about everything. But Will wasn't protecting her. Protecting her would imply that he actually cared about her, but obviously he didn't. He never even *tried* to have a relationship with her."

"Goddamn it, you're not listening. He didn't have a relationship with her *because* he cared about her! Fuck, Sylvie, I barely had a relationship with her because of how much I cared about her!"

My blood seemed to stall for the briefest of moments. "What are you talking about?" I asked.

Mom shook her head, her eyes shining with fresh tears. "I loved her more than anything in this world. She had both of us in her. She was proof of how deeply we loved each other."

When she blinked, a tear raced down her cheek. She cleared her throat, the sound like a cold car attempting to start.

"But I couldn't get too close to her," she continued. Then she looked up at me, her eyes wide and frantic. "I couldn't get too close to her just to *lose* her someday. I'd already gone through that once with Will. I couldn't survive it again. I had to—I had to watch her carefully, but I had to keep her at arm's length, too. I just, I never imagined I would lose her the way I did."

She lifted a finger to her chin, catching a tear on her knuckle. Then she wiped at her nose.

"Do you have any tissues in here?" she asked, looking around, but I was too stuck on what she'd said to answer.

I had to keep her at arm's length. When I pictured it, I saw Mom's hand on Persephone's shoulder, her arm stiff as it stretched out as far as it could go between them. It was just an expression—"arm's length"—but the image in my head felt right somehow, felt true. How many times had I burrowed into Mom on the couch, while Persephone sat alone in a chair? How many times had Persephone announced an accomplishment—that B+ on her English paper in high school, or her citizenship award in middle school—only for Mom to steamroll over it with something I had done, something I had achieved? How many times had Persephone told me we had two different mothers, or that Mom must have loved my father because of how much she clearly loved me? But now, Mom was insisting it was the opposite: it was Persephone's father she had loved beyond reason; it was Persephone who was the daughter—and here, a lump formed in my throat—she had cherished the most. Because of what she symbolized. Because of whose she was.

My mind flashed to Persephone's letter, the ease and candor with which she'd recounted her pain to Ben. *Shitty mother*, she'd written. *All that stuff with my shitty mother*. And I'd painted birds on her collarbones, clouds on her wrists. I'd covered up the bruises, turned them into teacups and trees and planets, and all the while, I never knew them for what they were—symptoms of the ache and loneliness no paint could ever cure.

How much of Persephone's relationship with Mom had I missed? How many small but accumulating hurts and dismissals had I filtered out over the years, swathed, as I'd been, in Mom's arms? How many times had Persephone watched us together and felt her skin grow cold? How much of the warmth I'd basked in had actually been real, and how much had been reallocated from love belonging to Persephone? Love Mom wouldn't allow herself to show. Love she kept, like a dangerous animal, at arm's length.

"Arm's length, huh?" I said now. "How'd that work out for you?"

She looked down at the floor and shrugged. Then she closed her eyes, and a tear dripped onto her lap.

"I wonder—" She shook her head. "I don't even know if she ever knew how much I loved her."

I watched her face, saw how her skin looked suctioned to bone, and I thought of how all the secrets she'd kept—who she'd loved and how much—had led Persephone to the place she'd ended up.

"She didn't . . ." I started to say.

Mom looked up at me, her eyes almost hopeful, as if she expected me to continue the sentence with something that would ease her guilt and pain. But instead, I said something terrible, something true, and a part of me—so removed from the part whose instinct was to protect her—hoped it would shatter her into shards.

"She didn't know you loved her."

27

I was counting the tiles on the floor of Mom's treatment room, and every time I got to ten, I looked toward the door, searching for Ben. I kept expecting every nurse that walked by to be him, but so far, he hadn't appeared. *Eight and nine and ten*—and it wasn't his tall frame filling up the doorway, wasn't his scar on the cheeks of the faces that passed. *Eight and nine and ten*—and the hours moved along, slow as the drugs that dripped into Mom's bloodstream. *Three and four and five*—and I glanced at Mom, saw her squeezed-shut eyes wringing out the light.

She hadn't spoken to me at all that morning, but I kept looking at her in her chair, her head tipped back, her lips dry and slightly parted. I even opened my mouth a couple times to apologize for what I'd said the night before, but then I clamped my teeth together, recalling all her secrets and everything they'd done.

I had to see Ben. *Eight and nine and ten*. He needed to know who Persephone was to him. I'd barely slept all night, filled with the urgency to tell him, to rewrite a history already dictated by pain. He would lose her all over again—lose whatever sacredness still colored his memories of their relationship—but he had to. He had to know. *Eight and nine and—*

My cell phone vibrated with a call, and for a second, I assumed that it was him. It was Lauren, though, and I shook my head, remembering that I'd never even given Ben my number.

I glanced at Mom, snoring gently beside me now. Then I looked back at my phone and sent the call to voicemail. I knew I needed to talk to her—I owed my best friend that much—and after my conversation with Ben the night before, I thought I might even be able to. But Mom's treatment room, the hospital itself, wasn't the place, and right then, I had only enough energy to devote myself to one difficult task.

I stood up and walked out of the room. I didn't see any nurses in the reception area, so I approached a woman at the front desk and waited as she wrapped up a conversation on the phone.

"Thanks for your patience," she said a minute later. "How can I help you?"

"Hi," I said. "I'm looking for Ben Emory."

"Hey."

A rush of warmth shot across my chest at the sound of his voice behind me. He'd startled me, I told myself—that's all it was—but when I turned and saw he was already smiling at me, my sternum felt lit up from inside. I raised my hand to my chest, trying to rub away the sensation.

"I found him," I said over my shoulder to the receptionist.

I heard her chuckle and then Ben's fingers wrapped around mine, tugging me away.

"I'm glad you're here," he said after we'd taken a few steps. He let go of my hand, the smile still stretched out on his face. "I was actually going to call you tonight, but then I realized I don't have your number."

Part of me wanted to laugh, having had the same realization only minutes ago—but the other part, which had no patience for bones that felt lit up inside, got right to the point.

"I need to talk to you," I said.

"Okay." Ben nodded. "Go ahead."

"No, I—" I looked around. "Not here. Can we get together after you get off of work?"

"Oh, sure. Of course. And actually—the reason I was going to call you is because I want to show you something."

I winced. "I don't think I can handle any more letters."

"No," Ben said, smiling again. "This is a good thing, I promise. Do you want to come over tonight? I'm done here at six."

Was it the light in the room or were his eyes just a simple shade of brown? I'd looked right into them several times over the last week, but in that moment, I couldn't see them as the impossibly black color they'd always been.

"Yeah." I swallowed down the thought. "That sounds good."

"Great," Ben said. "I can even whip something up for us, if you'd like. I can't promise it'll be better than frozen pizza, but—"

"No," I cut in. "That's okay. I'll just eat before I come."

His expression slackened, as if disappointed, but I couldn't let him plan a meal for us, imagining it as some sort of date, only for me to show up and destroy him. It would be too cruel—and after everything that had happened, everything I'd learned, I knew now that cruelty was not a thing Ben deserved.

"Okay," he said. "Well, just come when you can, then."

"Okay," I agreed, and I spun around before I could see him walk away. Heading back toward Mom's room, I felt stiff and heavy with dread. After tonight, Ben would never remember Persephone the same way again, and it wasn't fair that the messenger had to be me. He should have always known. We all should have.

When I walked back into the treatment room, Mom's eyes were open. She stared at me as I took my seat beside her.

"Who were you talking to?" she asked.

I looked at her, but her face revealed nothing—just a pale oval of bone and skin. I turned my eyes toward the doorway. There was no way she could have seen us from there; the view didn't reach that far. Still, there seemed no point in lying anymore. I was tired of it. I was so intolerably tired.

"Ben Emory," I said. "He works here."

Mom's mouth dropped open, but then she squeezed her eyes tightly and twisted her head away from me, leaning it back against the chair.

I felt no need to explain or apologize. I just looked at the floor—*eight and nine and ten*—and got back to counting tiles.

I didn't listen to the voicemail Lauren had left until Mom was back in her recliner at home, but by then it was too late.

"You're either at your mom's chemo," she'd said, "or you're still ignoring me. Either way, I'm leaving for work soon, but I'm out at seven thirty. You *better* call me back sometime after that." Then she'd softened her tone and added, "Oh, and Wolf Bro called Steve to complain about his last session. He's coming in today to discuss the issue with me—apparently the eyes don't look *beast*-y enough with the new shading—so at the very least, you're gonna want to hear that story. *If* I've forgiven you for ignoring me, that is."

It was just after seven when I got to Ben's, and I vowed to myself that I would call Lauren back as soon as I left. But for now, I was still carrying the weight of someone else's lies, and before I could feel unburdened enough to talk to Lauren about my own, I needed to tell Ben the unfathomable fact of who Persephone had been.

"Hey," Ben said when he opened his front door. "Come on in."

He was smiling at me again, and it was enough to make me hesitate. His expression should have been wary, not welcoming; he should have locked the door when he saw me coming. But he didn't know that yet, and I took a few extra seconds wiping my feet on the mat before walking inside, as if I could scrape off the truth.

"Can I take your coat?" he asked as he closed the door behind me.

"Uh, no, that's okay."

I didn't know how long I was staying—or, more accurately, I didn't know how long he'd want me to stay once I told him what I knew. If the situation were reversed, I'd ask him to leave immediately. Then I'd scream until the walls shook. I'd throw everything in the house to the floor.

"Okay," he said, sliding his hands into his pockets. "I have something to show you. Or—sorry, not show you—I'm giving it to you. I remembered it when you were talking to Tommy yesterday, and I was going to give it to you when we got back to my house, but then, honestly, I just forgot about it, after the letter, and everything."

I looked at my feet as my face flushed. "That's okay," I said quickly. "But can I just say my thing first?"

But he wasn't listening. He had walked into his bedroom and was now heading straight for his nightstand drawer. After a moment of watching from the doorway, I crossed the threshold and followed him into the room where, less than a day ago, we'd pressed our bodies together, desperate to feel something other than pain. I stopped myself a few feet from the bed, closing my eyes against the image of us—mouths on skin, fingers gripping hard. I willed the memory to dissolve, then forced myself to picture Persephone instead, her blonde hair trailing down her back as she got into Ben's car night after night.

Snapping my eyes open, I looked toward Ben, hunched over the nightstand, blocking my view.

How was I going to say it? I'd tried to rehearse it on the way over but I still didn't know where to start. I could keep it simple—*Ben, Persephone is your sister*—but how could he take that seriously? And if I told him, instead, the story of how I'd found out, would he even be able to follow? Or would the words become only syllables, and then only sounds?

"Got it," he said, turning toward me. He held his hand up in the air, palm toward the ceiling. Squinting into the space between us, I tried to translate the gesture—and then I saw it. At first I only noticed the delicate chain that dangled from his fingers, but as my eyes followed that down to the pendant hanging at the bottom, my pulse flickered.

It was the gold starfish swinging like a pendulum from his hand.

My eyes stretched wide. "Where did you get that?" I demanded.

Something flashed across Ben's face—satisfaction, maybe, or anticipation—and I saw he was still smiling at me. "I've had it since she died," he said.

My breath became shallow, the room teetering. I managed to take a couple steps backward. "No," I whispered.

"It's okay," Ben said, "you can have it. I didn't know until yesterday when you asked Tommy for it how much it would mean to you. But here—it's yours."

He held it out to me, his arm reaching through the air to close the gap between us. My feet continued to move backward, though the rest of my body felt frozen in place.

"Sylvie, what's wrong?"

The smile had faded from his face, but I could still see the ghost of it, lingering in the corners of his lips.

"It was you?" I murmured, my eyes glazing with tears.

He cocked his head to the side. "What was me?"

I spun away from him then, and in the fraction of a second before I'd fully turned around, I saw his eyes widen. When I yanked open the front door, I could feel him just behind me, his shoes thudding against the hardwood floor. I stumbled down the steps, fumbling for my keys in my coat pocket, and ran toward my car, his fingers brushing my coat as he tried to grab me.

"Sylvie, stop! Wait. Stop!"

I was almost there—just about to open the driver's side door—when he grabbed me by the shoulder and spun me around. His fingers dug into my arms like dead bolts locking into place, and he pressed my back against the car, his breath erupting in bursts against my cheek.

"What are you doing?" he asked.

I stared up at him. His eyes were blacker than I'd ever seen them, even with the light from his front door shining toward us. His pupils looked wildly dilated, like an animal about to pounce. I tightened my muscles, tried to wriggle free of him, but I couldn't move—his grip was that hard. Now, I could only stand there, helpless as Persephone once was, shaking.

But then, just as suddenly as he'd clasped onto my arms, he glanced down at his hands, and his mouth fell open. He let go.

"Sorry, I—" he started. Then he shook his head. "You're scared of me?"

"You killed her," I said, my voice husky with tears.

"What? Why would you say that? You know that's not true."

"You have her necklace. She was never without it. Ever."

"I—I know that, but—"

"She wasn't wearing it when they found her body. Which means that the person who has it was the last person to see her alive."

"No," Ben said, snapping his head back and forth. "No, no, no. You don't understand. I *found* the necklace. I didn't take it from her."

I heard a surge of voices then, not too far away from us. There were people, it seemed, just beyond the turn in the driveway back toward the main house. They were saying words I couldn't make out, words that sounded sharp and contentious. But I didn't care about that. Whatever it was, whoever was arguing, didn't matter to me then.

"You found it on her dead body!" I cried. "After you killed her!"

"No," he protested, looking back toward his father's house, the source of the sudden commotion. "No, I—" He thrust his eyes back onto mine. "I found it in my driveway. Right after she went missing. I was shoveling and I found it there, under the snow. I almost—"

"—*and your secretary's been giving me the runaround all fucking day.*"

"I almost shoveled it away."

"*I won't be ignored like this!*" the voice insisted. It was louder now, practically shouting, the boom of it echoing toward us.

"Why would it be in your driveway?" I demanded.

"I don't know." He glanced toward the voices again. "But I told you how we were fighting, how she was kicking all around, going nuts. It must have fallen off her then. And I don't know, I guess it fell out of my car some point after that."

"But—the police," I said. "I told them to check to see if you had it."

"They did."

"And?"

"And," Ben said, "I lied to them."

"*I need more. I didn't sign up to be harassed like this. People knocking on my door.*"

"They didn't ask me about the necklace until a couple weeks after her body was found," Ben continued. "And she was my girlfriend, Sylvie. It was her *necklace*. I wasn't just going to give it to them so they could—I don't know—hold it as evidence forever, or somehow use it as evidence against *me*. But, listen, if I'd known how much it meant to you—and I should have, I should have known—but I was nineteen and so stupid and I was only thinking of myself, of what *I'd* lost. So I kept it."

"*Get off my property right now or I will call the police,*" a second voice shouted.

"*Yeah, you do that. Go call the police. I'd love to have a chat with them.*"

My head was reeling, the sky whirling in circles above me, but I couldn't ignore it any longer.

"What's going on?" I asked, looking toward Will Emory's house. It was a couple hundred feet away, beyond the bend in the driveway. From where we stood, all I could see was the glow from the spotlight over the garage.

"I don't know," Ben said. "But that's my dad, and the other one sounds like . . ."

He started walking down the driveway, and despite how I'd just run away from him, how I could still feel the grip of his fingers on my arms, I followed him.

"*Look, I'm willing to make an even trade. Just like old times. They left this stuff at my house yesterday. Then they hauled ass out of there and—*"

"*They?*"

"*Haven't you been listening to me? They were harassing me, asking me all these questions. I need more money if I'm gonna have to deal with shit like that from now on.*"

As we crept down the driveway, we stayed close to a row of evergreen trees, careful not to crunch too loudly over the snow with our feet. When we drew near enough to make out their faces—Will's face, Tommy's face—I was about to take another step forward, but Ben held his arm in front of me. He put his index finger to his lips, then gestured for me to follow him to one of the larger evergreens a few feet closer to where they stood in the driveway. We crouched down behind it, my heart thumping.

"I'm not your personal savings account, Thomas. I've told you this."

"Just look," Tommy said. "Look—it's her blanket or whatever."

Through the branches, I watched as Tommy opened a box—*the* box, I saw through squinting eyes, the one I'd brought to his house the day before, then stupidly left behind when Ben dragged me out the door. I hadn't really thought about it—there had been too many other things tugging me this way and that—but now, seeing it in Tommy's arms, I could barely breathe. He pulled out a single corner of Persephone's afghan, and my stomach lurched.

"See?" Tommy said. "I bet she used this all the time. Way more often than an old sweater or a dingy copy of some dumbass book—and you paid for all that shit no problem."

It took me a moment to catch up—I was still staring at the afghan— but as I began to process Tommy's words, I felt the nausea slither up my esophagus. I tried to swallow it down, but everything inside me was stiffening, my throat heavy and immobile as stone.

Will had Persephone's things. Tommy had said he'd sold them to someone who needed them more than he did. But why would Will have needed them? My mind raced through possibilities. Had Persephone's death made him feel guilty for ignoring his daughter during her life? Had he sought, too late, to know her through the things that had been hers?

I looked at Ben, whose face was contorted by confusion and surprise. Still in the dark about his dad's relationship to Persephone, he had no context with which to make sense of it.

"You're not supposed to just show up like this," Will scolded. "There's a procedure."

"Yeah, well, fuck the procedure, because I called your secretary all day and she gave me nothing but bullshit. And I'm so sick of your rules. That was great and all when I needed a lawyer, or a place to live, or even back when it happened, but you know what I realized? I hold the fucking cards, and they're all coming up aces."

"Oh, is that right—you hold the cards?"

"Yep."

"Okay, let's call the police, then, shall we? I'll tell them how you're trespassing on my property, and then you can tell them . . . whatever it is you want, and we'll see who they believe—the mayor, or a convicted sex offender."

"They'll believe me," Tommy said, but there was something in his voice now that sounded unsure.

"All right, then," Will said. "Do you want to call or should I? Because to tell you the truth, you've never been anything but a headache, Thomas, and I'd be happy to see you arrested again. I only gave you money when it happened because you were so easily bought. Such a bargain. But I guess that's what happens when you never have any money—you have no idea what things are actually worth."

Will took a step toward Tommy, and his eyes, blacker than his son's, glinted in the light.

"You could have drained me of millions," he continued. "Although, at a certain point, I would have just found other ways of dealing with you, I suppose."

"Bullshit," Tommy spat. "I see what you're doing—you're trying to scare me—but I'm not afraid of you. I know you're not a killer."

"I'm not?"

"I saw your face that night. You were fucked up about it. Snot running down your nose. Crying all over her. Begging her to 'wake up, oh God, just please wake up,' even as you were dumping her on the ground. It was pathetic. You're not a killer. It was just what you've always said. You were pushed too far."

"I'd be careful, Thomas. I'm feeling a little pushed right now."

"Dad," Ben said. He stood up from behind the tree and walked toward his father. At the same time, as if we had choreographed the move, I followed him, my body in step with his as we stomped onto the driveway.

Tommy startled when he saw us. The box slipped from his hands, and I grabbed it.

Will, too, looked shaken, the fierceness in his expression now replaced with unmasked surprise. "Ben," he said, and then, looking at me, his eyes narrowing in on mine, he added, "You. What are you two doing—spying on me?"

"What are *you* doing?" Ben demanded. "What *did* you do?"

"I don't know what you're talking about."

"Cut the shit, Dad," Ben said through his teeth. He took a step toward his father, and even through his sweatshirt and jeans, I could tell that all the muscles in his body were tensed. "Please tell me you didn't do it."

"Do what?" Will asked. "You're babbling, son."

"Tell me you didn't kill her."

The air in my lungs solidified. I managed only the thinnest breath.

"Kill who?" Will asked. "That—that girlfriend of yours? Really, Ben, it's been *years*. You have to move on from that."

Ben grabbed Will by the shoulders and pushed him against the garage door. I heard Will's back slam against the wood.

"Take your hands off me, son. Right now," Will said.

His voice was as cold as I knew the air should have been—but I couldn't feel anything, not even my own body. I could only watch as the scene unfolded, as if I were in the audience of a play, as if I could leave anytime I wanted to, and the story would end right there.

"Right now, Ben," Will said again.

There was a part of Ben that almost obeyed his father—a flicker in his arms that seemed ready to let go—but then, his back rippling with the force of the movement, he pushed Will harder against the garage.

"Did you do it?" he yelled, smacking his hand against the door, inches from Will's head.

Will winced, closing his eyes for a second, but he opened them again at the sound that spewed from Tommy. At first, it sounded like he was choking, but then, when I looked at him, I saw he was laughing—a textured, guttural noise.

Ben turned his head toward Tommy, still holding his father to the garage.

"What's so funny?" he snapped.

"I'm sorry, this is just—oh man." Tommy covered his mouth, but then his fingers slipped from his face when another snicker burst from his lips. His laughter condensed in the air, his breath vivid and white as it rushed right out of him.

"Fuck the money, okay?" he continued. "I changed my mind. I don't want it. This right here is priceless." He laughed again. "And—holy shit—so worth the wait. I mean, your *face*, Benji."

"Thomas," Will warned, but Ben tightened his grip on his father's shoulder, his eyes never leaving Tommy's face.

"Nah, don't 'Thomas' me. I'm done with that. I mean, he heard us, right? Cat's out of the bag now. Cat's meowing up a fucking storm." His laughter doubled him over, his hands clutching his knees. "Oh man. This is so—" Then he cleared his throat, straightening back up and attempting a serious expression. "No, but it is true. Your dad killed your girlfriend."

And just like that, I felt the cold again.

28

The air bit at my skin, my bones glazed with ice, my blood freezing in my veins. To move right then would have been to shatter, so I stayed rooted to the ground, only a thread of air spooling in and out of my lungs.

As Tommy broke into laughter again, Ben let go of Will, his arms going slack at his sides.

"I saw it happen, man," Tommy said to Ben. "I saw you leave with her, even after you dropped her off at her house. And it took me a while to find my mom's car keys—that bitch was always hiding them from me—but I followed you anyway. Or I tried to. Tried to figure out where you might have gone. I mean, it was so *weird*, you know? You dropped her off, just like you always did, but then she came *back* and you guys left together again. That wasn't how you usually did it. I wanted to know where you were going. Where you were taking her. She should have been off to bed, Benji."

He sounded angry, like a parent scolding a child for missing curfew.

"I couldn't find you," he continued. "I drove around for a while, but I didn't know what route you took. What I *did* find, though . . ." He looked at Will and licked his lips. "Well, that was so much more interesting. Mind you, it was too late for Persephone by then. But if it's any consolation, your dad really was very pathetic that night. He was sitting in the snow beside her, sobbing into his hands like a little kid. It disgusted me. I mean, if you're going to do something like that, then fucking *do* it. Don't sit around and be a crybaby about it."

He shook his head, a grimace pulling at his lips. Then he looked at me, and I stared back, unable to blink.

"For the record," he said, "I never wanted your sister dead. She and I were the same, okay? But when I saw that she was gone, I realized it made sense for her to die."

He cocked his stare back toward Ben. "She wasn't yours anymore, Benji. She wasn't yours to pick up and drop off and drive to the park where you kept her locked up in your car for hours every night." His smile slithered across his face. "That's right—I followed you more than once. I knew it was only a matter of time before Persephone realized you were nothing but a rich kid, sucking off your daddy's teat for life—and when she did, I'd be there to show her we were the same. Only—you were so possessive of her, weren't you? Staring me down as you drove past my house at night, like I had no right to stand in my own yard and look at whatever I wanted. Waiting for me at the bus lane—Jesus, dude, you'd already *graduated*, and there you were, back at school—just to tell me to stop sending her letters, as if you were the only one allowed to speak to her."

Tommy snapped his eyes toward me again. "So, by dying, see, your sister was finally free of this asshole. She didn't belong to him anymore. She didn't belong to anyone. By dying, she became even more like me—neither of us had anybody—and you know what? In the end, that made her more mine than she'd ever been his."

He chuckled. "But your dad," he said, turning back to Ben. "Oh my God—that night—I finally saw where you got your patheticness from.

Once he finally noticed me standing there, noticed there was another fucking car idling in the street behind his, he scrambled to keep me quiet. He explained the whole thing." He licked his lips again. "His dirty little secret. Well, actually—at first he tried to play it off like he'd just found her there, but I'm not an idiot, I could see the marks on her neck. His hands were shaking—like this—" He demonstrated. "So I told him I knew that he'd strangled her, and then *that's* when he told me."

"Told you what?" Ben asked, his voice low and steady.

"Why he picked her up in the first place. Why he stopped the car. Why he put his hands around her neck. He was so stupid, though."

Tommy looked beyond Ben to the tall, black-eyed statue behind him. "Weren't you?" he demanded. "I guess you were just trying to justify what you'd done, but—" He returned his gaze to Ben. "He was just giving me more ammo. And he realized that himself, soon enough. That's when he offered to pay me off."

Tommy snorted at the memory.

"We were both shivering out there—the snow's coming down, Persephone's getting whiter and whiter—and he's pulling hundred-dollar bills out of his wallet, telling me there's more where that came from."

He looked at Will again.

"Pathetic," he said. "I probably wouldn't have even told the police anyway. I know how cops are in this town. They're all—"

"Is it true?" Ben cut in, and though I could only see him in profile, I could tell that his eyes, staring at Will, were as arctic as the air.

Will looked at his feet for a moment, then lifted his chin to meet Ben's gaze. "No," he said. "This story he's concocted, it's ludicrous. He doesn't even—"

"Stop." Ben took a step toward his father, his voice measured. "I'm giving you one more chance to tell me the truth." I watched his shoulders rise as he took a breath. "Did you kill Persephone?"

Staring at his son, Will's face sagged, his iron jaw seeming to soften, but when he finally spoke, his answer was unchanged. "No."

Ben punched him in the face. I heard the sound of it—like a loud crack of ice—before I processed the swinging of his arm. Tommy's laughter continued, high-pitched, but as soon as Will straightened up, his hand on his jaw, I couldn't even hear it anymore. Will's eyes flashed with a rage so bright that Ben actually took a step back.

"You want to know why I picked her up that night?" Will asked, all pretense dropped. "Because of you. This is on *you*, Ben."

It seemed to take a moment for words to come to him, but when they did, Ben spit them out as if they burned his tongue.

"Why? Because I let her out of my car when I shouldn't have? Fuck you. I made a mistake, one that I will always regret, but that doesn't mean I'm—"

Will put a hand up in the air to silence him. Ben's immediate compliance suggested it was a gesture he was accustomed to obeying.

"That's not what I'm talking about," Will said. "I'm talking about your insubordination."

"My *what*?"

"I told you I didn't want you dating her."

"Are you serious?" Ben asked. "I was nineteen."

"That doesn't matter!" Will bellowed. "In my day, I listened to my father. Even when what he wanted was in direct opposition with what I wanted. That's what a son *does*. But you—" He paused, a look of disgust curling his upper lip. "You failed me. And when I saw her walking that night, I took the opportunity to set things right."

"Set things *right*?"

"She accepted my offer of a ride, and when she got in the car, I simply told her I would drive her home as soon as she heard me out. She was polite at first. Respectful. She listened when I explained that the two of you were from different worlds and it would never work out. She nodded along and seemed to understand my points—that staying with you now would only mean greater pain in the future, that you were meant for more and she would only keep you from achieving everything you were destined to. It seemed—for a little while, at least—that we were on the same page. But then she said, and I quote, 'Go fuck yourself.' Classy girl you had there."

Ben shook his head, his body vibrating with rage or horror or even just cold, and when he spoke, his words trembled, too. "So you just *killed* her?"

"Do you think I meant for that to happen? Of course not. But she tried to get out of the car, and I still had things to say—I couldn't just let her *leave*. And then I don't, I don't really know what happened. I sort of blacked out, I think—she was being so impossible—and the next thing I knew, I had my hands around her neck and she was just limp."

"And then you just left her!" Ben exploded. "You just dumped her on the side of the road, let people think she was missing for three fucking days. You saw I was in agony worrying about her. And you didn't say a word!"

"I didn't say a word because I knew it would kill you."

"Oh, really, which part? That my girlfriend was dead, or that my father killed her?"

"Neither," Will said. "That it was your fault. That if you'd just listened to me from the start and done what I said, she would have still been alive. I was trying to save you from that, son. Because I love you."

Ben stared at him, his mouth slightly parted. "No," he said quietly—and then louder. "No. This isn't you throwing the knife at me in a rage. This is you *killing* someone. And you're going to stand there and say you were justified in what you did—that it was actually *my* fault—just because you didn't want us to be together? Just because you're such a narcissistic fuck who couldn't stand that I was dating someone from the other side of town? God, this fucking family, I—"

"This family is all that we are! You have never understood that, and that's why you continue to waste your time working for an embarrassing salary at that hospital. You—"

"Tell him," I said.

Ben and Will looked at me, and it was clear from their expressions that they had both forgotten I was there.

"Tell him why you didn't want them to be together." My voice was stiff as it scraped against the cold. "The real reason."

Tommy laughed, a quick, satisfied jab of sound. "Guess you finally talked to your mother," he said.

Will swept his eyes over my face, an incredulous look warping his features. Something inside me relished his surprise, the ways he was coming apart. His silver hair, previously slicked back, now fell across his forehead, and I stared at the bruise already coloring his jaw.

"You know?" he asked quietly. Then, with a surge of anger, he thundered, "She *told* you?"

"No," I said. "Don't worry. My mother kept your little secret, just like you made her believe she had to. I discovered it on my own. Last night."

I turned to Ben, whose eyes were wide with an effort to understand. "I wanted to tell you," I said to him. "Tonight. That's why I came."

Looking back at Will, I saw a tinge of fear tucked into the sneer in his lip.

"Tell him or I will," I insisted—but still, he said nothing.

I took a deep breath. "Tell him what Persephone was to you," I said. "Tell him how you had the right to take her life. Because that's what you think, isn't it? Your children are yours to do with as you wish. What's a knife across a cheek, what are hands around a neck, if they're not listening to you, not doing what you command?"

"I don't—" Will sputtered. "I don't know what your mother told you, but—"

"My mother told me nothing. You got what you wanted. Persephone never knew. Ben never knew. This town never knew. But that's over now. Tell him why you did it. Tell him who Persephone was."

I looked at Ben. His eyes were focused on the ground, shifting back and forth as if reading something off the pavement, but I could see in his face that he was piecing it together.

"No," Ben said after a moment. "No, that . . ." He chuckled a little, but then grew instantly serious. "No." He raised his eyes to stare at his father. "That can't be true. Because if it were, you wouldn't have kept that a secret—how could you have—when you saw we were—No. No way."

But I could see in his eyes—which were everything and nothing like his father's—that he knew it was true. It was on Will's face, even as he seemed perched to deny it, and there was a part of Ben, I knew, that had always understood his father was capable of anything.

I walked away then, back up the driveway, and no one made a move to stop me. I could hear Will rushing to explain, to redefine—"*As usual, you don't understand, because you've never made a single sacrifice for this family. I couldn't possibly tell you, because if I told you, then you'd tell her, and then everyone would . . .*"—but his words quickly dissolved into static. I could feel myself beginning to buckle, and I knew I only had a couple more minutes before I completely broke apart.

It wasn't until I reached for the door handle on the driver's side of my car that I realized I was still holding the box Tommy had dropped on the driveway. I blinked at it, the loops of Mom's handwriting as recognizable to me as Persephone's or my own, then I took out the afghan and let the box tumble to the ground.

Wrapping the blanket around me, my face numb to what would have been the scratch of wool against my face, I opened my car door and slid inside. I could feel a sob building up inside me, ready to break the dam and let all my loss and grief and love and relief come flooding out, but I quickly swallowed it down. I had one more thing to do.

Pulling my phone from my pocket, I held Persephone's afghan tightly in place with one hand, and I used the other to look up the number I needed. When I found it, I pressed the button that would connect the call.

Someone answered on the second ring.

"Spring Hill Police," the dispatcher said.

"Hi." My voice, I heard, was on the edge of caving in. "I need to speak to Detective Parker. I have important information about the death of Persephone O'Leary."

29

Mom didn't watch the news—didn't subscribe to the paper, either—so she didn't see the front-page story, the breaking news on every local channel: "Spring Hill mayor arrested, charged with murder."

Will and Tommy had been taken away for questioning the night before, and I'd let Detective Parker drive me to the police station to make my statement. When we got out of the car, he ushered me to the same interview room I'd been in twice before. We sat down, he set up a recording device, held a pen over a notepad, and in a voice that sounded scuffed and skinned, I spoke.

Now, as I sat up in bed, groggy from a marathon stretch of what felt like blackout sleep, blinking at the diluted sunlight filtering through the blinds, I could barely remember what I'd said to him.

What I did remember was Parker's somber expression when he came back into the room after having excused himself for several minutes. He sat down, leaned forward a little across the table, and clasped his hands together.

"I've spoken to my partner," he said.

"Detective Falley?" I asked dimly.

"Uh, no. She—"

"Doesn't work here anymore," I finished for him. "Right. Sorry. I forgot."

"It's okay," he said, waving away my apology. "Detective Hartwick is my partner now. He was at the scene tonight. Anyway, Ben Emory is corroborating your story."

"My story?" My voice was small and far away, like it came from someone in another room.

"Your version of what you heard tonight," Parker clarified. "Now, when it comes to incriminating statements made by family members of the victim, it doesn't always hold a lot of weight in court—for reasons I'm sure you understand."

I didn't.

"But when you've got the alleged murderer's son backing up everything you said," Parker continued, "that's a different story." He leaned back in his chair and folded his arms over his chest. "It's still only testimony, though. And listen—I believe you—I believe what you and the younger Mr. Emory said you heard tonight." He scratched his cheek and looked at the wall behind my head, as if unable to meet my gaze. "But we're still lacking direct evidence, and that could be a problem."

I felt my eyes expand, an old fear instantly resurrected.

"Now, with both of your statements," Parker rushed ahead, "we have enough to arrest Mr. Emory. But I want to warn you about the possibility that it may not stick. He'll be arraigned in the morning, and more than likely, he'll be able to post bail immediately." He changed his tone then, seeming to notice the panic on my face. "But that doesn't mean we won't try."

In the silence that followed, I felt tears begin to spill over onto my cheeks, wetting the salt that had dried there from tears I'd already cried.

When Parker spoke again, his voice was gruff but sincere. "I want to see him pay for this just as much as you do. I promise, Ms. O'Leary, that I will do my best for you and your sister."

"And my mother," I added. Even after everything, the words slipped out of my mouth like instinct, like breath.

Parker flicked his eyes toward mine and nodded. "And your mother."

And now, I would have to do my best for her. I had asked Detective Parker to let me be the one to tell Mom, but when I'd finally left the police station, fetched my car from Ben's and somehow driven it home, I hadn't trusted myself to speak to her. Instead, I'd shuffled past her closed door and crashed onto my bed. I'd been certain then, even as sleep tugged at my eyes and eased the ache in my muscles, that I'd be clearheaded enough in the morning to do it right.

So now I had to do it. I had to tell her that the man whose love she'd worn like a lead cape on her back was the same man who'd stolen her daughter, who'd plunged her entire life into darkness. I had to hold back my fury, keep myself from screaming that her relationship with Will was the root of our relentless pain. After all, I reminded myself, planting my feet onto the floor, if it hadn't been for that love embedded in my mother like a tick, I never would have had a sister in the first place. I never would have known the compromises I was capable of making.

So I had to be better than I wanted to be, better than I really was. The truth, I knew, would punish Mom enough.

Walking toward the door, I caught my reflection in the dresser mirror. My eyelids were swollen, my cheeks puffy, my hair matted against the side of my head. Shadows crouched beneath my eyes like bruises, and my lower lip looked bitten and chewed.

I moved closer to the glass, examining the shape of my nose, the curve of my chin, but it wasn't until I traced my jawline with my finger that I knew what I was looking for. Will's face the night before had been granite-hard and impenetrable, but thinking of it now, remembering the features that had been spotlighted by the bulb over the garage, I could see Persephone in it. Her blonde hair, gray eyes, and pointed chin were Mom's, but her nose—the sharp slope of it—was Will's. Her lips—their fullness like ripened fruit, their Cupid's bow—were Will's. Even her skin tone, like sunlit sand, seemed borrowed from him. It was a wonder I'd never noticed it before.

Scrutinizing my own features, I turned my head to look at every angle of my face, searching for even the slightest resemblance to Will. Mom had sworn he wasn't my father, and I'd believed her at the time, but it was possible, I realized now, that she was still protecting him. It was possible that—

A sound came from the living room that snatched my attention away from the mirror. I listened for it again, holding my breath, and when it came, I recognized it as Mom emitting a low moan before letting out a deep, echoing retch.

I yanked open my door and headed toward the living room. When I rounded the corner, I found Mom in her chair, holding a bucket to her chest as she leaned her head back, her skin slick with sweat. The room had a stale and sour smell, and I watched Mom close her eyes, groaning.

"Mom, what's going on? Should I call a doctor?"

I hadn't seen her like this since the day I'd come home late from picking up her medication. I reached for the phone on the table beside her chair, but she jerked out a hand, cold and moist, to stop me.

"I'm fine," she snapped. "It's just—" She stopped suddenly, then opened her eyes wide as she swallowed. I saw her throat move up and down in her neck. "It's just catching up to me. But I'm fine. It's already passing."

She pressed a palm into the arm of the chair and shifted her body, her other hand still holding on to the bucket. Then she looked me over, her eyes trailing from the top of my rumpled head, over the jeans and sweatshirt I'd slept in, all the way down to my sockless feet.

"What were you doing in there?" she asked.

"In where?"

"Your room." Her voice was laced with suspicion.

"I was sleeping," I said.

"It's the afternoon."

I looked at the sliding glass door, the dim light trickling through it, and I saw that she was right. I'd slept through most of the day.

"I had a rough night," I said.

"Well, maybe if you weren't so involved with Ben Emory, you wouldn't be having rough nights."

"I don't think you have any right to talk."

Mom set her lips into a firm line, looked into her bucket, and leaned her head back again.

"Why didn't you tell me?" she asked.

"Tell you what?"

"About Ben," she said, her voice brittle. "Working at the hospital."

The air pressed against me, and I slumped onto the couch, landing heavily against the cushions.

"I didn't want to upset you," I said.

"Oh, well, you did a great job."

"You know, can you just cut the sarcasm for, like, two seconds? You make it so difficult to talk to you about anything."

Mom narrowed her eyes at me but didn't speak, and I turned my head away from her, my gaze falling onto the wall that still, after all these years, remained a white sky to the metallic constellation I'd once painted. I could imagine a bomb going off, a fire swallowing up the whole house, and still, that wall would be standing, alone in the charred yard, Persephone's angry handprint gleaming like the stars she'd tried to wipe away.

"Why is that still there?" I asked.

I looked at Mom and saw that she was staring at it, too, her eyes a little gentler now. When she didn't respond, I continued.

"You got rid of everything Persephone ever owned, but you didn't get rid of the one thing that, to me, feels so much more like her than anything else."

"What do you expect me to do, Sylvie—tear down the wall?"

"I expect you to paint it. Why haven't you painted over it? She was *mad* at you when she wrecked the constellation. Why would you want to be reminded of that?"

She was quiet for a few moments, but her dry, parted lips seemed ready to respond. I pressed my teeth together, willing to wait her out, and when she finally answered me, her voice was soft as the sound of wind rustling grass.

"Because I have to be."

I hesitated. "You have to be what?"

"Reminded."

Her arm loosened around the bucket, her hand slipping into her lap.

"Why?" I asked.

"Because I deserve that," she said. "Don't you think?"

Her tone wasn't sarcastic, wasn't taunting or edged with any kind of malice. It seemed like an honest question—one I had no idea how to answer.

"Why do you say that?" I prompted.

She shrugged one shoulder. "You said it yourself, the other night— she didn't know I loved her. What kind of mother does that make me?"

She paused, leaving a space for me to respond, but when I didn't speak, she continued.

"The kind that deserves to be reminded," she answered for herself.

"Mom," I said. "I was angry when I said that. I had just found out that you'd—"

"I know what you were," she interrupted. "But I know that what you said was true. I've always known it. I just—" She looked back at the constellation, her eyes seeming to trace what was left of its stars. "I always tried so hard to be good to them."

"Them?"

"Your sister. Will."

At the sound of his name, my throat stiffened.

"I thought protecting her was the same as being good to her," Mom went on. "But I was wrong, maybe. I still don't know for sure. All I know is I got so caught up in all that protecting that I ended up protecting the wrong person."

"What do you mean?"

She looked at me sharply. "Me, obviously. I was so afraid of losing her that I pushed her away. I made that—" She gestured weakly toward the wall. "I made that happen. And, in the end, I lost her anyway— more than just physically—because, when I look back on my memories of her, they're all just . . ."

She closed her eyes, gripping the armrests, and after a wave of something—nausea or pain or guilt—seemed to rise and subside within her, she shook her head, letting out a breath.

"They're just her being mad at me," she said. "Or her reaching out to me, and me turning away."

She glanced down at the bucket in her lap, and with a look of revulsion, she picked it up and placed it on the floor.

"Mom," I started, "I have to tell you something. But first, I have to, I need to . . ."

Her eyes opened again, the gray of them like a shadow falling over snow.

I struggled to continue. "You said the other night that my father is someone named Eddie, someone you barely knew—and I believed you—but . . . I just need to know with absolute certainty that that's true, that Will is *not* my father."

Mom rolled her eyes. "This again," she said. "Of course he's not your father. I was never terrified of anyone taking *you* away, was I? That's why you and I were so close."

Her face changed then, quickly and starkly, her features going slack. It was as if she realized the vulnerability of her words, of mentioning something that neither of us had acknowledged out loud for a very long time. It was safer, somehow, to pretend that things had always been so broken between us. It hurt less to act as if we had no desire to go back to the way that things had once been.

"So you're positive, then," I said. "This Eddie guy was my father. Not Will."

"God, how many times are you going to make me say it? Will is not your father. He was furious with me when he found out I was pregnant with you. It hurt him terribly that I'd been with someone else."

"But—he was married! He had no right to be upset."

"That marriage meant nothing to him," Mom fired back.

I sighed. I didn't have it in me to argue with her anymore. We could go around and around in circles forever, and she'd never be able to see the past for what it had really been. Now, there was only one thing that could possibly save her from the inky depths of such a twisted love, and it was the same thing, I knew, that would destroy her.

"Mom," I started. "They've arrested someone for Persephone's murder."

Her head snapped upward. "What?" she said, sounding like someone who'd just been woken in the middle of the night. "Who?"

I took a deep breath and met her stare, which held my eyes in its grip. "Will," I said.

She squinted at me. "Will who?" she asked.

"What other . . . ? Will, Mom. Will Emory."

For a long while, she stared at me, her eyes unblinking, her expression blank as a gray winter sky. The clock ticked through her silence, time moving on while the two of us stayed frozen in our seats. I waited for what I knew would come—a sudden slump in her posture, tears in her eyes, something that would document the shock she felt as it punched inside her.

But when she finally spoke, her eyes were dry and her voice was the steadiest it had been in a while.

"That's a sick thing to joke about, Sylvie. Even for you. What the hell is wrong with you?"

"This isn't a joke, Mom. I promise you. I was there when he confessed."

"You're lying."

"I'm not. I saw the police take him away."

Her eyes narrowed, confusion spreading all over her face. "Well—it has to be some mistake, then. He's her *father*, Sylvie. Why the hell would he do such a thing?"

"Because he's the man that he is," I answered. "And I know you don't want to hear it, I know you might not be *able* to hear it, but he's not a good man, Mom. He's bad. He's really, really bad."

She shook her head, the wisps of her hair swishing through the air. "Stop it," she said. "Stop."

But I couldn't. I had to explain it to her. I had to tell her what he'd admitted—how he'd tried to reason with Persephone, and when that failed, he killed her. How it was as simple as that. And as I relayed his words, trying to remain as faithful to them as possible, I watched Mom's eyes, waiting for the tears that needed to fill them up.

"No," she kept saying as I poisoned the air with words that made it hard for us to breathe. But still, she didn't cry, her lips didn't tremble, her shoulders didn't shake.

When I finally finished, my throat was raw. I watched as Mom pinched her eyes shut and shook her head slightly, back and forth, back and forth. I waited for her to speak, but she just kept it up—back and forth, back and forth—until moments, or maybe minutes later, she went completely still.

I listened to the clock count away the seconds. I searched for any flicker of movement on her face, but she was immobile as a gravestone. Then, just when I thought she'd shut me out so completely that she'd managed to erase everything I'd just told her, her mouth opened.

"It was a mistake," she said quietly.

"What?" I blurted. "Mom, no, I just explained it all to you. He admitted it himself. He said—"

Her eyes opened, a soft but insistent plea fogging her irises.

"You said he hadn't planned to kill her," she said, "so that means he did it by mistake."

I was paralyzed, my wide eyes locked in place, my muscles completely unresponsive, but then, in a sudden rush, my breath spilled out of me, and I began to sputter.

"That—that's your response? You're fine with him killing your daughter as long as he didn't—didn't *mean* to?"

Her face didn't falter. Her expression was set in stone.

"Listen to me, Mom. Whether he meant to do it or not, he still covered it up for sixteen years. He lied to you."

"It isn't lying if I never asked him about it."

Her words shoved me backward. My throat creaked with attempts to speak, but only air came out.

"How," I finally managed, "how can you be *defending* him?"

"I love him," she said, as plainly as if she were stating her name or address.

"He killed Persephone," I said through clenched teeth.

She put her hand in the air like a shield. "I love him," she repeated, but her voice wobbled this time. "I love him."

She began to stand, her arms shaking with the effort of pushing against the chair. I felt no instinct to help her, to leap toward her and steady her. Instead, I watched her struggle, watched her rickety knees try to carry her weight, watched her nearly fall over as she reached for the bucket on the floor.

"I love him," she insisted, straightening back up, and I couldn't be sure if the sheen I saw across her eyes was a film of tears or a flash of light. "I love him, I love him."

Clutching the bucket to her chest, she turned away from me, and I watched her go, listening for the increasing rasp of her voice as it echoed those words: "I love him. I love him. I love him." Even as she disappeared down the hall, even as her bedroom door closed and the lock clicked into place, I could still hear her mumbling.

"I love him."

The words were becoming deeper and deeper—"I love him, I love him"—until they sounded like nothing more than a prolonged and agonized moan.

Then, finally, I heard a sob—low and cavernous, as if it welled up from the most buried part of her. And then it was two sobs, three sobs, four, one right after the other until it was too many to count.

I loosened with relief. Even as her pain thundered in my ears, I felt myself grow lighter, more buoyant, as if gravity were relaxing its grasp on me for the first time in years.

For a long while that afternoon, I sat on the couch, listening to my mother cry. At times, I even smiled, not at her sorrow or anguish, not at the fists I could hear beating against her bed. I listened to her sob so hard, so feverishly, that I imagined, the corners of my lips lifting, that the sobs might split her open, like a stem breaking through layers of darkness and soil into light.

30

That night, I called Aunt Jill to tell her everything I'd learned. I explained how Mom had been locked in her room since I told her, how she hadn't responded to my knocks at dinnertime, hadn't even come out for the plate of food I'd left in the hallway. When I finished speaking, Jill immediately started planning a trip to see us in a few days.

"No," I told her. "You should stay with Missy. She needs you."

"Carl's parents fly in on Tuesday. Missy and the baby will be fine until then."

"Yeah, but—"

"No buts. Nothing you say will stop me from showing up, okay? That's what family does, Sylvie. In times of crisis—or times of . . . unbelievable news—we show up."

I imagined it then—Jill at the front door, gathering me into a hug. The smell of her—cinnamon cookies and coconut lotion—would feel more like home than the house I'd been living in for the past couple weeks.

"How do you do it?" I asked, a tear wetting my cheek.

"Do what?"

"Bounce from person to person who needs you. You took care of me in high school, and spent years after that taking care of Mom. And now you're taking care of Missy and the baby and Mom and me, all at once. It's so much, Jill. I'd hate to think that you're sacrificing your own needs."

Jill sighed impatiently. "Oh, what do I need," she asked, "other than the people I love?"

I wiped at my cheek with my sleeve. "Well thank you," I said. "Seriously, thank you so much, Jill. I don't know how I ever would have—"

"Stop," she interrupted. "It's nothing. Now, let's hang up so I can text you a picture of the baby. She's sure to make you feel a little better."

And she was right. The picture that came in a few minutes later showed the baby wrapped tightly in a knitted blanket, her face poking out the top with wide, curious eyes. "Mallory Joy, our little potato," Jill had captioned it, and I laughed then, as effortlessly as breathing.

I stared at the picture for a little while longer, running my pinky finger over the baby's cheek. Then I took a deep breath, pulled up my list of contacts, and finally called Lauren back.

"You're lucky I'm even picking up at this point," she said by way of greeting. "And literally the only reason I am is because I have some news."

I was startled by the tone of her voice. Along with the impatience and frustration I'd been expecting, there was a note of excitement, too.

"Okay . . ." I said.

"And obviously we have a lot to talk about, but I've been dying to tell you this all day. Only—I promised myself that I wasn't gonna call you again until you called me. And yes, that sounds like something I'd say about a guy, but you're basically my wife at this point, so shut up."

"I wasn't gonna say anything."

"Okay, so . . . when I got into work this morning, Steve told me that some woman he knows is looking to hire a new tattoo artist at her parlor."

"Oh. And you're thinking of applying?"

"What? No, dummy. I already have a job. *You're* going to apply. Steve said he'd give you a *glowing* recommendation. Isn't that amazing?"

For a few moments, I didn't know what to say. The snap of the latex gloves against my wrists, the buzzing of the tattoo machine—they seemed like details from a movie I'd seen, not something I'd lived every day for the past several years. It was as if someone else had been in control of my life, telling my body what to do, my mouth what to say, and all that time, I'd just been hunched somewhere deep inside of myself, letting it all happen because it was easier and less exhausting than trying to live on my own.

Lauren barreled through my silence. "It's in East Providence," she added. "So, you know, gross—but at least you'll be doing what you love again, right?"

"Yeah," I said reflexively. "Right."

"What's wrong? Why aren't you more excited about this?"

"No, I am. But . . ."

"But *what?*"

"I'm not sure it's the right job for me anymore."

Actually, I knew that it wasn't.

"What are you talking about?" Lauren challenged. "Of *course* it's the right job for you. You're so good at it."

"Yeah, but I don't think I need it anymore."

"You don't *need* it anymore? What's going on? Did you win the lottery or something? Tap into some trust fund I don't know about?"

There was so much I would tell her, finally—and once I did, she would know what I meant. I no longer needed to watch a needle sink pigment into flesh, no longer needed to punish myself by reenacting what I'd done to Persephone, always seeing her arm instead of the client's, always seeing Ben's dark fingerprints instead of the blank canvas of the stranger's skin. Because I knew now that it wasn't me who deserved to be tortured by guilt and memory. I'd been fourteen years old—just a kid, as Ben had said—and none of what Will did to her that night had been my fault. Never mind the painted bruises, never mind the window I'd locked up tight. There'd still been a man—not a kid, but a full-grown man—who had used his hands as a noose around his daughter's neck, who had squeezed and squeezed until she—

My throat burned as I pictured it.

But still, I had to keep remembering; it had been his hands, not mine.

"The truth is," I said to Lauren, "I've just been going through the motions with that job for a long time now, and I don't want to anymore. I don't know what I'm going to do next, and I'm not really sure *what* I love doing or what kind of job is right for me. But I feel free for the first time to figure out what it is."

There was a pause on Lauren's end. "Wow," she said. "You're being really serious."

"Yeah, well, it's been a serious couple of weeks. And I'm really sorry I took so long to return your messages."

"Oh yeah," Lauren said dryly. "That."

"But you know what?" I continued. "I'm actually glad I didn't talk to you about it before now. Because I didn't know the whole story then. And you're my best friend, Lauren. You deserve to know the whole story."

She was quiet for a few moments, and I could hear her breathing against the phone. "You're talking about your sister now," she said.

"Yes," I replied. "Persephone. And if it's all right with you, I'd like to tell you all about her."

The next morning, I stood outside Mom's room holding my phone. I put my ear to the door, listening for a sound to confirm she was awake, and even though I heard none, I knocked.

"Come in," Mom said after a moment.

When I tried the doorknob, it turned easily, and though the curtains were still closed, Mom's light was on. She was sitting up in bed, a box of tissues in her lap.

"Hi," I breathed.

"Hi."

She was wigless and scarfless, her head all skin and skull, but she was up. She was speaking. She'd let me inside.

"Aunt Jill sent a new picture of the baby," I said, stepping toward her. "Can I show you?"

Mom hesitated, her eyes swollen and uncertain, but then she shrugged. "Okay."

I approached the side of her bed and held the picture up. She surprised me then by moving over a few inches so there was room for me to sit beside her. As the mattress creaked beneath our shared weight, she took the phone from my hand.

"Look at the caption," I said.

She didn't laugh or even smile as she read it, but her eyes softened a little. She used her fingers to zoom in on the baby's face, and then, quietly, she gasped.

"She's so pink," she said. "Just like Persephone when she was born."

I looked at the side of her face. "Really?" I said.

Mom nodded. "You were always so pale." She spoke without moving her eyes from the picture. "Like a sheet of paper held up to the light. And that was pretty, too. But Persephone . . ."

Her lips lifted slightly, the promise of a smile budding on her face. "She was the most beautiful pink I've ever seen."

I spent some time that afternoon tending to the driveway and front steps. A coating of snow had fallen overnight, and when I came back inside from clearing it, I saw I had a voicemail from an unfamiliar number.

"Hi, Sylvie," the caller said, a wary tinge to her voice. "It's Hannah Falley. I'm sorry to just call you like this, but I saw the news, and I spoke to Detective Parker, and now, I don't know, really. I just wanted to say . . ." She cleared her throat. "I'm sorry we never figured it out. We just didn't know to look at him. We should have. I want you to know we never dismissed what you said back then. But he just didn't seem connected in any way, other than being Ben Emory's father, so we missed it. And that's on us."

She made a soft chuckling sound, one without any humor in it at all.

"I mean, Tommy Dent pointed us right there, didn't he? 'Talk to the mother, talk to the mother.' And now that I finally know what he meant, I keep thinking: maybe if we'd just hit harder when we asked your mom about Persephone's father—who he was, how long since he'd been in the picture, all that—she would have told us the truth about your sister's paternity. And then we would have had reason to look closer at Will. And then . . ."

She sighed. "Anyway, I just called to say I'm so sorry I didn't catch it. But I'm glad you finally know. I hope this can be the start of some healing for you and your family. So take care, Sylvie, okay?"

For a while, I listened to the silence that followed Falley's message. I stood in the middle of my room, staring at the wall, and when I finally pulled the phone away from my face, its screen was black. Pressing the home button, I watched it light up with my new lock screen photo, the one of a bundled-up Mallory Joy, and I savored the sight of her—how new she was, how beautifully unwounded—until a tap on my bedroom window startled me into dropping the phone. It thudded against the rug as I whipped toward the glass.

Ben's face peered in at me.

"Jesus!" I breathed. And for just an instant, I saw him the way I used to, nights when he'd creep toward our window, waiting for Persephone to finish getting ready. I saw the scar on his cheek and felt that same old instinct to shudder.

But then I took a deep breath, unlocked the latch, and thrust the window open.

"What are you doing here?" I whispered, careful to keep my voice from reaching Mom in the living room.

"Sorry," Ben whispered back. "I'm sorry. I needed to see you, but I still don't have your number, and I didn't want to go to the door, just in case your mom . . . And so I went to the window to see if you were in your room, but then I saw you were on the phone, so I waited, and now I'm just beginning to realize how stalkerish I'm being. Shit. I'm sorry."

His cheeks reddened, and though I didn't know if it was with embarrassment or cold, my hesitation was brief. Waving him inside, I put a finger to my lips in warning as he hoisted himself through the window. I crossed the room to lock the door, and when I turned back around, he was already standing on the rug between the beds.

"That's a lot harder than it looks," he whispered, gesturing toward the window. "Persephone made it seem so easy."

"Persephone was an eighteen-year-old girl," I reminded him, walking back across the room to close the window and shut out the cold. "Now what are you doing here?"

"Right," he said, and he reached into his pocket. Pulling out his hand, he revealed Persephone's necklace in his palm. For a moment, the starfish caught the sun and winked.

"With everything that happened the other night," he said, "you never actually ended up taking this. But I still want you to have it." He stared down into his hand. "I think Persephone would want that, too."

Letting the chain dangle from his fingers, he held the necklace toward me, the same way he'd offered it at his house on Wednesday.

"I've been thinking about it," Ben whispered, "and I think it must have been in my dad's car that night, not mine. I think when he . . ."

He pressed his lips together and shook his head. "Maybe it fell off in the struggle. Maybe it was caught in his sleeve or something and it fell into the driveway when he got out of the car. So you might end up wanting to give it to the police as evidence, I don't know, but I wanted that to be your—"

"Ben, I'm sorry," I cut in.

Meeting my eyes, he cocked his head to the side. "For what?"

I sat down on the edge of my bed, gesturing for him to do the same.

"For accusing you the other night," I said as he settled down beside me. "For freaking out and running away before you had a chance to explain. I feel really stupid about that, especially given what happened after."

Ben reached for my hand, and for a second, I thought he was going to hold it. Instead, he flattened my palm, dropping the necklace onto it. The gold shimmered against my skin, and I marveled at how light it felt. All these years, I'd imagined it so much heavier.

"Don't worry about that," Ben said. "I get why you freaked out. But now we know." Even though he was already whispering, his voice grew quieter then. "We know for sure what happened."

I nodded. Closing my fingers into a fist, I felt the points of Persephone's starfish press into my palm. I looked at Ben, and the scar on his cheek was like the line of a mountain range on a map.

"How are you doing?" I asked.

His eyes were focused on my window.

"I'm okay," he said. "I'm moving out of the guesthouse. I haven't found a new place or anything yet, but I took today and tomorrow off to try to make some headway."

He chuckled dryly. "The hospital's cutting me some slack. 'Take all the time you need,' my supervisor said. But I wouldn't be surprised if they try to fire me. Son of an alleged killer and all that. Sort of a PR nightmare."

"They won't fire you," I assured him.

He blinked a few times and then looked at me, his eyes drilling into mine. "I think that bastard is going to get away with it," he said.

I felt the pinch of my lungs as I stopped breathing. Then, the air hitching between my lips, I asked, "Why do you say that?"

Ben shrugged and looked back toward the window. "I haven't talked to him," he said, "but I hear he's hired this whole team of lawyers. Some high-profile firm. And Tommy—well, suddenly this fancy attorney blows into town, offering to take on his case pro bono. But I bet my dad's tied up in that, too."

I gripped Persephone's necklace harder in my hand. "So Tommy's not going to testify against him?"

"Doesn't look like it."

The walls crept closer. The ceiling sagged toward our heads.

"Are *you* going to testify?" I asked. "I mean, I know he's your father, but—"

"That man is not my father," Ben declared. "Not anymore." He scratched his scar, scraping his nail slowly along the ridge of it. "Not ever, really."

As we sat in silence, I opened my fingers to glance at the starfish on my palm, and quickly closed them again. Then, Ben asked, "Is he yours?"

"My what?"

"Your father. Are we . . ."

"No. I asked my mom about that—twice, actually—and she insisted that he isn't."

"Well, good," Ben said. "Because that would be a little much, learning my dad's a murderer *and* sleeping with my sister, all in the same week?" He whistled so quietly the sound was mostly air. Then, as I lifted my eyebrows in surprise, he shook his head.

"I'm sorry," he said. "That was so inappropriate. I'm just not sure how to deal with all of this. It's so hard to even comprehend. I mean, first off—Persephone and I, we should have never been together in the first place, right? Someone should have told us the truth and stopped us. But, at the same time, it doesn't change the way I think of her, you know? If I remember her now, I still feel that same spasm of love, deep in my stomach. And then I feel sick about that."

I looked at him, saw the anguish and confusion in his eyes. Then I put my hand on top of his and squeezed. "Hey," I said. "It's only been a couple days since you found out. You just need time to process it all."

He stared down at my hand. "Time?" he scoffed. "Time has never been enough to make me stop loving her. It's been sixteen years, and I still haven't stopped." He sighed, his eyes scanning the back of my hand. "But maybe you're right, maybe now that I know, it'll be different."

He laced his fingers with mine and held my hand hard, his knuckles white, my own pinched and pressured. I winced at the pain of his grip, but I relished it, too. It made the ache in my lungs, my heart, my stomach—the ache I'd felt for days, or maybe even years—subside. But then I saw the danger in that, in trading one pain for another, and I slipped my hand out of his grasp.

He didn't fight it. He let me go.

"You don't have to stop loving her," I said. "I know I won't."

"That's different."

"It doesn't have to be. You were there for her, and I'm grateful to you for that. She deserved to have someone who understood her," I added. "We all do."

His eyes were unreadable as they shifted back and forth between my own. Then he nodded, blinking, and tears slipped down his cheek.

"I should go," he whispered, standing up. He took a couple muted steps toward the window before I stood, too.

"Wait," I said.

He turned around, slowly, as if the air were becoming too heavy for him to move through. "Yeah?"

"It's just—you know Tommy?"

He let out a short laugh. "I think I remember him, yeah."

"Right. Well, why do you think he kept telling the police—and telling us—that my mother knew something important? He was clearly hinting at Will being Persephone's father, but why would he point people in that direction? Your dad ended up bankrolling his whole life. He had a lot to lose if Will got arrested."

Ben took a deep breath and shook his head. "I don't know," he said. "I guess he just loved knowing something that no one else did. I mean, we were closest to Persephone, and we didn't have a clue. But maybe, maybe knowing this big, decades-old secret—it somehow proved to him that all that bullshit he'd said was true, about being the only one to actually see and know Persephone." He shrugged. "And it probably made him feel powerful for once, you know? He must have just thrived on showing that off, on taunting people with the fact that he knew something. I mean, think about his life. That ounce of power, or control, or whatever it was, probably meant a lot more to him than money. I know it always does for my father."

Ben shifted his feet, putting his hands in his pockets. "But speaking of Tommy," he said. "I found all the stuff he sold my dad. Persephone's stuff."

I stood up straighter. "You did?"

"Yeah. After I got back from the police station, I went inside the main house. I'm not even sure why. I guess I just figured my dad would be arraigned in the morning, and this would be the only chance I'd have to look around. I think I hoped I'd find something to help me reconcile the fact that my father murdered my . . ." He swallowed. "Anyway, I noticed that this room on the third floor—my mom's old office—was locked. And I kicked the door in. I didn't even know I was capable of that, but I just kept picturing his face as he said that what he did was all my fault, and it went a lot easier."

He paused, his mouth curling with a look of disgust, as if he were seeing his father in the room with us now.

"Anyway," he went on, "the room was filled with all these boxes. I opened one of them, and at first I didn't really know what I was looking at. Jeans, sweaters, stuffed animals. But then I saw a shirt that I recognized. It was that pink one, you know? With the gold stripes?"

My eyes closed around the image of Persephone standing in front of the mirror, holding her lip gloss up to the pink fabric, trying to see how well it matched.

"Yeah," I whispered, my throat stinging.

"So then I remembered what Tommy was saying when we first heard them arguing. And I searched through the rest of the boxes and every once in a while, I found something else I recognized."

A wave of dizziness spun the room around me. I closed my eyes, and when I opened them again, everything was still. "Why?" I asked. "Why would he want all of that?"

Ben shrugged, looking down at the space between our feet. "A part of me hopes it was guilt," he said. "Something that would make him just a little bit human. But I have no idea. And I've decided it's best not to wonder. Because I don't want to humanize him. I want to always see him the way I do right now. As a monster."

I nodded. I understood that feeling. How long had I held tight to the belief that my mother was beyond saving—just to make it easier to stay away? But she wasn't Will. She hadn't killed anyone. She'd simply swallowed her secrets like pills, then chased them with something she'd hoped would drown her.

"But listen," Ben said. "I took all that stuff back to the guesthouse. It's yours if you want it—unless the police end up taking it. You can come by anytime to go through it." He shifted his weight and put his hands into his coat pockets. "I mean, hopefully I'm moving out of there within the next few days or so, but I won't be far."

I tried my best to smile at him. "Thank you," I said. "And hey, let me give you my number, okay? That way, you can send me your new address when you know it."

He smiled back at me, weakly. "Your *number?*" he said. "I don't know, Sylvie. That feels like classified information at this point. Are you sure you trust me with that?"

His eyes—dark as a starless night, but deep, it seemed, as the sky itself—locked with mine.

"Yeah," I said. "I do."

On Saturday, I ran errands. When I returned home, Mom was just where I'd left her that morning—in her chair, wearing her robe and slippers. I brought my shopping bags into the living room and sorted through them, pulling out each item and setting them on the carpet. Then I split open the plastic that held a folded drop cloth and laid the canvas tarp across the floor.

"What are you doing?" Mom asked, eyeing me as I took a screwdriver to the lid of a paint can. "What's all this?"

"This," I said after a moment, mixing the paint and carefully pouring it into a plastic tray, "is our project for the day." I looked at the pool of color, milky and glistening in the light. "There were a lot of choices, but I went with Blossoming White. I'm not sure what makes it *blossoming* white instead of just white, but it sounds nice, right?"

"You're going to paint the wall?" Mom asked.

"No," I said. "*We* are."

She put her hand to her chest and clutched her robe closed. "But, you can't do that," she said, an edge of panic in her voice. "You'll—you'll make the other walls look all faded. What are you going to do then, paint the whole room?"

I clicked an orange roller into place on its handle and looked around at the rest of the room. "I don't know," I said. "Maybe." Then I shrugged. "Why not?"

After unplugging the TV and wheeling its stand away from the wall, I studied the constellation for what I knew would be the final time. Somewhere, in the silver paint that tornadoed through the dots I'd once placed so meticulously, were skin cells from Persephone's fingers. In that way at least, she was alive up there still, the paint laced with her desperate swipe for Mom's attention. But she'd been dead for so long—whether or not, in life, she'd wanted more from us. And we needed to let her be dead. We needed to let ourselves keep living, for as long as we both were allowed.

"Okay, come here," I said, and I walked over to Mom, holding my hands out for her.

She looked into my palms for a moment. Then, with a reluctant sigh, she put her hands into mine and I helped her out of her chair, her body feeling light as a stalk of wheat.

As she stood, something fell from the recliner, landing on the floor with a thump. We both looked down and saw the copy of *Wuthering Heights* I'd given her.

"Oops," I said, bending down to pick it up, but she tightened her grip on my hands, holding me in place.

"Leave it," she said. "You can take it out to the garbage bin later."

"You want to throw it away?" I asked, a familiar itch gathering on my skin. I had bought that for her. She had wanted it at the hospital, and when they didn't have it, I had gone out of my way to get her a copy of her own.

"I don't want to read that story ever again," she said.

She squeezed her eyes shut, her lids wrinkling with the effort, and it was then that I knew why she'd been drawn to that book in the first place.

"It reminds you of Will, doesn't it?"

Her hands, still gripping mine, flinched when I said his name. It had been almost fifteen years since I'd read *Wuthering Heights* in school, but I remembered the gist of it well enough—two lovers, from vastly different circumstances, spend much of their lives with other people, their obsessive love for each other still raging around inside them, turning one ill, the other withered and bitter.

"I don't want to read that story ever again," she repeated—and I nodded, relief filling up my lungs.

"Then let's do this," I said.

I led her to the tray of paint on the floor, and I bent down to roll the brush in the shallow pool of Blossoming White. When it was fully saturated with paint, I handed the roller to Mom, watching as she took it with a shaking hand.

"I don't know," she said softly, staring at the stars on the wall, her eyes wide and fearful. "I don't think I can."

"It's okay," I said. "I'll help you."

Placing my hand on top of hers, I felt the bones beneath her skin, felt the wrist I used to bring to my nose and smell when I was a child, inhaling her perfume as if it were the scent of a delicate flower.

Then, our hands holding on together, we touched the brush to the wall, and we painted.

acknowledgments

Thank you to my extraordinary agent, Sharon Pelletier, who has been an enthusiastic champion of this novel since I first pitched the idea to her. Without her guidance and expertise, this story would not be what it is today, and I am immeasurably grateful for all the time and effort she has invested in my work.

Thank you to the entire Touchstone team, especially my editor, Kaitlin Olson, whose sharp, insightful edits and thoughtful questions pushed me in ways I did not know I needed to be pushed. I am thankful that my book has been in such masterful hands.

There are not enough words to properly thank Maureen O'Brien for everything she has given me in this journey. From teaching me about the path to publication, to making me laugh after disappointing rejections, to sending me cheerleading emojis as I stared at the blinking cursor in a Word document, she has offered me unwavering support. Thank you, Maureen, for your artistic integrity and partnership.

Thank you to my colleagues in the Creative Writing/Media Arts department at the Greater Hartford Academy of the Arts. I love you all like family, and I am continuously inspired by you, both as teachers and artists.

Thank you to the incredible writing teachers I have had, especially Sue Standing, Deyonne Bryant, Robert Pinsky, Rosanna Warren, and the late Derek Walcott. I still can't believe how fortunate I am to have studied with you all.

Thank you to Sue Murray, who first taught me the myth of Persephone, and who instilled in me a passion for Greek mythology, without which this book would not exist.

I also want to express my immense gratitude for my family, particularly my sister and my parents, who never once told me that my dream of being a writer was an impractical one. I know what a gift that is, and I do not take it for granted. Mom and Dad, thank you for everything you've done to get me to this point, and for always being sure, especially when I wasn't, that this would happen.

Finally, thank you to my husband, Marc—my first reader and best friend. Thank you for your spot-on feedback, your game-changing suggestions, and your unparalleled support and encouragement every step of the way. I don't think I could have done this without you, but even if I could have, I'm so glad I didn't have to.

about the author

Megan Collins holds an MFA in creative writing from Boston University. She has taught creative writing at the Greater Hartford Academy of the Arts and Central Connecticut State University, and she is the managing editor of *3Elements Literary Review*. A Pushcart Prize and two-time Best of the Net nominee, she has been published in many print and online journals, including *Off the Coast*, *Spillway*, *Tinderbox Poetry Journal*, and *Rattle*. She lives in Connecticut.